Eiríkr Magnússon, William Morris

The Saga Library

Vol. III Heimskriingla, Vol. I

Eiríkr Magnússon, William Morris

The Saga Library
Vol. III Heimskriingla, Vol. I

ISBN/EAN: 9783744786164

Printed in Europe, USA, Canada, Australia, Japan

Cover: Foto ©Andreas Hilbeck / pixelio.de

More available books at **www.hansebooks.com**

THE STORIES OF THE KINGS OF NORWAY

CALLED THE ROUND

WORLD

(HEIMSKRINGLA)

BY SNORRI STURLUSON

DONE INTO ENGLISH
OUT OF THE ICELANDIC

BY

WILLIAM MORRIS

AND

EIRÍKR MAGNÚSSON

VOL. I

WITH A LARGE MAP OF NORWAY

LONDON

BERNARD QUARITCH, 15 PICCADILLY

1893

CHISWICK PRESS:—C. WHITTINGHAM AND CO., TOOKS COURT,
CHANCERY LANE.

CONTENTS.

TRANSLATORS' NOTE.

AS this work is to be published in four volumes, we think it best to keep the general body of Notes for the last; only printing in each volume an explanation of the metaphors contained in the staves of verse which occur in it. But the map of Norway with the names of the Saga period is given in this first portion of Heimskringla for the convenience of the reader.

Eiríkr Magnússon.
William Morris.

THE STORIES OF THE KINGS OF NORWAY, CALLED THE ROUND WORLD.

THE STORIES
OF THE
KINGS OF NORWAY,
CALLED THE ROUND WORLD.

THE PREFACE OF SNORRI STURLU-SON.

IN this book have I let write tales told concerning those chiefs who have borne sway in the Northlands, and who spake the Danish tongue, even as I have heard men of lore tell the same ; and also certain of their lines of kindred according as they have been taught to me. Some of this is found in the Tellings-up of Forefathers, wherein kings and other men of high degree have traced their kin ; but some is written after olden songs or story-lays, which men have had for their joyance. Now though we wot not surely the truth thereof, yet this we know for a truth, that men of lore of old time have ever held such lore for true.

Thiodolf of Hvin was skald to Harald Hairfair, and he did the lay concerning King Rognvald Higher-than-the-Hills, which is called the Tale of the Ynglings : Rognvald was son of Olaf Geir-

stead-Elf, the brother of Halfdan the Black. In
this song are thirty of his forefathers named, and
their deaths told of and the steads where they lie.
Fiolnir was he named who was son of Yngvi-Frey,
to whom for long time after have the Swedes done
sacrifice, and the Ynglings are named after his
name.

Eyvind the Skald-spiller also told up the tale of
the forefathers of Earl Hakon the Mighty, in the
lay called the Haloga Tale, which was done on
Hakon; therein is Sœming the son of Yngvi-Frey
named, and record is therein of the death of each
and of their howesteads.

After Thiodolf's tale are the lives of the Ynglings first written, and matters added thereto from
the tales of men of lore.

The first age is called the age of Burning,
whereas the wont was to burn all dead men, and
raise up standing-stones to them : but after that
Frey was laid in barrow at Upsala, many great
men fell to raising barrows to the memory of their
kin, no less often than standing-stones.

But after that Dan the Proud, king of the Danes,
let make for him a howe, and bade them bear him
thither dead with the kingly raiment and wargear,
and his horse with all its saddle-gear, and plenteous
wealth beside, then many men of his kin did even
so afterwards, and thence began the Mound age
in Denmark ; but long thereafter the Burning age
held on among the Swedes and Norwegians.

But when Harald Hairfair was king in Norway,
Iceland was settled, and with the king were skalds
whose songs folk yet know by heart, yea and all

songs on the kings who have since held sway in Norway; and most store we set by that which is said in such songs as were sung before the chiefs themselves or the sons of them; and we hold all that for true, which is found in these songs concerning their way-farings and their battles. Now it is the manner of skalds to praise those most whom they stand before while giving forth their song, but no one would dare to tell the king himself deeds, which all who hearkened, yea and himself withal, wotted well were but windy talk and lying; for no praise would that be, but mocking rather.

CONCERNING ARI THE LEARNED, THE MASS-PRIEST.

ARI the Learned, the mass-priest, who was the son of Thorgils, who was the son of Gellir, was the first man of this land who wrote down lore both old and new in the speech of the North: in the beginning of his book he wrote mostly of the settling of Iceland and the law-making therein; and then, concerning the Law-speakers, how long a time each had given forth the law; and began counting by years first till Christ's faith came to Iceland, and afterwards thence down to his own days.

He set off his lore of years by many other matters, both the lives of kings in Norway and Denmark, and in England also; yea, and by great tidings withal, that had befallen here in the land. And I deem his lore altogether most noteworthy,

for of exceeding wisdom he was, and so old, that
he was born the winter next after the fall of King
Harald Sigurdson. He wrote, as himself sayeth,
the lives of the kings of Norway after the telling
of Odd, the son of Kol, the son of Hall of the
Side; but Odd had learnt them from Thorgeir
Afradskoll, a man who was wise indeed, and so
old, that he dwelt at Nidness, when Earl Hakon
the Mighty was slain. Even in the same stead
King Olaf Tryggvison let build the cheaping
town that now is. Now Ari Thorgilson, the
priest, came seven winters old to Hawkdale, to
Hall, son of Thorarin, and abode there fourteen
winters. Hall was an exceeding wise man and
of keen memory; he bore in mind how Thaug-
brand the priest christened him at three years
old, the winter before Christ's faith was made law
in Iceland: Ari, the priest, was twelve winters
old whenas Bishop Isleif died. Hall had fared
from land to land, and was trading fellow of King
Olaf the Holy, whence he gat great furtherance;
and so his reign was well beknown to him. But by
the death of Bishop Isleif were worn away wellnigh
eighty years from the fall of King Olaf Tryggvison:
Hall died nine years after Bishop Isleif, and by
then were his years reckoned at ninety-four, and
he had set up house in Hawkdale in his thirtieth
year, and had dwelt there sixty-four winters, as
Ari writes. Teit, the son of Bishop Isleif, was
fostered at Hall's in Hawkdale, and kept house
there afterwards: he taught Ari the priest, and
told him manifold lore, which Ari wrote down
afterwards. Ari also got manifold knowledge

from Thurid, daughter of Snorri the Priest, a woman wise of wit; she remembered Snorri her father, who was near thirty-five whenas Christ's faith came to Iceland, and died one winter after the fall of King Olaf the Holy.

Therefore nought marvellous was it that Ari knew truly many ancient tales both of our land and of the outlands, whereas he had learnt them from old men and wise, and was himself a man of eager wit and faithful memory.

But the songs meseems are least misplaced, if they have been wrought aright, and are duly interpreted.

THE STORY OF THE YNGLINGS.

THE STORY OF THE YNGLINGS.

CHAPTER I. HEREIN IS TOLD OF THE PARTS OF THE EARTH.

THE ROUND WORLD, whereas manfolk dwell, is much sheared apart by bights : great seas go from the outer-sea into the earth ; and men know for sure that a sea goeth from Niorvi's sound right up to the land of Jerusalem ; from that sea goeth a long bight to the north-east which is called the Black Sea, and sundereth the two World-Ridings ; to the east is Asia, but to the west is called Europe of some, but of some Enea : but north of the Black Sea lies Sweden the Great or the Cold : Sweden the Great some men deem no less than Serkland the Great, and some make it even to Blueland the Great ; the northern parts of this Sweden lie unpeopled by reason of the frost and the cold, even as the southern parts of Blueland are waste because of the sun's burning. Mighty lordships there are in Sweden, and peoples of manifold kind, and many tongues withal ; there are giants, and there are dwarfs, yea and Blue-men, and folk of many kinds and marvellous, and there be savage beasts and drakes wondrous great. Out of the north, from those mountains which are without all the peopled parts, falls a river over Sweden, which is called aright Tanais, but of old was called Tanabranch or Vanabranch ; it comes unto the sea at the Black Sea ; the land betwixt the Vana-mouths was then called Vanland, or Vanhome. This water divides the two World-Ridings ; that to the east is called Asia, that to the west, Europe.

CHAPTER II. OF THE MEN OF ASIA.

EAST of Tanabranch in Asia was the land called As-land or As-home ; but the chief burg which was in that land they called As-garth, in which burg abode a chief called ODIN, and that was a great stead of blood-offerings. That was a custom there that twelve temple-priests were set the highest of all the people ; they were to rule the sacrifices, and judge betwixt man and man ; they were called DIAR or DROTTNAR, and all folk were bound to their service and worship. Odin was a great warrior, and exceeding far-travelled, and had made many realms his own, and so victorious was he, that in every battle he gained the day ; whence it befell, that his men trowed of him that he should of his own nature ever have the victory in every battle. His wont it was, if he sent his men to the wars or on other journeys, before they went to lay his hands on the heads of them, and to give them blessing, and they trowed that they would fare well thereby. So it was with his men withal, that whensoever they were hard bestead, either on sea or land, they called upon his name, and deemed that they had ease thereof, for they thought that in him they had all their trust. Now Odin often fared so far away, that he abode many seasons in his journeys.

CHAPTER III. OF ODIN'S BRETHREN.

ODIN had two brethren, one called Ve, and the other Vili : these brethren of his ruled the realm whiles he was away. But on a time whenas Odin was gone a long way off, and abided long away, the As-folk deemed they might never look to see him home again ; so his brethren fell to sharing his goods, but his wife Frigg they must needs have in wedlock betwixt them both ; but a little after came Odin home and took to himself his wife once more.

CHAPTER IV. WAR WITH THE VANIR.

NOW Odin fell with an host on the Vanir, but they bestirred them manly and warded their land, and now one, now the other prevailed ; either harried the land of the other and wrought scathe thereon ; but when at last either grew loth thereof, they bespoke a meeting of truce between them, and made peace and delivered hostages one to the other ; and the Vanir gave their noblest men, Niord the Wealthy and his son Frey, but the As-folk gave in return him who was called Hœnir, and said that he was well meet to be lord ; a big man he was, and the goodliest to behold. With him sent the As-folk a man hight Mimir, the wisest of men, but the Vanir in return him of the best wits in their company, Quasir by name. But when Hœnir came to Vanhome, then was he straightly made a lord, and Mimir taught him all good counsel. But when Hœnir was in his place at Things, or assemblies, whenso it befell that Mimir was not anigh him, and there came before him any hard matter, ever would he answer in one wise : " Let others give rule !" said he. Then the Vanir misdoubted them that the As-folk had beguiled them in the exchanging of men, and they took Mimir and cut his throat, and sent the head to the As-host : then Odin took the head, and smeared it with such worts that it might not rot, and sang words of wizardry thereover, and gave it such might that it spake to him and told him many hidden matters.

Odin made Niord and Frey temple-priests, and they became Diar among the As-folk. The daughter of Niord was Freya ; she was a temple-priestess, and was the first to teach wizardry among the As-folk according to the wont of the Vanir. While Niord was with the Vanir, he had had his sister to wife, for it was lawful there so to do, and their children were Frey and Freya. But it was forbidden among the As-folk to wed such near kin.

CHAPTER V. ODIN SHARES THE REALM; ALSO CONCERNING GEFION.

A GREAT mountain-wall goes from the north-east to the south-west; that parts Sweden the Great from other realms; south of those mountains there is no long way to the land of the Turks, and there had Odin wide lands of his own. Now in those days fared the Lords of the Roman Folk wide over the world and beat down all peoples under them, but many lords and kings fled away from their own before the trouble of them : so whereas Odin was foreseeing, and wise in wizardry, he knew that his offspring should people the Northern Parts of the World. So he set his brethren Ve and Vili over As-garth, but himself went his ways, and all the Diar with him, and much other folk withal ; and first he fared west into the Garth-realm, and then south into Saxland. He had many sons, and got for himself realms wide through Saxland, and there he set his sons over the heeding of the land. Then he fared north to the sea, and abode in a certain island that is now called Odin's-isle in Fion ; thence he sent Gefion north over the sound to seek new lands, and she came to Gylfi, and he gave her a day's plough-land. Then went she to the Giant-home, and there bore four sons to a certain giant, and turned them into the likeness of oxen, and yoked them to the plough, and drew the land out into the sea, and west over against Odin's-isle, and that land is called Selund, and there she dwelt afterward. Skiold, the son of Odin, wedded her, and they dwelt at Hleithra : there is a sea or water left behind which is called the Low. And so it is that the firths in the Low lie in such a wise that they answer to the nesses in Selund.

So sings Bragi the Old:

> Glad Gefion dragged from Gylfi,
> Great lord of the deep sea's-sun,
> Due increase unto Denmark,
> Hard drew the reeking beasts :
> Eight foreheads' moons shone forth
> From four heads as they went,
> And furrowed off the fair
> And friendly island home.

But when Odin heard that good land was to be gotten east in Gylfi's country, he went thither, and made peace with him, because Gylfi deemed he had no might to withstand the As-folk. Many dealings had Odin and Gylfi together in cunning tricks and wizardry, and ever were the As-folk the mightier therein. Odin took up his abode at the Low, at the stead which is now called Ancient Sigtown, and made there a great temple, with blood-offerings according to the custom of the As-folk ; he owned the land there as wide about as he called it Sigtown ; and there gave he abode to the temple-priests : Niord dwelt at Nois-town, but Frey at Upsala, Heimdall at Heavenberg, Thor at Thundermead, Balder at Broadbeam ; to all gave he good abiding-places.

CHAPTER VI. CONCERNING ODIN'S GREAT PROWESS.

IT is said soothly of Odin of the As-folk when he came into the North countries and the Diar with him, that they were the first to bring in and teach those crafts which men have long since plied. Odin was the noblest of all, and from him they all gat the crafts, for he was the first that knew them all and the greatest number thereof to boot. Now it is to be told that whereas he was so greatly worshipped, these were the things that brought it about : he was so fair and noble of visage when he sat amid his friends, that every man's heart laughed thereat ; whereas, when he was a-warring, then was his countenance terrible towards his foes. And this was the cause thereof, that he knew the art and craft whereby he could change his hue and shape in any wise that he would ; and this again, that the speech of him was so clear and smooth that all folk who listened thereto deemed that alone for true which he spake ; and in measures did he speak all things, even as that is now said which is called Skald-craft.

He and his temple-priests are called Lay-smiths, for that skill began through them in the North-lands. Such craft had Odin, that in battle he could make his foes blind or deaf or fear-stricken, and that their weapons would bite no more than wands ; but his own men went without byrnies, and were mad as dogs or wolves, and bit on their shields, and were as strong as bears or

III.

bulls; menfolk they slew, and neither fire nor steel would deal with them : and this is what is called Bareserks-gang.

CHAPTER VII. OF ODIN'S CRAFTS.

NOW Odin would change his shape; his body would lie there as of one sleeping or dead, while he himself was a fowl or a wild beast, a fish or a worm, and would go in the twinkling of an eye to far-away lands on his own errands or the errands of others.

Moreover, he knew how by words alone to slake the fire or still the sea, and how to turn the wind to whichso way he would. Odin had a ship called Skidbladnir, wherein he would fare over mighty seas; and that same ship might be folded together like a very napkin. Odin had ever Mimir's head by him, and that told him many tidings from other worlds : and whiles would he wake up dead men from the earth, or sit down under men hanged ; wherefore was he called the Lord of the Ghosts, or the Lord of the Hanged. Two ravens also he had which he had tamed to speak, and wide over the lands they flew, and told him many tidings ; and from all these things he became wondrous wise ; all this craft taught he by runes and songs called wizard songs, wherefore are the As-folk called smiths of wizardry. Odin was wise in that craft wherewith went most might, which is called spell-craft, and this he himself followed : wherefore he had might to know the fate of men and things not yet come to pass ; yea, or how to work for men bane or ill-hap or ill-heal, and to take wit or strength from men and give them unto others. But with this sorcery that is thus done goes so much lewdness, that it was not thought to be without shame for menfolk to deal therein, so that cunning was taught to the temple-priestesses. Odin knew of all buried treasures where they were hidden ; and he knew lays whereby the earth opened before him, and mountains and rocks and mounds, and how to bind with words alone whoso might be found dwelling therein ; and he would go in and take thence what he would.

From all this craft he became exceeding famed, and his foes dreaded him, but his friends put their trust in him, and had faith in his craft and himself ; but he taught the more part of his cunning to the temple-priests, and they were next to him in all wisdom and cunning : albeit many others got to them much knowledge thereof, and thence has sorcery spread far and wide and endured long. But to Odin and those twelve lords did men do sacrifice, and called them their gods, and trowed in them long afterwards.

Folk are called Audun after Odin's name, as men were wont so to call their sons, and Thorir or Thorarin are named after Thor ; or names are joined to it from other matters, as Steinthor or Hafthor, and so in many other wise.

CHAPTER VIII. OF ODIN'S LAW-MAKING.

ODIN settled such law in his land as had of old time gone among the As-folk ; and he laid down withal that all dead men should be burned, and that with them their chattels should be borne to bale ; for he said that with such wealth as a man brought to his bale should he come to Valhall ; and that there also should he enjoy whatsoever he had buried himself in the earth. But the ashes should men bear out to sea, or bury in the earth ; and over noble men should a mound be raised for the memory of them ; but in memory of all men of any mark should standing-stones be raised : and for long after did that wont endure.

Folk were to hold sacrifice against the coming of winter for a good year ; in midwinter for the growth of the earth ; and a third in the summer that was an offering for gain and victory. All over Sweden men paid Odin scat, to wit a penny for every head, but he was bound to ward their land from war, and to sacrifice for them for a good year.

CHAPTER IX. THE WEDDING OF NIORD.

NIORD wedded a woman called Skadi, but she would nought of him, and so was wedded to Odin, and many sons they had, one whereof was called Sœming, over whom hath Eyvind the Skald-spiller made this :

The reddener of shield,
The sire of As-folk,
Got the scat-giver
On a giant maiden,
While for more seasons
In Manhome dwelt
The warriors' friend
And Skadi with him.
But she of the rock-lands'
Rushing snow-skids,
Sons a-many
Bare unto Odin.

Earl Hakon the Mighty carried back the tale of his forefathers to this Sœming.

Now this Sweden they called Manhome, but Sweden the Great called they Godhome; and of Godhome are many tales told and many marvels.

CHAPTER X.   OF THE DEATH OF ODIN.

ODIN died in his bed in Sweden; but when he was come nigh to his death, he let mark him with a spear-point, and claimed as his own all men dead by weapon; and he said that he would go his ways to Godhome and welcome his friends there.   Now were the Swedes minded that he would be come to that As-garth of old days, there to live his life for ever; and then began anew the worship of Odin and the vowing of vows to him.   Oft thought the Swedes that he showed himself to them in dreams before great battles should be; and to some he gave victory there and then, and to others bidding to come to him; and either lot they deemed good enow.

Odin dead was burned, and his burning was done in the seemliest wise; but the troth of men was it in those days, that the higher the reek reached up aloft, the more exalted in heaven would he be who was burned there; yea, and the richer the more treasure was burned with him.

CHAPTER XI. OF NIORD.

SO then Niord of Noatown became ruler over the Swedes, and upheld the sacrifices, and the Swedes called him their Lord and he took free scat of them. In his days was there exceeding good peace, and years of all kinds of plenty, so great that the Swedes trowed thereby that Niord swayed the plenty of the year and the wealth-hap of mankind. In his days died the more part of the Diar, and to all of them were blood-offerings made, and they were burned thereafter. Niord died in his bed, and let him be marked unto Odin or ever he died; the Swedes burned him, and greeted sore over his grave.

CHAPTER XII. THE DEATH OF FREY.

FREY then took to him the realm after Niord; he was called Lord of the Swedes, and took free scat of them; he was well-beloved, and happy in good years even as his father. Frey raised a great temple at Upsala, and there had his chief abode, and endowed it with all his wealth, both land and chattels. Then began the weal of Upsala, which has endured ever

since.   In his days began the Peace of Frodi, and
then also were plenteous years throughout all lands;
and that the Swedes laid to the account of Frey;
and he was held dearer therefor than the other
gods, as in his days the people were wealthier
than aforetime from the good peace and plenteous
years.   Gerd, the daughter of Gymir, was Frey's
wife, and their son was called Fiolnir.   Frey was
called by another name, that is to say, Yngvi, and
this name of Yngvi was long used for a name of
honour in his blood, and his kindred were in aftertime called Ynglings.

Now Frey fell sick, but when his sickness waxed
on him, men took counsel and let few folk come
into him; and they built a great howe and made
a door therein, and three windows; and so when
Frey was dead they bore him privily into the
howe, and told the Swedes that he was still
alive, and there they guarded him for three
winters, and poured all the scat into the mound:
gold through the one window, silver through the
second, and copper pennies through the third.
And this while endured plenteous years and
peace.

CHAPTER XIII.   OF FREYA AND HER DAUGHTERS.

NOW Freya upheld the sacrifices, for she
alone of the gods was left behind alive;
and of the greatest fame she was, so that
by her name should all women of honour be called,
even as now they are called Fruvor (ladies): so

also every woman is called Freya who rules over her own, but House-freya she who rules a household.

Now Freya was somewhat shifting of mood; Odr was the name of her husband, but her daughters were Hnoss and Gersemi, and they were exceeding fair, and after them are called all things that are dearest to have.

But now when all the Swedes wotted that Frey was dead, and the plenteous years and good peace still endured, then they trowed that so it would be while he still abode in Sweden; neither would they burn him, but called him the God of the World, and sacrificed to him ever after, most of all for plenteous years and peace.

CHAPTER XIV. THE DEATH OF KING FIOLNIR.

FIOLNIR the son of Yngvi-Frey ruled next over the Swedes and the wealth of Upsala; he was a mighty man, and his years were full of plenty and peace. Peace-Frodi abode as then at Hleithra, and great friendship there was betwixt these twain and bidding from house to house. But whenas Fiolnir fared to Frodi in Selund, then was a great feast arrayed there against his coming, and folk were bidden there from lands far and wide. There had Frodi a great homestead, and therein was there wrought a mighty vat many ells high, which stood on mighty big beams; now this stood down in a certain undercroft, and there was a loft above it, the floor whereof was open, that the liquor might be poured down thereby; but the vat was full of mingled mead, and that drink was wondrous strong. A-night-time was Fiolnir brought to his lodging in the next loft, and his company with him. Amidst the night he went out unto the gallery to seek a privy place, and he was bewildered with sleep and dead-drunk; so when he turned back to his lodging he went along the gallery, and unto the door of another loft, whereinto he went, and missed his footing, and fell into the mead-vat and was lost there. So sings Thiodolf of Hvin:

> Now hath befallen
> In Frodi's house
> The word of fate
> To fall on Fiolnir:
> That the windless wave
> Of the wild bull's spears
> That lord should do
> To death by drowning.

CHAPTER XV. OF SWEGDIR.

SWEGDIR took the realm to him after his father, and he vowed a vow to go seek Godhome and Odin the Old. He fared with twelve men wide through the world; he came out to Turkland and Sweden the Great, and found there many of his kin and friends, and he was five winters about this journey; then he came home to Sweden, and dwelt there at home yet awhile. He had wedded a woman called Vana out in Vanhome, and their son was called Vanland. But Swegdir fared yet again a-seeking God-

home. Now in the east parts of Sweden is a great
stead called Stone, where is a rock as big as big
houses be ; so one evening-tide after sunset, whenas
Swegdir went from the drinking to his sleeping-
bower, he looked on the stone, and lo, there sat a
dwarf thereunder. Now Swegdir and his men were
very drunk, and they ran to the stone, and the
dwarf stood in the door thereof, and called on
Swegdir, and bade him come in there, if he would
find Odin. Swegdir ran into the stone and it shut
behind him straightway, and Swegdir never came
back again. So sings Thiodolf of Hvin :

There the day-shunning
Durnir's offspring,
The dark-halls' warden,
Won King Swegdir,
When into the stone
Leapt the strong-hearted,
The man all reckless,
After the dwarf kind ;
Then when the bright
Abode of giants,
Sokmimir's hall,
Gaped high o'er the king.

CHAPTER XVI. OF VANLAND.

THE son of Swegdir was Vanland, and he
took the realm after his father, and ruled
over the Wealth of Upsala ; he was a
great warrior, and fared wide about the world.
One winter-tide he abode in Finland with Snow
the Old, and there wedded his daughter Drift ; but
in the spring-tide he went his ways and Drift was
left behind, but he promised to come back after the

space of three winters, yet came he not back in ten
winters. Then sent Drift after Huld the witchwife,
but sent Visbur, the son of her and Vanland, to
Sweden. Drift made a bargain with Huld the
witchwife to this end, that she was to draw Vanland to Finland by spells or else slay him; but
when the spell was set forth, then was Vanland
at Upsala. Then he grew fain of faring to Finland,
but his friends and counsellors forbade him, and
said that the wizardry of the Fins was busy in his
desire. Then he became heavy with slumber, and
laid himself down to sleep, but when he had slept
but a short space, he cried out and said that the
Mare was treading him. His men went to him and
would help him; but when they went to his head,
she betrod his legs, so that they were nigh broken,
and when they went to the legs, she so smothered
the head of him, that there he died. The Swedes
took his corpse and burned it beside the river
called Skuta; and there standing-stones were set
up to him. So sings Thiodolf:

> Now the witch-wight
> Drave King Vanland
> Down to visit
> Vilir's brother.
> There the troll-wise
> Blind-night's witchwife
> Trod all about
> Men's over-thrower.
> The jewel-caster,
> He whom the mare quelled,
> On Skuta's bed,
> There was he burning.

CHAPTER XVII.   THE DEATH OF VISBUR.

VISBUR took to him the heritage of Van-land his father, and fell to wedding the daughter of Aude the Wealthy, to whom he gave as a dower three great towns and a gold necklace ; two sons they had, Gisl and Ondur. Then Visbur left her alone, and took to him another wife, and she fared to her father with her sons. Visbur had a son called Domald, and his step-mother let sing unluck at him. So when Visbur's sons were twelve and thirteen years old each, they went to him and claimed the dower of their mother, but he would not yield up the same. Then they cried out that that gold necklace should be the bane of the best man of his kin, and so went their ways home. Then was yet more sorcery set a-brewing and to this end, that they should have might to slay their father. Therewith Huld the witchwife declared unto them that even so she would work her spell, yea and moreover that the slaying of kin by kin should ever after follow the blood of the Ynglings ; and thereto they said yea. Then they gathered folk to them, and fell on Visbur unawares a-night-time, and burned him in his house. So sings Thiodolf :

> And King Visbur's
> Will-burg next
> Swallowed up
> The sea's hot brother.
> When the seat-warders
> Let loose the baneful
> Thief of the woodland

On Visbur their father.
And the roaring wolf
Of the red gleed bit
The mighty king
All in his hearth-keel.

CHAPTER XVIII. THE DEATH OF DOMALD.

DOMALD took to him the heritage of Visbur his father, and ruled the lands; and in his days there fell on the Swedes great hunger and famine. Then the Swedes set up great blood-offerings at Upsala: the first autumn they offered up oxen, but none the more was the earth's increase bettered; the next autumn they offered up men, and the increase of the year was the same, or worse it might be; but the third autumn came the Swedes flockmeal to Upsala whenas the sacrifices should be. Then held the great men counsel together, and were of one accord that this scarcity was because of Domald their king, and withal that they should sacrifice him for the plenty of the year; yea, that they should set on him and slay him, and redden the seats of the gods with the blood of him; and even so they did. So sayeth Thiodolf:

Of yore agone was it
That they the sword-bearers
Must redden the meadows
With blood of their lord:
When the land-folk were bearing
Their blood-wetted weapons
Away from the place
Where Domald lay life-spent.

When the Swedish people
Fain of plenty
Brought to undoing
The bane of the Jute-folk.

CHAPTER XIX.   THE   DEATH   OF DOMAR.

THE son of Domald was Domar, who next ruled the realm.   His rule over the land endured long, and there was good plenty and peace throughout his days ; of him is nought more told save that he died in his bed at Upsala, and was borne forth to Fyri's meads, and burned there on the river-bank whereas are his standing-stones.   So sayeth Thiodolf :

Oft have I
Of men of lore
Asked concerning
The corpse of Yngvi,
Where in earth Domar
Was down borne
By the roaring bright
Bane of Half.
Now wot I surely
That sickness-bitten
Fiolnir's offspring
By Fyri burned.

CHAPTER   XX.   THE   DEATH   OF DYGGVI.

DYGGVI was the name of his son, who ruled over the land after him : and of whom nought is told, save that he died in his bed ; as Thiodolf says :

Nought I misdoubt me
That Glitnir's goddess
Hath Dyggvi dead
For her own plaything ;
For the sister of Wolf,
The sister of Narfi,
Must come to choose
The kingly man.
And the over-ruler
Of Yngvi's people
Loki's sister
Has bewitchèd.

The mother of Dyggvi was Drott, the daughter of King Danp, the son of Rig, who was the first who was called King in the tongue of the Danes, and his kin have ever after held the name of King for the highest among names of honour.   Now Dyggvi was the first who was called King among his kin, but or his time they were called Drott-nar, and their wives, Drottningar, and the company of their court, Drott.   But Yngvi or Ynguni was everyone of that kin called through all the days of his life, and the whole race is called Ynglings. Queen Drott was sister of King Dan the Proud, after whom Denmark is named.

CHAPTER XXI.   OF DAY THE WISE.

THE son of King Dyggvi was Day, who took the kingdom after his time, and so wise a man he was, that he knew the speech of fowl ; and a certain sparrow he had which told him many tidings, and ever flew from land to land ; and on a time when the sparrow flew into Reith Gothland, to a stead called Vorvi, he flew into a carle's cornfield, and there gat his meat; but the carle came upon him, and caught up a stone, and smote the sparrow dead. Now King Day was ill at ease that his sparrow came not home, so he betook him to sacrifice of atonement, to know what had betid, and he had answer that his sparrow was slain at Vorvi. So he summoned to him a great host and went his ways to Gothland, and when he came to Vorvi, he went up into the country and harried there, and folk fled away far and wide before him. Now King Day turned back with his army to the ships as evening-tide drew on, and he had slain many folk and taken many; and as they crossed over a certain river at a place called Shooter's-ford, or Weapon-ford, a certain field-thrall ran out from the wood unto the river-bank, and cast a hayfork amidst their company, and it smote the king upon the head, and he fell from his horse straightway, and got his death therefrom; and his men went back to Sweden.

In those days a lord who went a-warring was called "gram," and the warriors were called "gramir." So sings Thiodolf:

> Of Day heard I,
> How forth he wended
> Fain of fame
> To his fated death;
> When unto Vorvi
> Came he that taineth
> The death-rod's hunger
> For his sparrow's avenging.
> Yea e'en that word
> All unto the eastways

The folk of the king
From fight must bear,
That the fork that pitcheth
The meat of Sleipnir
Hath laid alow
That lord of battle.

CHAPTER XXII. OF AGNI.

AGNI was the name of Day's son, who was king in his stead, a mighty man and far-famed, a great warrior, and a man of all prowess in all matters. On a summer King Agni went with his army to Finland, and went a-land and harried there; but the Fins drew together a great host and met him in battle, and Frosty was the name of their lord. So a fierce fight befell wherein King Agni gained the day, and Frosty fell there and many of his host with him. So King Agni fared, war-shield aloft, through Finland, and laid it under him, and gat mighty great booty; and he took and had away with him Skialf the daughter of Frosty, as well as Logi her brother.

So when he sailed from the east, he made for Stock-Sound, and pitched his tents south on the strand, whereas wood then was. Now King Agni had that gold necklace which Visbur had owned. But King Agni must needs wed Skialf, and she prayed him to hold a funeral feast over her father; and he did so, and bade to himself many mighty men and made a great feast: of mighty fame was he grown because of this way-faring. So at this feast were there great drinkings,

and when King Agni was merry with drink, then
Skialf bade him heed well the necklace which he
had on his neck ; so he fell to and bound it strongly
on his neck or ever he went to sleep.   But his
land-tent stood by the wood-side, and there was a
high tree over the tent to shade it from the sun's
heat.   So whenas King Agni was asleep, then
Skialf took a stout rope, and did it under the necklace.   But her men overthrew the tent-poles, and
cast a bight of the rope up into the tree-boughs,
and then hauled at it so that the king hung right
under the tree-limb, and gat his bane thereby ;
then Skialf and her men ran a-shipboard and rowed
away.   King Agni was burned there, and sithence
the place was called Agnis-thwaite, being in the
eastern part of the Taur and west of Stock-Sound.
So says Thiodolf :

> I count it wondrous
> If Agnis' men
> Deemed redes of Skialf
> For the redes of fate.
> When with the gold-gaud
> That goodly king
> Logi's sister
> Hove aloft :
> He who on Taur-mead
> Needs must tame
> The wind-cold steed
> Of Signy's husband.

CHAPTER XXIII.   OF ALREK AND ERIC.

ALREK and Eric, sons of Agni, were kings in his stead ; mighty men were they and great warriors, and skilled in manly deeds : their wont it was to ride horses and break them both to the amble and the gallop, and greater was their skill therein than of any other men ; and with the utmost eagerness they strove with each other which rode the better, and had the best horses.   On a time the two brethren rode away from other men, with their best horses, taking their way out into a certain mead, and never came back ; and when men went to seek them, they found them both dead, and the head of each one all to-broken, but no weapon had they save the bits of their horses ; and men deemed that they had slain each other therewith.   So sings Thiodolf :

Alrek fell
Whenas fell Eric
Brought to his bane
By his brother's weapons :
There with the headgear
Of riding-horses
Day's kin, 'tis said,
Did kill each other :
None yet had heard
Of horses' harness
Plied in the fight
By Frey's own offspring.

CHAPTER XXIV. OF ALF AND YNGVI.

YNGVI and Alf were the sons of Alrek, and took king's rule next in Sweden. Yngvi was a great warrior and ever happy in battle, fair and of the greatest prowess, strong and most brisk in fight, bountiful of his wealth, and one of cheerful heart, and from all this he became famed and beloved. But King Alf, his brother, sat at home, nor went to the wars, and he was called Altling; he was a moody man, masterful and rough; his mother was Daybright, the daughter of King Day the Mighty, from whom are come the Daylings.

King Alf had to wife Bera, the fairest and eagerest of women, a woman most gleesome of heart. Now Yngvi Alrekson was once again come in autumn-tide to Upsala from the viking wars, full of all fame, and oft he sat long a-drinking benights; but often would King Alf be going early to bed. Queen Bera sat full oft late of an evening, and Yngvi and she had privy talk together. Hereon would Alf oft be speaking to her and bidding her to go earlier to bed, for that he would not lie awake for her. Then said she that happy were the woman that had Yngvi to her husband rather than Alf, and Alf grew exceeding wroth when she spake that word full oft.

On a night Alf went into the hall, whenas Yngvi and Bera sat a-talking in the high-seat; and Yngvi had a sword across his knees. Now were men much drunken, and gave no heed to the king's coming in; but King Alf went up to the high-seat, and drew a sword from under his cloak and thrust it through Yngvi his brother. Then Yngvi sprang up and drew his glaive and smote Alf deadly, and they both fell dead to the floor : so Alf and Yngvi were laid in mound in Fyri's meads. So says Thiodolf :

There he the warden
Of holy stalls
Must lie dead, slaughtered
By Alf the Slayer,
Whenas Day's offspring
A-rage with envy
Must redden blade
In blood of Yngvi.

Unmeet that Bera
Should whet to battle
The slain men's lullers,
Whenas two brethren,
Each unto each grown
All unhelpful,
For jealous grudge
Must slay each other.

CHAPTER XXV. THE FALL OF KING HUGLEIK.

HUGLEIK hight the son of Alf, who had the kingdom of the Swedes after those brethren, because the sons of Yngvi were then but children in years. King Hugleik was no warrior, but sat at home in the seat of peace; he was exceeding wealthy, and niggard of wealth withal. He had in his court many of all kinds of minstrels, harp-players, and jig-players, and fiddlers; and spell-workers he had with him also, and all kind of cunning folk.

Now Haki and Hagbard were two brethren of great fame; sea-kings were they, and had a great company; and whiles they went both together, and whiles each one alone, and many champions there were with either. Now King Haki went with his army to Sweden against King Hugleik. So King Hugleik gathered together an host against him, and there came into his fellowship two brethren, Swipdag and Geigad, men of fame both, and the greatest of champions. King Haki had twelve champions with him, and Starkad the Old was then of his fellowship, and King Haki himself withal was the greatest of champions. They met on Fyri's meads, and a great battle befell there, and anon Hugleik's folk fell fast; then set on those chiefs, Swipdag and Geigad, but Haki's champions went six against each, and they were taken. Then went Haki into the shield-burg against Hugleik the king, and slew him there, and his two sons withal. Thereupon the Swedes fled; but King Haki now laid the lands under him, and became king over the Swedes, and sat at home by his lands for three winters; and amid that peace and quiet his champions went from him to the viking wars, and thus gat wealth to themselves.

CHAPTER XXVI. THE DEATH OF KING GUDLAUG.

JORUND and Eric were the sons of Yngvi, the son of Alrek; they lay out at sea in their warships all this while, and were great warriors. One summer they harried in Denmark, and there happened on Gudlaug, the King of Halogaland, and had a battle with him, which had such end, that Gudlaug's ship was cleared, and he himself taken. They brought him a-land at Stream-isle-ness, and there hanged him, and there his folk heaped up a mound above him. So says Eyvind the Skald-spiller:

> Gudlaug moreover,
> Borne down by the might
> Of the Eastland kings,
> Must tame the grim-heart
> Horse of Sigar;
> The sons of Yngvi
> On the tree they horsed him
> The jewel-waster.
>
> There then corpse-ridden
> Stands the windy tree
> On the Ness a-drooping
> Where the deep Lays sunder.
> 'Tis the ness of Stream-isle,
> Famed in story
> By the mark of a stone
> For the mound of a king.

CHAPTER XXVII. OF KING HAKI.

THOSE brothers Eric and Jorund won much fame from this deed, and they deemed themselves far greater men than aforetime. They heard that King Haki of Sweden had sent his champions from him, so they made for Sweden and drew an host together. As soon as the Swedes knew that the Ynglings were come thither, a countless host flocked to them. Then they laid their ships into the Low, and made for Upsala to fall on King Haki, but he went out into Fyri's meads against them, and his company was far less than theirs. Fierce fight befell there, and King Haki set on so hard that he felled all who were anigh him, and in the end slew King Eric, and hewed down the banner of the brethren. Then fled King Jorund away to his ships with all his folk. Now King Haki had gotten such sore hurts, that he saw that the days of his life would not be long; so he let take a swift ship that he had, and lade it with dead men and weapons, and let bring it out to sea, and ship the rudder, and hoist up the sail, and then let lay fire in tar-wood, and make a bale aboard. The wind blew offshore, and Haki was come nigh to death, or was verily dead, when he was laid on the bale, and the ship went blazing out into the main sea; and of great fame was that deed for long and long after.

CHAPTER XXVIII. THE DEATH OF JORUND.

JORUND, the son of King Yngvi, now became king at Upsala and swayed the realm, and ofttimes went hea-warring in the summer-tide; and on a summer he fared with his host to Denmark, and harried in Jutland, and in the autumn

went up Limbfirth, and harried thereabout, and
laid his ships in Oddsound. Then came thither
with a mighty host Gylaug, King of Halogaland,
the son of Gudlaug who is aforenamed, and he fell
to battle with Jorund. But the folk of that land
were ware thereof; they flocked thither from all
quarters with ships both great and small. So there
was King Jorund overborne by multitudes, and
his ships cleared, and he himself leaped overboard
a-swimming, but they laid hands on him, and
brought him a-land. Then let King Gylaug rear up
a gallows, and lead Jorund thereto, and hang him
thereon; and thus his life-days ended. So sings
Thiodolf:

> Jorund who died
> In yore-agone
> Must lay down life
> In Limafirth;
> When the high-breasted
> Hemp-rope Sleipnir
> Must needs bear up
> The bane of Gudlaug,
> And there the leavings
> Of Hagbard's goat
> Gripped hard the neck
> Of the Hersirs' ruler.

CHAPTER XXIX. THE DEATH OF KING AUN.

AUN, or Ani, was the son of Jorund, who
was king over the Swedes after his father.
He was a wise man, and held much by
blood-offerings; no warrior, but abode on his
lands in peace.

Now in the days when these kings aforesaid bare rule at Upsala, the kings over the Danes were, first, Dan the Proud, who lived to be exceeding old; then his son Frodi the Proud, or the Peaceful, and then Halfdan and Fridleif, the sons of him, and these were great warriors. Halfdan was the older, and the foremost in all matters; and he went with an army against King Aun of Sweden, and certain battles they had wherein Halfdan ever gained the day; and in the end King Aun fled into West Gautland, whenas he had been king at Upsala for five-and-twenty years; and for twenty-five winters he abode in Gautland, while King Halfdan ruled at Upsala. King Halfdan died in his bed at Upsala, and was laid in mound there. Thereafter came King Aun yet again to Upsala, and was then sixty years old. Then he made a great sacrifice for length of days, and gave Odin his son, and he was offered up to him. Then gat King Aun answer from Odin that he should live yet another sixty winters : so he reigned on at Upsala for twenty-five winters more. Then came Ali the Bold, the son of Fridleif, with an army to Sweden against King Aun, and battles they had, and King Ali ever had the better part; and again King Aun fled his realm, and went into West Gautland; and Ali was king in Upsala twenty-and-five winters or ever Starkad the Old slew him. After the fall of Ali, King Aun went back again to Upsala, and ruled the realm there yet five-and-twenty winters. Then he made yet another great sacrifice for the lengthening of his life, and offered up another of his sons; but Odin

answered him that he should live on ever, even so
long as he gave Odin one of his sons every tenth
year; and bade him withal give a name to some
county in his land, according to the tale of those
sons of his whom he should offer up to Odin. So
when he had offered up seven sons, then he lived
ten winters yet in such case that he might not go
afoot, but was borne about on a chair. Then he
offered up yet again the eighth son of his, and lived
ten winters yet, and then lay bedridden. Then
he offered up his ninth son, and lived ten winters
yet, and then must needs drink from a horn, even
as a swaddling babe. Now had he one son yet
left, and him also would he offer up, and give to
Odin Upsala withal and the country-side thereabout, and let call it Tenthland; but the Swedes
forbade it him, and there was no sacrifice So King
Aun died, and was laid in howe at Upsala; and
ever since is it called Aun's sickness when a man
dies painless of eld. So sings Thiodolf:

> In days agone
> At Upsala
> Must Aun sickness
> For Aun work ending:
> And he the king
> To life strong-clinging
> Sank back again
> To second childhood.
>
> Yea, the little end
> Of the long sword
> That the bull beareth,
> Beareth he mouthward.
> There the son-slayer
> Drank from the sword-point

Of the yoke reindeer,
Drank lying lowly.

No might had the East King
Hoary-headed
To hold aloft
The herd's head-weapon.

CHAPTER XXX. OF EGIL THE FOE OF TUNNI.

EGIL was the name of the son of Aun who was king in Sweden after his father; he was no warrior, but abode on his lands in peace. He had a thrall hight Tunni, who had been with Aun the Old, and was his treasurer; but when Aun the Old was dead, then took Tunni abundance of his wealth and buried it under the earth. But now when Egil became king he set Tunni amid the other thralls; and this he took exceeding ill, and ran away, and many other thralls with him; and they dug up the money which Tunni had buried, and he gave the same to his men, and they took him to be lord over them. Thereafter there flocked to him much folk of the runagates, and they lay abroad in the wild-wood; but whiles would they fall on the country-sides, and rob men or slay them. Now King Egil heard thereof, and went to seek them with his host; but on a night, when he had taken up his quarters, came Tunni with his folk and fell on them unawares, and slew many of the king's men. So when King Egil was ware that war was come upon him, he turned against Tunni, and set up his banner, but many of his folk fled away from him, so furiously as Tunni, he and

his, set on, and King Egil saw nought for it but to
flee. So Tunni and his folk drave the whole rout
to the wild-wood, and then fared back to the peopled
land, and harried and robbed, and found nought to
withstand them. All the wealth Tunni took in the
country-sides he gave to his men, whereof he became
well-beloved and followed of many.

Now King Egil gathered an army together and
went against Tunni; so they fought, and Tunni
prevailed, and King Egil fled away, and lost many
men : eight battles had King Egil and Tunni together, and in all of them Tunni gained the victory. So thereafter King Egil fled away from the
land, and made for Selund in Denmark and the
court of King Frodi the Bold ; and there he promised for King Frodi's helping seat from the
Swedes. So Frodi gave him an host and his champions withal, and Egil went his ways to Sweden.
And whenas Tunni knew thereof, he went against
him with his host, and they fought together a great
battle, wherein Tunni fell. So King Egil took his
realm to him, and the Danes went back home.
King Egil sent King Frodi good gifts and great
at each season, but paid no seat to the Danes, and
yet held good the friendship twixt him and Frodi ;
and after Tunni's fall King Egil ruled the realm
alone yet three winters.

It fell out in Sweden that there was a certain
bull set apart for sacrifice, that waxed old, and
was nourished so over abundantly that it grew
outrageous ; and so when men would take him, he
fled away into the woods, and went wild, and was
long time in the thicket, and dealt dreadfully with

men. Now King Egil was a mighty hunter, and
oft he rode day-long through the woods a-hunting
wild deer; and so on a time, whenas he had ridden
with his men to the hunting, the king chased a
certain deer a long while, and had followed after
it on the spur into the woods away from all his
folk: then was he ware of that bull, and rode to
him, and would slay him. The bull turned to meet
him, and the king got a thrust at him, but the spear
glanced from off him; then the bull thrust his horn
into the horse's flank, so that he fell flat, and the
king with him. The king leaped to his feet, and
would draw his sword, but the bull thrust his horns
into the breast of the king, so that they stood deep
therein. Then came the king's goodmen thereto,
and slew the bull. The king lived but a little while,
and was laid in mound at Upsala. Hereof says
Thiodolf:

> The happy of praise
> High kin of Tyr
> Must flee before
> The might of Tunni.
> The Jötun's yoke-beast
> Reddened thereafter
> The bull's head-sword
> In the breast of Egil;
>
> The beast who a great while
> Wide through the east-wood
> Had borne aloft
> The brow's high temple.
> Yea, and the sheathless
> Sword of the bull-beast
> Stood deep in the heart
> Of the son of the Skylfings.

CHAPTER XXXI. OF OTTAR VENDIL-
CROW.

OTTAR was the name of the son of Egil,
and he took the realm and kingdom after
him. No friendship he held with King
Frodi, so Frodi sent men to King Ottar to claim
the seat which Egil had promised him. Ottar
answered that the Swedes had never paid scat to
the Danes, and said that neither would he do so
now; and therewith the messengers went their
ways back. Now Frodi was a great warrior, and
so on a certain summer he went with his host
to Sweden, made the fray there, and harried,
and slew many folk, and took some captives.
There gat he exceeding great prey, and burnt
and wasted the dwellings of men, and wrought the
greatest deeds of war. But the next summer Frodi
the king went a-warring in the East-Countries, and
thereon King Ottar heard tell that King Frodi was
not in the land; so he went aboard his warships
and made for Denmark, and harried there, and found
nought to withstand him. Now he heard that men
were gathered thick in Selund, and he turned
west through Eyre-Sound, and then sailed south
to Jutland, and lays his keels for Limbfirth, and
harries about Vendil, and burns there, and lays
the land waste far and wide whereso he came.
Vatt and Fasti were Frodi's earls whom he had
set to the warding of the land whiles he was away
thence; so when these earls heard that the Swede
king was harrying in Denmark, they gathered force,
and leapt a-shipboard, and sailed south to Limb-

firth, and came all unawares upon King Ottar, and
fell to fighting; but the Swedes met them well,
and folk fell on either side; but as the folk of the
Danes fell, came more in their stead from the
country-sides around, and all ships withal were
laid to that were at hand. So such end the battle
had, that there fell King Ottar, and the more part
of his host.   The Danes took his dead body and
brought it a-land, and laid it on a certain mound,
and there let wild things and common fowl tear the
carrion. Withal they made a crow of tree and sent
it to Sweden, with this word to the Swedes, that
that King Ottar of theirs was worth but just so
much as that; so afterwards men called him Ottar
Vendil-crow.   So says Thiodolf:

> Into the ern's grip
> Fell the great Ottar,
> The doughty of deed,
> Before the Dane's weapons:
> When gledes of war
> With bloody feet
> Tore him about,
> And trod on Vendil.
>
> I hear these works
> Of Vatt and Fasti
> Were set in tale
> By Swedish folk:
> That Frodi's island's
> Earls between them
> Had slain the famous
> Fight-upholder.

CHAPTER XXXII. THE WEDDING OF KING ADILS.

ADILS was the name of King Ottar's son, who ruled in his stead. He was king a long while, an exceeding wealthy man, and went warring certain summers. Now King Adils came with his army to Saxland. A king reigned thereover called Gerthiof, and his wife was hight Alof the Mighty, but nought is told of their having children. This king was not in the land as then. So King Adils and his men rushed up to the king's stead and robbed there, and some drave down the herds to a strand-slaughtering. Certain bondfolk, both men and women, had had the warding of the herd, and all these the king's men took with them: among these folk was a maiden wondrous fair, named Yrsa. So King Adils fared home with his war-gettings, and Yrsa was not left among the bondmaids: men speedily found that she was wise and fair-spoken, plenteous in knowledge of all matters, so they held her in great account, but the king most of all; so that it came about that King Adils wedded her, and Yrsa was queen in Sweden, and was deemed the greatest of noble women.

CHAPTER XXXIII. THE DEATH OF KING ADILS.

KING HELGI, the son of Halfdan, ruled in Hleithra in those days, and he came to Sweden with so great an host that King Adils saw nought for it but to flee away. So King

Helgi went ashore with his host and harried, and got plenteous plunder, and laid hands on Yrsa the queen, and had her away with him to Hleithra, and wedded her, and their son was Rolf Kraki. But when Rolf was three winters old, then came Queen Alof to Denmark, and therewithal she told Queen Yrsa that King Helgi her husband was no less her father withal, and that she, Alof, was her mother. Then Yrsa went back to Sweden to King Adils, and was queen there ever after whiles she lived. King Helgi fell in battle whenas Rolf Kraki was eight winters old, who was straightway holden as king at Hleithra. King Adils had mighty strife with a king called Ali the Uplander from out of Norway. King Adils and King Ali had a battle on the ice of the Vener Lake, and Ali fell there, but Adils gained the day. Concerning this battle is much told in the Story of the Skioldungs, and also how Rolf Kraki came to Upsala to Adils; and that was when Rolf Kraki sowed gold on the Fyris-meads.

Now King Adils had great joyance in good horses, and had the best horses of that time: Slinger was the name of one of his horses, and another he had called Raven; him he took from Ali dead, and of him was begotten another horse who was called Raven, which he sent to Haloga-land to King Godguest; and King Godguest backed him, but might not stay him ere he was cast from his back, and gat his bane thereby: and this befell at Omd, in Halogaland.

Now King Adils happed to be at a sacrifice to the Goddesses, and rode his horse through the hall

of the Goddesses ; and the horse tripped his feet
under him, and he fell and the king fell forward
from off him, so that his head smote on a stone, and
he brake his skull, and the brains lay on the stones,
whereby he gat his bane.   Adils died at Upsala,
and was laid in mound there, and the Swedes
called him a mighty king.   So sings Thiodolf :

> Still have I heard
> Of Adil's life-days,
> How that the witch-wight
> Should waste them wholly ;
> How the doughty king,
> The kin of Frey,
> Must fall adown
> From the steed's shoulder,
>
> And that the brain-sea
> Of the son of king-folk
> Was mingled all
> With miry grit.
> And the deed-famed
> Foe of Ali
> Even at Upsala
> Had his ending.

CHAPTER XXXIV.   FALL OF ROLF KRAKI.

EYSTEIN was the name of the son of Adils,
who next ruled over the Swede-realm.
In his days fell Rolf Kraki at Hleithra.
At that time kings harried much in the realm of
Sweden, both Danes and Norsemen.   Many sea-
kings there were, who were at the head of many
folk, but had no lands : he alone was accounted
aright a sea-king, who never slept under sooty
roof-tree, nor ever drank in hearth-ingle.

CHAPTER XXXV.   OF EYSTEIN, AND OF SOLVI THE JUTE-KING.

THERE was a sea-king named Solvi, the son of Hogni of Niord's-isle, who in those days harried in the East-countries, and had a realm in Jutland withal.   He made with his host for Sweden ; and at that time was King Eystein a-feasting in the country-side which is called Lofund.   Thither came King Solvi on him unwares and a-night-time, and beset the king in his house, and burned him therein with all his court. Then went Solvi to Sigtown, and bade folk name him king, and take him for the same ; but the Swedes gathered an host, and would defend the land, and a fight befell, so great that it is told thereof that it brake off never for the space of eleven days.   Therein gat King Solvi the victory, and was king over the Swede-realm a long while, yea, until the Swedes betrayed him and he was slain. Hereof says Thiodolf :

> I know how Eystein's
> Ended life-thread
> Lieth hidden
> In Lofund country,
> And say the Swedes
> For sure, that Jute-folk
> Burnt indoors
> Their doughty ruler.
>
> The mountain-tangles'
> Biting sickness
> Ran on the king
> In the ship of the hearth-fires :

Then when the toft's-bark
Timber-strutted
Burnt o'er the king,
And crowds of warriors.

CHAPTER XXXVI. THE SLAYING OF KING YNGVAR.

THEREAFTER was Yngvar, the son of King Eystein, king over the Swede-realm; a great warrior was he, and was oft aboard warships, because in those days was the Swede-realm much troubled by war, both of the Danes and the men of the East-countries. Now King Yngvar made peace with the Danes, and then fell to warring in the East-countries. One summer he had out his host, and fared to Esthonia, and harried there summer-long in the part called Stone. Thither came down the Esthonian folk with a great army, and a battle befell; but by such odds were the folk of the land greater, that the Swedes might not withstand them, and King Yngvar fell there, but his folk fled away. He was laid in mound there down by the very sea, whereas it is called Adalsysla. So the Swedes fared home after this overthrow. So says Thiodolf:

Forth flew the news
How folk of Sysla
Had Yngvar done
To death a-fighting;
How Eastland folk
Beside the Sea-heart
Smote the fair-cheeked
Chieftain deadly.

Now the eastern sea
Ever singeth
Gymir's song
For the Swede-king's joyance.

CHAPTER XXXVII. OF KING ROAD-ONUND.

ONUND was the son of Yngvar; he was
the next to take the kingdom in Sweden.
In his day was there good peace in
Sweden, and he was very rich in chattels. King
Onund went with his army to Esthonia for the
avenging of his father. He went up a-land with
his host, and harried there far and wide, and got
great plunder, and went back in autumn-tide to
Sweden. In his days were there plenteous years
in Sweden, and King Onund was best beloved of
all kings. Now Sweden is a great woodland
country, and such great wild-woods are therein,
that it is many days' journey across them. So
King Onund set himself with great care and cost
to clearing the woods, and peopling the clearings;
he let also make ways through the wild-woods, and
wide about therein was found woodless land, and
thus great country-sides were peopled there. So
by this wise was the land widely settled, for the
folk of the land were enow for the peopling thereof.
King Onund let cut roads throughout all Sweden,
both through the woods and the mires, and the
mountain wilds; wherefore was he called Road-
Onund. King Onund set up a manor of his
in every shire of Sweden, and went through all the
land a-guesting.

CHAPTER XXXVIII. OF INGIALD EVIL-HEART.

ROAD-ONUND had a son hight Ingiald. Now in those days was Yngvar king in Fiadrundaland, and he had two sons by his wife, one hight Alf, the other Agnar, and they were much of an age with Ingiald. Wide about Sweden in that time were there county-kings of Road-Onund, and Swipdag the Blind ruled over Tenth-land. Upsala is in that county, and there is the Thing of all the Swedes holden; and there also were great blood-offerings, and many kings sought thither: and that was about mid-winter. So on a certain winter were many folk come to Upsala, and King Yngvar was there, and his sons; and both Alf, the son of King Yngvar, and Ingiald, the son of King Onund, were six winters old. So these fell to sporting as children use, and each was to rule over his own band, and so when they played together, then was Ingiald proven feebler than Alf, and so ill he deemed that, that he wept sore thereover. Then came to him Gautvid his foster-brother, and led him away to Swipdag the Blind his foster-father, and told him how it had gone ill with him, and that he was feebler and of less pith in the play than Alf, the son of King Yngvar. Then answered Swipdag that it was great shame thereof. So the next day Swipdag let take the heart out of a wolf and roast it on a spit, and gave it thereafter to Ingiald, the king's son, to eat: and thenceforth became he the grimmest of all men, and the evilest-hearted.

Now when Ingiald was come to man's estate, then King Onund wooed a wife for him, even Gauthild, the daughter of King Algaut, who was the son of King Gautrek the Bounteous, the son of Gaut, after whom is Gautland named. King Algaut thought assuredly that his daughter would be exceeding well wedded if she were given to the son of King Onund, if so be he was of the same mind as his father. So the may was sent to Sweden, and Ingiald wedded her in due time.

CHAPTER XXXIX. THE DEATH OF ONUND.

NOW King Onund went from manor to manor of his in the autumn-tide with his court, and journeyed to a place called Heavenheath, where there are certain strait mountain-valleys, with steep mountains on either side thereof. Heavy rain was falling at that tide, but before had snow fallen on the hills. So now there tumbled down a mighty slip with stones and clay; but King Onund and his folk were in the way of that slip, and the king gat his death thereby, and many of his men with him. So says Thiodolf:

Onund the king
Was caught by the bane
Of Jonaker's sons
Under the Heaven-fell.
All unsparing
On the Eastman's foeman

Came the wrathful
Corpse destroyer.

There the handler
Of Hogni's bulrush
By the world's bones
Was overwhelmèd.

CHAPTER XL.   A BURNING AT UP-SALA.

THEN Ingiald, the son of King Onund, took the kingdom at Upsala. Now the Upsala kings were the master-kings in Sweden, whenas there were many county-kings therein, from the time that Odin was lord in Sweden; but the chiefs that abode at Upsala were sole lords over the Swede-realm until that Agni died. But then was the realm first apportioned between brethren, as is afore writ; and afterwards the realm and kingdom drifted apart amongst kin, even as these were sundered; but some of these kings cleared great woodlands and peopled them, and thereby eked out their realms. But when King Ingiald took the realm and kingdom, were there many county-kings, as is written afore. Now King Ingiald let set afoot a great feast at Upsala, with the mind to hold the heirship feast over his father, King Onund; and he let array a certain hall, neither less nor less seemly than the hall at Upsala, and he called it the hall of the Seven Kings, and there were made therein seven high-seats.

King Ingiald sent men all over Sweden, and

bade to him kings and earls, and other men of
note. To this feast came King Algaut, the father-
in-law of Ingiald, and King Yngvar of Fiadrundaland, with his two sons, Alf and Agnar; King
Sporsniallr withal of Nerick, and Sigvat, King of
Eighth-land. But Granmar, King of Southman-
land, was not come. So six kings were set down in
the new hall; but one high-seat of those that King
Ingiald had let make was empty. All the folk that
had come thither had place in the new hall; but
King Ingiald had settled his own court and goodmen in the hall of Upsala. Now the custom it was
of those days that when an heirship feast was to be
holden over kings or earls, he who made the said
feast, and was to be brought to his heritage, should
sit on a stool before the high-seat, until such time
as the cup was borne in, which was called the
Bragi-cup: then should he stand up to meet the
Bragi-cup, and take oath, and drink out the cup
thereafter, and then be led into the high-seat
that was his father's, and thus was he fully come
into the heritage of all things after him.

Now in like ways was it done here, for when
the Bragi-cup came in, uprose Ingiald the king,
and took a great bull's horn, and took even such an
oath that he would increase his realm by the half on
every one of the four quarters of heaven, or else
would die; and therewithal he drank out the horn.
But when men were drunken a-night-time, then
spake King Ingiald to Gautvid and Hulvid, the
sons of Swipdag, and bade them arm with all their
folk, even as had been laid down aforehand that
same night. So they went out to the new hall

and bare fire thereto; and so then the hall fell
ablaze, and the six kings were burned therein with
all their folk, but all those who sought to come out
were slain speedily.

Thereafter King Ingiald laid under him all the
dominions that these kings had owned, and took
seat therefrom.

CHAPTER XLI. THE WEDDING OF HIORVARD.

KING GRANMAR heard the tidings of
all this bewrayal, and he deemed it might
well be that the same fate was brewing
for him, if he paid not good heed thereto. That
same summer Hiorvard the king, who was called
the Yling, came with his host to Sweden, and
laid his ships in the firth called Mirk-firth. But
when King Granmar knew that, he sent men to
him, and bade him come feast with him with all
his men; and he took the bidding gladly, because
he had not harried the realm of King Granmar.
So when he came to the feast, there was the welcome goodly. And so in the evening when the cup
came in, it was the wont of those kings who abode
at home that at the feasts which they let make, folk
should drink benights two and two, to every man
a woman, as far as men and women would pair,
and then the odd tale of them apart together; but
the viking law was it that they should drink all in
company, even when they were a-guesting. Now the
high-seat of King Hiorvard was dight over against
the high-seat of King Granmar, and all his men

sat on that dais. Then King Granmar bade his
daughter Hildigunna to array herself and bear ale
to the vikings ; and she was the fairest of all
women. So she took a silver bowl and filled it,
and went before King Hiorvard, and spake :
" Hail to ye all, O Ylfings! This in memory of
Rolf Kraki!" And therewith she drank the half
of the cup, and then gave it unto King Hiorvard.

Now he took the cup, yea, and her hand withal,
and bade her sit beside him ; but she said it was
not the use of vikings to drink sitting paired with
women. Hiorvard answered and said, it was
more like that now he would for a shift do this, to
let the viking law go somewhat, and drink paired
with her. Then sat Hildigunna beside him, and
they drank together, and talked of many things
that evening. But the next day when the kings
met, even Granmar and Hiorvard, Hiorvard fell
to his wooing, and bade for Hildigunna.

King Granmar laid the matter before Hild his
wife, and other great folk of his realm, and said that
they would have great avail in King Hiorvard.
Good rumour there was thereat, and to all it
seemed well counselled, and so the end was that
Hildigunna was betrothed to King Hiorvard, and
he wedded her. Hiorvard was to dwell with King
Granmar, because he had no son born to ward his
realm for him.

CHAPTER XLII. BATTLE IN SWEDEN
BETWEEN INGIALD AND THE KINS-
MEN-IN-LAW, GRANMAR AND THOR-
VARD.

THAT same autumn King Ingiald gathered
force with the mind to fall on those folk
allied; he had an host out from all those
realms which he had aforetime laid under him.
But when those kin-in-law heard thereof, they
gathered force in their realm, and there came to
their helping King Hogni and Hildir his son, who
ruled over East Gautland: Hogni was the father
of Hild, whom Granmar had to wife. So King
Ingiald went up a-land with all his host, and had
overwhelming odds against them. Now they
meet in battle, and of the hardest it was; but when
they had fought a little while, there fled away the
lords who ruled over Fiadrundaland and West
Gautland and Nerick and Eighth-land, with all
the host that were come from those lands, and gat
them to the ships. Then was Ingiald hard bestead
and gat many wounds, and therewith fled away to
his ships; but Swipdag the Blind, his foster-father,
fell there, and both his sons, Gautvid and Hulvid.
King Ingiald fared back to Upsala with things in
such a plight, and was ill-content with his journey,
and deemed it well to be seen that the host which he
had from his realm conquered by war would be but
untrusty. Sore war there was afterwards betwixt
King Ingiald and King Granmar; but when a long
while things had thus gone on, the friends of either
of them brought it so about that they made truce,

and the kings appointed a meeting between themselves, and they met and made peace together, even King Ingiald and King Granmar and King Hiorvard his son-in-law; and the peace should hold good betwixt them whiles they all three lived; and it was bound by oath and troth. The next spring went King Granmar to Upsala to the blood-offering, as the wont was at the coming of summer, for good peace; and suchwise the lot fell to him thereat that he would not live long: so he went back home to his realm.

CHAPTER XLIII.   DEATH OF THE KINGS GRANMAR AND HIORVARD.

THE next autumn fared King Granmar and King Hiorvard his son-in-law to guesting in the isle called Sili at their own manor therein; and so while they were at this feasting, thither came King Ingiald with his army on a night, and took the house over them, and burned them therein with all their folk. Thereafter he laid under him all the realm which those kings had had, and set lords over it.   But King Hogni and Hildir his son would oft ride up in the Swede-realm, and slay those men of Ingiald's whom he had set over the realm of King Granmar their kinsman-in-law.   So for a long while was there mighty strife betwixt King Hogni and King Ingiald; nevertheless King Hogni held his realm in King Ingiald's despite even to his death-day.

King Ingiald had two children by his wife, the eldest (a daughter) was called Asa, and the other,

Olaf the Tree-shaver; but this lad Gauthild, the wife of King Ingiald, sent to Bovi her foster-father in West Gautland, and there was he reared along with Saxi, the son of Bovi, who was called the Splitter.

Now men say that King Ingiald slew twelve kings, and betrayed them all whenas they trusted in him; he was called Ingiald Evil-heart, and was king over the greater part of Sweden. Asa, his daughter, he wedded to Gudrod, King of Scania; she was of like mind to her father. Asa brought it about that Gudrod slew his brother Halfdan; but Halfdan was the father of Ivar Wide-fathom. Withal Asa accomplished the death of Gudrod her husband, and then fled away to her father; and she was called Asa Evil-heart.

CHAPTER XLIV. THE DEATH OF INGIALD EVIL-HEART.

IVAR WIDE-FATHOM came to Scania after the fall of Gudrod, his father's brother, and straightway gathered together a great host, and went his ways up Swedenward. Now Asa Evil-heart was before that gone to her father; but King Ingiald was a-feasting at his manor of Ræning when he knew that the host of King Ivar was come anigh; nor did he deem that he was of might to meet King Ivar in battle; and, on the other hand, he deemed it certain that, if he fled away, his foes would gather together against him from every side. So he and Asa fell to that counsel which has now become far-famed,

for they made all their folk dead drunk, and then
let lay fire in the hall, and the hall burned there,
and all the folk that were therein, along with King
Ingiald and Asa. So says Thiodolf:

> There was Ingiald
> Trod to his ending
> By the reek-flinger
> At Ræning manor:
> When the house-thief
> Fiery footed
> Stalked through and through
> The God-sprung king.

> And such betiding,
> All the people
> Of Swedes must deem it
> Most seldom told of ;
> When he himself
> His life of valour
> The first of all men
> Must make nought of.

CHAPTER XLV. OF IVAR WIDE-FATHOM.

IVAR WIDE-FATHOM laid under him all
the Swede-realm, and he gat to him all Denmark withal, great part of Saxon-land and all
the East-realm, and the fifth part of England. Of
his kin are all who since him have been kings of
Denmark, and Sweden also, such as have been
sole kings thereof; for after Ingiald Evil-heart
the dominion of Upsala fell from the kin of the
Ynglings, that may be told up by the straight line
of forefathers.

CHAPTER XLVI.　OF OLAF TREE-SHAVER.

OLAF, the son of King Ingiald, when he heard tell of the fall of his father, fared with such folk as would follow him ; because the whole assembly of the Swedes rose up with one accord for the driving away of the kin of King Ingiald and all his friends. Olaf fared first into the parts of Nerick. But when the Swedes heard of him, where he was, then he might no more abide there; so he went west by the wild-wood ways to the river which falls from the north into the Vener, and is called the Elf. There he dwelt with his folk, and they fell to clearing of the woods and burning them, and there sithence they abode ; and in a little there grew up there great peopled country-sides, and they called the land Vermland, and exceeding good land was there. But when it was told of King Olaf in Sweden that he was clearing the woods, then they called him Olaf Tree-shaver, deeming his ways worthy of mocking. Olaf had to wife her who is called Solveig or Solva, the daughter of Halfdan Gold-tooth west of Sol-isles. Halfdan was the son of Solvi, the son of Solvar, the son of Solvi the Old, who first cleared Sol-isles. The mother of Olaf Tree-shaver was Gauthild; but her mother was Alof, daughter of Olaf the Far-sighted, King of Nerick. Olaf and Solveig had two sons, Ingiald and Halfdan ; and Halfdan was reared in Sol-isles with Solvi, his mother's brother, and was called Halfdan White-leg.

CHAPTER XLVII.   THE BURNING OF OLAF TREE-SHAVER.

NOW there were much folk who were outlaws that fled from Sweden from King Ivar, and they heard that Olaf Tree-shaver had good land in Vermland; and there flocked to him so many folk that the land might not bear them, so that there befell great famine and hunger; which evil they laid to the account of their king, as is the wont of the Swedes forsooth, to lay upon their kings both plenty and famine.

Now King Olaf was a man but little given to blood-offering, and the Swedes were ill content therewith, and deemed that thence came the scarcity. So they drew together a great host, and fell on King Olaf, and took the house over him, and burned him therein, and gave him to Odin, offering him up for the plenty of the year. This befell by the Vener; as says Thiodolf:

> By the side of the lake
> The temple-wolf swallowed
> The body of Olaf,
> Of him the tree-shaver:
> And there the glede-wrapt
> Son of Forniot
> Did off the raiment
> Of the king of the Swede-realm.
>
> So the high king
> Sprung from the kin
> Of the Upsal lords
> Died long ago.

CHAPTER XLVIII. HALFDAN WHITE-LEG TAKEN FOR KING.

SUCH as were wisest among the Swedes now found out that what had wrought the famine was, that the folk were more than the land might bear, and that the king had nought at all to do with it. Now they fall to and fare with all their host west over the Eidwood, and come down upon Sol-isles all unawares. There they slew King Solvi, but laid hands on Halfdan White-leg, and took him to be lord over them, and gave him the name of king, and he subdued Sol-isles to him. Thereafter he went with his host out to Raumrick, and warred there, and won that folk in war.

CHAPTER XLIX. OF HALFDAN WHITE-LEG.

HALFDAN WHITE-LEG was a mighty king: he had to wife Asa, the daughter of Eystein the Terrible, King of the Uplands, who ruled over Heathmark. Halfdan and Asa had two sons, Eystein and Gudrod. Halfdan gat to him much of Heathmark and Thotn and Hadaland, and great part of Westfold withal: he lived to be old, and died in his bed at Thotn, but was afterwards brought out to Westfold, and laid in mound in Skæreid at Skiringsal. So says Thiodolf:

All folk know it
How fate bereft
The law-upholders
Of Lord Halfdan;

How the hill-wards'
Helpsome daughter
There in Thotn
Took the folk-king.
Lo now, Skæreid
In Skiringsal
Hangs over the bones
Of the elf of the byrny.

CHAPTER L. OF INGIALD THE BROTHER OF HALFDAN.

INGIALD, the brother of Halfdan, was king of Vermland; but after his death Halfdan laid Vermland under him, and took seat thereof, and set earls thereover whiles he lived.

CHAPTER LI. THE DEATH OF KING EYSTEIN.

EYSTEIN, son of King Halfdan, was king after him in Raumrick and Westfold. He had to wife Hild, the daughter of Eric, son of Agnar, who was king of Westfold. Agnar, the father of Eric, was the son of Sigtrygg, the king of Vendil. King Eric had no son, and died while King Halfdan White-leg was yet alive. So Halfdan and Eystein his son took to them all Westfold, and Eystein ruled Westfold while he lived. In that time was Skiold king of Varna, and a mighty wizard he was. Now King Eystein went with certain warships over to Varna and harried there, and took whatso he came across, both raiment and other goods, and the gear of the bonders withal, and had a strand-slaughtering

there, and then he went his ways. Then came
King Skiold down to the strand with his host, but
King Eystein was gone away, and had crossed
over the firth, and Skiold beheld the sails of him.
Then he took his cloak and waved it abroad, and
blew therewith. And so as they sailed in past
Earl's-isle, King Eystein sat by the tiller, and
another ship was sailing anigh, and so amid a certain cross-sea, the sail-yard of the other ship smote
the king overboard, and he gat his bane thereby.
His men got his dead corpse, and it was brought
to Borro, and a mound heaped up over it at the
ending of the land out by the sea beside Vadla.
So says Thiodolf :

> King Eystein, smitten
> By stroke of sail-yard,
> To the may of the brother
> Of Byleist fared :
> The feast's bestower
> His rest now findeth
> Neath the sea's bones
> By the shore's ending,
>
> Where by the Goth-king
> Cometh ever
> The stream of Vadla
> Ice-cold to the great sea.

CHAPTER LII.   OF KING HALFDAN THE BOUNTEOUS AND THE MEAT-GRUDGING.

HALFDAN was the name of King
Eystein's son, who took the kingdom
after him. He was called Halfdan the
Bounteous and the Meat-grudging ; for it is told of

him that he gave in pay to his warriors as many
pennies of gold as other kings were wont to give
pennies of silver, yet he kept men short of meat.
A great warrior he was, and long time cruised a-
warring, and gat wealth to him. He had to wife
Hlif, the daughter of King Day of Westmere.
Holtar in Westfold was his chief manor. Here he
died in his bed, and was laid in mound at Borro :
even as Thiodolf says :

> To the Thing of Odin
> Was the king then bidden
> By Hvedrung's Maiden
> From the homes of men-folk ;
> Whenas King Halfdan,
> Dweller at Holtar,
> The doom of Norns
> Had done fulfilling.

> And battle-winners
> Their warrior-king
> Buried in mound
> At Borro later.

CHAPTER LIII. OF GUDROD, THE HUNTER-KING.

GUDROD was the name of Halfdan's son,
who took the kingdom after him. He
was called Gudrod the Proud, but some
called him the Hunter-king. He had a wife called
Elfhild, the daughter of Alfarin of Elfhome, and
had with her one half of Vingulmark. Their son
was Olaf, who was afterwards called Geirstead Elf.
Elfhome was then the name of the land betwixt
Raumelf and Gautelf. Now when Elfhild was
dead, then sent King Gudrod his men west to

Agdir, to the king who ruled thereover, who was
named Harald Red-lip, and they were to woo of
him for their king Asa his daughter ; but Harald
said them nay. So the messengers came back and
told the king of the speeding of their errand.   So
a little after King Gudrod thrust his ships into the
water, and went with a great host out to Agdir.
He came all unwares, and raised the fray,
coming a-night-time to King Harald's dwelling ;
but he, when he knew that war was upon him,
went out with such folk as he had, and a fight
there was, but over-great were the odds betwixt
them, and King Harald fell there with his son
Gyrd.   King Gudrod took great booty, and had
home with him Asa, daughter of King Harald,
and wedded her, and they had a son called Halfdan.   But when Halfdan was one winter old, in
the autumn-tide fared King Gudrod a-guesting,
and lay on his ship in Stifla-sound, and great
drinkings there were, and the king was very merry
with drink.   So in the evening when it was dark
the king went from the ship, but whenas he came
to the gangway end, then ran a man against him
and thrust him through with a spear, and that was
his bane ; but the man was slain straightway.
But in the morning when it was light the man was
known for Queen Asa's footpage ; neither did she
hide that it was done by her rede.   So says
Thiodolf :

> Lo, King Gudrod,
> Great of heart,
> Dead yore agone,
> By treason died ;

A head revengeful,
False rede and evil,
Wrought on the king,
By ale made merry;

And Asa's man,
The evil traitor,
Won by murder
The mighty king:
So e'en the king
On the ancient bed
Of Stifla-sound
Was stung to dying.

CHAPTER LIV. THE DEATH OF KING OLAF.

OLAF took the kingdom after his father. He was a mighty man and a great warrior; the fairest and strongest of all men, and great of growth. Westfold he had, because in those days King Elfgeir took under him all Vingulmark, and set thereover King Gandalf his son. Then the father and son drave hard into Raumrick, and gained the more part of that realm and people. Hogni was the son of King Eystein the Mighty, King of the Uplands; and he laid under him all Heathmark and Thotn and Hadaland; and therewithal fell Vermland from the sons of Gudrod, and that folk turned them to paying tribute to the Swede king. Now Olaf was twenty years old whenas Gudrod died, but when Halfdan his brother came to the realm along with him, then they shared the realm betwixt them; Olaf had the eastern part, but Halfdan the southern. King

Olaf had his abode at Geirstead, but he gat a disease in his foot, and died thereof, and is laid in mound at Geirstead. So sings Thiodolf:

A line descended
From Thror the mighty
Had thriven well
Thus far in Norway.
Wide through Westmere
While agone
King Olaf ruled
The land right proudly;

Until the foot-ache
By the earth's ending,
Brought unto nought
That battle-dealer.
The bold in warfare
At Geirstead bideth:
There is the howe heaped
Over the host-king.

CHAPTER LV. OF ROGNVALD HIGHER-THAN-THE-HILLS.

ROGNVALD was the son of King Olaf, who was king in Westfold after his father. He was called Higher-than-the-Hills, and of him did Thiodolf of Hvin make the Yngling-Tale. And so sayeth he:

That know I best
Neath the blue heavens
Of eke-names ever
Owned of king,
Whereas King Rognvald,
Who rules the rudder,
Higher-than-the-heaths
Is hight most fitly.

THE STORY OF HALFDAN THE BLACK.

THE STORY OF
HALFDAN THE BLACK.

CHAPTER I. HALFDAN FIGHTS WITH GANDALF AND SIGTRYGG.

HALFDAN was one winter old when his father fell. Asa, his mother, went forthwith west to Agdir, and straightway betook her to the realm her father Harald had had. There waxed Halfdan, and was big and strong even in his early years, and black-haired withal ; he was called Halfdan the Black. When he was eighteen winters old he took the rule in Agdir, and straightway he went to Westfold and shared the realm with Olaf his brother.

That same autumn he went with an army to Vingulmark against King Gandalf, and many battles they had together, and now one, now the other had the victory ; but in the end they made peace in such wise, that Halfdan was to have the half of Vingulmark that his father Gudrod had had. Thereafter fared King Halfdan up into Raumrick, and laid it unto him ; whereof heard King Sigtrygg, the son of King Eystein, who as then abode in Heathmark, and had aforetime subdued Raumrick. Then went King Sigtrygg with an host against

King Halfdan, and a great battle befell, and King Halfdan gained the day. So as the host broke into flight was King Sigtrygg smitten by an arrow under the left armpit, and he fell there. Thereafter King Halfdan laid all Raumrick under him. Eystein was another son of King Eystein, and the brother of King Sigtrygg, and was then king in Heathmark; and whenas King Halfdan was gone west to Westfold, King Eystein went with his host west to Raumrick, and laid the land there under him far and wide.

CHAPTER II. BATTLES BETWEEN HALFDAN AND EYSTEIN.

HALFDAN THE BLACK heard that there was war in Raumrick, so he drew an host together, and fared into Raumrick to meet King Eystein, and they had a battle there, and Halfdan gained the day, and Eystein fled away up into Heathmark. King Halfdan followed after him up into Heathmark with his host, and they had another battle there, and Halfdan prevailed; but Eystein fled north into the Dales to Gudbrand the Hersir. Thence he gat together men, and went in the winter out into Heathmark, and met Halfdan in a great island which lies amidst the lake of Miors; there had they battle, and many men fell on either side, but Halfdan gained the day. There fell Guthorm, the son of Gudbrand the Hersir, who was deemed the hopefullest man of the Uplands. Then Eystein fled again north into the Dales, and sent Hallvard Rascal, his kinsman, to meet King

Halfdan and bespeak peace with him. So for kinship's sake King Halfdan gave up to King Eystein the half of Heathmark even as those kinsfolk had owned it aforetime; but Halfdan brought Thotn under him, and the place called the Land, and he gained to him Hadaland also, and was withal an exceeding mighty king.

CHAPTER III. THE WEDDING OF HALFDAN THE BLACK.

HALFDAN THE BLACK took to wife a woman named Ragnhild, the daughter of Harald Gold-beard, King of Sogn; a son they had, to whom the king Harald gave his own name, and the child was reared at Sogn, in the house of King Harald, his mother's father. But whenas Harald was clean worn out by years, and was childless, he gave his realm to Harald, his daughter's son, and let him be made king, and a little after died Harald Gold-beard. That same winter died Ragnhild his daughter; and the spring after King Harald the Young fell sick and died in Sogn, when he was already ten years old. But as soon as Halfdan the Black heard of his death, he went his ways with a great host, and came north to Sogn, and was well taken to by folk; so there he claimed for himself the kingdom and heritage after his son, nor was there any to withstand him, and so he brought that realm under him. Then came to him Atli the Slender, Earl of Gaular, who was a friend of King Halfdan, and the king set this Earl Atli over the folk of Sogn to be judge

there by the law of the land, and to gather together
the scat for the king's hands.　Then went King
Halfdan thence to his kingdom in the Uplands.

CHAPTER IV.　BATTLE BETWIXT HALFDAN AND GANDALF'S SONS.

KING HALFDAN went in the autumn
out to Vingulmark ; and so on a night
whenas King Halfdan was a-feasting,
there came to him at midnight the man who
had holden the horse-ward, and told him that an
host was come nigh to the stead.　Then the king
arose straightway, and bade his men arm, and
therewith he went without and arrayed them.　But
even therewith were come thither Hysing and
Helsing, the sons of Gandalf, with a great host, and
there was a great battle.　But whereas King Halfdan was overborne by multitude, he must needs
flee away to the woods, having lost many men :
there fell Olvir the Sage, his foster-father.　Thereafter much folk drew toward King Halfdan, and
he went to seek the sons of Gandalf, and met them
at Eydi by the Eyna-skerries, and there they
fought, and Hysing and Helsing fell, but Haki
their brother fled away.　After that King Halfdan
laid all Vingulmark under him; but Haki fled into
Elfhome.

CHAPTER V. THE LATER WEDDING OF KING HALFDAN WITH THE DAUGHTER OF SIGURD HART.

SIGURD HART was the name of a king of Ringrick; he was bigger and stronger than any other man, and the fairest to look on of all men. His father was Helgi the Keen, but his mother was Aslaug, the daughter of Sigurd Worm-in-Eye, the son of Ragnar Lodbrok.

So tells the tale, that Sigurd was but twelve winters old when he slew Hildibrand the Bareserk and the whole twelve of them in single combat; many a work of fame he won, and long is the tale told of him. Now Sigurd had two children: Ragnhild was the name of his daughter, the grandest of all women, and she was at this tide twenty years old; but Guthorm, her brother, was but a youngling. Now it is told about the death of King Sigurd, that he would ride out alone into the wild-woods, even as his wont was: for he would hunt beasts great and hurtful to men, and exceeding eager he was herein.

So on a day whenas Sigurd had ridden a long way, he came into a certain clearing near by Hadaland, and there came against him Haki the Bareserk with thirty men, and they fought there. There fell Sigurd Hart, and twelve men of Haki, and he himself lost his hand and had three other wounds. Thereafter rode Haki with his men to the dwelling of Sigurd, and took there Ragnhild his daughter, and Guthorm her brother, and had

III.   G

them away with him, with much wealth and many
goodly things, and bore them home to Hadaland,
where he had great manors.   Then he let array a
feast, and was minded to wed Ragnhild, but the
matter was stayed, because it went ill with his
hurts.

So Haki the Hadaland-bareserk lay wounded
through harvest-tide, and till winter began.

But at Yuletide King Halfdan was guesting in
Heathmark, and had heard all these tidings.   So
on a morning early, when the king was clad, he
called to him Harek the Wolf, and bade him fare
over to Hadaland, and bring him Ragnhild, the
daughter of Sigurd Hart.   Harek arrayed him,
and had a company of an hundred men.   So he sped
his journey, that in the grey of the morning they
came over the water to Haki's stead, and took all
the doors of the hall wherein the housecarles slept.
Then went they to Haki's sleeping-bower, and brake
it open, and took thenceaway Ragnhild and Guthorm her brother, and all the wealth that was there,
and the hall and all men therein they burnt up.
Then they tilted over a wain in most seemly wise,
and set Ragnhild therein and Guthorm, and so
went their ways back unto the ice.

Haki arose and went after them awhile, but
when he came to the frozen water, then he set the
hilts of his sword downward, and fell on the point
thereof, so that the sword ran through him, and
there he gat his bane ; and he is buried there on
the water-bank.

Now King Halfdan saw how they fared over
the ice, for he was the keenest-eyed of all men,

and when he saw the tilted wain, he deemed full surely that their errand had sped as he would have it; so he let lay out the tables, and sent men wide through the country-side and bade many men to him; and good feast there was holden that day, for at that feast King Halfdan wedded Ragnhild, and she was a mighty queen thereafter. Now the mother of Ragnhild was Thorny, daughter of Klack-Harald, the King of Jutland, and sister of Thyri Denmark's Weal, the wife of King Gorm the Old, King of the Danes, who swayed the Dane-realm in those days.

CHAPTER VI. OF RAGNHILD'S DREAM.

QUEEN RAGNHILD dreamed great dreams, for wise of wit she was; and this was a dream of hers: She thought she stood in her grass-garth, and took a thorn out of her smock; and even whiles she held it, it waxed so, that it grew into a great rod, so that one end smote down into the earth and struck fast root therein; but the other end of the tree went high up aloft; and even therewith it seemed to her a tree so great that she might scarce see over it; yea, and wondrous thick it was: now the lower part of this tree was red as blood, but the bole thereof fair-green, and goodly, and the limbs up about as white as snow. Many and great branches there were on the tree, some aloft and some alow; and the limbs of the tree were so great, that she deemed they spread all over Norway; yea, and far wider yet.

CHAPTER VII. THE DREAM OF HALF-DAN.

KING HALFDAN dreamed never; and he deemed that a wondrous thing, and opened his mind on it to a man named Thorleif the Sage, and sought rede of him how to amend it. Thorleif told him what he was wont to do if he were curious in any matter, to wit, that he went to sleep in a swine-sty, and then lacked not ever of dreams. So the king did so, and this dream came to him: for he thought he had the fairest hair of any man, and it all fell in locks, some low down till they touched the earth, some to mid-leg, some to the knee, some to the loins or the midst of his side, some to the neck of him, and some but just springing up from his head like little horns; of diverse hues were these locks, but one lock prevailed above all the others for fairness and brightness and greatness.

So he told his dream to Thorleif, and he areded it in such wise, that great offspring would come of him, and that his kin would rule over lands with great honour, yet not all with the like honour, and that one would come of his kin greater and higher than all: and men hold it for sooth that that lock must betoken King Olaf the Holy.

Now King Halfdan was a wise man, trusty and upright; he made laws, and heeded them himself, and made all others heed them, lest the high hand should overthrow the law. He himself made a tale of blood-guilts, and settled duly the weregilds for each man after his birth and dignity.

Now Queen Ragnhild bore a son, and he was sprinkled with water and named Harald, and he speedily grew big, and the fairest that might be: there he waxed, and was of right great prowess from his early days, and well stored with wit and wisdom; his mother loved him much, but his father not so much.

CHAPTER VIII.   THE VANISHING OF HALFDAN'S MEAT.

KING HALFDAN was abiding through Yule-tide in Hadaland, and a marvel befell there on Yule-eve, whenas men had gone to table, and there were many men there. For lo, all the victual vanished from off the boards and all the good drink withal: so the king sat behind heavy of mood, and every man else made for his own home. But the king, to the end that he might know what had brought this thing about, let take a certain Finn, who was a great wizard, and would wring a true tale out of him, and tormented him, but gat nought of him.

Now the Finn cried ever for help on Harald, the king's son, and Harald prayed grace for him and gat it not; yet Harald delivered him, and let him go his ways, against the will of the king, and followed after him himself. So they came on their journey to where a lord held a great feast, and by seeming had goodly welcome there. So when they had abided there till spring-tide, then

spake the Lord to Harald on a day, and said :
"Great todo maketh thy father of his loss,
in that we took a little victual from him last
winter ; but with a fair tale will I reward thee
that. Lo now, thy father is dead, and thou shalt
go thy ways home, and thou wilt get to thee all
the realm that thy father had, and therewith shalt
thou become the Lord of all Norway."

CHAPTER IX. THE DEATH OF KING HALFDAN.

HALFDAN THE BLACK drave from
a feast at Hadaland, and the road led
him in such wise that he drave over the
water of Rand. Spring-tide it was, and the sun
was thawing all swiftly ; so as they drave over
Rykinswick, there in the winter-tide had been
wakes for the neat, but the muck had fallen on
the ice and made holes therein by reason of the
sun's thawing; but when the king drave thereover,
the ice brake under him, and there was King
Halfdan lost and much folk with him : he was by
then forty years old.

He had been of all others a king of plenteous
years ; and so much men made of him, that when
they heard he was dead, and his body brought to
Ringrick, where folk were minded to bury it,
then came great lords from Raumrick and Westfold and Heathmark, and all prayed to have the
corpse with them, to lay it in mound among their
own folk, deeming that they who got it might look
to have plenteous years therewith : so at last they

agreed to share the body in four, and the head was laid in mound at Stone, in Ringrick. Then of the others each took away their share, and laid it in mound; and all the mounds are called Halfdan's mounds.

THE STORY OF HARALD HAIRFAIR.

THE STORY OF
HARALD HAIRFAIR.

CHAPTER I. HARALD'S FIGHT WITH HAKI AND GANDALF HIS FATHER.

KING HARALD took the kingdom after his father when he was but ten winters old; he was the biggest of all men, the strongest, and the fairest to look on; a wise man, and very high-minded. Guthorm, his mother's brother, was made ruler of his bodyguard, and of all matters pertaining to his lands; withal he was duke of the host.

Now after the death of King Halfdan the Black many chieftains fell on the realm he had left, and the first man of these was King Gandalf, and those brethren Hogni and Frodi, the sons of King Eystein of Heathmark; Hogni Karason also was abroad far and wide through Ringrick. Then Haki Gandalfson also arrayed him to fare out to Westfold with three hundred men, and went the inland roads through certain dales, being minded to fall on King Harald unawares; but King Gandalf abode with his host in his land with intent to put across the firth, he and his army, into Westfold. But

when Duke Guthorm heard thereof he gathered an
army and went his ways with King Harald. And
first he goes to meet Haki up country, and they met
in a certain dale, and there was a battle fought, and
King Harald had the victory, but King Haki fell
there, and a great part of his folk, even at the
place sithence called Hakisdale. Then back wend
King Harald and Duke Guthorm, but by then
was King Gandalf come into Westfold, and so
each goes to meet the other, and when they met
was a hard fight foughten, but thence away fled
King Gandalf, and lost the more part of his men,
and came home to his own realm with things in
such a plight. And when these tidings come to
the sons of King Eystein of Heathmark, they looked
to have an host upon them speedily, so they send
word to Hogni Karason and Hersir Gudbrand,
and appoint a meeting between them at Ringsacre
in Heathmark.

CHAPTER II. KING HARALD OVER-COMES FIVE LORDS.

AFTER these battles fared King Harald
and Duke Guthorm with all the host
they may get, and wend toward the Uplands, going much by the woodland ways, and
they hear where the Upland kings have appointed
their muster, and come thither a-midnight, nor
were the warders aware of them till an host was
come before the very house wherein was Hogni
Karason, yea, and that wherein slept Gudbrand;
so they set fire to both of them, but Eystein's sons

got out with their men and fought a while, and there fell both Hogni and Frodi.

After the fall of these four lords, King Harald, by the might and furtherance of Guthorm his kinsman, got to him Ringrick and Heathmark, Gudbrand's-dales and Hadaland, Thotn, and Raumrick, and all the northern parts of Vingulmark. Thereafter had King Harald and Duke Guthorm war and battles with King Gandalf, with such end that Gandalf fell in the last battle, and King Harald got to him all his realm south away to Raumelf.

CHAPTER III.   OF GYDA, ERIC'S DAUGHTER.

KING HARALD sent his men after a certain maiden called Gyda, the daughter of King Eric of Hordaland, and she was at fostering at Valldres with a rich bonder. Now the king would fain have her to his bed-mate, because she was a maiden exceeding fair, and withal somewhat high-minded. So when the messengers came there, they put forth their errand to the maiden, and she answered in this wise :

"I will not waste my maidenhood for the taking to husband of a king who has no more realm to rule over than a few Folks. Marvellous it seems to me," she says, "that there be no king minded to make Norway his own, and be sole lord thereof in such wise as Gorm of Denmark or Eric of Upsala have done."

Great words indeed seemed this answer to the

messengers, and they ask her concerning her words, what wise this answer shall come to, and they say that Harald was a king so mighty, that the offer was right meet for her. But yet though she answered to their errand otherwise than they would, they see no way as at this time to have her away but if she herself were willing thereto, so they arrayed them for their departing, and when they were ready, men lead them out ; then spake Gyda to the messengers :

"Give this my word to King Harald, that only so will I say yea to being his sole and lawful wife, if he will first do so much for my sake as to lay under him all Norway, and rule that realm as freely as King Eric rules the Swede-realm, or King Gorm Denmark ; for only so meseems may he be called aright a King of the People."

CHAPTER IV. OF KING HARALD'S BOUNDEN OATH.

THE messengers fare back to King Harald and tell him of this word of the maiden, calling her overbold and witless, and saying withal that it would be but meet for the king to send after her with many men, for the doing of some shame to her. Then answered the king that the maid had spoken nought of ill, and done nought worthy of evil reward. Rather he bade her much thank for her word; "For she has brought to my mind that matter which it now seems to me wondrous I have not had in my mind heretofore."

And moreover he said: "This oath I make fast, and swear before that god who made me and rules over all things, that never more will I cut my hair nor comb it, till I have gotten to me all Norway, with the seat thereof and the dues, and all rule thereover, or else will I die rather."

For this word Duke Guthorm thanked him much, and said it were a work worthy of a king to hold fast this word of his.

CHAPTER V. BATTLE IN ORKDALE.

AFTER this the kinsmen gather much folk and array them to go into the Uplands, and so north through the Dales, and thence north over the Dofrafell; and when they came down into the peopled country, they let slay all men and burned the country. So when the folk were ware of this all who might fled away; some down to Orkdale, some to Gauldale, some into the woodland; and yet othersome sought for peace, and all got that who came to the king and became his men. Nought they found to withstand them before they came to Orkdale, and there was a gathering against them, and there they had their first fight with a king called Gryting. King Harald had the victory, and Gryting was taken, and much of his folk slain; but he gave himself up to King Harald, and swore oaths of fealty to him: thereafter all the Orkdale folk submitted them to King Harald and became his men.

CHAPTER VI. HOW KING HARALD LAID LAW ON THE LAND.

SUCH law King Harald laid on all land that he won to him, that he made all free lands his own, and he caused the bonders pay land dues to him, both the rich and the unrich. He set up an earl in each county, who should maintain law and right in the land, and gather all fines and land dues; and each earl was to have a third of the scat and the dues for his board and costs. Each earl was to have under him four hersirs or more, and each of these was to have twenty marks for his maintenance. Each earl was to bring sixty men-at-arms to the king's host at his own costs, and each hersir twenty; but by so much had King Harald increased the taxes and land dues, that his earls had more wealth and might than the kings had had aforetime. So when this was heard of about Thrandheim, then many rich men came to King Harald and became his men.

CHAPTER VII. BATTLE IN GAUL-DALE.

IT is told that Earl Hakon Griotgard's son came to King Harald from the west from Yriar with a great company for the helping of King Harald; and after that went King Harald to Gauldale, and had a battle there, and slew two kings, and gat their realms to him, that is to say, the Gauldale-folk and the Strind-folk. Then he gave to Earl Hakon the lordship over the Strind-folk. Thereafter King Harald went into Stior-dale and had there a third battle, and won the victory, and gat that folk to him. After these things the upcountry Thrandfolk gathered to-gether, and four kings with their hosts were assembled; whereof one ruled over Verdale, the second over Skaun, the third the folk of the Sparbiders, and the fourth from Inner-isle who ruled the Isles'-folk: these four kings went with their host against King Harald, and he fell to battle with them and gained the day, and of these kings, some fell, and some fled. King Harald had eight battles in all, yea, or more, in Thrandheim, and when eight kings had been slain, he gat to him all Thrandheim.

CHAPTER VIII. HARALD WINS THE NAUMDALE FOLK.

NORTH in Naumdale were two brethren kings, Herlaug and Hrollaug, and they had been three summers at the making of a howe, and that howe was built of stone and lime, and roofed with timber; and so when it was all done, those brethren heard the tidings that King Harald with his host was coming upon them. Then let King Herlaug gather to the howe much victual and drink, and thereafter went into the howe with eleven men, and then let cover up the howe again.

But King Hrollaug went on the top of the howe whereon the kings were wont to sit, and let array

the kingly high-seat, and sat down therein ; then
he let lay pillows on the footpace whereon the
earls were wont to sit, and tumbled himself down
from the high-seat on to the earl's seat, and gave
himself the name of earl.

After that fared Hrollaug to meet King Harald,
and gave him up all his realm, and prayed to become his man, and told in what wise he had done
in all things ; then King Harald took a sword and
did it on to his girdle, then hung a shield about the
neck of him, and made him his earl, and led him
to the high-seat; then he gave him the Naumdale
folk, and made him earl over them.

CHAPTER IX.   HOW KING HARALD MANNED SHIP.

THEREWITH King Harald fared back
to Thrandheim, and abode there the winter
through, and called it his home ever after,
and there he set up his chiefest stead, which was
called Ladir.

That winter he wedded Asa, the daughter of
Earl Hakon Griotgard's son, and Hakon had
beyond all men the greatest honour of the king.
In the spring Harald gat a-shipboard, for he had
let make in the winter a dragon-galley, great, and
arrayed in the seemliest wise. The said dragon he
manned with his court-guard and bareserks; the
stem-men were the men most tried, because
they had with them the king's banner; aft from
the stem to the baling-place was the forecastle,
and that was manned by the bareserks. Those

only could get court-service with King Harald
who were men peerless both of strength and good
heart, and all prowess ; with such only was his ship
manned, whereas by now he had good choice of
men to pick out for his bodyguard from every folk.
He had a great company of folk, and big ships, and
many mighty men followed him.   Hereof tells
Hornklofi in Glymdrapa how that King Harald had
fought in the Updale Woods with the Orkdalers
or ever he led out his folk on this voyage :

> The king for ever wrathful
> With them that crave the singing
> Of the fight-fish on its home-road,
> Had battle high on the heathland,
> Ere the high-heart war-din's raiser
> With sea-skates fell a-faring
> To the battle of the horses
> In wind-swept hall that welter.
>
> The host of the war-din's heeder,
> Who showeth hell to robbers,
> Set battle-din a-roaring
> Over the wolf-pack's highway,
> Ere that manscathe that meeteth
> The home-way unto the sea-log
> Drave the proud-gliding dragon
> And sundry ships out seaward.

CHAPTER X. BATTLE AT SOLSKEL.

KING HARALD led out his folk from
Thrandheim, and turned south toward
Mere ; but Hunthiof was the king's
name who ruled over the Mere-folk, and Solfi
Klofi was his son's name, and mighty men of war
they were. But the king who ruled Raumsdale was

called Nockvi, and he was the father of Solfi's mother. These kings drew together a great host when they heard tidings of King Harald, and went against him, and they met at Solskel. There then was battle, and King Harald gained the day. Thereof singeth Hornklofi:

> Storm drave from the north the board-steed;
> So that the wargear's wielder
> Was borne aboard amidward
> The battle of two war-kings.
> There then the kings all valiant
> Wordless each other greeted
> With din-shots midst the murder;
> The red shields' voice long lasted.

Both the kings fell, but Solfi fled away; and both these folks did Harald lay under him, and dwelt there long that summertide. There he set up law and right for men, and established rulers over them, and took the fealty of folk; but, autumntide come, he arrayed him to fare northaway unto Thrandheim. Rognvald the Mere Earl, son of Eystein Glumra, had become King Harald's man that summer, and him King Harald made lord over the two folks, Northmere and Raumsdale, and strengthened his hands thereto both with lords and franklins; and ships he gave him withal that he might ward the land against war: he was called Rognvald the Mighty, or the Keen-counselled, and as folk say it was good sooth of either name. So King Harald abode the next winter in Thrandheim.

CHAPTER XI.   FALL OF THE KINGS ARNVID AND AUDBIORN.

NOW the spring thereafter King Harald gathered a mighty host out of Thrandheim, and said that he was minded to lead it to Southmere. Solfi Klofi had abided in warships out at sea the winter long, and he had harried in Northmere; many men of King Harald's he slew there; othersome he robbed, othersome he burned out of house and home, and wrought there all deeds of war. Nathless in the winter he had whiles been with King Arnvid, his kinsman, in Southmere.

So when these get news of King Harald, they gathered together their folk, and were no few; whereas many deemed that they owed hatred to King Harald. Now fared Solfi Klofi south into the Firths unto King Audbiorn, who ruled thereover, and bade his help, to fare with his host for the strengthening of him and Arnvid, and in this wise he spake:

"Easy it is for us all to see how that we have but one choice: either to rise up all against King Harald, and might enow we shall have then, and in the hands of Hap shall the victory be; or otherwise there is this, a thing forsooth not to be chosen by folk named and holden no less nobly-born than this Harald, to wit, to become his thralls. My father deemed it a better choice to fall in battle, a very king, than to be the underling of King Harald."

So thus prevailed the redes of Solfi that King Audbiorn gave his word to go, and gathered an host together, and went north to meet King Arnvid; and a full mighty host they had. Now heard they tidings of King Harald, that he was newcome from the north, and they met inward of Solskel.

Now in those days the wont was, when men fought a-shipboard, to bind the ships together and fight from the forecastle; and even so was it now done. King Harald laid his ship against King Arnvid's ship, and keen enow was the battle, and much folk fell of either side; but in the end waxed King Harald so wood-wroth that he went forth on to the forecastle of his ship, and there fought so fiercely that all the forward fighting-folk of Arnvid's ship gave back before him to the mast, and some there were that fell. Then did King Harald follow after on to their ship, and Arnvid's men took to flight, but he himself fell on his own ship. There also fell King Audbiorn, but Solfi fled away; as singeth Hornklofi:

> Our lord stirred up the spear-storm
> Where the byrny's fowl rent armour
> Amidst the din of Skögul,
> And blood the red wound snorted.
> Where on the Work the warriors
> Sank life-bereft before him.
> Mad yelled on shields the weapon
> While dyer of edges triumphed.

Of Harald's folk fell Asgaut and Asbiorn, the king's earls, Griotgard withal and Herlaug, his wife's brothers, the sons of Hakon, the Earl of Ladir.

A long while hereafter was Solfi a viking, and

oft wrought great scathe in the realm of King Harald.

CHAPTER XII. THE BURNING OF KING VEMUND.

THEREAFTER King Harald laid Southmere under him. But Vemund, brother of King Audbiorn, held the Firth-folk, and became king thereover; and now was autumn far spent. So men gave counsel to King Harald that he should not fare south about the Stad of an autumn day. Then King Harald set Earl Rognvald over either Mere and Raumsdale, and a many folk had the earl about him as then; and therewithal King Harald turned back north to Thrandheim.

That same winter fared Earl Rognvald by the inner course through Eid, and then southward past the Firths : he espied the goings of King Vemund, and so came a-night-tide to a certain stead hight Naust-dale, whereat was King Vemund a-feasting. There took Earl Rognvald the house over their heads, and burned King Vemund therein with ninety men. Thereafter came Kari of Berdla to Earl Rognvald with a long-ship all manned, and they went both together north to Mere. Earl Rognvald took the ships which King Vemund had owned, and all the chattels that he gat there. Kari of Berdla went north to Thrandheim unto King Harald, and became his man; he was a mighty bareserk.

CHAPTER XIII. THE FALL OF EARL HAKON AND EARL ATLI THE SLENDER.

THE springtide hereafter went King Harald south along the land with his host of ships, and subdued to him the Firth-folk; then east along the land he sailed till he hove-to at Wick in the east. But he left behind Earl Hakon Griotgard's son, and gave him rule in the Firths. But when the king was gone east, then sent Hakon word to Earl Atli the Slender, bidding him get him gone from Sogn and be earl in Gaular, as he had been aforetime; for he said that King Harald had given him Sogn; but Earl Atli sent word again that he would hold both Sogn and Gaular to boot until he should see King Harald. Hereof the earls strove till either gathered an host together, and they met at Fialir in Staffness-bay, and there fought a great fight. There fell Earl Hakon, and Atli was hurt deadly, whose men fared with him to Atlis-isles, where he died. So saith Eyvind the Skald-spoiler:

There Hakon, stem
Of Hogni's daughter,
All a-fighting
Was stripped of weapons.
Mid edges'-din
Frey's offspring there
At Fjalir laid
His life adown.

Where fell the friends,
The kin of the Stonegarth,
Mid mighty din

Of the friend of Lodur,
There it was
That the wave of Staffness
With blood of men
Was all to-blended.

CHAPTER XIV. OF KING HARALD AND ERIC THE SWEDE KING.

KING HARALD led his host east into Wick, and laid his ships up for Tunsberg, which was a cheaping-stead in those days; he had then dwelt four years in Thrandheim, nor had been for that while in the Wick. Now he heard tidings that Eric, son of Eymund, King of the Swedes, had laid under him Vermland and took scat there of all the woodland folk; and how that he had called the land West Gautland north-away to Swinesound, and west-away to the sea: all that the Swede-king claimed as his own, and took scat of; and an earl he had set there called Rani the Gautlander, who ruled all between Swinesound and Gaut-elf, and was a mighty earl. Now King Harald was told that the word of the Swede-king was that he would leave not till he had as much rule in the Wick as Sigurd King had aforetime, or Ragnar Lodbrok his son, Raum-realm to wit, and Westfold right out to Grenmar, Vingulmark also, and thenceaway south; and many great chiefs and other folk all about these folk-lands had already turned to the rule of the Swede-king. King Harald was full ill content herewith, and forthwith gathered together a mote

of the bonders there at Fold, and bore witness
against them of treason. Some put the charge
from them; some paid money therefor, and some
were punished; and in such wise he dealt with all
that folk-land that summer; and in autumn he
went up into Raum-realm, and dealt in like wise,
laying all the country under him. But in the beginning of winter he heard how Eric the Swede-king
rode abroad guesting with his court in Vermland.

CHAPTER XV. THE KINGS FEAST WITH AKI: THE DEATH OF HIM.

KING HARALD got ready and went his
ways east over the Eid-wood, and so
came out into Vermland, and let array
feasts before him. Now there was a man named
Aki, the mightiest bonder of Vermland, exceeding
wealthy, but now much stricken in years; he sent
men to King Harald, and bade him to a feast, and
the king gave his word to go at the day appointed.
King Eric also did Aki bid to feast on the self-same
day. Aki had a great guest-hall, now waxen old; so
he let build another one anew, nowise lesser, and
arrayed it in the best wise. The new hall he let
hang with gear all new, but the old one with old
gear; and when the kings came to the feast, King
Eric and his court were marshalled in the old hall,
but King Harald in the new hall with his men;
and such wise was the fashion of the table-gear,
that Eric and his men had old beakers and horns,
gilt though they were, and full fairly fashioned;
but King Harald and his men had new beakers

and horns, all done about with gold, fair-graven
withal, and shining as clear as glass; but in either
hall was the drink of the best that might be. But
goodman Aki had aforetime been liegeman of
Halfdan the Black.

Now when the day came that the feast was
ended, the kings arrayed them for departure, and
the horses were saddled. Then went Aki before
King Harald, having with him his son of twelve
winters old, Ubbi by name, and spake: "If thou
deemest me, lord, worthy of thy friendship for the
goodwill's sake I have shown to thee in this thy
guesting, reward my son therefor; and I give
him to thee for thy servant."

Then the king thanked him for his welcome
with many fair words, and promised him his full
friendship in return thereof. Then brought forth
Aki great gifts, which he gave to the king; and
therewithal they kissed, Aki and the king.

Thereafter went Aki to the Swede king, and
there was King Eric clad and ready for the road,
but was somewhat moody withal. So Aki took
good gifts, which he gave to the king; but the
king answered little, and leapt a-horseback, and
Aki went on the way with the king, and talked
with him. A wood lay anigh to the house, and the
road went therethrough; and when Aki came to
the wood the king asked him: "Why didst thou
deal so diversely between me and Harald in our
guesting, so that he had the better part in all
things, whereas thou wottest that thou art my
man?" Says Aki: "I was deeming, lord, that
neither thou nor thy men lacked aught of welcome

at this feast ; but whereas the gear where ye drank was old, it was because thou art now old, and Harald is in the very flower of his life-days ; therefore gat I the new gear for him. And whereas thou wouldst bring to my mind that I am thy man, I wot not but that thou art just so much mine." Then the king drew his sword and smote him to death, and went his ways.

But when King Harald was ready to leap a-horseback, he bade call Master Aki to him. So when men ran to seek him, some came on the road whereby King Eric had ridden, and found Aki lying dead there. So they went back and told King Harald. But when he heard it he called on his men to avenge Master Aki, and so he and his rode by the way King Eric had ridden afore, till either side were ware of other. Then both rode all they might till they came to the wood that parteth Gautland from Vermland. Then King Harald turned back into Vermland, and laid it all under him, and slew King Eric's men wheresoever he might come on them.

And so King Harald went back in the winter to Raum-realm, and abode there a while.

CHAPTER XVI. KING HARALD FARES TO TUNSBERG.

KING HARALD went in the winter-tide out to Tunsberg, and to his ships there ; and he dight his ships and crossed the Firth eastward and laid all Vingulmark under him; and all the winter long he lay out in his war-ships, and harried in Ran-realm; as saith Thorbiorn Hornklofi:

> Our lord the high-hearted
> If his own will rule only
> Out a-doors drinketh Yule,
> All Frey's game a-faring.
> E'en young was he loathing
> The fire-bake, the hall-nook;
> Loathed the bowers of women,
> And warm downy mittens.

Now the Gautlanders had been drawing together throughout all the country-side.

CHAPTER XVII. BATTLE IN GAUT-LAND.

BUT in the spring, when the ice was gone, the Gautlanders staked the Gaut-elf that King Harald might not bring his ships up into the land. But King Harald brought his ships up the Elf and laid them by the stakes, and harried on either shore, and burned the steads; as singeth Hornklofi:

> The feeder of the fight-mew
> Hath land and men laid under,
> All southward of the deep sea,
> The king in battle hardy!
> The great king the high-hearted,
> Wont to the Helm of Aweing,
> Let bind the linden's wild-deer
> Unto the stakes off shore there.

Then rode the Gautlanders down with a mighty host, and joined battle with King Harald, and great was the fall of men; but such end there was

thereof that King Harald prevailed; as singeth
Hornkloſi :

> Throve roar of upreared axes,
> The spears fell on a-howling,
> Bit men the swords black-gleaming
> Of the followers of the mighty.
> Where the Gautfolk's foe prevailéd,
> High then arose the singing
> Of the spears to flight commanded
> About the necks of warriors.

CHAPTER XVIII. THE FALL OF RANI THE GAUTLANDER.

KING HARALD fared a-warring wide
about Gautland, and had many battles
on either side the Elf, and oftenest gained
the day; till in a certain fight fell Rani the Gautlander. Then King Harald subdued to him all
the land north of the Elf and west of the Venner-
Water, and all Vermland to wit; and when he
turned away thence he set Duke Guthorm over the
land with a great company; but he himself turned
toward the Uplands, and dwelt there awhile. Then
he fared north over the Dofra-fell to Thrandheim,
and abode there a long while.

And now began children to be born to King
Harald. By Asa he had these sons: Guthorm was
the eldest; then Halfdan the Black and Halfdan
the White, twins; and Sigfrod the fourth: all
these were nourished in Thrandheim in great
honour.

CHAPTER XIX. BATTLE IN HAFURS-FIRTH.

NOW came tidings from the south that the men of Hordaland and Rogaland, they of Agdir and Thelmark, had arisen and gathered together with great plenty of weapons and ships and many men; and their captains were Eric, king of Hordaland, Sulki, king of Rogaland, and Earl Soti his brother, Kiotvi the Wealthy, king of Agdir, and Thorir Long-chin; from Thelmark came two brethren, Roald and Rig, and Hadd the Hardy to wit.

But when King Harald heard these tidings he gathered an host, and put forth his ships into the sea. Then he arrayed a great host, and fared south along the land, and gat many men from every folk-land. But when he was come south about the Stad, King Eric heard thereof; and he had by then gotten together all the folk he looked to have. So he fared south to meet the host that he wotted would come from the east to his helping; and the whole host of them met north of Jadar and made for Hafursfirth, where lay King Harald with his host awaiting them. There a great fight befell, and both long and hard it was; but such was the end thereof that King Harald had the victory, and King Eric fell there, and King Sulki, and Earl Soti his brother. Thorir Long-chin had laid his ship against King Harald's; and a great bareserk was Thorir. Hard was the brunt before Thorir fell, when his ship was cleared utterly. Then fled away King Kiotvi to a certain holm where was good vantage for fighting. Then all their host fled away, some by ship, and some ran up country, and so inland south about Jadar. So singeth Hornklofi :

Heardst thou in Hafursfirth
How there fell the battle
Twixt the king of high kindred
And Kiotvi the Wealthy?
From east-away came the ships
All eager for battle,
With grim gaping heads
And prow-plates fair-graven.

Of wight-men was their lading
And shields white-shining ;
Spears of the Westlands
And Welsh-wrought swords.
Roared there the bareserks,
Battle-wood was the host,
Loud howled the Wolf-coats
And clattered the iron.

The strong master tried they,
Bold lord of the Eastmen,
The bider at Outstone,
But fleeing he taught them.
Beached ships he ran out
When of battle he wotted ;
Fast shields were a-clashing
Ere Long-chin fell dead.

The brawny-necked king
Waxed a-weary of warding
His land from the Shock-head,
And let the holm shield him.
Down neath the decks then
Dived the lads wounded,
Their buttocks uphoven,
Their heads by the keel laid.

Bold men stone-battered,
Blenched from the battle,

Hung Odin's hall-tiles
Behind them to glitter.
Home then from Hafursfirth
Hied they by Jadar ;
Trembled the gold-staves,
And set heart on the mead-horn.

CHAPTER XX. KING HARALD BE-COMETH ONLY LORD OF NORWAY. OF THE PEOPLING OF THE WASTE LANDS.

AFTER this battle King Harald found nought to withstand him in all Norway; for all his greatest foemen were fallen. But certain fled away from the land, and a many folk were these ; for then were the waste lands peopled far and wide. Jamptland and Helsing-land were peopled, though either of them in-deed had been somewhat peopled by Northmen aforetime.

Amid this unpeace, whenas King Harald was fighting for the land in Norway, were the Outlands found and peopled, the Faroes and Iceland to wit ; also was there much faring of Northmen to Shetland. And many mighty men of Norway fled as outlaws before King Harald, and fell to the warring of the West : in the winter they abode in the South-isles or the Orkneys, but a-summer harried in Norway, and wrought great scathe on the land.

Nevertheless there were many mighty men who did fealty to King Harald and became his men, and abode in the land along with him.

III.   I

CHAPTER XXI. OF THE CHILDREN OF KING HARALD, AND OF HIS WEDDINGS.

AND now when King Harald was gotten to be only Lord of Norway, he called to mind the word that the great-hearted maiden had spoken to him, and sent men after her, and had her to him, and bedded her. These were their children : Alof the eldest, then Rœrek, then Sigtrygg, then Frodi and Thorgils.

King Harald had many wives and many children. He wedded her who is called Ragnhild, daughter of Eric, king of Jutland. Ragnhild the Mighty was she called, and their son was Eric Blood-axe. Moreover, he had to wife Swanhild, daughter of King Eystein, and these were their sons : Olaf Geirstead-elf, Biorn, and Ragnar Ryckil ; and again had King Harald to wife Ashild, daughter of Ring Dayson down from Ring-realm, and their children were Day and Ring, Gudrod Skiria, and Ingigerd.

So folk say that when King Harald wedded Ragnhild the Mighty he put away from him nine of his wives. Hereof singeth Hornklofi :

> The king of high kindred
> When his Dane-wife he wedded,
> Put from him the Holmfolk,
> And Hordaland maidens,
> Each woman of Heathmark,
> All kindred of Holgi.

King Harald's children were nourished ever whereas their mothers' kin dwelt. Duke Guthorm

sprinkled the eldest son of King Harald with water,
and gave him his own name. He set the lad on his
knee, and became his fosterer, and had him away
with him east into the Wick. There he was
nourished with Duke Guthorm. Duke Guthorm
had all rule of the land about the Wick and the
Uplands when King Harald was not nigh.

CHAPTER XXII. OF KING HARALD'S FARING TO THE WESTLANDS.

NOW heard King Harald how the vikings
harried wide about the midmost of the
land, even such as were a-wintertide West-
over-sea. So he had out his host every summer,
and searched isles and out-skerries; and whenso
the vikings were ware of his host they fled away;
yea, the more part right out to sea. But when the
king grew a-weary of this work, this betid, that on
a summer he sailed with his host West-over-sea,
and came first to Shetland, and there slew all the
vikings who might not flee before him. Then he
sailed south to the Orkneys, and cleared them utterly
of vikings. And thereafter he fared right away to
the South-isles, and harried there, and slew many
vikings who were captains of bands there. There
had he many battles, and ever gained the day.
Then he harried in Scotland, and had battles there.
And when he came west to Man, the folk thereof
had heard already what warfare King Harald had
done in the land aforetime, and all folk fled into Scotland, so that Man was all waste of men, and all the
goods that might be were flitted away. So when

King Harald and his folk went a-land they gat no prey there.   So sayeth Hornklofi :

> Bore the much-wise gold-loader
> To the townships shields a-many —
> The grove of Nith-wolves' land-lace,
> In the land prevailed in battle —
> Ere needs must flee the Scot-host
> Before the fight-proud waster
> Of the path of the fish that playeth
> Around the war-sword's isthmus.

In these battles fell Ivar, son of Rognvald the Mere-Earl.   But to boot the loss of him King Harald, when he sailed from the West, gave Earl Rognvald the Orkneys and Shetland.   But Rognvald straightway gave both the lands to Sigurd his brother, who abode behind in the West.   And the king or ever he fared back east gave the earldom to Sigurd.   Then there joined him to Sigurd, Thorstein the Red, son of Olaf the White and Aud the Deeply-wealthy, and they harried in Scotland, and won to them Caithness and Sutherland all down to the Oikel-Bank.   Now Earl Sigurd slew Tusk-Melbrigda, a Scottish earl, and bound his head to his crupper; but he smote the thick of his leg against the tooth as it stuck out from the head, and the hurt festered so that he gat his bane therefrom, and he was laid in howe in Oikel-Bank.   Then Guthorm his son ruled the lands for one winter, and then died childless, and thereafter many vikings, Danes and Northmen, sat them down in his lands.

CHAPTER XXIII. THE CUTTING OF KING HARALD'S HAIR.

NOW King Harald was a-feasting in Mere at Earl Rognvald's, and had now gotten to him all the land. So King Harald took a bath, and then he let his hair be combed, and then Earl Rognvald sheared it. And heretofore it had been unshorn and uncombed for ten winters. Aforetime he had been called Shockhead, but now Earl Rognvald gave him a by-name, and called him HARALD HAIRFAIR, and all said who saw him that that was most soothly named, for he had both plenteous hair and goodly.

CHAPTER XXIV. ROLF WEND-AFOOT MADE AN OUTLAW.

ROGNVALD the Mere-Earl was a friend most well beloved of King Harald, and the king held him in great honour. Earl Rognvald wedded Hild, daughter of Rolf Nefia, and their sons were Rolf and Thorir. Earl Rognvald had also three children from his bedmates, to wit, Hallad the first, Einar the second, Hrollaug the third; and these were already come to man's estate when their lawfully gotten brethren were but children.

Rolf was a great viking, and a man so great of growth that no horse might bear him, wherefore he went afoot wheresoever he fared, and was called Rolf Wend-afoot. He would be ever a-harrying in the Eastlands; and on a summer

when he came to the Wick from his Eastland
warring he had a strand-slaughtering there. King
Harald was in the Wick at that time, and was
very wroth when he heard hereof, for he had laid
a great ban upon robbing in the land. Wherefore
at a Thing he gave out that he made Rolf outlaw
from all Norway. But when Hild, the mother
of Rolf, heard thereof, she went to the king and
prayed him for peace for Rolf; but the king was
so wroth that her prayers availed nought. Then
sang Hild:

> Thou hast cast off Nefia's namesake ;
> Brave brother of the barons,
> As a wolf from the land thou drivest.
> Why waxeth, lord, thy raging ?
> Ill to be wild in quarrel
> With a wolf of Odin's war-board.
> If he fare wild in the forest
> He shall waste thy flock right sorely.

Rolf Wend-afoot fared thereafter west-over-sea
to the South-isles. Thence west he went to
Valland, and harried there, and won therein a
mighty earldom, and peopled all the land with
Northmen, and thenceforward has that land been
called Normandy.

The son of Rolf Wend-afoot was William, the
father of Richard, the father of Richard the second,
the father of Robert Long-sword, the father of
William the Bastard, king of the English ; and
from him are come all the English kings thenceforward. From Rolf's kin also are come earls in
Normandy.

Queen Ragnhild the Mighty lived three winters

after she came to Norway. After her death Eric, the son of her and Harald, went to the Firths to be fostered of Hersir Thorir, the son of Roald, and there was he nourished.

CHAPTER XXV. OF SWASI THE WIZARD AND KING HARALD.

ON a winter went King Harald a-guesting in the Uplands, and let array his Yule-feast at the Tofts. Yule-eve it is when cometh Swasi to the door, whenas the king is set down to table. He sendeth bidding to the king to come out to him, but the king waxed wroth at the bidding; and the same man bore the king's wrath out that bore the bidding in. No less bade Swasi bear in again his errand, saying that he was that Finn unto whom the king had said yea to set up his cot on the other side the brent. So went the king out, and needs must say yea to faring home with him, and went across the brent into his cot; with the egging of some men of his, though some letted him. There rose to meet him Snowfair, daughter of Swasi, fairest of women, and gave to the king a cup full of honey-mead. Then took he together the cup and the hand of her, and straightway it was as if hot fire came into his skin, and therewith would he be by her that very night; but Swasi says it may not be, but if need sway him, but if the king betroth him to her, and take her lawfully. So King Harald betrothed him to Snowfair, and wedded her; and with such longing he loved her, that he forgat his kingdom, and all

that belonged to his kingly honour. Four sons
they had: Sigurd a-Bush, Halfdan High-leg,
Gudrod Gleam, and Rognvald Straight-leg.

Then died Snowfair, but nowise changed her
hue, and as red and white she was as when
she was alive; and the king sat ever by her and
thought in his heart that she lived yet. So wore
away three winters, while the king sorrowed for
her dying, and all the folk of the land sorrowed
for his beguilement. But now to the leech-craft
of laying this wildness came Thorleif the Sage,
and with wisdom vanquished it, first with soft
words, saying thus:

"No marvel, O king, although thou mindest so
fair a woman and so mighty, and honourest her
with the down-pillow and the goodly web, even as
she would have of thee; yet is thine honour less
than what behoveth both thee and her, whereas
overlong in one raiment she lieth; more meet it
were that somewhat thou move her, and shift the
cloths beneath her."

But, lo! so soon as she was turned out of the
bed sprang up ill savour, rose up rottenness, and
all manner of stink from the dead corpse. Speedy
were they with the bale-fire, and therein was she
burned; but first her body waxed all blue, and
thence crawled worms and adders, frogs and paddocks, and all the kind of creeping things. So
sank she into ashes; but the king strode forth
into wisdom, and cast his folly from his heart, and
stoutly ruled his realm, and strengthened him
of his thanes and waxed glad of them, and his
thanes of him, and all the land of them both.

CHAPTER XXVI. OF THIODOLF OF HVIN.

FTER King Harald had proven the beguiling of the Finn-wife, he was so wroth that he drave from him the sons of him and the Finn-wife, and would not look on them. But Gudrod Gleam went to Thiodolf the Hvindweller, his foster-father, and bade him go with him to the king, because Thiodolf was a well-loved friend of King Harald; but the king was as then in the Uplands. So they went whenas they were arrayed, and came to the king late of an evening-tide, and took an outer place, and kept hidden. Now the king went up the hall-floor, and looked on the benches; but some feast or other was toward, and the mead was mixed. So he sang muttering:

> My warriors of old seasons
> For the mead are much o'er-eager;
> Yea, here are come the hoary,
> What make ye here so many?

Then answered Thiodolf:

> Our heads bore oft in old time
> Hard strokes from out the edge-play,
> Along with the wise gold-waster;
> And were we *then* o'er-many?

Therewith Thiodolf took the hat from his head, and then the king knew him and gave him fair welcome. Then Thiodolf prayed the king not to set aside his sons: " For fain had they been of a better-born mother hadst thou gotten them one."

So the king said yea thereto, and bade him have
Gudrod home with him even as he had had aforetime; but Sigurd and Halfdan he bade fare to Ring-
realm, and Rognvald he bade fare to Hadaland;
and they did as the king bade. They became full
manly men, and well endowed with prowess. So
sat King Harald at home in his own land, amid
good peace and plenteous seasons.

CHAPTER XXVII. THE UPRISING OF EARL TURF-EINAR IN THE ORKNEYS.

ROGNVALD, the Earl of Mere, heard
of the fall of Sigurd his brother, and
how the vikings abode in his lands. So
he sent his son Hallad west-away, who took the
name of earl on him, and had a great company of
men; and when he came to the Orkneys he sat
him down in the land. But both autumn, winter,
and spring fared the vikings about the isles, and
lifted on the nesses, and slaughtered beasts on the
strand. So Earl Hallad grew a-weary of sitting
in the isles and cast aside his earldom, and took a
franklin's dignity, and so fared east to Norway;
and when Earl Rognvald heard thereof, he was ill
content with Hallad's journey, and said that his
sons would become all unlike their forefathers.
Then spake Einar: "I have had little honour of
thee, and but little love have I to part from. I
will fare west to the isles if thou wilt give me some
help or other; and then I will promise thee, what
will gladden thee exceedingly, never to come back
again to Norway."

Earl Rognvald said he should be well content if he never came back : " For small hope have I that thy kin will have honour of thee, whereas all thy mother's kin is thrall-born." So Earl Rognvald gave Einar a long-ship all manned, and in the autumn-tide Einar sailed West-over-sea ; but when he came to the Orkneys there lay before him two ships of the vikings Thorir Wood-beard and Kalf Scurvy. Einar fell to battle with them straightway, and won the victory, and they both fell. Then was this sung :

> Tree-beard to the trolls he gave there,
> Scurvy there Turf-Einar slaughtered.

For this cause was he called Turf-Einar, because he let cut turf and use it instead of firewood, whereas there were no woods in the Orkneys.

Thereafter Einar became earl over the isles, and was a mighty man there. He was an ugly man, and one-eyed, howbeit the sharpest-sighted of men.

CHAPTER XXVIII. THE DEATH OF KING ERIC EYMUNDSON.

DUKE GUTHORM abode for the most part in Tunsberg, and bore sway all over the Wick whenas the king was not thereby; and he was charged with the warding of the land withal. In those days was there great trouble of the vikings, and there was war also up in Gautland while King Eric Eymundson lived. But he died whenas King Harald Hairfair had been king of Norway for ten winters.

CHAPTER XXIX. DEATH OF DUKE GUTHORM.

AFTER Eric, Biorn his son was king in Sweden for fifty years. He was father of Eric the Victorious, and Olaf, the father of Styrbiorn.

Duke Guthorm died in his bed in Tunsberg, and King Harald gave the sway over all that land to Guthorm his son, and he set him up for lord thereover.

CHAPTER XXX. THE BURNING OF ROGNVALD THE MERE-EARL.

WHEN King Harald was forty years old, many of his sons were well waxen up, and men early ripened were they all. And so it befell that they were ill content that the king gave them no rule, but set an earl in every county, which earls they deemed less nobly-born than themselves.

So one spring, Halfdan High-leg and Gudrod Gleam went their ways with a great company of men, and came unwares on Rognvald the Mere-Earl, and took the house over him, and burned him therein with sixty men. Then took Halfdan three long-ships, and sailed West-over-sea; but Gudrod set him down in the lands that Rognvald had aforetime owned. But when

King Harald heard hereof he went with a great host against Gudrod, and Gudrod saw that there was nought for it but to give himself up into the power of King Harald. So the king sent him east-away to Agdir. But King Harald made lord over Mere, Thorir, the son of Earl Rognvald, and gave him Alof his daughter, who was called the Years-heal. So Earl Thorir the Silent had the same rule that his father Rognvald had before him.

CHAPTER XXXI. DEATH OF HALF-DAN HIGH-LEG.

HALFDAN HIGH-LEG came west to the Orkneys all unwares, and Earl Einar fled straightway from the isles over into Caithness; but he came back again in the autumn and fell unwares on Halfdan. They met, and short was the battle ere Halfdan fled against the very fall of night; and Einar and his folk lay tentless through the night. But in the morning at daybreak they fell a-searching the fleers about the islands, and every man was slain where he was taken. Then spake Earl Einar: "I wot not," says he, "what it is I see out on Rinan's-isle, whether it be a man or a fowl; whiles it cometh up, and whiles it lieth down." So thither went they, and found Halfdan High-leg there, and laid hands on him. Now Earl Einar had sung this song the eve before, or ever he joined battle:

From the hand of Rolf my brother,
From Hrollaug's hand nought see I
The spears fly gainst the foemen.

> And our father cries for vengeance.
> Yea, and on this same evening,
> While we thrust on the battle,
> In Mere by the beakers' river
> Earl Thorir sitteth silent.

So now went Earl Einar to Halfdan, and cut an erne on the back of him in such wise, that he thrust his sword into the hollow of the body by the backbone, and sheared apart all the ribs down to the loins, and thereby drew out the lungs; and that was the bane of Halfdan.

Then sang Einar:

> Wreaked have I Rognvald's slaying,
> I for my fourth part fully,
> For the stay of hosts is fallen;
> The Norns have ruled it rightly.
> Heap stones then upon High-leg,
> High up, brave lads of battle,
> For we in strife were stronger,
> And a stony seat I pay him.

Then took Earl Einar the Orkneys to him as he had before had them. But when these tidings were known in Norway, then were the brethren of Halfdan exceeding ill content thereat, and said that it must be avenged, and many others said that sooth it was. But when Earl Einar heard thereof, then sang he:

> A many nought unmighty
> There are in many countries,
> For many a due cause doubtless,
> Full fain my death to compass;
> Yet ere to field they fell me,
> They know not who is fated
> Meanwhile to fall before me
> Neath foot-thorn of the eagle.

CHAPTER XXXII. PEACE BETWEEN KING HARALD AND EARL EINAR.

KING HARALD called out his men and drew together a great host, and so went west to the Orkneys; and when Earl Einar heard that King Harald was come from the east, he got him over to Caithness.

Then he sang this song:

> For the slaughtering of the sheep-kind
> Are some with beards made guilty;
> But I for a king's son's slaying
> Amid the sea-beat island.
> Comes peril, say the franklins,
> From the wrath of a king redoubled,
> And surely of my shearing
> Is the shard in the shield of Harald.

Then went men and messengers between the king and the earl; and it was so brought about that a meeting was bespoken, and they themselves met, and the earl handselled all to the king's judgment. So King Harald doomed Earl Einar and all the folk of Orkney to pay him sixty marks of gold. Over-great the bonders deemed the fine; so the earl offered to pay it all himself, and that he should have in return all the odal lands in the isles. Hereto they all assented, mostly for this cause, that the poor folk had but little land, but the rich thought to redeem their land when they would. So the earl paid all the fine to the king; and the king went back east in the autumn-tide. So a long while thereafter in the Orkneys the earls owned all the odal lands; yea, until the time when Sigurd, son of Lewis, gave them up again.

CHAPTER XXXIII. FALL OF GUTHORM AND HALFDAN THE WHITE, SONS OF HARALD.

GUTHORM, the son of King Harald, had the warding of the land about the Wick, and would fare with his war-ships out beyond the skerries; and on a time whenas he lay in the mouth of the Elf, came Solfi Klofi and joined battle with him, and Guthorm fell there.

Halfdan the Black and Halfdan the White lay out sea-roving, and harried in the Eastlands; and on a time they had a great battle in Esthonia, and Halfdan the White fell there.

CHAPTER XXXIV. THE WEDDING OF KING ERIC.

ERIC, Harald's son, was fostered with the Hersir Thorir, Roald's son, in the Firth-land. Him King Harald loved and honoured the most of all his sons. When Eric was twelve winters old Harald gave him five long-ships, and he went a-warring; first in the Eastlands, then south about Denmark and Friesland and Saxland, in which warfare he abode for four winters; thereafter he went West-over-sea, and harried in Scotland, Wales, Ireland, and Normandy, and another four winters he wore away thus; then he fared north-away to Finland, and right up to Biarmland, and had a great battle there, and won the day.

Now when he came back to Finmark his men found a certain woman in a cot there, the like of whom they had never seen for fairness; she named her Gunnhild to them, and said that her father dwelt in Halogaland, and was called Ozur Tot. "For this cause have I abided here," said she, "that I might learn cunning from two Finns here, the wisest of all the wood. Now are they gone a-hunting; but they both of them are fain of my love. So wise are they, that they may follow a track as hounds, both over thaw and hard ice; and so cunning are they on snow-shoes that nought may escape them, neither man nor beast; and whatso they shoot at they hit without fail. Thus have they overcome every man that has come anigh here; and if they be angry, the earth turneth inside outward before the eyes of them; but if aught quick be before their eyes, straightway it falleth down dead. Now may ye in no wise cross their way, but I will hide you here in the hut, and then ye shall try if we may compass their slaying."

That took they with thanks, and so she hid them there. She took a linen sack, wherein them-seemed were ashes; that took she in her hand, and strawed it about the hut both within and without.

A little after the Finns come home, and ask her what is come thither, and she says that nought at all is come. Marvellous that seemeth to the Finns, who have followed the slot right up to the hut, but may find nought thereafter.

So they make them fire, and cook some meat ; and when they had had their fill Gunnhild arrays their bed. But so matters had gone for three nights past, that Gunnhild had slept, but either of them had watched waking over the other for jealousy's sake ; but now she spake to the Finns : "Come hither, and lie one of you on either side of me."

Hereof were they full fain, and did so ; and she cast an arm about the neck of either, and they fell asleep straightway. But she woke them again ; yet speedily they fell asleep once more, and that so fast, that she might scarcely wake them ; once again they slept, and then she might nowise get them awake. So she set them up withal, and still they slept on ; then she took two great seal-skin bags, and did them over their heads, and bound them strongly underneath their arms. Then she gave a sign to the king's men, and they leap forth and bear weapons against the Finns and destroy them, and drag them out of the hut ; and all that night was there fierce thundering, so mighty that they might not go their ways; but in the morning they fared to the ship, and had Gunnhild with them, and brought her to Eric. So Eric and his folk fare south thence to Halogaland ; and there Eric summoned Ozur Tot to him, and says that he would wed his daughter. He said yea thereto, and Eric wedded Gunnhild, and had her with him into the South-country.

CHAPTER XXXV.   KING HARALD SHARES HIS REALM WITH HIS SONS.

NOW was King Harald fifty years old, when some of his sons were fully grown, or dead, other some of them ; they were waxen now riotous men in the land, yea, and were not at one among themselves. They drave the king's earls away from their lands, or some they slew. So King Harald summoned a Thing of many men in the South-country, bidding thereto all the Upland-men. Thereat he gave his sons the name of king, and established by law that all his very kin should each take the kingship after his father, but all they who were come of him on the distaff side should be held for earls.

He shared the land betwixt them ; Vingulmark, Raumrealm, Westfold, Thelmark, this he gave to Olaf, Biorn, Sigtrygg, Frodi, and Thorgils. Heathmark and Gudbrandsdale gave he to Day and Ring and Ragnar. To the sons of Snowfair gave he Ring-realm, Hadaland, Thotn, and all that appertains thereto. To Guthorm had he aforetime given all rule from the Elf to Swinesound, and Ran-realm to wit, and had set him up for the warding of the land to the easternmost end thereof.

King Harald himself was most oft in the midmost of the land. Rœrek and Gudrod were ever in the court with the king, and held great bailiwicks about Hordland and Sogn. King Eric abode ever with King Harald ; to him gave he Halogaland and Northmere and Raumsdale. North-away in Thrandheim he gave the rule to

Halfdan the Black and Halfdan the White and
Sigrod. In each of these counties he gave to his
sons half of the dues against himself, and therewithal seat in the high-seat a step higher than
the earls and a step lower than he himself. That
seat of his, in sooth, each of his sons was minded
himself to have after his father's day; but he himself was minded that Eric should have it. And
the Thrandheim folk would have Halfdan the
Black to sit there; and the folk of the Wick and
the Upland-men would give the rule each unto
the one who was nighest at hand to them; and
from all this waxed dissension anew betwixt the
brethren. And whereas they deemed themselves
to have but little dominion, they went a-warring,
as is aforesaid, and how Guthorm fell in the
mouth of the Elf before Solfi Klofi; and after
him Olaf took the dominion he had had. Halfdan
the White also fell in Estland, and Halfdan High-
leg in the Orkneys.

To Thorgils and Frodi gave King Harald war-
ships, and they went a-warring in the West, and
harried about Scotland and Wales and Ireland;
and they were the first of the Northmen who gat
to them Dublin. So say folk that to Frodi was
deadly drink given; but Thorgils was a long while
king over Dublin, and was bewrayed of the Erse-
folk and so died there.

CHAPTER XXXVI. DEATH OF ROGNVALD STRAIGHT-LEG.

ERIC BLOOD-AXE was minded to be king over all his brethren, and even so would King Harald have it; and at most times were he and his father together. Now Rognvald Straight-leg had Hadaland, and he fell to wizardry and became a spell-worker; but King Harald was a foe to wizards. In Hordland dwelt a wizard called Vitgeir; to him sent the king word bidding him leave his wizard-craft, but he answered and sang this song:

> Little weighs it
> Though wizards we be,
> We carle-begotten
> On very carlines;
> When Rognvald Straight-leg,
> Dear son of Harald,
> Raiseth the witch-lay
> In Hadaland.

But when King Harald heard thereof, Eric Blood-axe fared at his bidding to the Uplands, and came to Hadaland; and there he burned in his house Rognvald his brother and eighty wizards, and much was that work praised.

CHAPTER XXXVII. DEATH OF GUDROD GLEAM.

GUDROD GLEAM abode in the winter with his foster-father Thiodolf of Hvin for old friendship's sake; a cutter he had all-manned, and therein would he fare north to

Rogaland. Great storms were about that tide, but Gudrod was eager to go, and loth to abide. Then sang Thiodolf:

> Go not from hence, O Gudrod,
> Ere the ship's plain groweth better;
> For Geitir's way is wafting
> The stones in wash of billows.
> Await here, O thou wide-famed,
> The turmoil and wind's wonder:
> Bide with us for fair weather!
> Surf-washed is all round Jadar.

But Gudrod went as he was minded, whatsoever Thiodolf might say; but when they were come off Jadar the ship foundered under them, and there they all perished.

CHAPTER XXXVIII. THE FALL OF BIORN THE CHAPMAN.

BIORN, the son of King Harald, ruled in those days over Westfold, and abode oftest at Tunsberg, and went a-warring but little. To Tunsberg came many ships, both from the Wick and thereabouts, and from the North-country; from south-away also from Denmark and Saxland. King Biorn also had ships a-voyaging to other lands, and he gathered thus to him dear-bought things and other goods that he deemed he had need of; and his brethren called him Biorn the Sea-farer, or the Chapman. Biorn was a wise man and a peaceful, and was deemed to have in him the makings of a good lord; he wedded well and meetly, and had a son named Gudrod.

Now came Eric Blood-axe from the Eastlands with war-ships and a great company of folk, and bade Biorn his brother give up to him the seat and dues which King Harald had in Westfold; but the wont was aforetime for Biorn to bring the seat to the king himself, or send men therewith; and even so he will have it now, and will not pay it out of hand, but Eric deemed he had need of victuals and tents and drink. The brethren contended hereover with high words, but nowise might Eric get his needs, so he fared away from the town. Biorn also fared away from the town in the evening, and up to Seaham. So Eric turned back a-night-time after Biorn, and came on Seaham as Biorn and his men sat over the drink. Eric took the house over their heads, and Biorn went out to fight, he and his; and there fell Biorn and many men with him. Eric took great booty there, and so went north-away up country.

The Wick-folk were full evil content with this deed, and Eric was evil spoken of therefor; and the word went about that King Olaf would avenge Biorn his brother when occasion served.

King Biorn lieth in Sea-farer's Mound at Seaham.

CHAPTER XXXIX. PEACE BETWEEN THE KINGS.

THE winter after King Eric fared north to Mere, and took guesting at Solvi inward of Agdanes. But when Halfdan the Black heard thereof he fared thither with an host of men, and took the house over their heads; but Eric slept in an outbower, and gat him away to the wood with four other men, while Halfdan and his men burned up the house and all the folk therein. So came Eric to King Harald with these tidings. The king was wood-wroth thereat, and gathered an host together against the Thrandheimers. But when Halfdan the Black heard thereof he bade out folk and ships, and waxed full many, and put out to the Stad inward of Thorscliff; and the king lay with his host out by Reinfield. Then went men betwixt them; and there was one Guthorm Cinder, a noble man among the folk of Halfdan the Black, who had aforetime been with King Harald, and was well loved of either. Guthorm was a great skald, and he had done a song on both father and son, and they had bidden him a reward therefor; which thing he refused, and craved that they should one time grant him a boon, and they promised him. So now he went to King Harald and bare words of peace between them, and now claimed his boon of either, to wit, that they should be at one again; and the kings deemed him worth so much honour that at his prayer they were appeased. And many other noble men also pleaded this cause along

with him ; and the peace was this, that Halfdan
should have still the dominion he had had aforetime, but he was to give no trouble to Eric his
brother. After this tale Jorun the Skald-maiden
hath made somewhat in the Sentbit :

> I learned how Harald Hairfair
> Heard the hard deeds of Halfdan.
> To him that deals with sword edge
> Dark looking shall the deed be.

CHAPTER XL.   BIRTH OF HAKON THE GOOD.

HAKON GRIOTGARDSON, Earl of
Ladir, had had all rule in Thrandheim
whenas King Harald was otherwhere in
the land, and Hakon had had the greatest honour
from the king of all the Thrandheim folk.   After
the fall of Hakon, Sigurd his son took all his
dominion, and became earl in Thrandheim, and
had his abode at Ladir ; with him had been
nourished the sons of King Harald, Halfdan the
Black and Sigrod, who had before been in the hands
of Earl Hakon his father. They were much of an
age, the sons of King Harald and Earl Sigurd.
Earl Sigurd wedded Bergliot, daughter of Earl
Thorir the Silent, and whose mother was Alof
the Years-heal, daughter of Harald Hairfair.
Earl Sigurd was the wisest of men.

But when King Harald grew old he abode
often at his great manors which he had in Hordland, at Alrek-stead or Seaham, at Fitiar, at Outstone, or at Ogvalldsness in Kormt-isle.   When

King Harald was now nigh seventy years old he
begat a son on a woman named Thora Most-staff,
whose kin were of Most; good kin she had, and
might tell Horda-Kari amongst them. The tallest
of women was she, and the fairest, and was called
the king's bondwoman; for in those days there were
many of good blood, both men and women, that
owed homage to the king. Now the wont it was
then concerning the children of noble men, to
seek carefully one who should sprinkle the child
with water and give it a name. So when the
time came that Thora looked to bear a child she
was fain to go seek King Harald, who was as
then north in Seaham, and she was in Most; so
she fared north in Earl Sigurd's ship. And on a
night when they lay off the land Thora brought
forth a child on the cliff's side hard by the gang-
way-head, and a man-child it was; so Earl Sigurd
sprinkled the boy with water, and called him Hakon
after his father Hakon the Ladir-earl. The boy
was early fair to look on, and great of growth, and
most like unto his father. King Harald let the lad
abide with his mother, and they were about the
king's manors while the lad was yet young.

CHAPTER XLI. THE MESSAGE OF KING ATHELSTANE.

THE king in England of those days was
called Athelstane, who was but newcome
to the kingdom; he was called the Victorious, or the Faithful.

Now he sent men to Norway to King Harald,

with this-like message, that the messenger should go before the king and deliver to him a sword done with gold about the hilts and the grip thereof, and all its array wrought with gold and with silver, and set with dear-bought gems. So the messenger reached out the sword-hilt to the king and said : " Here is a sword which King Athelstane sendeth thee, bidding thee take it withal."

So the king took the grip, and straightway spake the messenger : " Now hast thou taken the sword even as our king would ; wherefore now wilt thou be his thane, since thou hast taken his sword."

Then saw King Harald that this was done to mock him ; but no man's thane would he be. Nevertheless, he called to mind his wont, that whensoever swift rage or anger fell on him, he held himself aback at first, and let the wrath run off him, and looked at the matter unwrathfully ; and even so did he now, and laid the matter before his friends, who all found a rede hereto, and this above all things, that they should let the messenger go his ways home unhurt.

CHAPTER XLII. THE JOURNEY OF HAWK INTO ENGLAND.

THE next summer King Harald sent a ship west to England, and made Hawk High-breech captain thereof, a great champion and most well-beloved of the king ; into his hands gave the king Hakon his son. So Hawk fared west to England to see King Athelstane, and found the king in London, and thereat was there a bidding and a feast full worthy. Hawk told his men whenas they came to the hall, how they shall deal with their entering, saying that he shall go out first who came in last, and that all shall stand abreast before the board, and each man with his sword at his left side, but their cloaks so set on that the swords be not seen. So they went into the hall, thirty men in company. Hawk went before the king and greeted him, and the king bade him welcome. Then took Hawk the lad Hakon and laid him on King Athelstane's knee; the king looked on the lad and asked Hawk why he did so. Says Hawk: "King Harald biddeth thee foster the child of his bondwoman."

The king was exceeding wroth, and caught up his sword that lay beside him, and drew it, as if he would slay the lad. Then said Hawk: "Thou hast set him on thy knee, and mayst murder him if thou wilt, but not thus withal wilt thou make an end of all the sons of King Harald."

Therewith went Hawk out and all his men, and they go their ways to their ship and put to sea, when they were ready, and so came back to Norway to King Harald; and now was he well content, for men ever account the fosterer less noble than him whose child he fostereth. By such-like dealings of the kings may it be seen how either would fain be greater than the other; yet not a whit for all this was any honour of either spilt, and either was sovereign lord of his realm till his death-day.

CHAPTER XLIII. THE CHRISTENING OF HAKON, ATHELSTANE'S FOSTER-LING.

KING ATHELSTANE let christen Hakon and teach him the right troth, and good manners with all kind of prowess. Athelstane loved him more than any of his kin, yea, moreover, and all men else loved him who knew him. He was sithence called Hakon Athelstane's Fosterling: he was a man of the greatest prowess, bigger and stronger and fairer than any man else. He was a wise man and of fair speech, and a well-christened man. King Athelstane gave Hakon a sword whose hilts and grip were all of gold; yet was the brand itself better, for therewith did Hakon cleave a quern-stone to the eye, wherefore was it called sithence Quern-biter, and it was the best sword that ever came to Norway; and Hakon kept it till his death-day.

CHAPTER XLIV. ERIC LED INTO KINGSHIP.

NOW was King Harald eighty years old, and waxen heavy of foot, so that he deemed he might no more fare through the land or rule the kingly matters; so he lead Eric his son into the high-seat, and gave him dominion over all the land. But when the other sons of King Harald knew thereof, then Halfdan the Black set himself down in the king's high-seat, and took on him all rule in Thrandheim;

and all the Thrandheimers were consenting to that rede with him.

After the fall of Biorn the Chapman, Olaf his brother took the dominion of Westfold, and fostered Gudrod Biorn's son. Tryggvi was Olaf's son, and he and Gudrod were foster-brothers, and much of an age; both were most hopeful and full of all prowess: Tryggvi was the biggest and strongest of men. So when the folk of the Wick heard that the Hordlanders had taken Eric for sovereign king, then they in like wise took Olaf for sovereign king in the Wick, and he held that dominion; and full ill content was Eric thereat. Two winters thereafter Halfdan the Black died a sudden death at a feast in Thrandheim, and it was the common talk of men that Gunnhild Kings'-mother had struck a bargain with a witch-wife to give him a deadly drink. But thereafter the Thrandheimers took Sigrod for king.

CHAPTER XLV. THE DEATH OF KING HARALD.

KING HARALD lived three winters after he had given Eric sole dominion over his realm, and that while he abode in Rogaland or Hordland at the great manors he had there. Eric and Gunnhild had a son whom King Harald sprinkled with water, and gave his own name to, saying that he would have him be king after his father Eric.

King Harald gave the more part of his daughters

to his earls in his own land, and great stocks are come thence.

King Harald died in his bed in Rogaland, and was buried at the Howes by Kormt-sound. In Howe-sound a church standeth to-day, and just to the north-west of the churchyard is the howe of King Harald Hairfair; but west of the church lies the tombstone of King Harald, which lay over his grave in the mound, and the said stone is thirteen feet and a half long, and near two ells broad. In the midst of the howe was the grave of King Harald, and one stone was set at the head, and another at the feet, and on the top thereof was laid the flat stone, while a wall of stone is builded below it on either side: but those stones which were in the howe stand now in the churchyard, as is aforesaid.

Now so say men of lore that Harald Hairfair was the fairest of face of all men that have ever been, the biggest and the strongest, the most bounteous of his wealth, and the friendliest to his men. In his early days he was a great warrior; and common rumour goeth about that great tree that his mother saw in her dream, how that it fore-shadowed his deeds therein, whereas the lower half of the tree was red as blood: and whereas the stem thence upward was fair and green, that betokened the flourishing of his realm; but whereas the topmost of the tree was white, that betokened that he should come to old age and hoary hairs. The boughs and limbs of the tree showed forth his descendants who were scattered wide about the land; yea, and of his kin also have all kings in Norway been sithence.

CHAPTER XLVI. THE FALL OF OLAF AND SIGROD.

KING ERIC took all the dues which the king owned amidmost of the land the next winter after the death of King Harald; but Olaf ruled east-away in Wick, and Sigrod their brother ruled all in Thrandheim. Eric was right ill content hereat, and the rumour ran that he would seek by the strong hand to get from his brethren the sovereign rule over all the land which his father had given him; and when Olaf and Sigrod heard thereof, messengers fared between them, and thereon they made trysting, and Sigrod fared east in the spring-tide to the Wick, and there met his brother Olaf in Tunsberg, and there they abode awhile. That same spring-tide Eric called out a great host of men and ships, and turned east-away to Wick. King Eric gat so fair a wind that he sailed night and day; nor was there any espial of his coming. So when he came to Tunsberg, Olaf and Sigrod fared with their folk from the town eastward on to the brent and there arrayed them. Eric had much the greater host, and he won the day, and Olaf and Sigrod fell both, and the howes of them both are on the brent whereas they lay slain.

Then King Eric fared all about the Wick and subdued it to him, and abode there long that summer; but Tryggvi and Gudrod fled away to the Uplands.

Eric was a big man and a fair; strong, and most stout of heart; a mighty warrior and victorious, fierce of mind, grim, unkind, and of few words.

Gunnhild his wife was the fairest of women, wise and cunning in witchcraft; glad of speech and guileful of heart, and the grimmest of all folk.

These are the children of Eric and Gunnhild: Gamli the eldest, Guthorm, Harald, Ragnfrod, Ragnhild, Erling, Gudrod, and Sigurd Slaver. And all Eric's children were fair and full manly.

THE STORY OF HAKON THE GOOD.

THE STORY OF
HAKON THE GOOD.

CHAPTER I.   HAKON TAKEN FOR KING.

HAKON, Athelstane's foster-son, was in England when he heard of the death of King Harald his father. He straightway arrayed him for departure ; and King Athelstane gave him both folk and fair great ships, and arrayed all for him in the seemliest wise. So he came to Norway in the autumn-tide.

Then heard he of the fall of his brethren, and therewith how that King Eric was as then in the Wick. So Hakon sailed north to Thrandheim, and came to Sigurd, the Earl of Ladir, the wisest of all men of Norway, and gat good welcome of him; and they made covenant together, and Hakon promised him great dominion if he might get to be king. Then they let summon a Thing of many men, and at the Thing Earl Sigurd spake on Hakon's behoof, and offered him to the bonders for king, and thereafter Hakon himself stood up and spake. Then fell a-talking man to man that here was come back Harald Hairfair grown young a second time.

Now the beginning of Hakon's word was that he bade them take him for king, and so name him, and therewithal to give him help and strength to hold his kingdom ; but in return he offered to make them all as free-born bonders, and that they should dwell every man on his free lands.

At this harangue was there so great a stir that the whole throng of bonders shouted, and cried out that they would take him for king.

And so it came to pass that they of Thrandheim took Hakon for king over all the land ; and in those days was Hakon fifteen winters old.

So he took to him a body-guard and went through the land. Now came tidings to the Uplands that the Thrandheimers had taken one for king like in all wise to Harald Hairfair, if it were not that Harald had enthralled and oppressed all the folk of the land, whereas this Hakon willed good to every man, and offered to give back to the bonders the odal rights which King Harald had taken from them. All were glad at those tidings, and one man told the other, till it ran like wild-fire all through the land to the land's-end. Many bonders fared from the Uplands to go see King Hakon ; some sent men, some sent messengers and tokens ; and all to one end, to wit, that they would be his men ; and the king took all with thanks.

CHAPTER II. KING HAKON'S JOURNEY THROUGH THE LAND.

KING HAKON fared in the beginning of winter to the Uplands, and summoned Things there, and all folk that might come came thronging to meet him; and at all Things was he taken for king. Then he fared east to the Wick; and Tryggvi and Gudrod, his brothers' sons, came to meet him, and many others, who told over the sorrows they had borne from King Eric his brother. So ever the more waxed the enmity against Eric as to all men King Hakon grew dearer, and each felt more emboldened to speak as he thought.

King Hakon gave a king's name to Tryggvi and Gudrod, and the same dominion which Harald his father had given to their fathers; to Tryggvi gave he Van-realm and Vingulmark, and to Gudrod, Westfold. But whereas they were young and but children, he set noble men and wise to rule the land with them; and he gave the land to them on that covenant aforesaid, that they should have half of the dues and scat against him.

So King Hakon went north in the spring-tide through the Upper Uplands to Thrandheim.

CHAPTER III. ERIC FLEETH FROM THE LAND.

KING HAKON drew together a great host in spring-tide, and arrayed his ships; and the folk of the Wick also had a great company afield, and were minded to meet him.

Then King Eric too called out men from the mid
land, but was ill-furnished with folk, because many of
the great men had turned from him and gone over to
Hakon. But when he saw that he had no might to
withstand the host of Hakon, he sailed West-over-
sea with such folk as would follow him. He fared
first to the Orkneys, and had thence a great company; then he sailed south toward England, and
harried about Scotland wheresoever he made land;
and then he harried all about the north parts of
England. Now Athelstane, the English king, sent
word to Eric, bidding him take dominion of him;
saying that King Harald his father had been a
great friend of his, wherefore he was fain thus to
make it avail to his son. So men went between
the kings, and they made peace with sworn troth
on such covenant that King Eric should take
Northumberland to hold of King Athelstane, and
should ward the land from the Danes and other
vikings; he should let himself be christened also,
with his wife and children, and all the folk that had
followed him thither. That choice took Eric, and
was christened and took the right troth.

Now Northumberland is accounted the fifth
part of England. Eric had his abode at York,
whereas, say folk, Lodbrok's sons had aforetime
abided. Northumberland was mostly peopled by
Northmen after Lodbrok's sons had won the
land. Full oft had Danes and Northmen harried
therein since the dominion thereof had departed
from them. Many steads in that land are named
after the Northern tongue, Grimsby to wit, and
Hawkfleet, and many others.

CHAPTER IV.   THE FALL OF KING ERIC.

KING ERIC had many men about him; for he kept there many Northmen who had come from the East with him, and more-over many of his friends came afterward from Norway.   But whereas he had but little land, he fared ever a-warring in summer-tide; he harried in Scotland and the South-isles, Ireland and Wales, and so gat wealth to him.

King Athelstane died in his bed whenas he had been king fourteen winters and eight weeks and three days.   After him was Edmund his brother king of England.   He could not away with Northmen, nor was King Eric beloved of him, and the word went about King Edmund that he would set another king over Northumberland; and when King Eric heard that, he went a-warring in the West, and had with him from the Orkneys Earls Arnkel and Erland, the sons of Turf-Einar. Then he went to the South-isles, and found there many vikings and kings of hosts, and they joined themselves to King Eric, and with the whole host he went first to Ireland, and had thence such folk as he might get.   Thereafter he fared to Wales, and harried there; thence he sailed south under England, and harried there as in other places, and all the people fled away wheresoever he came.

Now whereas Eric was a most daring man, and had a great host, he trusted so well to his folk that he went a long way up into the land, and harried and followed up the fleers; but there was a king

called Olaf whom King Edmund had set there for
the warding of the land, and he drew together an
army not to be withstood, and fell on King Eric,
and there was a great battle ; many of the English
folk fell, but ever whereas one fell, came three in
his place down from the land, and by the latter end
of the day the fall of men turned toward the side
of the Northmen, and there died full many folk ;
and ere this day was ended fell King Eric and
five kings with him, which are named, Guthorm
and his two sons, Ivar and Harek. There fell
also Sigurd and Rognvald, and there fell withal
Arnkel and Erland, the sons of Turf-Einar. Yea,
and there was an exceeding great fall of the Northmen, but they who escaped fared back to Northumberland and told Gunnhild and her sons of
these tidings.

CHAPTER V. THE JOURNEY OF GUNNHILD'S SONS.

NOW when Gunnhild and her sons knew
that King Eric was fallen, and that he
had before that harried the land of the
English king, they deemed full surely that they
might look for no peace there ; so they straightway got them gone from Northumberland, and had
all the ships that King Eric had had, and such
folk as would follow them, and plenteous wealth
withal, which they had gotten together, part by the
tribute of England and part by warring. They
turned their host first north-away to the Orkneys
and took up their abode there awhile, and the earl

there in those days was Thorfinn Skull-cleaver, son
of Turf-Einar. So Eric's sons took to them the
Orkneys and Shetlands, and had scat from them,
and abode there a-winter-tide and harried in
summer about Scotland and Ireland.

Hereof telleth Glum Geirason :

> The bairn-young wise wayfarer,
> The rider of the strand-steed,
> A goodly way had wended
> Thence, and all on to Skaney.
> The upright fight-fires speeder
> Won sons of men in Scotland,
> And sent therefrom to Odin
> Hosts of the men sword-smitten.

> The folk's friend drave the fight-flames
> To gladden choughs of the Valkyrs ;
> Of the Erse folk many a war-host
> Betook them unto fleeing.
> The Frey of the land of people,
> Of victory well-belovèd,
> In man's blood reddened edges,
> And felled folk in the Southland.

CHAPTER VI. A BATTLE IN JUT-LAND.

KING HAKON, Athelstane's foster-son, subdued to him all Norway, when
King Eric his brother had fled the land.
King Hakon abode the first winter in the West-country, and thereafter went north to Thrandheim
and abode there ; but whereas that he doubted of
war if perchance King Eric should come with an
host from West-over-sea, for that cause he sat
with his host in the mid land of the Firth-country,

or Sogn, or Hordaland, or Rogaland. Hakon set Earl Sigurd, the Earl of Ladir, over all Thrandheim whereas he had been lord aforetime, and Hakon his father also under King Harald Hairfair.

But when Hakon heard of the fall of Eric his brother, and withal that Eric's sons durst not abide in England, he deemed there was little need to dread them, and so fared with his folk one summer east into the Wick. In these days the Danes harried much in the Wick, and wrought full oft great scathe there; but when they heard that King Hakon was come thither with a great host, they fled all away, some south to Halland, but others who were nigher to King Hakon stood out to sea, and so south to Jutland. And when King Hakon was ware of this, he sailed after them with all his host, and, coming to Jutland, harried there. And when the folk of the land were ware of it, they drew together an host and would defend their land, and joined battle with King Hakon. There was a great battle, and King Hakon fought so mightily that he went on before his banner unhelmed and unbyrnied. King Hakon won the day, and followed the chase far up into the land.

So sayeth Guthorm Cinder in the Hakon's-drapa:

> The ship's blue stream now wended
> The king with oars spray-washen;
> The high lord felled the Jute-folk
> In the drift of battle's maiden.
> The feeder of swans of Odin
> Drave flight e'en as his will was,
> The covering of the lurers
> To crows' wine brake asunder.

CHAPTER VII. BATTLE IN ERE-SOUND.

THENCE King Hakon made south with his host for Selund, and sought the vikings there. He rowed with two cutters forth into Eresound, and there fell in with eleven cutters of the vikings, and straightway joined battle with them, and the end thereof was that he won the day, and cleared all the craft of the vikings.

So sayeth Guthorm Cinder:

> Speeder of gales of bow-drifts'
> Fires from the South came faring
> To the green ness of the Seal-wound
> With but two plate-decked sea-steeds,
> Whenas the all-wroth sender
> Of the wand of slaughter cleared them,
> Eleven keels of Dane-folk,
> Far famed therefor e'er after.

CHAPTER VIII. KING HAKON'S WARRING IN DENMARK.

THEREAFTER King Hakon harried wide about in Selund, and plundered many folk and slew some, and had away some as captives, and took great fines from some, nor found aught to withstand him.

So sayeth Guthorm Cinder:

> The blackthorn of the onset
> Gat this, to conquer Selund,
> And the safe-guard of the Vend-host
> Along the side of Skaney.

Then went King Hakon east along Skaney-

side, and harried all, and took fines and scat from
the land, and slew all vikings wheresoever he
found them, were they Danes or Vends.

Then went he east-away beyond Gautland and
harried there, and gat great tribute from the land.

So sayeth Guthorm Cinder:

> Shielded by skirt of Odin
> He won scat of the Gautfolk;
> Gold-hewer the all-bounteous
> Won spear-storms in that faring.

King Hakon went back in autumn-tide with his
folk, and had gotten to him exceeding great wealth.
He abode that winter in the Wick, against onsets,
if perchance the Danes or Gautlanders should do
the same.

CHAPTER IX. OF KING TRYGGVI.

THAT same autumn had King Tryggvi
Olafson come from warring in the West;
and he had as then been harrying in
Ireland and Scotland. In the spring King Hakon
went into the North-country, and set Tryggvi his
brother's son over the Wick to guard it against
war, and to get what he might from those lands of
Denmark whereas King Hakon had taken scat the
summer before.

So sayeth Guthorm Cinder:

> The helmet's ice-rod's reddener
> Hath set the brave mind-gladdener
> Over the maid of Onar,
> The oak-green of the Southland;
> The ever-nimble breaker

Of Swegdir's hall of battle,
Who erst had come from Ireland
With a host on the Swan-mead's runners.

CHAPTER X. OF THE SONS OF GUNN-HILD.

KING HARALD GORMSON ruled in those days over Denmark; and he was exceeding ill content that King Hakon had harried in his land, and rumour ran that the Dane-king would fain avenge it; but nought so speedily came that about.

But when Gunnhild and her sons heard hereof, that unpeace was toward betwixt Denmark and Norway, they arrayed their departure from the west: they gave Ragnhild, the daughter of King Eric, to Arnfinn, the son of Thorfinn Skull-cleaver. So Thorfinn abode still earl in the Orkneys when Eric's sons went away. Gamli Ericson was somewhat the eldest of them, yet was not he fully come to manhood.

So when Gunnhild came to Denmark with her sons she fared to meet King Harald, and had good welcome of him. King Harald gave them lands in his realm so great that they might well keep them there in good fortune, they and their men; but he took into fostering Harald Ericson, and set him on his knee, and he grew up there in the court of the Dane-king. Some of Eric's sons fared a-warring as soon as they were of age thereto, and so gathered wealth; they harried about the East-lands. They were early fair to look on, and of manhood in strength and prowess beyond their years.

Hereof telleth Glum Geirason in the Greycloak's Drapa :

> A many in the Eastlands
> Gat them a war-shrine smitten,
> The mighty skalds' gift-giver
> Gained victory in the journey.
> The king set there a-singing,
> The sheath-tongues gold bewrappèd,
> And hosts of the wight sword-players
> Unto the ground he sent them.

Then turned Eric's sons also north to the Wick with their host, and harried there ; but Tryggvi called out his folk and turned to meet them, and they had many battles, wherein now one, now the other prevailed ; and whiles Eric's sons harried in the Wick, whiles Tryggvi harried in Selund or Halland.

CHAPTER XI. KING HAKON'S LAW-MAKING.

WHENAS Hakon was king in Norway was there good peace amidst bonders and chapmen, so that none did hurt to other, nor to other's wealth, and plenteous were the seasons both by land and by sea.

King Hakon was the blithest of all men, and the sweetest-spoken, and the kindest ; he was a very wise man, and turned his mind much to law-making. He set forth the Gula-things Laws with the help and counsel of Thorleif the Wise, and also the Frosta-things Laws, with the rede of Earl Sigurd and other Thrandheimers of the wisest ; but the Heidsævis Law Halfdan the Black had set forth aforetime, as is written afore.

CHAPTER XII.   BIRTH OF EARL HAKON THE MIGHTY.

KING HAKON held his Yule-feast in Thrandheim, which feast Earl Sigurd arrayed for him at Ladir. Thereon the first night of Yule, Bergliot, the earl's wife, brought forth a man-child; and the next day King Hakon sprinkled the lad with water, and gave him his own name, and he waxed up and became a mighty man and a noble, and became earl after Sigurd his father.

Earl Sigurd was the dearest of friends to King Hakon.

CHAPTER XIII.   OF EYSTEIN THE EVIL.

EYSTEIN, King of the Uplands, whom some called the Mighty and some the Evil, harried in Thrandheim, and laid under him Isles'-folk and Spar-biders-folk, and set his son Onund over them; but the Thrandheimers slew him. King Eystein fared a-warring the second time into Thrandheim, and harried wide there, and laid folk under him. Then he bade the Thrandheimers choose whether they would have for king his thrall, who was called Thorir Faxi, or his hound, who was called Saur; so they chose the hound, deeming they would then the rather do their own will. Then let they bewitch into the hound the wisdom of three men, and he barked two words and spake the third. A collar was wrought for

him, and chains of gold and silver ; and whenso the
ways were miry, his courtmen bare him on their
shoulders.   A high-seat was dight for him, and he
sat on howe as kings do ; he dwelt at the Inner
Isle, and had his abode at the stead called Saur's
Howe.   And so say folk that he came to his death
in this wise, that the wolves fell on his flocks and
herds, and his courtmen egged him on to defend
his sheep ; so he leaped down from his howe, and
went to meet the wolves, but they straightway tore
him asunder.

Many other marvellous deeds wrought King
Eystein with the Thrandheimers ; and from the
warring and trouble of him fled away many lords,
and other folk also, a many, fled away from their
free lands.

CHAPTER XIV.   THE PEOPLING OF JAMTLAND AND HELSINGLAND.

KETIL JAMTI, the son of Earl Onund
of the Spar-biders, went east-away over
the Keel, and a great company of men with
him, who had their households with them.   They
cleared the woods, and peopled great country-sides
there, and that was called sithence Jamtland.

The son's son of Ketil was Thorir Helsing, who
for slayings he wrought fled from Jamtland and
east-away through the woods of that land and
settled there, and many folk resorted thither to
him, and that land is called Helsingland, and
goeth east right down to the sea ; but all easternmost Helsingland down by the sea the Swedes

peopled. Also when King Harald Hairfair cleared
the land before him, then fled away because of him
many men from the land, men of Thrandheim and
Naumdale. Then befell anew peopling of the east
parts of Jamtland, and some went right into
Helsingland. The folk of Helsingland dealt in
chaffer with the Swedes, and were altogether
bound in tribute to them; but they of Jamtland
were much betwixt and between folk, and none
took heed thereof until King Hakon established
good peace and chaffer with Jamtland, and made
friends there with the great men. So they came
from the east to meet him, and assented to the
obeying of him and giving him scat, and so became the king's thanes, because they had heard
tell good of him; and they would liefer be under
his rule than under the sway of the Swede king,
whereas they were come of the blood of the Northmen. So he set law amongst them and good ruling
of the land.

And in this wise did all they of Helsingland
who were come of kin north of the Keel.

CHAPTER XV.   OF KING HAKON'S
HOLDING AND PREACHING CHRIST'S
FAITH.

KING HAKON was a well-christened
man when he came to Norway; but
whereas all the land was heathen, and
folk much given to sacrificing, and many great
men in the land, and that he deemed he lacked
men sorely and the love of all folk, he took such

rede that he fared privily with his Christian faith.
Sunday he held and the Friday fast, and held in
memory the greatest high-tides, and he made a
law that Yule should be holden the same time as
Christian men hold it, and that every man at that
tide should brew a meal of malt or pay money else,
and keep holy tide while Yule lasted.   But aforetime was Yule holden on Hogmanay night, that
is to say, mid-winter night, and Yule was holden
for three nights.

Now he was minded that when he was set fast in
the land, and had gotten it all to him freely to hold,
he would then set forth the Christian faith.   And
at the beginning he wrought in such wise that he
lured such as were best beloved by him to become
Christians, and so much did his friendship prevail
herein, that very many let themselves be christened, and othersome left off blood-offering.

He abode for the more part in Thrandheim
because the most strength of the land was therein.

So at last when King Hakon deemed he had
gotten strength enough in certain mighty men to
uphold the Christian faith, he sent to England for
a bishop and other teachers ; and when they came
to Norway, then did King Hakon lay bare that
he would bid all the land to the Christian faith.
But they of Mere and Raumsdale put the matter
wholly on them of Thrandheim ; so King Hakon
let hallow certain churches, and set priests thereto.
And when he came to Thrandheim, he summoned
the bonders to a Thing, and bade them take the
Christian faith.   They answered that they would
put off the matter to the Frosta Thing, and that

they will that thither come men from all the
countries that are in Thrandheim, and they say
that then will they answer this hard matter.

CHAPTER XVI. OF BLOOD-OFFERINGS.

EARL SIGURD of Ladir was much
given to blood-offerings, and so had been
Hakon his father. Earl Sigurd upheld
all feasts of blood-offering there in Thrandheim
on the king's behoof. It was the olden custom
that when a blood-offering should be, all the
bonders should come to the place where was the
Temple, bringing with them all the victuals they
had need of while the feast should last; and at
that feast should all men have ale with them.
There also was slain cattle of every kind, and horses
withal; and all the blood that came from them
was called hlaut, but hlaut-bowls were they called
wherein the blood stood, and the hlaut-tein a rod
made in the fashion of a sprinkler. With all the
hlaut should the stalls of the gods be reddened,
and the walls of the temple within and without, and
the men-folk also besprinkled; but the flesh was to
be sodden for the feasting of men. Fires were to be
made in the midst of the floor of the temple, with
caldrons thereover, and the health-cups should be
borne over the fire. But he who made the feast
and was the lord thereof should sign the cups and
all the meat; and first should be drunken Odin's cup
for the victory and dominion of the king, and
then the cup of Niord and the cup of Frey for
plentiful seasons and peace. Thereafter were many

men wont to drink the Bragi-cup ; and men drank
also a cup to their kinsmen dead who had been
noble, and that was called the cup of Memory.
Now Earl Sigurd was the most bounteous of men,
and he did a deed that was great of fame, whereas
he made great feast of sacrifice at Ladir, and
alone sustained all the costs thereof. Hereof
telleth Kormak the son of Ogmund in the Sigurd's
Drapa :

> Let none bear bowl nor basket
> Unto Thiassi's offspring,
> E'en to the great gold-wounder,
> When gods have feast before them.
> What creature would encumber
> The greatness of the glaive-god,
> When the lord of fen-fire feasteth
> All folk ? For gems the king fought.

CHAPTER XVII. THE THING AT FROSTA.

KING HAKON came to the Frosta-Thing,
and thither were come also great throngs
of the bonders ; and when the Thing
was duly ordered King Hakon spake, and began
in this wise : That it was his bidding and prayer
to bonders and farming thanes, to mighty and
unmighty, yea, to all the people, young men and old,
rich and poor, men and women, that they all should
be christened and believe in one God, Christ to
wit, the son of Mary ; that they should put from
them all blood-offering and the heathen gods ;
that they should keep holy every seventh day from
all work, and fast also every seventh day. But

as soon as the king had put this before the people
there uprose a great murmur, of the bonders
murmuring how the king would take from them
their work; saying that in this wise the land might
have no husbandry. And the workmen and
thralls cried out that they might not work if they
lacked meat. They said also that such was the
turn of mind of King Hakon and his father, and
of his kin withal, that they were niggard of their
meat, howso bountiful of gold they might be.

Therewith stood up Asbiorn of Middlehouse in
Gauldale, and answered the king's harangue, and
spake: "So deemed we bonders, King Hakon,"
says he, "when thou didst hold that first Thing
here in Thrandheim, and we took thee for king,
and had of thee our free lands, that we had
verily taken hold of heaven; but now wot we
not whether we have any the more gotten our
freedom, or whether rather thou wilt not enthrall
us anew in wonderful wise, that we should cast
away the troth that our fathers have held before
us, and all our forefathers, first in the Burning
Age, and now after in the Age of Howes; and far
mightier they were than we, and this their troth
has availed us well. Such love have we given
thee that we have let thee have thy way amongst
us in all laws and ruling of the land. But now
this is our will, and the common consent of the
bonders, that we will hold to those laws which
thou gavest us here at the Frosta-Thing, and to
which we assented; we will all follow thee and
hold thee for king while we have life, each and all
of us bonders here at this Thing, if thou, O king,

wilt forbear somewhat with us, and bid us such
things only as we may give thee, and are not unmeet
for us to do.   But if thou wilt take up this matter
in so headstrong a wise as to deal with us with
might and mastery, then are we bonders of one consent to depart us from thee and to take us another
lord, who shall rule us in such wise that we may
hold in peace the troth that is most to our mind.
Now shalt thou, O king, choose between these
two ways before the Thing be come to an end."

At these words was there great stir among the
bonders, and they cried out that so would they
have it as he spake.   But when silence was gotten,
then answered Earl Sigurd: "It is the will of
King Hakon to be of one accord with you, O
bonders, and never to depart the friendship between you and him."

Then said the bonders that they would have the
king do blood-offering on their behoof for plenteous seasons and peace, as his father did before
him.   And therewith the murmur abated and they
brake up the Thing.   Then talked Earl Sigurd to
the king, praying him not to deny utterly to do as
the bonders would, and saying that there was
nought else for it; "For this is, O king, as thou
thyself mayst hear, the will and longing of the
lords, and of all folk besides; and some good rede
shall we find hereto, O king."

So the king and the earl accorded hereon.

CHAPTER XVIII. THE BONDERS COMPEL KING HAKON TO BLOOD-OFFERING.

IN the autumn-tide at winter-nights was there a blood-offering held at Ladir, and the king went thereto. Heretofore he had ever been wont, if he were abiding at any place where was a feast of blood-offering going on, to eat his meat in a little house with but few folk, but now the bonders murmured at it, that he sat not in his own high-seat, where the feast of men was greatest; and the earl said to the king that so he would not do as now. So it was therefore that the king sat in his high-seat. But when the first cup was poured, then spake Earl Sigurd thereover, and signed the cup to Odin, and drank off the horn to the king. Then the king took it, and made the sign of the cross thereover; and Kar of Griting spake and said: "Why doeth the king thus, will he not do worship?" Earl Sigurd answers: "The king doth as they all do who trow in their own might and main, and he signeth the cup to Thor. For he made the sign of the hammer over it before he drank." So all was quiet that eve. But on the morrow, when men went to table, the bonders thronged the king, bidding him eat horse-flesh, and in no wise the king would. Then they bade him drink the broth thereof, but this would he none the more. Then would they have him eat of the dripping, but he would not; and it went nigh to their falling on him. Then strove Earl Sigurd to appease them, and bade them lay the storm; but the king he

bade gape over a kettle-bow, whereas the reek of
seething had gone up from the horse-flesh, so that
the kettle-bow was all greasy. Then went the king
thereto, and spread a linen cloth over the kettle-
bow, and gaped thereover, and then went back to
the high-seat; but neither side was well pleased
thereat.

CHAPTER XIX. A FEAST OF BLOOD-OFFERING AT MERE.

THE next winter was the Yule-feast
arrayed for the king in Mere. But when
time wore towards Yule, the eight lords
who had most dealing in blood-offerings of all
Thrandheim appointed a meeting between them;
four were from the Outer Thrandheim, to wit, Kar
of Griting, Asbiorn of Middlehouse, Thorberg of
Varness, and Worm of Lioxa; but they from the
Inner Thrandheim were Botolf of Olvirshowe,
Narfi of Staff in Verdale, Thrand o' Chin from
Eggia, and Thorir Beard from Houseby in the
Inner Isle. So these eight men bound themselves
to this, that the four of Outer Thrandheim should
make an end of the Christian faith in Norway,
and the four of Inner Thrandheim should compel
the king to blood-offering.

So the Outer Thrandheimers fared in four ships
south to Mere, and there slew three priests, and
burned three churches, and so gat them back
again. But when King Hakon came to Mere with
his court and Earl Sigurd, there were the bonders
come in great throngs. The very first day of the

feast the bonders pressed hard on the king bidding him offer, and threatening him with all things ill if he would not.   Earl Sigurd strove to make peace between them, and the end of it was that King Hakon ate some bits of horse-liver, and drank crossless all the cups of memory that the bonders poured for him.   But so soon as the feast was ended, the king and the earl went out to Ladir. Of full little cheer was the king, and straightway he arrayed him for departing from Thrandheim with all his court, saying that he would come with more men another time, and pay back the bonders for the enmity they had shown him.

But Earl Sigurd prayed the king not to hold them of Thrandheim for his foes for this ; and said that no good would come to the king of threatening or warring against the folk of his own land, and the very pith of his realm, as were the folk of Thrandheim.   But the king was so wroth, that no speech might be held with him.   He departed from Thrandheim, and went south to Mere, and abode there that winter and on into spring ; and as it summered he drew together an host, and rumour ran that he would fall on the Thrandheimers therewith.

CHAPTER XX. BATTLE AT OGVALDS-NESS.

BUT when King Hakon was come aboard ship with a great host, there came to him tidings from the South-country, to wit, that the sons of King Eric were come north from Denmark into the Wick, and therewithal that they had chased King Tryggvi Olafson from his ships east-away by Sotanes. They had harried wide about in the Wick, and many men had submitted them-selves to them. So when King Hakon heard these tidings him-seemed he needed folk, and he sent word to Earl Sigurd to come to him, and other lords from whom he looked for help.

Earl Sigurd came to King Hakon with a very great host, wherein were all they of the Thrand-heimers who in the winter-tide laid hardest on the king to worry him to blood-offering; and all these were taken into peace of the king at the pleading of Earl Sigurd.

Then fared King Hakon south along the land, and when he was come south round about the Stad, he heard that Eric's sons were come into North Agdir. Either side fared against the other, and they met by Kormt Isle. There went both sides from out their ships, and they fought at Ogvaldsness; and either host was of very many men, and there befell a great fight. King Hakon fell on fiercely, and King Guthorm, Eric's son, was before him with his company, and the two kings came to handy-strokes. There fell King Guthorm, and his banner was smitten down and many of his people died about him. Thereon fell the folk of Eric's sons to flight, and they gat them away to their ships and rowed away, and had lost a many men.

Thereof telleth Guthorm Cinder:

The eker of din of Valkyr
Let fight-moons clash together

> Over the heads of slain ones,
> Erst wasters of the hand-warp.
> The Niord of the fire of wide-lands
> Of sound-steeds then departed
> From the Niord of the moon of roaring
> Of the swords, left weapon-wounded.

King Hakon fared to his ships and sailed south after Gunnhild's sons, and either side did their most might till they were come into East Agdir. Thence sailed Eric's sons into the main, and so south to Jutland ; as saith Guthorm Cinder :

> The brethren of the awer
> Of bow-draught now full often
> Must learn of might down-crushing
> At the hands of wound-fires' Balder.
> I mind me how fight-seeker
> Of the flood-craft steered ships seaward,
> And drave all sons of Eric,
> His brother, off before him.

Then fared King Hakon back into Norway, and Eric's sons abode again in Denmark for a long while.

CHAPTER XXI. LAW-MAKING OF KING HAKON.

AFTER this battle King Hakon made a law for all the land by the sea-side, and so far up into the land as a salmon swimmeth furthest, whereby he ordered all the peopled lands, and divided them into ship-raths, and settled the tale of ship-raths in each folk-land.   In every folk-land was it appointed how many ships and how great should be fitted out from each, when the common muster of all men should be, which muster afore-

said should be made whensoever outland war was
come to the land ; and along with the said muster
beacons should be made on high mountains so
that each might be seen from the other.   And
so say men that in seven days ran the tidings of
war from the southernmost beacon to the northern-
most Thing-stead in Halogaland.

CHAPTER XXII. OF ERIC'S SONS.

ERIC'S sons fared oft a-warring in the Eastlands, but whiles they harried in Norway
as is aforewrit.   When King Hakon
ruled over Norway were there plenteous seasons
in the land ; and most well-beloved he was.
Withal there was good peace. Now whenas King
Hakon had been king in Norway twenty winters
came Eric's sons north from Denmark with an
exceeding great host ; a great company indeed
was that which had followed them in their warring,
but far greater was the host of the Danes that
King Harald Gormson had given into their hands.
They gat a fair wind and sailed out from Vendil
and hove up from the main to Agdir, and thence
sailed north along the land day and night.   But
the beacons were not lighted up for this cause :
the wont was, that the beacon-fires went west-along
the land, but east-away had none been ware of
their going. This went to bring it about moreover,
that the king had laid heavy penalty for the wrong-
ful lighting of the beacons, on such as should be
found and proven guilty thereof ; because war-
ships and vikings would be a-harrying in the

outer isles, and the folk of the land would be thinking that these were none else than the sons of Eric; and then would the bale-fires be lighted, and all the land would run to weapons; but Eric's sons would go back to Denmark, having no Danish host, nought save their own following. Or indeed would it whiles be other kind of vikings; and hereof was King Hakon exceeding wroth, whereas toil and cost came thereof and no profit; and withal the bonders for their part cried out when it went thus.

So for this cause it was that no tidings of Eric's sons went before them till they came north to Wolf-sound. There they lay seven nights; then fared tidings in-land over Eid and so north across Mere; but King Hakon was as then in North-mere in the isle of Frædi, at a stead called Birch-strand, a manor of his, and had no folk save his own courtmen and the bonders who had been bidden to the guesting.

CHAPTER XXIII.   OF EGIL WOOL-SARK.

THE spies came to King Hakon and told him their errand, to wit, that Eric's sons were south of the Stad with a great host. Then he let call to him such men as were wisest and sought counsel of them, whether he should fight with Eric's sons for all their greater multitude, or should flee away north, and get him more men. Now there was a bonder there hight Egil Woolsark, a very old man now, but once bigger and stronger than any man, and the greatest of warriors, and a long while had he borne the banner of King Harald Hairfair. So Egil answered the king's word and said : "I have been in certain battles with King Harald thy father, and whiles he fought with more folk, whiles with less, yet ever had he the victory ; nor ever did I hear him seek counsel of his friends to teach him how to flee ; and no such lesson will we learn thee, king, for a stout-hearted lord we deem we have, and of us thou shalt have trusty following."

Many others there were also who stood by him in his speech. Yea, and the king also said that this was what he was fainest of, to fight with such folk as might there be gotten. So was it settled, and the king let shear up the war-arrow, and sent it out on all sides, and let gather what host he might get. Then spake Egil Woolsark :

"A while was I dreading amid this long peace that I should die of eld within doors on my straw-bed, for as fain as I was to fall in battle a-following my own lord : and lo ! now may it be even so, ere all is over."

CHAPTER XXIV. BATTLE BY FRÆ-DISBERG.

THE sons of Eric sailed north round about the Stad as soon as they had wind at will ; but when they were come north of the Stad, they heard where King Hakon was, and fare to meet him. King Hakon had nine ships ; he lay under the north side of Frædisberg in Sheppey

Sound. But Eric's sons lay-to south of the berg and had more than twenty ships. King Hakon sent them word, bidding them go aland, and saying that he had pitched a hazelled field for them at Rast-Kalf. There are there flat meads and wide, and above them a long brent somewhat low. So Eric's sons go forth from their ships and fare over the neck inward of Frædisberg and so on to Rast-Kalf. Then spake Egil to King Hakon, bidding him give him ten men and ten banners; and the king did so, and Egil went with his men up under the brent. But King Hakon went on to the fields with his folk, and set up his banner, and arrayed them, saying: "We will have a long array, so that they may not encompass us, though they have the more folk." So did they, and there befell a great battle, and full sharp was the onset. Then let Egil Woolsark set up those ten banners that he had, and ordered the men that bare them in such wise that they went as nigh the brent's top as might be, and let there be a certain space between each man of them. So did they, going right by the brow of the brent, even as they would fall on the back of the folk of Eric's sons. That saw the hindermost of Eric's sons' array, how many banners came on flying apace and fluttering over the brow of the brent, and they deemed that a great host would be coming after, and would fall on their backs, and cut them off from their ships. Then arose a great cry, and either told other what was betid, and thereon fell flight among their array; and when the kings saw that, they fled away. King Hakon set on hard, and followed up the fleers and slew much folk.

III.   N

CHAPTER XXV. OF KING GAMLI.

GAMLI ERICSON, when he came up on to the brow of the brent, turned back and saw that no more folk were following them than they had dealt with afore, and that this was but a beguiling. Then let King Gamli blow up the war-blast, and set up his banner and drew his folk into array; and all the Northmen turned thereto, but the Danes fled to the ships. So when King Hakon and his folk came up with them, then was there anew the fiercest fight. Now had King Hakon the more folk, and the end of it was that Eric's sons fled, making south from the neck; but some of their men ran south on to the berg, and King Harald followed them. A flat field is to the east of the neck and goeth west toward the berg, and sheer rocks cut it off on the westward. Thither on to the berg ran Gamli's men; but King Hakon fell on them so fiercely that he slew some, and some leapt west over the berg, and either band died; and King Hakon left not till every man of them was slain.

CHAPTER XXVI. FALL OF KING GAMLI AND OF EGIL WOOLSARK.

GAMLI ERICSON fled from the neck down on to the plain south of the berg. Then yet again turned King Gamli and upheld the battle, and yet again drew folk unto him. Thither also came all his brethren, each with a great company. Egil Woolsark was as then

leading Hakon's men, and set on full fiercely, and
Gamli and he gat to handy-strokes, and King
Gamli was sore wounded, but Egil fell, and many
men with him. Then came up King Hakon with
the company that had followed him, and there was
yet again a new battle. Full hard then set on King
Hakon, and smote men down on either hand, and
felled one on the top of other. So singeth
Guthorm Cinder :

> Afeard before gold-waster
> Fled all the host of sword-song ;
> The dauntless warflames'-speeder
> Went forth before his banner.
> The king who gat great plenty
> Of the breeze of Mani's darling,
> He spared himself in no wise
> Amidst the fray of spear-maids.

Eric's sons saw their men falling on all sides
for all they could do, and so they turned and fled
away to their ships ; but they who had fled afore to
the ships had thrust out from the shore, and some
ships were yet left high and dry by the ebb. Then
Eric's sons leapt into the sea, and swam with
such folk as was with them. There fell Gamli
Ericson, but the other brethren gat to the ships,
and went their ways with such of their folk as was
left, and so sailed south to Denmark, and tarried
there a while, and were full evil content with their
journey.

CHAPTER XXVII. EGIL WOOLSARK LAID IN HOWE.

SO King Hakon let take all the ships of Eric's sons which had been beached, and let draw them up aland. There King Hakon let lay Egil Woolsark in a ship, and all those of his folk with him who were fallen, and let heap over them stones and earth. Then King Hakon let set up yet more ships, and bear them to the field of battle; and one may see the mounds to-day south of Frædisberg.

Eyvind Skald-spiller made this stave whenas Glum Geirason boasted in his song over the fall of King Hakon:

The flight-shy king aforetime
Hath reddened Fenrir's jaw-gag
In Gamli's blood; there waxèd
The hearts of the trees of steel-storm,
When seaward the unslumbering
Drave down the heirs of Eric.
Great grief on all spear-warders
For the king's fall lieth heavy.

High standing-stones there are by the howe of Egil Woolsark.

CHAPTER XXVIII. TIDINGS OF WAR TOLD TO KING HAKON.

WHEN King Hakon, Athelstane's foster-son, had been king in Norway six and twenty winters since his brother Eric fled the land, it befell that he was abiding in

Hordland, and took guesting in Stord at Fitiar, and there had he his court and many bonders as guests. Now whenas the king sat a-breakfasting, the warders who were without saw a many ships sailing from the south, and come no long way from the island. Then spake one to other that the king should be told, how they deemed that war was coming on them; but it seemed easy to none to tell the king tidings of war, for he had laid heavy penalty on whoso should so do lightly. Yet deemed they it was in no wise to be done that the king should know not thereof; so one of them went into the hall, and bade Eyvind Finnson come out quickly with him, saying that there was the greatest need thereof. So Eyvind went out, and as soon as he came whence he might see the ships, forthwithal he saw that there was a great host a-coming. So he went straightly back into the hall and before the king, and spake: "In a little while the hour doth fleet, and a long space here sit men at meat."

The king looked on him and said: "What is toward?"

Eyvind sang:

> Avengers now of Blood-axe,
> Keen in the play of sheath-staff,
> Men say crave byrny-meeting.
> Scant cause have we to tarry.
> A trouble-bringing telling
> To tell our lord of battle!
> But well I willed thy glory.
> Swift don we the old weapons.

The king said: "Thou art too good a man,

Eyvind, to tell me tidings of war but they be sooth."
Then said many that sooth the tale was. So
the king let take away the board, and he went out
and beheld the ships, and saw that they were war-
ships. Then the king asked his men what rede
to take, whether they should fight with such folk
as they had, or go to their ships and sail away
north. " It is well seen," says he, " that we shall
now have to fight with an host outnumbering us far
more than we had to do with aforetime, though forsooth we have oft deemed that we dealt few against
many when we fought with the sons of Gunnhild."

Men were not swift to answer hereto, till Eyvind
Finnson answered and sang :

> Niord of the shaft-rain, nowise
> The bold thane it beseemeth
> North on to urge the sea-steed.
> All dallying be accursèd !
> Lo, now a fleet wide-spreading
> From south-away drives Harald
> On Rakni's roaring highway.
> Now grip in gripe the war-board !

The king answers : " Manfully is it spoken,
Eyvind, and after mine own heart; yet will I
hearken the mind of more men about this matter."
But when men thought they wotted what the
king would have, then many said that they had
liefer fall with manhood, than flee before Danes
without trying it ; saying that oft had they gotten
the victory when they had been the fewer folk in the
fight. The king thanked them well for their words,
and bade them arm ; and men did so. The king did
a byrny on him, and girt himself with the sword

Quern-biter, set a forgilded helm on his head, and took a glaive in his hand, and had his shield by his side. Then he ordered his body-guard in one battle and the bonders with them, and set up his banners.

CHAPTER XXIX. OF THE ARRAY OF THE SONS OF ERIC.

NOW King Harald Ericson was lord over the brethren after the fall of Gamli. The brethren had there a great host from out of Denmark; and there were in their company their mother's brethren, Eyvind Braggart and Alf Ashman, both strong men and stout, and the greatest of man-slayers. Eric's sons laid their ships by the island and went aland and arrayed their men; and so it is said that so great were the odds that the sons of Eric must have been six to one.

CHAPTER XXX. BATTLE AT FITIAR IN STORD.

NOW King Hakon arrayed his folk; and as men say he cast his byrny from him or ever the battle was joined. So sayeth Eyvind Skald-spiller in the Hakon's-song:

> There found they Biorn's brother
> A-donning his byrny,
> The king the most goodly
> Come neath the war-banner.
> The foemen were drooping,
> Shaken the shafts were,
> When uphove the brunt of the battle.

The Halogaland folk,
The Holmroga people,
The earls' bane was cheering
As he wended to battle.
Good gathering of Northmen
The noble one mustered ;
Neath bright-shining helm
Stood the dread of the Isle-Danes.

War-weed he did off him,
On field cast his byrny,
The war-warders' leader,
Ere the fight had beginning.
There he played with the people
The land's peace a-winning,
The king merry-hearted
Neath gold helm a-standing.

King Hakon chose men diligently for his court
for their might's sake and stoutness, even as King
Harald his father had done. There was Thoralf
Skolmson the Strong going on one hand of the
king, dight with helm and shield, glaive and sword,
which same was called Foot-broad ; and, as folk
said, he and Hakon were of like strength. Hereof
telleth Thord Siarekson in the drapa he made
about Thoralf :

The host went fain to the sword-clash,
There where the battle-hardy
Urgers of steed of land's belt
Fought on in Stord at Fitiar.
He, flinger of the glitter
In she-giant's drift on lee-moon
Of sea-stead, dared the nighest
To the Northmen's king to wend there.

So when the battle was joined was the fight wild
and slaughterous ; and when men had shot their

spears, they drew their swords. And King Hakon
went forth before the banner and Thoralf with
him, and smote on either hand. So sayeth Eyvind
the Skald-spiller:

So bit the sword
In the king's hand swayed
Through Vafad's weed
As through the water.
Crashed there the sword-points,
Shivered the shields there,
Rattled the axe-clash
On skulls of the people.

Trodden were targes
And skulls of the Northmen
Before the hard feet
Of the hilt of the Ring-Tyr,
War rose in the island
Where the kings reddened
The shield-bright burgs
In blood of warriors.

CHAPTER XXXI. THE FALL OF EY-VIND BRAGGART AND ALF ASHMAN.

KING HAKON was easy to know above
other men, for his helm flashed again
when the sun shone on it; so, great brunt
of weapons was about him. Then took Eyvind
Finnson a hat and did it over the king's helm.
But forthright Eyvind Braggart cried out on high:
" Doth now the king of the Northmen hide? or is
he fled away? where is gotten the golden helm?"

Forth then went Eyvind and Alf his brother
with him, smiting on either hand, and making
as they were mad or raging. But King Hakon

cried on high to Eyvind : " Keep thou the
road wherein thou art, if thou wouldst find the
king of the Northmen."

So sayeth Eyvind Skald-spiller :

> Man's friend to gold unfriendly,
> The speeder of the tempest
> Of slaughter-hurdles' Gefn,
> Bade Braggart nowise turn him.
> If thou for victory yearning
> Wouldst find the deft crafts-master
> Of Odin's brunt, hold hither !
> To the king of the doughty Northmen.

But little was the while to bide ere thither came
Eyvind and hove up sword and smote on the king ;
but Thoralf thrust forth his shield against him, so
that Eyvind staggered; and the king took his sword
Quern-biter in both hands, and smote down on Eyvind's helm, and clove helm and head down to the
shoulders.   Therewith Thoralf slew Alf Ashman.

So sayeth Eyvind Skald-spiller :

> I wot that in both hands brandished
> Sharp bit King Hakon's wound-wand
> On him, the middling doughty
> Dweller in hulk sea-gliding.
> The fearless one that eketh
> The squall of the boar of Ali,
> The Dane's hurt, clave the hair-mounds
> With war-brand golden-hilted.

After the fall of those brethren, King Hakon
went forth so hard, that all folk shrank aback
before him ; and anon therewith fell terror and
fleeing among the folk of Eric's sons.   But King
Hakon was in the vanward of his array, and

followed fast on the fleers, and smote oft and hard. Then flew forth a shaft, such as is called a dart, and smote King Hakon on the arm up in the muscle below the shoulder. And the talk of many men it is, that a foot-page of Gunnhild, one named Kisping, ran forth into the press crying out : "Give room to the king's-bane!" and so shot the arrow at King Hakon. Yet some say that none knoweth who shot; as may well be, because arrows and spears, and all kind of shot were flying as thick as the snow drifts.

Many men fell of the folk of Eric's sons, both on the field of battle, and on the way to the ships, yea, and on the very beach; and many leapt into the deep sea. Many there were who came aboard the ships, amongst whom were all Eric's sons, and they rowed away forthwith, yet followed of King Hakon's men.

So sayeth Thord Siarekson :

> Wolves' slayer wards the coast-folk :
> Thus duly peace is broken.
> That king all men were wishing
> At home to grow eld-hoary.
> But toil forsooth hove upward
> When Gunnhild's heir from the Southland,
> The gold's well-wonted scarer,
> Fled, and the king was fallen.

> Now fainting was and fleeing,
> When no few wounded bonders
> Sat by the strong-rowed gunwale,
> And a man and another perished.
> Sure this to prowess pointeth,
> When the all-rich Niord of Gondul
> Who giveth drink to Hugin,
> Went next the king in battle.

CHAPTER XXXII. THE DEATH OF KING HAKON.

KING HAKON went forth unto his ship, and let bind his hurt; but so fast the blood ran from it that it might not be staunched; and as day wore the king's might waned. Then he tells his men that he would fare north to his house at Alrek-stead; but when they came to Hakon's crag they brought-to there, for the king was nigh departing. Then he calls his friends to him, and tells them how he will have his realm ordered. He had one child, a daughter named Thora, but no son; so he bade send word to the sons of Eric, saying that they shall be kings in the land, but bidding them hold his kin and friends in honour.

"For," said he, "though life be fated me, yet will I get me from the land unto Christian men, and atone for what I have misdone against God. Yet if I die here amongst the heathen, then give me grave such as seemeth good to you."

A little thereafter King Hakon gave up the ghost, there on the very rock whereas he had been born.

So was King Hakon sorrowed for, that both friends and foes wept his death, and said that never again would so good a king come to Norway. His friends brought his body north to Seaham in North Hordland, and raised there a great howe, and laid the king therein, all armed with the best of his array, but set no wealth therein beside. Such words they spake over his grave as heathen men had custom, wishing him welfare to Valhall.

Eyvind Skald-spiller did a song on the fall of King Hakon, and of how he was welcomed to Valhall. It is called Hakon's Song, and this is the beginning thereof :

> Gondul and Skogul
> Sent forth the Goth-god
> From the king-folk to choose him
> What kindred of Yngvi
> Should fare unto Odin
> For Valhall's abiding.

> There found they Biorn's brother
> A-donning his byrny,
> The king the most goodly
> Come neath the war-banner.
> The foemen were drooping,
> Shaken the shafts were,
> When uphove the brunt of the battle.

> The Halogaland folk,
> The Holmroga people,
> The earls' bane was cheering
> As he wended to battle.
> Good gathering of Northmen
> The noble one mustered ;
> Neath bright-shining helm
> Stood the dread of the Isle-Danes.

> War-weed he did off him,
> On field cast his byrny
> The war-warders' leader,
> Ere the fight had beginning.
> There he played with the people
> The land's peace a-winning,

The king merry-hearted
Neath gold helm a-standing.

So bit the sword
In the king's hand swayed
Through Vafad's weed
As through the water.
Crashed there the sword-points,
Shivered the shields there,
Rattled the axe-clash
On skulls of the people.

Trodden were targes
And skulls of the Northmen
Before the hard feet
Of the hilt of the Ring-Tyr;
War rose in the island
Where the kings reddened
The shield-bright burgs
In blood of warriors.

Burnt there wound-fires
Amid the wounds bloody;
There were the long swords
At men's lives a-lowting.
High swelled the wound-sea
About the swords' nesses;
The flood of spears fell
On the foreshore of Stord.

Blended were they
Neath the red shield's heaven;
Neath Skogul's cloud-storm
For rings they strove there.

Roared the spear-waves
In Odin's weather;
Fell many a man
Before the sword-stream.

There sat the lords
With swords all naked,
With sharded shields,
And shot-pierced byrnies.
This was the host
With hearts down-fallen
Who had to wend
Their ways to Valhall.

So Gondul spake,
On spear-shaft steadied:
  "Great now the gods' folk groweth,
Whereas Hakon the high
And a mighty host
  They bid to their home, to abide."

That heard the king
What the Valkyrs spake,
  The glorious ones from a-horseback.
Wise ways they had
As helmed they sat there,
  And hove up shield before them.

Spake Hakon:
"Why sharest thou war's lot
In such wise, Geir-skogul?
  Worthy we were of the gain of the gods."

Spake Skogul :
" Yea, and have we not wrought
That the field thou hast held,
    And fled are thy foemen away ? "

" Come ride we away then,"
Quoth the rich Skogul,
    " To the green homes of god-folk.
Come tell we to Odin
How a great king is coming
    To gaze on his godhead itself."

Spake out the high god :
" Ye, Hermod and Bragi,
    Go forth now the mighty to meet ;
For this is a king,
And a champion far-faméd,
    Who fareth his way to our hall."

Spake now the king
From the battle-roar come,
    And he stood with blood bedrifted :
" Odin, meseems,
Looketh awfully on us ;
    Grim of heart we behold him to-day."

" Nay, the peace of all heroes
Here hast thou gotten.
    Come, drink of the ale of the Æsir !
O foe of the Earl-folk,
Herein shalt thou find
    Eight brethren of thine," quoth Bragi.

The good king spake :
" Our own, our wargear
   Here will we have as of old.
Helm and byrny
Are good for heeding ;
   Full seemly to handle the spear."

Now was it wotted
How well the king
   Had upheld holy places,
Whereas all powers
And all the god-folk
   Bade Hakon welcome home.

On a goodly day
Were a great one born
   To get him such good will,
And the days of his life
Shall be told of for good
   For ever and evermore.

Till free, unbound,
Mid folk of men
   The Fenrir's wolf shall fare,
No one so good
To his empty path
   Of the kingly folk shall come.

Now dieth wealth,
Die friends and kin,
   And lea and land lie waste.
Since Hakon fared
To the heathen gods
   Are a many folk enthralled.

THE STORY OF KING HARALD GREYCLOAK AND OF EARL HAKON THE SON OF SIGURD.

THE STORY OF KING HARALD GREYCLOAK AND OF EARL HAKON THE SON OF SIGURD.

CHAPTER I. THE UPRISING OF ERIC'S SONS: AND OF EYVIND SKALD-SPILLER.

SO Eric's sons took to them the kingdom of Norway after that King Hakon was fallen. Harald was the most accounted of amongst those brethren, and the eldest of them yet alive. Gunnhild, their mother, had much to do with the ruling of the land along with them, and she was called the Kings' Mother. These were lords in the land in those days: to wit, Tryggvi Olafson, in the East-country; Gudrod Biornson in Westfold; and Sigurd the Earl of Ladir in Thrandheim. But Gunnhild's sons held but the mid land the first winter. Then went word betwixt Gunnhild's sons and Tryggvi and Gudrod, and all that was said went toward peace, to wit, that they should hold such like share of the realm of Gunnhild's sons as they had aforetime held of King Hakon.

There was one named Glum Geirason, the skald of King Harald, and a man of great daring, and he made this song on the fall of King Hakon :

> Good vengeance then gat Harald
> For Gamli. But sword-bearers
> Lost life whenas the fight-strong
> War-leader fame was winning.
> When Battle-god's black falcons
> Drank of the blood of Hakon,
> I heard how the ruddy wound-reed
> Beyond the sea was reddened.

Right dear was this song deemed; but when Eyvind Finnson heard thereof, he made this song, which is aforewrit :

> The flight-shy king aforetime
> Hath reddened Fenrir's jaw-gag
> In Gamli's blood ; there waxed
> The hearts of the trees of steel-storm,
> When seaward the unslumbering
> Drave down the heirs of Eric.
> Great grief on all spear-warders
> For the king's fall lieth heavy.

And this stave also was given forth far and wide. But when King Harald heard thereof, he laid a death-guilt on Eyvind, till at last their friends brought peace about between them, so that Eyvind should become King Harald's skald, even as erst he had been the skald of King Hakon. They were nigh akin, for Gunnhild, the mother of Eyvind, was the daughter of Earl Halfdan. But her mother was Ingibiorg, daughter of King Harald Hairfair.

So Eyvind made this stave on King Harald :

> Hord's land-ward, little say they
> Thou lettedst thine heart falter
> When burst wound's hail on byrnies
> And bows were bent against thee,
> That tide the full-edged sheath-ice
> Naked screamed out in battle,
> In hands of thine, O Harald,
> For the hungry wolf's fulfilling.

The sons of Gunnhild abode mostly in the mid land; for they trusted not to abide under the hands either of the Thrandheim men, or of those of the Wick, who had been the greatest friends of King Hakon, and withal there were many great men in either country.

But now men went about to make peace between Gunnhild's sons and Earl Sigurd, for hitherto had they gotten no dues from Thrandheim; and so at last they made peace between them, the kings and the earl, and bound the same with oaths. Earl Sigurd was to have such dominion in Thrandheim from them as he had had aforetime from King Hakon. And so they were at peace in words at least.

All Gunnhild's sons were called miserly, and it was said of them that they buried treasure in the earth; whereof made Eyvind Skald-spiller a stave:

> Uller of leek of battle,
> Through all the life of Hakon,
> The seed of Fyri's meadows
> On the falcon-fells we carried.
> But now the folk's foe hideth
> The meal of the woeful maidens
> Of Frodi, in the fair flesh
> Of the troll-wives' foeman's mother.

And this :

> The coif-sun of the brow-fields
> Of Fulla shone on the mountains
> Of Uller's keel for skald-folk
> All through the life of Hakon.
> Now the sun of the deep river
> In the mother's corpse is hidden
> Of the giants' foe—so mighty
> Are the spells of the folk strong-hearted.

But when King Harald heard of these staves he sent word to Eyvind to come to him. But when Eyvind came before him, the king laid guilt on him and called him his foe. "And it befitteth thee ill," said he, "to be untrusty to me, whereas thou hast now become my man."

Then sang Eyvind a stave :

> Dear king, I had one master
> Or ever thee I gat me ;
> I pray for me no third one,
> For eld, lord, 'gainst me beateth.
> True to the dear king was I,
> With two shields played I never ;
> O king, of thy flock am I,
> Now on my hands eld falleth.

King Harald made Eyvind handsel him self-doom in the case. Now Eyvind had a gold ring great and goodly, which was called Mouldy, and had long agone been taken from out the earth. This ring the king saith he will have, and there was nought else for it.

Then sang Eyvind :

> Surely from henceforth should I,
> Speeder of skates of isle-mead,

> Find setting fair to me-ward
> Thy breeze of giant-maidens.
> Since now we needs must hand thee,
> Chooser of hawk-land's jewels,
> That very lair of the ling-worm
> Which long time was my father's.

Therewith fared Eyvind home, nor is it told that he ever met King Harald again.

CHAPTER II. OF GUNNHILD'S SONS, AND HOW THEY HELD THE CHRISTIAN FAITH.

GUNNHILD'S sons had been christened in England, as is aforewrit; but when they came to the ruling of Norway they might nowise bring about the christening of men in the land. But whensoever they might compass it, they brake down temples and undid the feasts of offerings, and gat great hatred thereby. Early in their days came to nought the plenteous seasons; for many kings there were, and each with his court about him; and much they needed, and at great cost, and withal they were most greedy of wealth. Neither held they the laws that King Hakon had set up, save when it pleased them.

They were all the goodliest of men, strong and big, and great of prowess. So sayeth Glum Geirason in that drapa which he made on Harald Gunnhildson:

> The terror-staff of the jaw-teeth
> Of Heimdall, he that ofttimes
> Pressed on in fight, was master
> Of twelve-fold kingly prowess.

Oft those brethren went about all together, but
whiles each by himself. They were men hard-
hearted and bold, great warriors and right happy
in battle.

CHAPTER III.   THE PLOTTING OF GUNNHILD AND HER SONS.

GUNNHILD, the Kings' Mother, and her
sons would oft be meeting for talk and
counsel, and turned over the matters of
the land thereby. And on a time Gunnhild asked
of her sons, " What way are ye minded to let things
fare in the matter of the dominion of Thrandheim ?
Ye bear the name of kings, indeed, as your fathers
did before you ; but little have ye of land or folk,
and yet are ye many to share.   East in the Wick
Tryggvi and Gudrod bear rule, but they indeed
may have some claim thereto, seeing of what kin
they be ; but Earl Sigurd rules alone over all
Thrandheim, nor wot I how this may be meet, to
suffer but a very earl to take so great dominion
from under you ; and marvellous meseemeth, that
year by year ye go a-warring in other lands, while
ye let an earl of your own country take from you
the heritage of your fathers.   A little matter had it
seemed to King Harald, thy namesake, thy father's
father, to take from one earl life and land, when
he won all Norway and held it unto eld."

Harald answers : " It is nought so easy," says
he, "to end the days of Earl Sigurd's life, as
it is to cut the throat of a kid or a calf. Earl
Sigurd is of high blood, and hath much kin, and

is well-beloved and wise. We may wot well that if
he know surely that he may look for enmity at our
hands, all the Thrandheimers will be as one man
with him; and then we have no errand thither
but an ill one. Withal meseemeth none of us
brethren deems it safe to abide under the hand of
the Thrandheimers." Then spake Gunnhild:
"Fare our redes then by clean another way, and
let us betake us to a lesser business. Ye, Harald
and Erling, shall abide this autumn in North-
mere, and I also may fare with you; and then shall
we try all together what may be done."

So in this wise did they.

CHAPTER IV. THE PLOTTING OF GUNNHILD'S SONS WITH GRIOT-GARD.

THE brother of Earl Sigurd was called
Griotgard. He was far the youngest, and
the least accounted of withal; no title of
honour had he, but kept a company of men about
him, and went a-warring in the summer-tide and so
gat him wealth.

Now King Harald sent men into Thrandheim
to Earl Sigurd with friendly gifts and friendly
words, and the messengers said that King Harald
would strike up such friendship with the earl as
had been aforetime betwixt him and King Hakon;
and therewith bidding the earl come see King
Harald that they might bind their friendship
fast and fully. Earl Sigurd received well the
king's messengers and the king's friendship, but

said that he might not go see him because of his much business; but he sent the king friendly gifts and good words and kindness in return for his friendship. So fared away the messengers, and fared to find Griotgard, and bare him the same errand, the friendship of King Harald to wit, and the bidding to his house, and goodly gifts withal; and by then the messengers departed for home, Griotgard had promised to go. And so on a day appointed came Griotgard to meet King Harald and Gunnhild, and a right blithe welcome he had of them. There was he holden in the greatest well-liking, and was with them in the closest talk and many hidden matters: till it came to this, that the matter of Earl Sigurd came uppermost, even as was afore agreed betwixt the king and the queen. Then they showed forth to Griotgard, how Earl Sigurd had long held him of small account; and if he would be with them in this rede, then says the king that Griotgard should be his earl, and have all the dominion which Earl Sigurd had had heretofore. So it came about that they agreed to this with solemn words, that Griotgard should spy out a likely time for falling on Earl Sigurd, and send word to King Harald thereof. So Griotgard fared home with so much done, and had good gifts of the king.

CHAPTER V. THE BURNING OF EARL SIGURD.

EARL SIGURD fared in autumn-tide in to Stiordale, and abode there a-guesting. Thence he fared out to Oglo, there to guest. Now ever would the earl have many men with him, for he trusted the kings but little ; yet now, whereas such friendly words had passed betwixt him and King Harald, he had no great company of men. So now Griotgard did King Harald to wit, that there would be no hopefuller time to fall on Earl Sigurd. So the self-same night the kings, Harald and Erling, went up the Thrandheim-firth with four ships and a great company, and sailed in by night and starlight. Then came Griotgard and met them ; and when the night was far spent, they came to Oglo, whereas Earl Sigurd was a-guesting. There they set fire to the house, and burned the stead and the earl therein, and all his folk with him. So then early in the morning they went their ways down the firth and so south to Mere, and dwelt there a long while.

CHAPTER VI. THE UPRISING OF EARL HAKON SIGURDSON.

HAKON, the son of Earl Sigurd, was up in Thrandheim when he heard of these tidings. Then was there forthright great running to arms throughout all Thrandheim, and every keel that was anywise meet for war was thrust into the sea ; and when the host came

together they took for earl and captain of their
host Hakon, son of Earl Sigurd, and therewith
the host put out down the Thrandheim-firth. But
when the sons of Gunnhild knew thereof they
fared south to Raumsdale and South-mere; and
either side kept watch on the other.

Earl Sigurd was slain two winters after the fall
of King Hakon.

Eyvind Skald-spiller says thus in the Haloga-tale:

And Sigurd, he
The swans that feedeth
Of the Burden-Tyr
With the rooks' beer
From Hadding's chosen,
The land's wielders
Left life-bereft
Down there at Oglo.

There then the giver
Of the arm's gold-worm,
Who nourished never
Fear of the fish-land,
Laid his life down,
Whenas the land's lords
In trust betrayed
Tyr's very kindred.

Earl Hakon held Thrandheim with the might
of his kin to help him for three winters, so that
the sons of Gunnhild gat no dues from Thrandheim. Hakon had many battles with Gunnhild's
sons, and each slew many men for the other.
Hereof telleth Einar Jingle-scale in the Gold-lack,
which he made about Earl Hakon:

The troth-fast spear-point dealer,
Wide sea-host out he drew there.

> The merry king laid sleeping
> All sloth in storms of Gondul.
> The trier of the red moon
> That is of Odin's elbow,
> Eager uphove the fight-sail
> For the kings' fight-mood's allaying.

And again he saith :

> The gladdener of the swan-fowl
> Of the heavy sword-stream nowise
> Had any wite laid on him
> For the shaft-storm of the spear-wife.
> Stoutly the lord of fight-crash
> Shook from Hlokk's sail the bow-hail,
> And he of the sword unsparing
> Goodly the wolves' life nourished.

> Full many a storm of Ali
> Most mighty was befalling
> Ere the deft grove of the shield-leek
> Took the Eastland at the gods' will.

And moreover Einar telleth how Earl Hakon
avenged his father :

> Loud praise I bear forth herewith
> For that vengeance for his father
> Which the warder of waves' raven
> Wreaked with the sword of battle.

> Mail-rain of the sword-storm's urger
> Rained wide on the life of hersirs,
> And he, for battle minded,
> Gave many a thane to Odin.
> The Vidur of gale of sea-steads
> Let wax the life-cold sword-storm
> 'Gainst the shelter of the warriors
> That raise the High-one's tempest.

After these things the friends of either side went
between them with words of peace ; for the bonders

were weary of war and unrest in the very land.
And so it was brought by the redes of wise men,
that peace was made between them, and Hakon
was to have such dominion in Thrandheim as
Earl Sigurd his father had had, but the kings the
dominion therein that King Hakon had had before
them; and this was bound with full oath and troth.
And now befell great love betwixt Earl Hakon
and Gunnhild, though now and again they baited
each other with guile. And so time wore for
other three winters, and Hakon abode in peace in
his dominion.

CHAPTER VII. OF GREYCLOAK.

KING HARALD abode oftenest in Hordland and Rogaland, and yet more of the
brethren also; and oft was their dwelling
at Hardang. Now on a certain summer came a
ship of burden from Iceland and owned of Icelanders, and laden with grey cloaks. They brought
the ship up to Hardang, because they had heard
that there already was the greatest concourse of
men; but when men came to deal with them they
would not buy their grey cloaks. So went the
skipper to King Harald, for he had known him to
speak to aforetime, and told him of his trouble. The
king said he would come to them, and did so. King
Harald was a kindly-mannered man and a merry-
hearted. He was come there in a cutter all manned;
he looked on their lading, and spake to the skipper:
"Wilt thou give me one of thy grey cloaks?"
"With a good will would I," said the skipper,

" yea, and even more." Then the king took a grey cloak, and cloaked him therewith, and so went down into the barge ; and before they rowed away every one of his men had bought a cloak. Moreover, a few days thereafter came thither so many men every one of them wanting to buy a grey cloak, that not the half of them that wanted them could get them.

So ever after was the king called Harald Greycloak.

CHAPTER VIII. THE BIRTH OF EARL ERIC.

EARL HAKON fared on a winter to the Uplands to a feast, and there, as it happed, he lay with a certain woman, and she lowly of kin ; and as time wore the woman went with child, and when it was born it was a man-child ; so it was sprinkled with water and called Eric. The mother brought the lad to Earl Hakon, and said that he was the father thereof; so the earl let the lad be nourished at the house of one called Thorleif the Sage. He dwelt up in Middledale, and was a wise man and a wealthy, and a great friend of the earl's. Eric speedily waxed hopeful ; he was of the fairest aspect, and great and strong from his earliest days. The earl had but little to say to him. Earl Hakon was the goodliest to look on of all men, not high of stature, yet strong enow, and well skilled in all prowess, wise of wit, and the greatest of warriors,

CHAPTER IX.   THE   SLAYING   OF KING TRYGGVI.

ON a certain autumn Earl Hakon fared to the Uplands, and when he came on to Heathmark there came to meet him King Tryggvi Olafson and King Gudrod Biornson, and thither also came Gudbrand a-Dale.   These held counsel together, and sat long in privy talk, whereof this came uppermost, that each should be friend of the other ; and therewith they parted and went home each to his own realm.   Now Gunnhild and her sons hear hereof, and misdoubt them of it, that they have been plotting against the kings ; so often they talk hereof together.   But in spring-tide King Harald and King Gudrod his brother give out that they will be a-faring a war-voyage in the summer West-over-the-sea, or into the East-countries, as their wont was.   So they gather their folk together and thrust their ships into the water and array them for departure ; but when they drank their ale of departure, great drinking there was, and a many things spoken over the drink ; and so they gat to the sport of likening man to man, and the talk fell on the kings themselves.   Then spake a man, saying that King Harald was the foremost of those brethren in all matters.   Then waxed King Gudrod very wroth, and says so much as that he will be none the worse in any wise than King Harald, and that he is ready to prove the same.   Then speedily were they full wroth either of them, so that either bade other come and fight, and ran to their weapons withal.   But they who had their wits about them, and were the less drunken, stayed them and ran betwixt. So they went both to their ships, but it was no longer to be looked for that they should sail together. Gudrod sailed east along the land, and Harald made out into the main, saying that he would sail West-over-the-sea; but when he was gotten without the isles, he turned and sailed east along the land, keeping out to sea. King Gudrod sailed by the common course east-away to the Wick, and so east across the Fold. Thence he sent word to King Tryggvi to come and meet him, and they would go both together that summer a-warring in the Eastlands. King Tryggvi took the message well and hopefully. He had heard that King Gudrod had but few folk; so he went to meet him with but one cutter, and they met at the Walls, east of Sotaness. But when they came to the council, King Gudrod's men leapt forth and slew King Tryggvi and twelve men with him; and he lieth at the place which is now called Tryggvi's Cairn.

CHAPTER X.   THE FALL OF KING GUDROD,

NOW King Harald sailed far out to sea, and he made in for the Wick, and came a-night-time to Tunsberg. There heard he that King Gudrod was a-guesting a little way up the country. So King Harald and his folk went thither, and came there a-night-time, and took the house over their heads. King Gudrod came forth, he and his; but short was the stour or ever King Gudrod fell, and many men with him. Then King Harald fared away to find King Gudrod his brother, and they twain laid all the Wick under them.

CHAPTER XI. OF HARALD THE GRENLANDER.

KING GUDROD BIORNSON had wedded well and meetly, and had a son by his wife called Harald; he was sent into Grenland to Roi the White, a lord of the land, to be fostered there. The son of Roi was Rani the Wide-faring, and Harald and he were foster-brethren and much of an age. After the fall of Gudrod his father, Harald, who was called the Grenlander, fled away to the Uplands with Rani his foster-brother and but few other men, and Harald tarried awhile with his kin. Now Eric's sons pried closely into all such as had enmity against them, and on those the most whom they deemed like to rise up against them. Harald's kindred gave him the rede that he should depart from the land; so Harald the Grenlander fared east to Sweden, and sought for himself a crew, so that he might fall into company with such men as went a-warring to gather wealth; and Harald was the doughtiest of men. There was one Tosti in Sweden, the mightiest and noblest of all men of that land who lacked title of dignity; he was the greatest of warriors, and was for the most part a-warring, and he was called Skogul-Tosti. Into his fellowship Harald the Grenlander betook himself, and was with Skogul-

Tosti a-warring in the summer, and every man
deemed well of Harald, and Harald abode behind
with Tosti through the winter.   Sigrid was the
name of Tosti's daughter ; young and fair she was,
and exceeding high-minded.   She was afterward
wedded to Eric the Victorious, the Swede-king,
and their son was Olaf the Swede, who was king
in Sweden in after-times.   King Eric died of sickness at Upsala ten winters after Styrbiorn fell.

CHAPTER XII.   THE WARRING OF EARL HAKON.

THE sons of Gunnhild drew a great host
out of the Wick, and so fare north along
the land, gathering ships and folk from
every country ; and they lay it bare that they
are bringing that same host north to Thrandheim
against Earl Hakon.

Thereof heareth the earl, and gathereth folk
and goeth a-shipboard ; but when he heard of the
host of Gunnhild's sons how many they were, he
led his folk south to Mere, and harried whereso
he came, and slew much folk.   Then he sent back
the host of Thrandheim and the whole crowd of
the bonders, but himself fared a-warring all about
either Mere and Raumsdale, and had spies abroad
south of the Stad on the host of Gunnhild's sons.
But when he heard that they were come into the
Firths, and abode a wind there to sail north about
the Stad, then sailed Earl Hakon south of the
Stad, but out to sea, so that none might behold
his sails from the land.   Then he held his course

by the open sea east along the land till he came
right on to Denmark ; thence he sailed for the
Eastlands, and harried there the summer long.

The sons of Gunnhild led their host north into
Thrandheim, and abode there a long while through
the summer, and took all scat and dues there ;
but when summer was far spent, Sigurd Slaver
and Gudrod abode behind there, and King Harald
and the other brethren went into the East-country
with the host that had gone with them in the
summer season.

CHAPTER XIII.   OF EARL HAKON AND THE SONS OF GUNNHILD.

EARL HAKON fared in autumn-tide
to Helsingland, and laid up his ships
there, and then fared by land through
Helsingland and Jamtland, and so west over the
Keel down into Thrandheim.   Much folk drew
unto him, and he gat a-shipboard.   But when
Gunnhild's sons hear thereof they get aboard their
ships and make down the firth ; but Earl Hakon
goeth to Ladir, and abode there the winter, while
Gunnhild's sons dwelt in Mere ; and either made
raids on the other, and slew men each of the other.
Earl Hakon held dominion in Thrandheim, and
was there oftest in winter-tide, but whiles in the
summer he fared east into Helsingland, and took
his ships there, and went into the Eastlands, and
harried there in summer-tide.   But whiles he abode
in Thrandheim, and had his host out, and then Gunnhild's sons might not hold them north of the Stad.

CHAPTER XIV. THE SLAYING OF SIGURD SLAYER.

HARALD GREYCLOAK fared on a summer north to Biarmland, and harried there, and had a great battle with the folk of the land at Dwina side. There had King Harald the victory, and slew much folk; then he harried wide about in the land, and gat to him exceeding great wealth. Hereof telleth Glum Geirason:

The word-strong king's oppressor
Reddened the fire-brand east there,
All northward of the township,
Where saw I Biarm-folk running.
Spear-gale the youthful Atheling
Gat him on that same journey.
Good word the men's appeaser
Found on the side of Dwina.

King Sigurd Slayer came to the house of Klypp the Hersir; he was the son of Thord, the son of Horda-Kari, and was a mighty man and of great kin. Now Klypp was not at home as then, but Alof his wife gave the king good welcome, and there was noble feast and great drinking. Alof was the daughter of Asbiorn, and the sister of Jarnskeggi from Yriar in the North-country. Hreidar, the brother of Asbiorn, was the father of Styrkar, the father of Eindrid, the father of Einar Thambarskelfir.

Now the king went a-night-time to the bed of Alof, and lay with her against her will; and thereafter fared the king away. Thereafter in the

autumn-tide King Harald and Sigurd his brother
fared up to Vors, and there summoned the bonders
to a Thing ; at which Thing the bonders fell on
them to slay them, but they escaped and went
their ways. King Harald went to Hardanger, but
King Sigurd to Alrek-stead. But when Hersir
Klypp heard thereof, he called together his kinsmen to set on the king ; and the captain of the
company was Vemund Knuckle-breaker. And so
when they came to the house they fell on the
king. And so tells the tale that Klypp thrust the
king through with a sword, and slew him ; but
forthright Erling the Old slew Klypp on the
spot.

CHAPTER XV. THE FALL OF GRIOT-GARD.

KING HARALD GREYCLOAK and
Gudrod his brother drew together a great
host from out the East-country, and made
for Thrandheim with that folk. But when Earl
Hakon heard thereof he gathered folk to him, and
made for Mere and harried there. There was
Griotgard his father's brother, and was charged
with the warding of the land for Gunnhild's sons ;
he drew out folk even as the kings had sent him
word. Earl Hakon went to meet him, and joined
battle with him ; there fell Griotgard and two earls
with him, and much other folk. Hereof telleth
Einar Jingle-scale :

> The hardy king caused helm-storm
> To fall upon his foemen.

Thereof were friends a-waxing
In Loft's friend's hall of friendship.
Three earls' sons fierce were fallen
In fiery rain of Odin,
Whereof the pride of the people
Great praise and fame hath gotten.

Thereafter Earl Hakon sailed out to sea, and so by the outer course south along the land. So came he south right on to Denmark to King Harald Gormson the Dane-king; there had he good welcome, and abode with him the winter through.

There also with the Dane-king was a man called Harald, who was son of Knut, the son of Gorm, and was the brother's son of King Harald. He was new-come from warring, wherein he had long been, and had gotten thereby very great wealth; so he was called Gold Harald. He was deemed to have good right to be king in Denmark.

CHAPTER XVI. THE FALL OF KING ERLING.

KING HARALD GREYCLOAK and those brethren brought their folk north to Thrandheim, and found nought to withstand them there; so they took scat and dues, and all king's revenues, and made the bonders pay great fines, for the kings had now for a long while gotten but little money from Thrandheim, since Earl Hakon had abided there with many men, and had been at war with the kings.

In the autumn King Harald went into the South-country with the more part of the folk that were

home-born there ; but King Erling abode behind
with his folk, and he had yet again plenteous goods
of the bonders, and dealt them out hard measure.
Thereof the bonders bemoaned them sore, and took
their scathe ill. And so in the winter they gathered
together and gat a great company, and went against
King Erling as he was out a-guesting, and had
battle with him. There fell King Erling, and a
many men with him.

CHAPTER XVII. FAMINE IN NORWAY.

IN the days when Gunnhild's sons ruled over
Norway befell great scarcity, and ever the
greater it grew the longer they ruled over
the land ; and the bonders laid it to the account of
the kings, whereas they were greedy of money,
and dealt hardly with the bonders. To such a
pitch it came at last, that all up and down the land
folk well-nigh lacked all corn and fish. In Halogaland was there such hunger and need, that well-
nigh no corn grew there, and the snow lay all over
the land at midsummer, and all the live-stock was
bound in stall at the very midsummer. Thus sang
Eyvind Skald-spiller when he came forth from his
house, and it was snowing hard :

> On Swolnir's dame it snoweth,
> And so have we as Finn-folk
> To bind the hind of birch-buds
> In byre amidst of summer.

CHAPTER XVIII. OF THE ICE-LANDERS AND EYVIND SKALD-SPILLER.

EYVIND made a drapa on all the men of Iceland, and they gave him this reward, that each bonder gave him a scat-penny of the weight of three silver pennies, and which would cut white. But when this silver came forth at the Althing, men took counsel to get smiths to refine the silver; and thereafter was a cloak-clasp made thereof, and, the smithying being paid for, the clasp was worth fifty marks, and this they sent to Eyvind. But now Eyvind let shear the clasp asunder, and bought him stuff therewith. That same spring withal came a shoal of herring to certain outward-lying fishing-steads; so Eyvind manned a row-boat of his with his house-carles and tenants, and rowed thither whereas the herring were being netted; and he sang:

> Now did we set our sea-horse
> Be spurring from the northward
> After the terns fin-tailèd,
> Foreboders of the long nets,
> To wot, O dear fire-goddess,
> If silver-weeds of the ice-fields,
> Through which the wave-swine rooteth,
> My friends be fain to sell me?

So utterly were his goods expended, that he must needs buy herring with the arrows of his bow; as he singeth:

> We fetched the fair cloak-buckle
> The sea-heaven's folk had sent us

From over the sea, and sold it
For store of the swimming firth-herd.
The more part of the herrings
That leap from hands of Egil,
To Mar for sea-shafts sold I,
And all this came of hunger.

THE STORY OF KING OLAF
TRYGGVISON.

THE STORY OF KING OLAF TRYGGVISON.

CHAPTER I. THE BIRTH OF OLAF TRYGGVISON.

ASTRID was the name of the woman whom King Tryggvi Olafson had had for wife; she was the daughter of Eric Biodaskalli, who dwelt at Ofrustead, a mighty man. Now after the fall of King Tryggvi, Astrid fled away, and fared privily with such chattels as she might have with her. In her company was her foster-father, Thorolf Louse-beard by name. He never departed from her, but other trusty men of hers went about spying of tidings of her foes, and their comings and goings.

Now Astrid went with child of King Tryggvi, and she let herself be flitted out into a certain water, and lay hidden in a holm thereamidst with but few folk in her company. There she brought forth a child, a man-child, who was sprinkled with water and named Olaf after his father's father. There lay Astrid hidden through the summer-tide; but when the nights grew dark and the days grew short, and the weather waxed cold, then Astrid gat her gone thence with Thorolf and few other folk,

but they went into peopled parts only when they
might be hidden by the night, and met no men.

So on a day in the even they came to Ofrustead,
to Eric, the father of Astrid, and fared privily.
There Astrid sent men to the house to tell Eric,
who let bring them to a certain out-bower, and
spread a table for them with the best of cheer.
And when Astrid had been there a little while
her folk gat them gone, and she abode behind
with two serving-women of hers, her son Olaf, and
Thorolf Louse-beard, with his son Thorgils, of six
winters old; and there they dwelt through the
winter.

CHAPTER II. OF GUNNHILD'S SONS.

HARALD GREYCLOAK and Gudrod
his brother after the slaying of Tryggvi
Olafson fared to the steads he had
owned; but Astrid was gone, and they might hear
no tidings of her. But the rumour reached them
that she was with child of King Tryggvi. So in
autumn-tide they went into the North-country, as
is aforewrit; and when they saw Gunnhild their
mother, they told her all matters concerning what
had betid them in their journey; and she asked
closely of all that had to do with Astrid, and they
told her such babble as they had heard thereof.
But now whereas that autumn Gunnhild's sons
had strife with Earl Hakon, yea and the winter
thereafter, as is writ afore, withal there was no
search made after Astrid and her son that winter.

CHAPTER III.   THE JOURNEYING OF ASTRID.

THE next spring Gunnhild sent spies to the Uplands, and all the way to the Wick, to spy what Astrid would be doing; who, when they came back, had chiefly to tell Gunnhild that Astrid would be with her father Eric; and they said that it was more like than not that she would be nourishing there the son of her and King Tryggvi.

Then Gunnhild sped messengers, and arrayed them well with weapons and horses; and they were thirty men in company, and their leader was a man of might, a friend of Gunnhild's, Hakon by name. She bade them fare to Eric at Ofrustead, and have thenceaway this son of King Tryggvi's, and bring him to her. So the messengers go all the way, and when they were come but a little way from Ofrustead, the friends of Eric were ware of them, and bare him tidings of the goings of them at eve of the day. So straightway at night-tide Eric arrayed Astrid for departure, and gave her good guides, and sent her east-away into Sweden to Hakon the Old, a friend of his, and a man of might; so they departed while the night was yet young, and came by eve of the next day into a country called Skaun, and saw there a great stead, and went thereto, and craved a night's lodging. They had disguised them, and their raiment was but sorry. The bonder thereat was called Biorn Poison-sore, a wealthy man but a churlish; he drave them away. So they went that

III.   Q

eve to another thorp hard by, which was called Attwood; one Thorstein was the bonder there, who lodged them and gave them good entertainment that night, and so they slept there well cared for.

Now Hakon and the men of Gunnhild came to Ofrustead betimes in the morning, and asked after Astrid and her son; but Eric says she is not there. So Hakon and his men ransacked all the stead, and abode there far on into the day, and had some inkling of Astrid's goings. So they ride away the selfsame road that she had gone, and come late in the evening to Biorn Poison-sore in Skaun, and there take lodging. Then Hakon asks of Biorn if he had aught to tell him of Astrid. Biorn says that certain folk had come there that day craving lodging: "But I drave them away, and they will be lodged somewhere or other in the township."

Now a workman of Thorstein's went that eve from the wood, and came to Biorn's because it lay on his road. So he found that guests were come there, and learned their errand, and so goes and tells Master Thorstein. And so when the night had yet one third to endure, Thorstein waked his guests, and bade them get them gone, speaking roughly to them; but when they were come their ways out from the garth, Thorstein told them that Gunnhild's messengers were at Biorn's, and were about seeking them. They prayed him to help them somewhat, and he gave them guides and some victual, and their guide brought them forth away into the wood where was a certain water, and a holm therein grown about with reeds; thither to the holm might they wade, and there they lay hid in the reeds.

Betimes on the morrow rode Hakon from Biorn's into the country-side, asking after Astrid wheresoever he came; and when he came to Thorstein's he asked if they were there.   Thorstein says that certain folk had come thither, but had gone away against daybreak east into the wood.   So Hakon bade Thorstein go with them, seeing that he knew the wood, both way and thicket; so he went with them, but when he came into the wood he brought them right away from where Astrid lay, and they went about seeking all day long, and found them nowhere.   So they went back and told Gunnhild how their errand had sped.

But Astrid and her fellows went their ways, and came forth into Sweden to Hakon the Old; and there abode Astrid and Olaf her son in all welcome a long while.

CHAPTER IV.   HAKON SENT INTO SWEDEN.

NOW Gunnhild the Kings' Mother hears that Astrid and Olaf her son are in the Swede-realm; so she sent Hakon yet again, and a goodly company with him, east to Eric the Swede-king, with good gifts and fair words and friendly.   There had the messengers good welcome, and abode there in good entertainment.   Then Hakon laid his errand before the king, saying that Gunnhild sent this word,

that the king should be to Hakon of such avail
that he might have Olaf Tryggvison back with
him to Norway, where Gunnhild would foster
him.

So the king gave him men, and they ride unto
Hakon the Old. There Hakon craved for Olaf to
fare with him with many friendly words. Hakon
the Old answered him well, but said that Olaf's
mother should order his going; but Astrid will in
no wise suffer the boy to go. So the messengers go
their ways, and tell King Eric how matters stand.
Then they array them for their journey home,
but crave somewhat of force of the king to have
the lad away whether Hakon the Old will or not.
So the king gave them again a company of men,
and the messengers go therewith to Hakon the
Old, and crave once more for the lad to fare with
them; but whereas the message was taken coldly,
they fall to big words and threats, and grow right
wroth. Then sprang forth a thrall named Bristle,
and would smite Hakon, and scarce may they get
away unbeaten of the thrall. Then home they
fare to Norway, and tell Gunnhild of their journey,
and how they have seen Olaf Tryggvison.

CHAPTER V.   OF SIGURD ERICSON.

SIGURD, son of Eric Biodaskalli, was the
brother of Astrid; he had been a long
while away from the land east in Garth-
realm with King Valdimar, where he dwelt in great
honour. Now Astrid would fain go thither to
Sigurd her brother; so Hakon the Old gave her a

goodly fellowship, and all fair array, and she went with certain chapmen. She had now been two winters with Hakon the Old, and Olaf was three winters old.

But now as they made into the Eastern sea, vikings fell on them, Estlanders, who took both men and money; and some they slew, and some they shared between them for bond-slaves. There was Olaf parted from his mother, and an Estlander called Klerkon gat him along with Thorolf and Thorgils. Klerkon deemed Thorolf over old for a thrall, and could not see any work in him, so he slew him, but had the lads away with him, and sold them to a man named Klerk for a right good he-goat. A third man bought Olaf, and gave therefor a good coat or cloak; he was called Reas, and his wife Rekon, and their son Rekoni. There abode Olaf long, and was well served, and the bonder loved him much. He was six winters exiled thus in Estland.

CHAPTER VI. THE FREEING OF OLAF FROM ESTLAND.

SIGURD ERICSON came into Estland on a message of King Valdimar of Holmgarth, to wit, the claiming of the king's scat in that land. He fared like a mighty man with many men and plenteous wealth.

Now he saw in a certain market-place a lad full fair, and knew him for an outlander, and asked him of his name and kin. He named himself Olaf, and called his father Tryggvi Olafson, and his

mother Astrid, daughter of Eric Biodaskalli. So
Sigurd knew that the lad was his sister's son ; so
he asked the lad what made him there, and Olaf
told him all that had befallen in his matter. So
Sigurd bade him show the way to the goodman
Reas ; and when he came there he bought both
the lads, Olaf and Thorgils, and had them with
him to Holmgarth, but gave out nought about the
kinship of Olaf, though he did well to him.

CHAPTER VII. THE SLAYING OF KLERKON.

OLAF TRYGGVISON was standing one
day in the gate, and there were many
men about, amongst whom he saw Klerkon, who had slain his fosterer, Thorolf Louse-
beard. Olaf had a little axe in his hand, which
same he drave into Klerkon's head, so that it
stood right down in the brain of him ; then he fell
to running home to the house, and told Sigurd his
kinsman thereof. So Sigurd straightway brought
Olaf into the queen's house, and told her these
tidings. She was called Allogia. Her Sigurd
prayed help the lad. She answered, looking on
the lad, that they should not slay so fair a child,
and bade call to her men all armed.

Now in Holmgarth was the p ace so hallowed,
that, according to the law thereof, whoso slew a
man undoomed should himself be slain. And now
all the people made a rush together, according to
their custom and law, and sought after the lad,
where he were ; and it was told that he was in the

queen's garth, and that there was an host of men
all armed.

Hereof was the king told, and he went thereto
with his folk, and would not that they fought, and
so brought about truce and peace thereafter; and
the king adjudged the weregild, and the queen paid
the fine.

Thereafter abode Olaf with the queen, and was
right dear to her.

It was law at that time in Garth-realm that kingly-
born men might not abide there, save by the king's
counsel. So Sigurd told the queen of what kin
Olaf was, and for why he was come thither, and
how he might not abide in his own land because of
his foes, and prayed her deal with the king concerning this. She did so, praying him to help
this king's son so hardly dealt with, and she did
so much by her words, that the king assented
hereto, and took Olaf under his power, and did
well and worthily to him, as was meet for a king's
son to be served.

Olaf was nine winters old when he came into
Garth-realm, and he abode with King Valdimar
other nine winters.

Olaf was the fairest and tallest and strongest of
all men, and in prowess surpassing all men told of
among the Northmen.

CHAPTER VIII. OF EARL HAKON.

EARL HAKON SIGURDSON abode with Harald Gormson the Dane-king the winter after he had fled from Norway before the sons of Gunnhild. So great imagining had Hakon through the winter season, that he lay in his bed, and waked long, and ate and drank not save to sustain his might. Then he sent men of his privily north into Thrandheim to his friends there, and gave them counsel to slay King Erling if they might compass it; and said withal that he would come back to his realm when summer was again. That winter they of Thrandheim slew Erling as is aforewrit.

Now betwixt Hakon and Gold Harald was dear friendship, and Harald showed all his mind to Hakon, saying that he would fain settle in the land, and lie out no more in war-ships; and he asked Hakon what he thought of it, whether King Harald would be willing to share the realm with him if he craved it.

"Meseemeth," said Hakon, "that the Dane-king would not deny thee any rights; but thou wilt know the uttermost of the matter if thou lay it before the king; and I ween thou wilt not get the realm if thou crave it not."

So a little after this talk Gold Harald fell to talk hereover with King Harald, whenas there were standing by many mighty men, friends of either of them. There craved Gold Harald of the king to share the realm in half with him, even as his birth warranted, and his kin there in the Dane-realm.

At this asking grew King Harald exceeding wroth, saying that no man had craved it of King Gorm, his father, that he should become half-king over the Dane-realm ; nay, nor of his father Horda-knut, nor of Sigurd Worm-in-eye, nor of Ragnar Lodbrok ; and therewith he waxed so wood-wroth that none might speak to him.

CHAPTER IX. OF GOLD HARALD.

NOW was Gold Harald worse content than afore, whereas he had gotten the king's wrath, and of realm no whit more than erst. So he came to Hakon his friend, and be-wailed his trouble to him, and prayed him for wholesome rede, if such could be, how he might get the realm to him ; and said withal, that it had come uppermost in his mind to seek his realm with might and weapons. Hakon bade him not speak that word before any, lest it become known. Said he : " Thy life lieth on it. See thou to it, of what avail thou art herein. Needs must he who dealeth with such big deeds be high-hearted and dauntless, and spare neither for good nor ill in bringing to pass what he hath set his hand to ; but it is unworthy to take up high counsels and then lay them down with dishonour." Gold Harald answers : " In such wise shall I take up this claim of mine, that I will not spare to slay the king himself with mine own hand, if occasion serve, since he must needs gainsay me this realm which I ought of right to have." Therewith they left talking.

Now King Harald went to Hakon, and they

fall a-talking, and the king tells the earl what claim Gold Harald had made on him for the realm, and how he had answered it, saying withal that for nought would he diminish his realm: "Yea, if Gold Harald will yet hold by this claim, I shall deem it but a little matter to let slay him, for I trust him ill, if he will not give this up."

The earl answers: "Meseemeth that Harald hath put this matter forth then only when he will by no means let it fall; and I must needs deem that if he raise war in the land he will not lack for folk, chiefly for the dear remembrance of his father. Yet is it most unmeet for thee to slay thy kinsman, when, as the matter now is, all folk shall call him sackless. Nevertheless I would not have thee think that I counsel thee to become less of a king than was Gorm thy father, who indeed brought increase to his realm, and minished it in no wise."

Then said the king: "What is thy rede then, Hakon? Must I needs neither share the realm then, nor have this bugbear off my hands?"

"We shall be meeting a few days hence," said Hakon, "and I will turn my mind before that to this trouble, and clear it up in some wise."

Then the king went his ways with all his men.

CHAPTER X. THE COUNSEL OF KING HARALD AND EARL HAKON.

EARL HAKON now fell again to the greatest brooding and plotting; and let few men be in the house with him. But a few days thereafter came King Harald to the

earl, and they fell a-talking, and the king asked if
the earl had bethought him on that matter they
were on the other day.

Says the earl : " I have waked day and night
ever since, and the best rede meseemeth is that
thou hold and rule all the realm which thou hadst
from thy father, but get for Harald thy kinsman
another kingdom, whereof he shall be a man well
honoured."

" What realm is that," said the king, " that I
may lightly give to Harald, keeping the Dane-
realm whole the while ? "

The earl says : " Norway is it.   Such kings as
are there, are ill-beloved of all the folk of the
land ; and every man wishes them ill, as is but
meet."

The king says : " Norway is a great land and
a hardy folk, an ill land to fall on with an outland host.   Such hap we had when King Hakon
defended the land, that we lost much folk, and
won no victory ; and Harald Ericson is my foster-
son, and hath sat on my knee."

Then saith the earl : " I knew this long while
that thou hadst oft given help to the sons of Gunnhild ; yet have they rewarded thee with nought but
ill ; but we shall come far lightlier by Norway than
by fighting for it with all the host of the Danes.
Send thou for thy foster-son Harald, bidding him
take from thee the lands and fiefs which they had
aforetime here in Denmark, and summon him to
meet thee ; and then may Gold Harald in that little
while win him a kingdom in Norway from Harald
Greycloak."

The king says that it will be called an evil deed to betray his foster-son.

Saith the earl: "The Danes will account it a good exchange, the slaying a Norse viking rather than a brother's son, a Dane."

So they talk the matter over a long while till it was accorded between them.

CHAPTER XI. THE MESSAGE OF HARALD GORMSON TO NORWAY.

YET again came Gold Harald to talk with Earl Hakon; and the earl tells him that he has been so busy in his matter that most like a kingdom would be ready at hand for him in Norway. "And now," saith he, "let us hold by our fellowship, and I will be a trusty and great help to thee in Norway. Get thou first that realm; but then moreover is King Harald very old, and hath but one son, a bastard, whom he loveth but little."

So the earl talks hereof to Gold Harald till he says he is well content therewith. Thereafter they all talk the thing over together full often, the king to wit, the earl, and Gold Harald.

Then the Dane-king sent his men north into Norway to Harald Greycloak Right gloriously was that journey arrayed, and good welcome had they, when they came to Harald the king. There they tell the tidings that Earl Hakon is in Denmark, lying hard at death's door, and well-nigh witless; and these other tidings withal, that Harald the Dane-king biddeth Harald Greycloak, his foster-son to him, to take such fiefs from him as the brethren had aforetime in Denmark, and biddeth Harald come and meet him in Jutland.

Harald Greycloak laid this message before Gunnhild his mother and other of his friends; and men's minds were not at one thereon; to some the journey seemed nought to be trusted in, such men as were awaiting them yonder; yet were the others more who were fain to fare, whereas there was so great famine in Norway, that the kings might scarce feed their own household; wherefrom gat the firth wherein the kings abode oftest that name of Hardanger; but in Denmark was the year's increase of some avail. So men deemed that there would be something to be got thence if King Harald had fief and dominion there.

So it was settled before the messengers went their ways, that King Harald should come to Denmark in the summer-tide to meet the Daneking, and take of him the fortune he offered.

CHAPTER XII. THE TREASON OF KING HARALD AND EARL HAKON AGAINST GOLD HARALD.

HARALD GREYCLOAK fared in the summer-tide to Denmark with three long-ships; Arinbiorn the Hersir of the Firths sailed one of them.

So King Harald sailed out from the Wick to the Limbfirth and put in there at the Neck; and it was told him that the Dane-king would speedily come thither. But when Gold Harald heard thereof he made thither with nine long-ships, for he had aforetime arrayed his host for war-sailing. Earl Hakon also had arrayed his folk for war, and had twelve ships, all great.

But when Gold Harald was gone, then spake Earl Hakon to the king : " Now see I nought but that we are both pressed to row, and paying fine. Gold Harald will slay Harald Greycloak, and take the kingdom in Norway ; and deemest thou then that thou mayst trust him, when thou hast put such might into his hands, whereas he spake this before me last winter, that he would slay thee, might but time and place serve ? Now will I win Norway for thee and slay Gold Harald, if thou wilt promise me easy atonement at thy hands for the deed. Then will I be thine earl, and bind myself by oath to win Norway for thee with thy might to aid, and to hold the land thereafter under thy dominion and pay thee scat. Then art thou a greater king than thy father, when thou rulest over two great peoples." So this was accorded betwixt the king and the earl, and Hakon fared with his host a-seeking Gold Harald.

CHAPTER XIII. THE FALL OF HARALD GREYCLOAK AT THE NECK.

GOLD HARALD came to the Neck in the Limbfirth, and straightway bade battle to Harald Greycloak. Then, though King Harald had the fewer folk, he went aland straightway, and made him ready for battle, and arrayed his folk. Then before the battle was joined Harald

Greycloak cheered on his folk full hard, and bade them draw sword, and so ran forth before the van-ward battle and smote on either hand. So sayeth Glum Geirason in Greycloak's Drapa :

> The god of hilts made meetly,
> E'en he who durst to redden
> The green fields for the people,
> A doughty word hath spoken.
> There Harald the wide-landed
> Gave bidding to his king's-men
> To swing the sword for slaughter ;
> That word his men deemed noble.

There fell King Harald Greycloak, as sayeth Glum Geirason :

> The heeder of the garth-wall
> Of Glammi's steeds, the ship-wont,
> Alow he needs must lay him
> On the wide board of Limbfirth.
> The scatterer of the sea's flame
> Fell on Neck's sandy stretches ;
> He, the word-happy kings' friend
> It was who wrought this slaughter.

There fell the more part of King Harald's men with him ; Arinbiorn the Hersir fell there.

Now was worn away fifteen winters from the fall of Hakon Athelstane's Foster-son, and thirteen winters from the fall of Sigurd, the Earl of Ladir. So sayeth Ari Thorgilson the priest, that Earl Hakon had ruled for thirteen winters over his heritage in Thrandheim before Harald Greycloak was slain ; but the last six winters of Harald Grey-cloak's life, saith Ari, Gunnhild's sons and Hakon were at war together, and in turn fled away from the land.

CHAPTER XIV. THE DEATH OF GOLD HARALD.

EARL HAKON and Gold Harald met a little after Harald Greycloak was fallen; and straightway Earl Hakon joined battle with Gold Harald. There gat Hakon the victory, and Harald was taken, whom Hakon let straightway hang up on a gallows. Thereafter fared Earl Hakon to meet the Dane-king, and had easy atonement from him for the slaying of Gold Harald, his kinsman.

CHAPTER XV. THE SHARING OF NORWAY.

THEN King Harald called out an host from all his realm, and sailed with six hundred ships; and in his fellowship was Earl Hakon Sigurdson, and Harald the Grenlander, son of King Gudrod, and many other mighty men who had fled their free lands in Norway before the sons of Gunnhild.

The Dane-king turned his host from the south into the Wick, and all the folk of the land submitted them to him; but when he came to Tunsberg drew much folk to him, and all the host that came to him in Norway King Harald gave into the hands of Earl Hakon, and made him ruler over Rogaland and Hordland, Sogn, the Firth-country, South-mere, North-mere, and Raumsdale. These seven counties gave King Harald unto Earl Hakon to rule over, with such-like investiture as had King Harald Hairfair to his sons; with this to boot, that Earl Hakon should have there and in Thrandheim also all kingly manors and land-dues, and have of the king's goods what he needed if war were in the land.

To Harald the Grenlander gave King Harald Vingul-mark, Westfold, and Agdir out to Lidandisness, and the name of king withal; and gave him dominion therein with all such things as his kin had had aforetime, and as Harald Hairfair gave to his sons. Harald the Grenlander was as then eighteen winters old, and was a famed man thereafter. So home again fared Harald the Daneking with all the host of the Danes.

CHAPTER XVI. GUNNHILD'S SONS FLEE THE LAND.

EARL HAKON fared with his host north along the land; and when Gunnhild and her sons heard these tidings they gathered an host, yet sped but ill with the gathering. So they took the same rede as erst, to sail West-over-sea with such folk as will follow them; and first they fared to the Orkneys and abode there a while, wherein were ere this the sons of Thorfinn Skull-cleaver earls, Lodver to wit, and Arnvid, Liot, and Skuli.

So Earl Hakon laid all the land under him, and sat that winter in Thrandheim. Hereof telleth Einar Jingle-scale in the Gold-lack:

> Evil-shunning heeder
> Of eyebrow's field's silk-fillet,

Seven counties now hath conquered ;
To all the land good tidings.

Now Earl Hakon, when he went north along the
land that summer, and all folk came under him,
had bidden sustain the temples and blood-offerings
throughout all his dominions ; and so was it done.
So sayeth Gold-lack :

The wise one let Thor's shrine-lands
Once harried, and all steads truly
Unto the gods a-hallowed,
Lie free for all men's usage.
Ere Hlorrid of the spear-garth,
He whom the gods are guiding,
The wolf of the death of the giant
Over the sea-waves ferried.

Fight-worthy folk of Hlokks' staff
To offering-mote now turn them,
And the mighty red-board's wielder,
Thereby a fair fame winneth.
Now as afore earth groweth,
Since once again gold-waster
Lets spear-bridge wielders wend them
Gladheart to the Holy Places.

Now from the Wick all northward
Under Earl Hakon lieth.
Wide stands the rule of Hakon,
Who swells the storm of fight-board.

The first winter that Hakon ruled over the
land, the herring came up everywhere high into
the land, and in the autumn before had the corn
grown well wheresoever it had been sown ; but
the next spring men gat them seed-corn, so that
the more part of the bonders sowed their lands,
and speedily the year was of good promise.

CHAPTER XVII. BATTLE BETWIXT EARL HAKON AND RAGNFROD, SON OF GUNNHILD.

KING RAGNFROD, son of Gunnhild, and Gudrod, another son of hers, these were now the only two left of the sons of Eric and Gunnhild. So sayeth Glum Geirason in Greycloak's Drapa:

> Half of wealth's hope fell from me,
> Then when the spear-drift ended
> The king's life. For no good hap
> To me was Harald's death-day.
> Yet nathless both his brethren
> Behote me somewhat goodly,
> For all the host of manfolk
> For good luck looketh thither.

Now Ragnfrod gat him ready in spring-tide, when he had been one winter in the Orkneys; then he made east for Norway with a chosen company and big ships. And when he came to Norway he heard that Earl Hakon was in Thrandheim. So he made north about the Stad, and harried in South-mere. There some men came under him, as oft befalleth when warring bands come on the land, that they whom they fall in with seek help for themselves whereso it seems likeliest to be gotten.

Earl Hakon hears these tidings, how there was war south in Mere. So he dight his ships and sheared up the war-arrow, and arrayed him at his speediest, and sailed down the firth, and sped well with his gathering of folk.

So they met, Ragnfrod and Earl Hakon, by the northern parts of South-mere, and Hakon straightway joined battle. He had the more folk, but the smaller ships. Hard was the battle, and the brunt was heaviest on Hakon. They fought from the forecastles, as was the wont of those days. The tide set in up the sound, and drave all the ships landward together. So the earl bade backwater toward shore, where it looked handiest to go aland; and so when the ships took ground the earl and all his host went from their ships, and drew them up, so that their foes might not drag them out. Then the earl arrayed his battles on the mead, and cried on Ragnfrod to come ashore. Ragnfrod and his folk stood close in, and they shot at each other a long while; yet would he not go up aland, but departed at this pass, and stood with his host south about the Stad, for he dreaded the land-host if folk should perchance flock to Earl Hakon.

But the earl would not join battle again, because he deemed the odds of ship-boards over-great. So he fared north to Thrandheim in the autumn, and there abode winter-long. But King Ragnfrod held in those days all south of the Stad; Firthland, to wit, Sogn, Hordland, and Rogaland. He had a great multitude about him that winter, and when spring came, he bade to the muster, and gat a mighty host. Then fared he through all those parts aforenamed to gather men and ships and other gettings, such as he needed to have.

CHAPTER XVIII. ANOTHER BATTLE BETWEEN EARL HAKON AND KING RAGNFROD IN SOGN.

EARL HAKON called out folk in the spring-tide from all the North-country. He had much folk from Halogaland and Naumdale. Right away, moreover, from Byrda to the Stad had he folk from the seaboard lands; and a multitude flocked to him from all Thrandheim and from Raumsdale. So tells the tale that he had an host drawn from four folk-lands, and that seven earls followed him, each and all with a very great company. So sayeth it in Gold-lack:

Further the tale now tell I,
How the Mere-folks' war-fain warder,
Now let his folk be faring
From the Northland forth to Sogn.
The Frey of Hedin's breezes
From four lands manfolk levied.
Soothly the war-brands' Uller
Therein saw goodly helping.

Seven lords of land came sweeping
On hurdles smooth of Meiti,
Unto the mote of gladdener
Of the sparrow of the shield-swarf.
All Norway clattered round them,
When the god of the wall of Hedin
Rushed on to meet in edge-thing.
Dead men by the nesses floated.

Earl Hakon brought all this host south about the Stad. There he heard that King Ragnfrod was gone with his host into the Sogn-firth. So he turned thither with his folk, and there was the

meeting of him and Ragnfrod. The earl brought-
to his ships by the land, and pitched a hazelled
field for King Ragnfrod, and chose there a battle-
stead. So saith Gold-lack :

> The Wend-slayer on King Ragnfrod
> Came once again in battle,
> Sithence betid a man-fall
> Far-famed in that meeting.
> The Narvi of the screaming
> Of shield-witch bade turn landward ;
> The need of Jalk of snow-shoes
> He laid by the sea-ward folk-land.

There befell a full hard battle ; but Earl Hakon
had many more folk, and he won the day. At
Thing-ness this was, where Sogn meeteth Hordland.

So King Ragnfrod fled away to his ships, and
there fell of his folk three hundred men. As saith
Gold-lack :

> Strong fight ere the fight-groves' queller,
> That fierce one, there brought under
> The claws of the carrion vulture
> Three hundred fallen foemen.
> The king, the victory-snatcher,
> Who giveth growth to battle,
> O'er the heads of the host of the ocean,
> Strode thence. 'Twas a deed right gainful.

After this battle King Ragnfrod fled away from
Norway ; but Earl Hakon gave peace to the
land, and let fare back northward that great host
that had followed him through the summer ; but
he himself abode there the autumn, yea, and the
winter-tide withal.

CHAPTER XIX. THE WEDDING OF EARL HAKON.

EARL HAKON wedded a woman called Thora, the daughter of Skagi Skoptison, a wealthy man, and Thora was the fairest of all women. Their sons were Svein and Heming, and Bergliot was their daughter, who was wedded thereafter to Einar Thambarskeltir.

Earl Hakon was much given to women, and had a many children. Ragnfrid was a daughter of his, whom he gave in marriage to Skopti Skagison, brother of Thora. The earl loved Thora so well, that he held her kin dearer than other men, and Skopti his son-in-law was more accounted of than any other of them. The earl gave him great fiefs in Mere; and whensoever the earl's fleet was abroad, Skopti was to lay his ship alongside the earl's ship; neither would it do for any to lay ship betwixt them.

CHAPTER XX. THE FALL OF SKOPTI OF THE TIDINGS.

ON a summer Earl Hakon had out his fleet, and Thorleif the Sage was master of a ship therein. Of that company also was Eric, the earl's son, who was as then ten or eleven winters old. So whenever they brought-to in havens at night-tide, nought seemed good to Eric but to moor his ship next to the earl's ship.

But when they were come south to Mere, thither came Skopti, the earl's brother-in-law, with a long-

ship all manned; but as they rowed up to the
fleet, Skopti called out to Thorleif to clear the
haven for him, and shift his berth. Eric answered
speedily, bidding Skopti take another berth. That
heard Earl Hakon, how Eric his son now deemed
himself so mighty that he would not give place to
Skopti. So the earl called out straightway, and
bade them leave their berth, saying that somewhat
worser lay in store for them else, to wit, to be
speedily beaten. So when Thorleif heard that, he
cried out to his men to slip their cables; and even
so was it done. And Skopti lay in the berth
whereas he was wont, next the earl's ship to wit.

Now Skopti was ever to tell all tidings to the
earl when they two were together; or the earl would
tell tidings to Skopti, if so be he wotted first of
them. So Skopti was called Skopti of the Tidings.

The next winter was Eric with Thorleif his foster-
father, but early in spring-tide he drew to him a
company of men; and Thorleif gave him a fifteen-
benched cutter with all gear, tents, and victuals.
And Eric sailed therewith down the firth, and so
south to Mere; but Skopti of the Tidings was
a-rowing from one manor of his to another in
a fifteen-benched craft, and Eric turned to meet
him, and joined battle with him. There fell
Skopti, and Eric gave quarter to all those who yet
stood upon their feet. So sayeth Eyjolf Dadaskald in Banda-drapa:

> Yet very young he gat him,
> One eve on Meiti's sea-skate,
> Well followed, 'gainst the heisir
> High-hearted of the sea-marge.

Whenas the one that shaketh
The flickering flame of targe-field
Made Skopti fall, wolf-gladdener
Gave meat enow to blood-hawks.

Wealth-swayer, fiercely mighty,
Made fall Sand-Kiar in battle.
Yea there the life thou changedst
Of the land's belt's-fire's giver.
So strode off the steel-awer
Away from the dead din-bidder
Of the storm of stem-plain's ravens.
The land at gods' will draweth. . . .

Then sailed Eric south along the land, and came right forth to Denmark, and so fared to meet King Harald Gormson, and abode with him the winter; but the spring thereafter the Dane-king sent Eric north into Norway, and gave him an earldom with Vingul-mark and Raum-realm to rule over, on such terms as the scat-paying kings had aforetime had there. So sayeth Eyjolf:

Few winters old, folk-steerer
Bode south there at the ale-skiff
Of the sea-worm, one while ownèd
By the Finn of serpent's seat-berg,
Ere the wealth-scatterers willed it
To set adown the helm-coifed,
The whetter of the Hild-storm,
Beside the bride of Odin.

Earl Eric became a mighty chieftain in after days.

CHAPTER XXI. THE JOURNEY OF OLAF TRYGGVISON FROM GARTH-REALM.

ALL this while was Olaf Tryggvison in Garth-realm, amid all honour from King Valdimar, and loving-kindness from the queen. King Valdimar made him captain of the host which he sent forth to defend the land. So sayeth Hallstone :

> The speech-clear foe of the flame-flash
> Of the Yew-seat had twelve winters,
> When he, stout friend of Hord-folk,
> Dight warships out of Garth-realm.
> The king's men, there they laded
> Prow-beasts with weed of Hamdir,
> With the clouds of the clash of sword-edge,
> And with the helms moreover.

There had Olaf certain battles, and the leading of the host throve in his hands. Then sustained he himself a great company of men-at-arms at his own costs from the wealth that the king gave to him. Olaf was open-handed to his men, whereof was he well beloved. Yet it befell, as oft it doth when outland men have dominion, or win fame more abundant than they of the land, that many envied him the great love he had of the king, and of the queen no less. So men bade the king beware lest he make Olaf over-great : " For there is the greatest risk of such a man, lest he lend himself to doing thee or the realm some hurt, he being so fulfilled of prowess and might and the love of men ; nor forsooth wot we whereof he and the queen are evermore talking."

Now it was much the wont of mighty kings in those days, that the queen should have half the court, and sustain it at her own costs, and have thereto of the seat and dues what she needed. And thus was it at King Valdimar's, and the queen had no less court than the king; and somewhat would they strive about men of fame, and either of them would have such for themselves.

Now so it befell that the king trowed those redes aforesaid which folk spake before him, and became somewhat cold to Olaf, and rough. And when Olaf found that, he told the queen thereof, and said withal that he was minded to fare into the Northlands, where, said he, his kin had dominion aforetime, and where he deemed it like that he should have the most furtherance.

So the queen biddeth him farewell, and sayeth that he shall be deemed a noble man whithersoever he cometh.

So thereafter Olaf dight him for departure, and went a-shipboard and stood out to sea in the East-salt-sea.

But when he came from the east he made Borgund-holm, and fell on there and harried. Then came down the landsmen on him, and joined battle with him; and Olaf won the victory, and a great prey.

CHAPTER XXII. THE WEDDING OF KING OLAF TRYGGVISON.

OLAF lay by Borgund-holm, but there gat they bitter wind and a storm at sea, so that they might no longer lie there, but sailed south under Wendland, and gat there good haven, and, faring full peacefully, abode there awhile.

Burislaf was the name of the king in Wendland, whose daughters were Geira, Gunnhild, and Astrid. Now Geira, the king's daughter, had rule and dominion there, whereas Olaf and his folk came to the land, and Dixin was the name of him who had most authority under Queen Geira. And so when they heard that alien folk were come to the land, even such as were noble of mien, and held them ever in peaceful wise, then fared Dixin to meet them, with this message, that she bade those new-come men to guest with her that winter-tide; for the summer was now far spent, and the weather hard, and storms great. So when Dixin was come there, he saw speedily that the captain of these men is a noble man both of kin and aspect. Dixin told them that the queen bade them to her in friendly wise. So Olaf took her bidding, and fared that autumn-tide unto Queen Geira, and either of them was wondrous well seen of the other; so that Olaf fell a-wooing, and craved Queen Geira to wife. And it was brought to pass that he wedded her that winter, and became ruler of that realm with her. Hallfred the

Troublous-skald telleth of this in the Drapa he made upon Olaf the king :

> The king, he made the hardened
> Corpse-banes in blood be reddened
> At Holme and east in Garth-realm.
> Yea, why should the people hide it?

CHAPTER XXIII. EARL HAKON PAYETH NO SCAT TO THE DANE-KING.

EARL HAKON ruled over Norway, and paid no scat, because the Dane-king had granted him all the scat which the king owned in Norway for the labour and costs that the earl was put to in defending the land against the sons of Gunnhild.

CHAPTER XXIV. THE KEISAR OTTO HARRIETH IN DENMARK.

KEISAR OTTO was lord of Saxland in those days, who sent bidding to Harald the Dane-king to take christening and the right troth, both he and the folk he ruled over, or else, said the Keisar, he would fall upon them with an host.

So the Dane-king let array his land-wards and sustain the Dane-work, and dight his war-ships ; and therewith he sent bidding to Earl Hakon in Norway to come to him early in spring with all the host he might get. So Earl Hakon called out his host from all his realm in the spring-tide,

and gat a great following, and sailed with that folk
to Denmark to meet the Dane-king, and goodly
welcome the king gave him.

Many other lords were come to the help of the
Dane-king at that tide, and a full mighty host he
had.

CHAPTER XXV. THE WARRING OF OLAF TRYGGVISON.

OLAF TRYGGVISON had abided that
winter in Wendland, as is afore writ; and
that same winter he fared into those lands
of Wendland that had been under Queen Geira,
but now were clean turned away from her service
and tribute.

There harried Olaf, and slew many men, and
burned some out of house and home, and took
much wealth, and, having laid under him all those
realms, turned back again to his own stronghold.
Early in spring-tide Olaf dight his ships and sailed
into the sea ; he sailed to Skaney, and went aland
there. The folk of the land gathered together and
gave him battle, but Olaf had the victory, and gat
a great prey.

Then sailed he east to Gothland and took a
cheaping-ship of the Iamtlanders. They made a
stout defence forsooth, but in the end Olaf cleared
the ship and slew many men, and took all the
wealth of them.

A third battle he had in Gothland, and won the
victory and gat a great prey. So sayeth Hallfred
the Troublous-skald :

> The great king, the shrine's foeman,
> There felled the Iamtland dwellers
> And Wendland folk in fight-stour.
> So in young days his wont was.
> Sword-hardy lord of hersirs
> To Gothland lives was baneful;
> I heard it of gold-shearer,
> That he raised spear-gale on Skaney.

CHAPTER XXVI. BATTLE AT THE DANE-WORK.

KEISAR OTTO drew together a mighty host; he had folk from Saxland, and Frankland, from Frisland and Wendland. King Burislaf followed him with a great company, and thereof was Olaf Tryggvison his son-in-law. The Keisar had a mighty host of riders, and yet more of footmen; from Holtsetaland also had he much folk.

King Harald sent Earl Hakon with the host of Northmen that followed him to the Dane-work to ward the land there, as it saith in Gold-lack:

> It fell, too, that the yoke-beasts
> Of the ere-boards ran from the Northland
> Neath the deft grove of battle,
> Down south to look on Denmark.
> The lord of the folk of Dofrar,
> The ruler of the Hord-men,
> Becoifed with the helm of aweing,
> Now sought the lords of Denmark.
>
> The bounteous king would try him,
> Amidst the frost of murder,
> That elf of the land of mirkwoods,
> New-come from out the Northland.

> When bade the king the doughty
> Heeder of storm of war-sark
> Hold walls against the fight-Niords
> Of Hagbard's hurdles' rollers.

Keisar Otto came from the south with his host against the Dane-work ; and Earl Hakon warded the burg-wall with his company. Now such is the fashion of the Dane-work that two firths go up into the land on either side thereof, and from end to end of these firths had the Danes made a great burg-wall of stones and turf and timber, and dug a deep and broad ditch on the outer side thereof ; and castles are there before each burg-gate.

So there befell a great battle ; as is told in Gold-lack :

> "Twas not an easy matter
> To go against their war-host,
> Though Ragnir of garth of spear-flight
> Wrought there a stour full hardy,
> Whenas fight-Vidur wended
> From the south with the Frisian barons
> And the lords of the Franks and Wend-folk,
> Egged on the sea-horse rider.

Earl Hakon set companies all over the burg-gates ; but the more part of his folk he let wend up and down the wall, and withstand the foe where-soever the onset was hottest. Fell many of the Keisar's host, and they gat nought won of the burg-wall. So the Keisar turned away, and tried it no longer. So saith it in Gold-lack :

> Rose din of the flame of Thridi
> When the dealers in the point-play
> Laid shield to shield. Fight-hardy
> Was the stirrer of ernes' craving.

The fray-Thrott of the sound steed
Turned Saxons unto fleeing;
The king, he and his goodmen,
The Work from the aliens warded.

After the battle fared Earl Hakon back to his ships, and was minded to sail back north to Norway; but the wind was foul for him, and he lay out in the Limbfirth.

CHAPTER XXVII. THE CHRISTENING OF KING HARALD GORMSON AND EARL HAKON.

KEISAR OTTO wended back with his host to Sleswick, and there drew a fleet together, and so flitteth his host over the firth to Jutland. But when Harald Gormson the Dane-king heard thereof, he went against him with his host, and there was a great battle, wherein the Keisar prevailed at the last; so the Dane-king fled away to the Limbfirth and out into Mars-isle.

Then went men betwixt the King and the Keisar, and truce was brought about, and a meeting appointed. So Keisar Otto and the Dane-king met in Mars-isle, and there Bishop Poppo preached the holy faith before King Harald, and bare glowing iron in his hand, and showed King Harald his hand unburnt thereafter.

So King Harald let himself be christened with all the host of the Danes.

King Harald had sent word afore to Earl Hakon, whenas the king was abiding in Mars-isle, to come and help him; but Earl Hakon came to the isle

III   S

when the king had already got christened, who
sent word to the earl to come and meet him; and
when they met the King let christen Earl Hakon
will he nill he. So the earl was christened, and all
the men who followed him; and the king gave
him priests and other learned men, and bade the
earl to do christen all folk in Norway.

Therewith they sundered, and Earl Hakon fared
down to the sea and abode a wind there.

CHAPTER XXVIII. EARL HAKON CASTETH ASIDE HIS FAITH, OFFERETH BLOOD-OFFERING, AND HARRYETH IN GAUTLAND.

NOW when the wind came and he deemed
he might stand out to sea, he cast up
aland all those learned men, and so
sailed out to sea; but the wind veered round to
the south-west and west, and the earl sailed east
through Ere-sound, harrying on either land; then
he sailed east-away by Skaney-side, and harried
there, yea, and wheresoever he made land; but
when he came east off the Gaut-skerries he made
for land and made there a great sacrifice. Then
came flying thither two ravens and croaked with a
high voice; whereby the earl deemed surely that
Odin had taken his blood-offering, and that he
would have a happy day of fight. So thereon the
earl burnt all his ships, and went up aland with his
host, and wended the war-shield alway. Then
came to meet him Earl Ottar, who ruled over Gautland, and they had a great battle together, and

Hakon won the day, but Earl Ottar fell, and a many of his folk with him. Then fared Earl Hakon through either Gautland, and all with the war-shield aloft, till he came to Norway; then he went by the land-road north-away to Thrandheim.

Hereof is said in Gold-lack:

> The feller of the fleeing
> For the god's rede forth on mead went;
> The bole of the gear of Hedin
> Gat happy day for battle.
> And the bidder of war-waging
> Had sight of corpse-fowl mighty;
> The Tyr of pine-rod's hollow
> Longed for the lives of Gautfolk.
>
> The earl there held a folk-mote
> Of the wild-fire of the sword-vale
> Where none erst came to harry,
> With Sorli's roof above him.
> None bare the shield bedizened
> With the sleeping-loft of ling-fish,
> So far up from the sea-shore
> The lord o'erran all Gautland.
>
> The god of the gale of Frodi
> The fields with dead men loaded;
> Gain might the gods' son boast of,
> Gat Odin many chosen.
> What doubt but gods be ruling
> The lessener of kings' kindred?
> I say that gods strong-waxen
> Make great the sway of Hakon.

CHAPTER XXIX. KEISAR OTTO GOETH HOME AGAIN.

KEISAR OTTO fared back to his own realm of Saxland, and he and the Dane-king parted in friendly wise. So say men that Keisar Otto became gossip of Svein, the son of King Harald, and gave him his name, so that he was christened Otto Svein.

King Harald held the Christian faith well unto his death-day.

So fared King Burislaf back to Wendland, and Olaf his son-in-law with him.

Of this battle telleth Hallfred the Troublous-skald in the Olaf's Drapa :

The speeding-stem of the horses
Of rollers there was hewing
The birch of fight-sark barkless
In Denmark south of Heathby.

CHAPTER XXX. DEPARTURE OF OLAF TRYGGVISON FROM WENDLAND.

OLAF TRYGGVISON was three winters in Wendland ; and then Geira his wife fell sick, and that sickness brought her to her bane. Such great scathe did Olaf deem this, that he had no love for Wendland ever after. So he betook him to his war-ships, and fared yet again a-warring ; and first he harried in Friesland, and then about Saxland, and so right away to Flanders. So sayeth Hallfred the Troublous-skald :

The king the son of Tryggvi
At last let fast be hewen
To troll-wife's steed ill-waxen
The bodies of the Saxons.
The king the well-befriended
Gave drink to the dusky stallion,
Whereon Night-rider fareth,
Brown blood of many a Frisian.

Fierce feller of fight's people
Drew from its skin the corpse-awl ;
Let host-lord flesh of Flemings
Be yolden unto ravens.

CHAPTER XXXI. THE WARRING OF OLAF TRYGGVISON.

THEN sailed Olaf Tryggvison to England, and harried wide about the land ; he sailed north all up to Northumberland, and harried there, and thence north-away yet to Scotland, and harried wide about. Thence sailed he to the South-isles, and had certain battles there ; and then south to Man, and fought there, and harried also wide about the parts of Ireland. Then made he for Bretland, and that land also he wasted wide about, and also the land which is called of the Kymry ; and again thence sailed he west to Valland, and harried there, and thence sailed back east again, being minded for England, and so came to the isles called Scillies in the western parts of the English main. So sayeth Hallfred the Troublous-skald :

The young king all unsparing
Fell unto fight with English ;
The nourisher of spear-shower
Made murder for Northumbria.

The war-glad wolf-greed's feeder,
Wide then the Scot-folk wasted ;
Gold-slayer wrought the sword-play
In Man with sword uplifted.

The bow-tree's dread let perish
The Isle-host and the Irish ;
The Tyr of swords be-worshipped
Of fame was sorely yearning.
The king smote Bretland's biders,
And hewed adown the Kymry.
There then the greed departed
From the choughs of the storm of spear-cast.

Olaf Tryggvison was four winters about this
warfare, from the time he fared from Wendland till
when he came to Scilly.

CHAPTER XXXII. THE CHRISTEN-ING OF OLAF TRYGGVISON IN SCILLY.

NOW when Olaf Tryggvison lay at Scilly
he heard tell that in the isle there was a
certain soothsayer, who told of things not
yet come to pass; and many men deemed that things
fell out as he foretold. So Olaf fell a-longing to
try the spaeing of this man ; and he sent to the wise
man him who was fairest and biggest of his men,
arrayed in the most glorious wise, bidding him say
that he was the king; for hereof was Olaf by then
become famed in all lands, that he was fairer and
nobler than all other men. But since he fared from
Garth-realm, he had used no more of his name than
to call him Oli, and a Garth-realmer. Now when
the messenger came to the soothsayer and said he

was the king, then gat he this answer : " King art thou not ; but my counsel to thee is, that thou be true to thy king."

Nor said he more to the man, who fared back and told Olaf hereof ; whereby he longed the more to meet this man, after hearing of such answer given ; and all doubt fell from him that the man was verily a soothsayer. So Olaf went to him, and had speech of him, asking him what he would say as to how he should speed coming by his kingdom, or any other good-hap.

Then answered that lone-abider with holy spaedom : " A glorious king shalt thou be, and do glorious deeds ; many men shalt thou bring to troth and christening, helping thereby both thyself and many others ; but to the end that thou doubt not of this mine answer, take this for a token : Hard by thy ship shalt thou fall into a snare of an host of men, and battle will spring thence, and thou wilt both lose certain of thy company, and thyself be hurt ; and of this wound shalt thou look to die, and be borne to ship on shield ; yet shalt thou be whole of thy hurt within seven nights, and speedily be christened thereafter."

So Olaf went down to his ship, and met un-peaceful men on the way, who would slay him and his folk ; and it fared with their dealings as that lone-biding man had foretold him, that Olaf was borne wounded on a shield out to his ship, and was whole again within seven nights' space.

Then deemed Olaf surely that the man had told him a true matter, and that he would be a soothfast soothsayer, whencesoever he had his spaedom. So he went a second time to see this soothsayer, and talked much with him, and asked him closely whence he had the wisdom to foretell things to come. The lone-dweller told him that the very God of christened men let him know all things that he would, and therewithal he told Olaf many great works of Almighty God; from all which words Olaf yeasaid the taking on him of christening; and so was he christened with all his fellows. He abode there long, and learned the right troth, and had away with him thence priests and other learned men.

CHAPTER XXXIII. OLAF WEDDETH GYDA.

IN the autumn-tide sailed Olaf from the Scillies to England. He lay in a certain haven there, and fared peacefully, for England was christened, as he was now become christened.

Now went through the land a bidding to a certain Thing, and all men should go thither; and when the Thing was set on foot, thither came a queen hight Gyda, sister of Olaf Kuaran, who was King of Dublin in Ireland; she had been wedded in England to a mighty earl, who was now dead, and she held his realm after him. Now there was a man in her realm named Alfwin, a great champion and fighter at holmgangs. This man wooed Gyda, who answered that she would make choice of one to wed her from out the men of her realm; and for this cause was the Thing aforesaid assembled, and there was Gyda to choose herself a husband. Thither was come Alfwin decked out with the best of raiment, and many other well attired were there. Thither also was come Olaf, clad in his wet-weather gear, and a shag-cloak over all, and he stood with his company outward from other folk.

Now went Gyda, here and there looking at everyone who seemed to her of the mould of a man; but when she came whereas Olaf stood, and looked up into the face of him, she asked what man he was. He named himself Oli: " I am an outland man here," said he.

Gyda said : " Wilt thou have me ? then will I choose thee."

" I will not gainsay that," said he. And therewith he asked her of her name, and what was her kin, and the house of her.

" Gyda am I called," said she, "a king's daughter of Ireland, but I was wedded here in the land to an earl who had dominion here. But now since he is dead have I ruled the realm, and men have wooed me ; neither have I seen any to whom I list to be wedded."

She was a young woman, and full fair ; so they talked the matter over, and were of one mind on that. So now Olaf betrothed him to Gyda.

CHAPTER XXXIV. HOLMGANG BE-TWIXT ALFWIN AND KING OLAF.

BUT now is Alfwin full ill content. And it was the custom of those days in England that if any two contended about a matter, they should meet on the Island; wherefore Alfwin biddeth Olaf Tryggvison to the Island on this matter. So time and place were appointed for the battle; and they were to be twelve on either side. So when they met, Olaf gave the word to his men to do as he did. He had a great axe, and when Alfwin would drive his sword at the king, he smote the sword from the hand of him, and then a stroke on the man himself; so that Alfwin fell, and therewith Olaf bound him fast. In like wise fared all Alfwin's men, and they were beaten and bound, and so led home to Olaf's lodging. Then Olaf bade Alfwin depart from the land, and never come back again, and Olaf took all his wealth.

Then Olaf wedded Gyda and abode in England, or whiles in Ireland.

CHAPTER XXXV. KING OLAF TRYGG-VISON GETTETH THE HOUND VIGI.

NOW when Olaf was in Ireland, he was warring on a time; and a-shipboard they fared, and needed a strand-slaughtering. When the men go up aland, and drive down a many beasts, then came to them a certain goodman, who prayed Olaf give him back his own cows. Olaf bade him take them if he might find them, "But let him not delay the journey!" Now the goodman had there a great herd-dog, to which dog he showed the herd of neat, whereof were being driven many hundreds. Then the hound ran all about the herd, and drave away just so many neat as the goodman had claimed for his, and they were all marked in one wise; wherefore men deemed belike that the hound verily knew them aright, and they thought him wondrous wise. Then asked Olaf of the goodman if he would sell his hound. "With a good will," said the goodman.

But the king gave him a gold ring there and then, and promised to be his friend.

That dog was called Vigi, and was the best of all dogs. Olaf had him for long afterward.

CHAPTER XXXVI. OF KING HARALD GORMSON, AND HIS WARRING IN NORWAY.

NOW Harald Gormson the Dane-king heard how Earl Hakon had cast aside his christening, and harried wide in the realm of the Dane-king. So he called out an host, and fared away for Norway. And when he came to the realm of Earl Hakon he harried there, and laid waste all the land, and then brought-to by the isles called Solunds. But five steads only were left standing unburned by him in Læradale of Sogn, and all folk fled to the fells and woods with such of their chattels as they might bear away. And now was the Dane-king minded to sail with

that mighty host to Iceland, and avenge him of
the shame which the Icelanders, one and all, had
laid upon him. For it had been made a law in
Iceland that for every nose in the land should a
scurvy rime be made on the Dane-king. And
this was the cause thereof, that a ship owned of
Icelandmen had been cast away in Denmark, and
the Danes took all the goods for lawful drift, and
one Birgir, a bailiff of the king's, had been chief
dealer in this matter. And the scurvy rimes were
done on both of them. This is in the said rimes :

> When strode fight-wonted Harald
> From the south to the mew of Mornir,
> The Wend's-bane then as wax was
> In no shape but a stallion's.
> But unrich Birgir out cast
> By the powers of the Hall of Mountains,
> In the land in mare's shape met him ;
> And that beheld the people.

CHAPTER XXXVII. WIZARDRY WROUGHT AGAINST ICELAND.

NOW King Harald bade a wizard shape for
a skin-changing journey to Iceland, and see
what tidings he might bring him thereof.
So he fared in the likeness of a whale. And whenas
he came to the land he went west round about the
north country ; and he saw all the fells and hills full
of land-spirits both great and small. But when he
came off Weapon-firth he went into the firth, and
would go up aland ; but lo, there came down from
the dale a mighty drake, followed of many worms
and paddocks and adders, and blew venom at him.

So he gat him gone, and went west along the land till he came to Eyjafirth. Then he fared up into the firth. But there came against him a fowl so great that his wings lay on the fells on either side, and many other fowl were with him, both great and small. So he fared away thence, and west along the land, and so south to Broadfirth, and there stood in up the firth. But there met him a great bull that waded out to sea and fell a-bellowing awfully, and many land-spirits followed him. Thenceaway he gat him, and south about Reckness, and would take land on the Vikars-Skeid. But there came against him a mountain-giant, with an iron staff in his hand, and who bore his head higher than the fells, and with him were many other giants. So thenceaway fared the wizard east endlong of the south country. "And there," says he, "was nought but sands, and land haven-less, and a huge surf breaking round about without them; and so great is the main betwixt the lands," said he, "that all unmeet it is for long-ships."

Now in those days was Brodd-Helgi abiding in Weapon-firth; Eyjolf Valgerdson in Eyjafirth; Thord the Yeller in Broadfirth; and Thorod the Priest in Olfus.

So the Dane-king stood south along the land with his host, and so went south to Denmark. But Earl Hakon let build all the land again, and none the more ever paid scat to the Dane-king.

CHAPTER XXXVIII. THE FALL OF KING HARALD GORMSON.

SVEIN, the son of King Harald, who was afterwards called Twibeard, craved dominion of King Harald his father; but it was as afore that King Harald would not share the Dane-realm, nor give his son dominion. Then Svein gathers war-ships to him, and says that he will go a-warring; but when they were all come together, and Palnatoki, to wit, of the Jomsburg vikings was come to help him, then Svein stood toward Sealand and in up Icefirth, where lay King Harald his father with his ships, all ready to fare to the wars. So straightway Svein fell on him, and there was a great battle. But so much folk drew to King Harald that Svein was overborne by odds, and fled away.

Notwithstanding, there gat King Harald the hurts which brought him to his bane.

So thereafter was Svein taken for king in Denmark.

In those days was Earl Sigvaldi captain over Jomsburg in Wendland. He was son of King Strut-Harald, sometime King of Skaney. The brethren of Earl Sigvaldi were Heming and Thorkel the High.

Then also was a lord among the Jomsburg vikings Bui the Thick of Borgund-holm, and Sigurd his brother. Vagn also, the son of Aki and Thorgunna, and sister's-son of Bui.

Now Earl Sigvaldi and his brother had laid hands on King Svein, and brought him to Joms-

burg in Wendland, and driven him perforce to
make peace with Burislaf the Wend-king, in such
wise that Sigvaldi was to make peace between them
—Earl Sigvaldi had then to wife Astrid, daughter
of King Burislaf—"either else would the earl," said
he, "deliver King Svein to the Wends." Now
King Svein knew full well that then would the
Wends torment him to death, so he assented to
this peace-making of the earl.

So Earl Sigvaldi laid down that King Svein
should wed Gunnhild, daughter of King Burislaf;
and King Burislaf, Thyri, Harald's daughter, sister
of King Svein; and either king to hold his dominion,
and peace to be between the lands of them.

So King Svein fared home to Denmark with
Gunnhild his wife, and their sons were Harald
and Knut the Mighty.

In those days did the Danes make great threats
of sailing with an host to Norway against Earl
Hakon.

CHAPTER XXXIX. THE AVOWING OF THE JOMSBURG VIKINGS.

KING SVEIN held a famous feast, and
bade to him all lords of his realm, for
he would hold his grave-ale after King
Harald his father; and a little before had died
Strut-Harald in Skaney, and Veseti of Borgund-
holm, the father of Bui and Sigurd. So King
Svein sent word to the Jomsburgers bidding Earl
Sigvaldi and Bui, and the brethren of each, come
hold the grave-ale of their fathers at this same

feast which the king was arraying.   So to the feast fared the Jomsburgers with all the valiantest of their folk; eleven ships from Jomsburg had they, and twenty from Skaney.   So thither was come together a full great company.   The first day of the feast, before King Svein stepped into the high-seat of his father, he drank the cup of memory to him, swearing therewith that before three winters were outworn he would bring an host to England, and slay King Æthelred, or drive him from his realm.   And that cup of memory must all drink who were at the feast.

Thereupon was poured forth to those lords of Jomsburg; and ever was borne to them brimming and of the strongest.   But when this cup was drunk off, then must all men drink a cup to Christ.   And then were borne to the Jomsburgers the biggest horns of mightiest drink that was there.   The third cup was Michael's memory, and that also must all drink.   But thereafter drank Earl Sigvaldi the memory of his father, swearing oath therewith that before three winters were worn away he would come into Norway, and slay Earl Hakon, or else drive him from the land.

Then swore Thorkel the High, the brother of Sigvaldi, that he would follow his brother to Norway, nor ever flee from battle leaving Sigvaldi fighting.

Then swore Bui the Thick that he would fare to Norway with them, and in no battle flee before Earl Hakon.

Then swore Sigurd his brother that he would fare to Norway, and not flee while the more part of the Jomsburgers fought.

Then swore Vagn Akison that he would fare with them to Norway, and not come back till he had slain Thorkel Leira, and lain a-bed by his daughter Ingibiorg without the leave of her kin.

Many other lords also swore oath on sundry matters. So that day men drunk the heirship-feast.

But the morrow's morn, when men were no more drunken, the Jomsburgers thought they had spoken big words enough; so they met together and took counsel how they should bring this journey about, and the end of it was that they determined to set about it as speedily as may be. So they arrayed their ships and their company; and wide about the lands went the fame of this.

CHAPTER XL. THE WAR-GATHERING OF ERIC AND EARL HAKON.

NOW Earl Eric, son of Hakon, heard these tidings as he abode in Raum-realm. So he straightway gathered folk to him, and fared to the Uplands, and so north over the fells to Thrandheim to meet Earl Hakon, his father. Hereof telleth Thord Kolbeinson in Eric's Drapa:

> Now fared great soothfast war-tales
> Of the steel-stems wide around there
> Out from the south, and therewith
> Good bonders woe foreboded.
> The stem of the steed of the meadow
> Of Sveidi heard how the boardlong
> Dane-ships o'er the well-worn rollers
> In the south were run out seaward.

So Earl Hakon and Earl Eric let shear up the war-arrow all about the Thrandheim parts; bid-

ding also they sent to either Mere, and to Raumsdale, north also into Naumdale and Halogaland;
therewith they called out their whole muster both
of ships and men. So saith it in Eric's Drapa:

> Shield-maple set his cutters,
> Round-ships and great keels many
> Into the surf a-rushing
> (Grows the skald's song praise-bounteous).
> Off shore were ships a-many,
> When the point-hardener mighty
> Seaward drew garth about it,
> His father's land, with war-shields.

Earl Hakon went straightway into Mere to hold
espial there, and gather folk; but Earl Eric drew
his host together, and led it from the north.

CHAPTER XLI. THE JOURNEY OF THE JOMSBURGERS INTO NORWAY.

THE Jomsburgers brought their host into
the Limbfirth, and sailed out thence into
the main with sixty ships, and came in to
Agdir; thence they brought their host to Rogaland, and fell a-harrying so soon as they came into
the dominion of Earl Hakon; and so fare they
toward the North-country doing all deeds of war.

Now there was a man named Geirmund, who
was sailing in a skiff, and certain men with him,
and he came on north to Mere, and there fell in
with Earl Hakon, and went in before the board
and told the earl the tidings of an host in the
South-country come from Denmark.

The earl asked if he had any soothfast token
hereof to show. So Geirmund drew forth his

other arm with the hand smitten off at the wrist, and saith that by that token was an host in the land. Then asked the earl closely concerning this host, and Geirmund saith they were the vikings of Jomsburg, and had slain many men, and robbed far and wide: "Swift fare they though, and full eagerly, and belike no long time will wear by or they are come upon thee here."

So thereon the earl rowed through all the firths in along one shore and out along the other; night and day he fared, and had espial holden inland about the Eid-reaches right away south to the Firths on one side, and north away on the other, whereas Eric went with his host. This is told of in Eric's Drapa:

> The war-wise earl who driveth
> The fifth-board steeds far seaward,
> Now set his prows high-fashioned
> Against Sigvaldi's coming.
> There shook the oars a-many,
> But the solacers of wound-fowl
> Who rent the sea with oar-blade,
> They feared the bane in nowise.

Earl Eric meanwhile fared south with his host at his swiftest.

CHAPTER XLII. OF THE JOMS-BURGERS AND THEIR WARFARE.

EARL SIGVALDI led his host north about the Stad, and brought-to first at Her-isles. Here, though the vikings fell in with the folk of the land, these told them never the truth of what the earl was about. The Jomsburgers harried wheresoever they came; they brought-up west of Hod-isle, and went ashore there and harried, driving down to their ships both thrall and beast, but slew all carles fit for fight.

But now as they came down to their ships there came to meet them a certain bonder afoot, and this was hard by where went the company of Bui. Spake the bonder: "Nought like men-at-arms fare ye, driving to the strand cow and calf; better prey to take the bear, now nigh come to the bear's den."

"What says the carle?" said they. "Canst thou tell us aught of Earl Hakon?"

Said the bonder: "He fared yesterday in to Hiorund-firth. One ship or two he had, or at the most not more than three; nor had he heard aught of you."

Then straightway Bui and his folk fell a-running to the ships and let loose all their booty; and Bui said: "Make we the most of it that we have espied on the earl, and so be we the nighest to the victory."

So when they come to their ships, straightway they row out; and Earl Sigvaldi called out to them, asking what tidings; and they said that Earl Hakon was there in the firth. So Earl Sigvaldi weighed, and rowed out north of the isle of Hod, and so in about the isle.

CHAPTER XLIII. THE BEGINNING OF THE JOMSBURGERS' BATTLE.

BUT Earl Hakon and Eric his son lay in Halkell's-wick, with all their host now come together, being an hundred and eighty ships, and they had tidings how the Jomsburgers had stood from the west in to Hod. So the earls rowed from the south to seek them.

But when they came to Hiorung-wick they met, and either side arrayed them for the battle. In the midst of the array of the Jomsburgers was set forth the banner of Earl Sigvaldi; and over against him was arrayed the battle of Earl Hakon. Earl Sigvaldi had twenty ships and Earl Hakon sixty. In Earl Hakon's battle were these two captains, Thorir Hart of Halogaland and Styrkar of Gimsar.

On the one wing of the Jomsburgers was Bui the Thick and Sigurd his brother, and over against him fell on Earl Eric Hakonson with sixty ships, and these lords to aid, Gudbrand the White of the Uplands, to wit, and Thorkel Leira, a man of the Wick.

Again, on the other wing of the Jomsburgers was arrayed Vagn Akison with twenty ships, and against him was Svein Hakonson, and with him Skeggi from Uphowe in Yriar, and Rognvald of Ærwick in Stad, with sixty ships. So is it told in Eric's Drapa:

> Far down along the coast-land
> Sped the sea-host, but the sea-mews
> Of the glow-home fight-ways glided
> To meet the keels of Denmark.
> Them most in Mere the earl cleared;
> Neath the seekers of gold's plenty
> The steed of the sea-brim drifted
> Deep laden with warm slain-heap.

And thus saith Eyvind Skald-spiller in the Halogaland Tale:

To the hurt-wreakers
Of Yngvi Frey
Least of all things
Was that day's dawning
A joyous meeting,
When the land-rulers
Sped their fleet
Against the wasters.
Whereas the sword-elf
Thrust the sea-steeds
Forth from the southland
Against their war-host.

So then they brought the fleets together, and there befell the grimmest of battles, and many fell on either side, but many the more of Hakon's folk, for hardily, hard, and handily fought the vikings of Jomsburg, and clean through shields they shot, and so great was the brunt of weapons about Earl Hakon that his byrny was all rent and perished, so that he cast it from him. Thereof telleth Tind Hallkelson :

The sewing, that the flame-Gerd
Wrought for the earl with bent-boughs
Of the shoulder, grew ungainly.
Waxed din of Fiolnir's fires,
Whereas the byrny's Vidur
Must shed the ring-bright, clattering
War-sark of Hangi. Cleared were
The weltering steeds of sea-stream.

Where the ring-weaved shirt of Sorli
From the earl was blown to tatters
On the sound ; whereof a token
That friend of warriors showeth.

CHAPTER XLIV.   THE FLIGHT OF EARL SIGVALDI.

NOW the Jomsburgers had the bigger ships and the higher of bulwark; but either side fought most fiercely. Vagn Akison lay so hard on the ship of Svein Hakonson that Svein let back-water and was on the point of fleeing. Then thither turned Earl Eric, and thrust into the battle against Vagn; and Vagn gave back and the ships lay where they had been at the first. So Earl Eric gat him back to his own battle, where his men now were giving aback, and Bui having cut himself adrift from the lashings, was about driving them to flight. So Earl Eric lay Bui's ship aboard, and a battle of handy-strokes betid of the sharpest, and two of Eric's ships or three were on Bui's ship alone. And therewithal came down foul weather with so great hail, that a hailstone weighed an ounce. Even therewith Earl Sigvaldi cut his lashings and turned his ship about with the mind to flee. Vagn Akison cried out at him bidding him not to flee away; but Earl Sigvaldi gave no heed thereto, whatsoever he might say. Then Vagn shot a spear at him, and it smote the man who sat by the tiller. So rowed away Earl Sigvaldi with five-and-thirty ships, and but five-and-twenty were left lying behind.

CHAPTER XLV. BUI THE THICK LEAPETH OVERBOARD.

THEN laid Earl Hakon his ship on the other board of Bui, and many strokes in short space befell Bui's men. Vigfus, son of Slaying Glum, took up a snout-anvil that lay on the forecastle of Earl Hakon's ship, whereon some man had been a-driving home the rivet of his sword-hilt. A strong man was Vigfus ; and he cast the anvil with both hands and smote it on the head of Aslak Holm-pill-pate, so that the spike drave into his brain. By no weapon had Aslak been bitten afore, as he fought on smiting with either hand ; he was foster-son of Bui, and his forecastle-man. There was another of them, hight Howard the Hewer, the strongest and valiantest of men. Now in this stour Eric's men gat up aboard Bui's ship, and made aft to the poop toward Bui. Then Thorstein Midlang smote Bui right athwart the nose through the nose-guard, and a very great wound was that ; but Bui smote Thorstein round-handed on the flank, so that the man fell asunder in the midst.

Then caught up Bui two chests full of gold, and called on high, "Overboard all folk of Bui !" and himself leapt overboard with those chests. And therewith many men of his leapt overboard, and others fell on the ship, for as to peace it availed not to pray it. So was Bui's ship cleared from stem to stern, and then the rest of them one after other.

CHAPTER XLVI. THE JOMSBURGERS BOUNDEN IN A STRING.

THEN fell Earl Eric on Vagn's ship, and was met full valiantly ; but in the end was the ship cleared, and Vagn laid hands on, and thirty men with him, and they were brought aland bound. Now Thorkel Leira went up to them and said : " Vagn, thou swarest oath to slay me, but now meseemeth I am more like to slay thee."

Now Vagn and his folk sat all together on a tree-trunk ; and Thorkel had a great axe, wherewith he smote down him who sat outermost on the trunk. Vagn and his fellows were so bound that a rope was done about the feet of them all, but their hands were loose. Now spake one of them : " Lo here my cloak-clasp in my hand, and I will thrust it into the earth if I wot of aught after my head is off." So the head was smitten from him, and down fell the clasp from his hand.

Hard by sat a very fair man with goodly hair. He swept his hair up over his head, and stretched forth his neck saying : " Make not my hair bloody ! " So a certain man took his hair in his hand and held it fast. Thorkel hove up his axe, but the viking snatched his head sharply, and he who held his hair lowted forward with him, and the axe came down on both his hands, and took them off, so that it struck into the earth. Therewith came Earl Eric thither and asked : " Who is this goodly man ? " " Sigurd the lads call me," saith he; " I am a bastard son of Bui; not yet are all the vikings of Jomsburg dead."

Eric saith : " Verily wilt thou be a son of Bui. Wilt thou have peace ? " says he.

" That hangs on who biddeth it," said Sigurd.

" He biddeth," said the earl, " who hath might thereto; Earl Eric to wit."

" Then will I take it," says he. So he was loosed from the tether.

Then spake Thorkel Leira : " Though thou, earl, will give peace to all these men, yet never shall Vagn Akison depart hence alive ! "

And he ran at him with brandished axe; but the viking Skardi let himself fall in the tether and lay before Thorkel's feet, and Thorkel fell flatling over him. Then Vagn caught up the axe, and smote Thorkel his death-blow.

Spake the earl then : " Wilt thou have peace, Vagn ? " " Yea will I," saith he, " so be we all have it."

" Loose them from the tether then," saith the earl. And so was it done; eighteen were slain, but twelve had peace.

CHAPTER XLVII. THE SLAYING OF GIZUR OF VALDRES.

NOW sat Earl Hakon with many men on a tree-bole, and there twanged a bowstring from Bui's ship, and therewith came an arrow and smote Gizur of Valdres, a lord of land, who sat next to the earl clad in brave raiment. Then went men out to the ship and found there Howard the Hewer, standing on his knees out by the bulwark, for the legs had been smitten from him; and in his hand he had a bow. So when they came out to the ship Howard asked, " Who fell from the log ?" " Gizur," they said. " Then was my luck lesser than I would," said he.

" Ill luck enough," said they, " but thou shalt win no more." And they slew him. Then were the slain searched, and all wealth brought together for sharing.

So was it said that twenty and five ships of the Jomsburg vikings were cleared. Thus Tind sayeth

> He, Hugin's fellows' feeder,
> Now laid the sword-edge foot-prints
> Upon the host of Wend-folk.
> There bit the dog of thong-sun
> Or ever the wight spear-stems
> Might clear a five-and-twenty
> Of the long-ships of their war-host.
> That was a deed of peril.

Then departed the host this way and that; and Earl Hakon went to Thrandheim, and was exceeding ill-content that Eric had given peace to Vagn Akison.

The talk of men it is that in this battle Earl Hakon offered up his son Erling to Odin for victory, and thereafter came down that hail-storm, and fall of men therewith betid to the Jomsburgers.

Earl Eric fared up to the Uplands, and thence to his own realm; and Vagn Akison fared with him. And Eric wedded Vagn to Ingibiorg, daughter of Thorkel Leira, and gave him a goodly long-ship well found in all things, and gat a crew for him. In all friendship they parted, and Vagn fared home south to Denmark. He grew of great fame afterwards, and many great men are come of him.

CHAPTER XLVIII. THE DEATH OF KING HARALD THE GRENLANDER.

HARALD the Grenlander was king in Westfold, as is aforewrit. He had to wife Asta, daughter of Gudbrand Kula. Now on a summer whenas Harald the Grenlander was a-warring in the East-lands to get him goods, he came into Sweden. Olaf the Swede was king there in those days, the son of Eric the Victorious and Sigrid, daughter of Skogul-Tosti. Sigrid was now a widow, and had many and great manors in Sweden. So when she heard that Harald the Grenlander, her foster-brother, was come off the land, she sent men to him, bidding him come guest with her. And he slept not over his journey, but went thither with a great company of men. Goodly welcome abode him, and the king and queen sat in the high-seat and drank together through the evening, and in noble wise were all his men treated. At night-tide also, when the king went to his bed-chamber, the bed was all hung with pall and arrayed with dear-bought cloths. In that lodging were but few men; and when the king was unclad and gotten into bed, then came thither the queen to him, and poured out to him herself and pressed the drink on him hard, and was exceeding kind unto him. The king was full

merry with drink; yea, and she too. Then fell the
king asleep, and she also went her ways to bed.

Now Sigrid was the wisest of women, and foreseeing about many matters.

The next morning was the feast still most noble.
But it befell, as oft it doth, that whereas men are
exceeding drunk, on the morrow they are for the
more part wary of the drink. Yet was the queen
joyous, and she and the king talked together; and
she fell a-saying how she deemed her land and
dominion in Sweden there to be no less worth
than his kingdom in Norway and his lands.
Amidst this talk waxed the king heavy of mood
and short of speech, and so got him ready to
depart with a heart full sick; but ever was the
queen most merry of mood, and brought him on his
way with great gifts. So Harald fared back to
Norway in the autumn, and abode at home that
winter in joyance little enough.

But the next summer he fared toward the
East-lands with his host, and made for Sweden.
Then he sent word to Queen Sigrid that he would
see her, and she rode down to meet him, and they
fell to speech together. Speedily his words came
to this, whether she would wed with him; but she
said that were a fool's wedding for him, he being
so well wedded already, as better might not be.

Harald saith that Asta is a good woman and
of noble blood; "yet is she not so high-born as
I be."

Sigrid answereth: "Maybe thou art come of
higher kin than she; yet none the less meseemeth
with her lieth the good-hap of you both."

And there were but few more words spoken between them ere Sigrid rode away.

Then waxed King Harald heavy-hearted, and he arrayed him to ride up into the land and meet Queen Sigrid yet again. Many of his men would have stayed him, but he went his way none the less with a great company of men, and came to the manor-house where the queen was lady.

Now the self-same evening came east-away from Garth-realm another king, hight Vissavald, and he also was about wooing Queen Sigrid.

So both the kings were lodged in a great chamber, and all their company. Old was the chamber, and all the array of it in like wise; but there was no lack that night of drink, so mighty that all men were drunken, and the head-guard and the out-guard were all asleep.

Then amidst the night let Queen Sigrid fall on them with fire and sword, and the hall burned up there, and they who were therein; but they who won out were slain.

Said Sigrid hereat that she would weary these small kings of coming from other lands to woo her. So she was called Sigrid the Haughty thereafter.

CHAPTER XLIX. THE BIRTH OF KING OLAF HARALDSON.

THE winter before these things, was foughten the battle with the vikings of Jomsburg in Hiorung-wick.

Now one Hrani had been left behind with the

ships when Harald had gone up aland, and he was captain of those folk that were left behind.

But when they heard that Harald had lost his life, they gat them away at their swiftest and back to Norway, where they told these tidings. Hrani went to Asta and told her what had betid, and therewith on what errand King Harald had gone to Queen Sigrid. So straightway Asta fared into the Uplands to her father, so soon as she had heard these tidings; and he gave her good welcome. And full wroth were they both at the guiles that had been toward in Sweden, and that Harald had been minded to put her away.

So Asta Gudbrand's daughter brought forth a man-child there that summer, who was named Olaf when he was sprinkled with water; but Hrani sprinkled the water on him. And at the first was the lad nourished with Gudbrand and with Asta his mother.

CHAPTER L. OF EARL HAKON.

EARL HAKON ruled all the outer parts of Norway along the sea, and had sixteen folk-lands under his dominion. But since Harald Hairfair had ordained an earl to be over every county, that order endured for long, and Earl Hakon had sixteen earls under him, as is said in Gold-lack:

> Where tell the folk of such like,
> A land where earls are lying
> Sixteen neath one land-ruler,
> Hereof should all folk ponder.

The sea limes' urger's folk-play
Of the fire of head of Hedin
Goes forth on high bepraisèd
Unto the heavens' four corners.

Whiles Earl Hakon ruled in Norway was the year's increase good in the land. And good peace there was betwixt man and man among the bonders.

Well beloved of the bonders was the earl the more part of his life ; but as his years wore, it was much noted of the earl that he was mannerless in dealing with women ; and to such a pitch this came, that the earl let take the daughters of mighty men and bring them home to him, and would lie by them for a week or twain, and then send them home. Whereof he won great hatred from the kin of such women, and the bonders fell a-murmuring sore against it, even as they of Thrandheim are wont to do when aught goeth against their pleasure.

CHAPTER LI. THE JOURNEY OF THORIR KLAKKA TO SEEK OLAF TRYGGVISON.

NOW Earl Hakon heard some rumour to this end, that there would be a man West-over-sea who called himself Oli, and that they held him for king there. And the earl had a deeming from the talk of certain folk that this man would be come of the blood of the Norse kings. Now he was told that Oli called himself of the kin of Garth-realm, and the earl had heard how Tryggvi Olafson had had a son who had fared east into Garth-realm and been nourished there at King Valdimar's, and that he was called Olaf. The earl had sought far and wide for this man, and now he misdoubted he would be this man come there into the Westlands.

Now there was a man called Thorir Klakka, a great friend of Earl Hakon, who was long whiles at viking work, but whiles would go cheaping voyages, and was of good knowledge of lands. Him Earl Hakon sent West-over-sea, bidding him go a cheaping voyage to Dublin, as many folk were wont, and look into it closely what this man Oli was; and if he found that he verily was Olaf Tryggvison, or any other offspring of the kingly stem of the North, then was Thorir to entangle him with guile if he might bring it to pass.

CHAPTER LII. OLAF TRYGGVISON COMETH INTO NORWAY.

SO thereon gat Thorir west unto Ireland to Dublin, and learned that Oli was there, who was as then with King Olaf Kuaran, his brother-in-law. Speedily then gat Thorir speech with Oli, and a man wise of speech was Thorir.

Now when they had talked oft and right long together, Oli fell to asking concerning Norway, and first of the Upland kings, and who of them were yet alive, and what dominion they had. Of Earl Hakon also he asked, and how well beloved he might be in the land. Thorir answered: "The earl is so mighty a man that none durst to speak but as he will. Yet this somewhat bringeth it

about, that there is none to seek to otherwhere.
And yet, to say thee sooth, I know the mind of
many mighty men, yea, of all the people, that
they would be most fain and eager to have a
king for the land come of the blood of Harald
Hairfair; but none such have we to turn to, and
chiefly for this cause, that it is now well proven
how little it availeth to contend with Earl
Hakon."

Now when they had oft talked in this wise, Olaf
bringeth to light before Thorir his name and kin,
and asked his rede, what he thought of it, if Olaf
should fare to Norway, whether the bonders would
take him for king. But Thorir egged him on full
fast to the journey, and praised him much and his
prowess. So Olaf fell a-longing sorely to fare to
the land of his fathers; and he saileth from the
west with five ships, first to the South-isles, and
Thorir was in company with him. Thence he
sailed to the Orkneys, and there lay as then Earl
Sigurd Hlodverson by Rognvaldsey in Asmunds-
wick with one long-ship, being minded to fare
over to Caithness. Even therewith King Olaf sailed
his folk from the west to the islands, and brought-
to there, whereas he might not win as then
through the Pentland Firth. And when he knew
that the earl lay there already, he let summon
him to talk with him. But when the earl came to
speech with the king, few words were spoken
before the king sayeth this, that the earl must let
himself be christened, and all the folk of his land,
or die there and then. And the king said that he
would fare through the isles with fire and sword,

and lay waste the whole land, but if the folk would
be christened. So the earl, being thus bestead,
chose to take christening, and he was christened
and all the folk that were with him. Then swore
the earl oath to the king, and became his man,
and gave him his son for hostage, who was called
Whelp or Hound, and Olaf had him home to Norway with him.

Then sailed Olaf east into the sea, and came
from out the main to Most-isle, and there first he
went aland in Norway, and let sing mass in his
land-tent, and in the aftertime was a church built
in that same place.

Now Thorir Klakka told the king that there
was nought for him to do but to keep it hidden
who he was, and let no espial go forth of him, but
to fare with all diligence to meet the earl, in such
wise that he shall come on him unawares.

Even so did King Olaf, and fared north day
and night as weather served, nor let the folk of
the land wot of his ways, whether he was bound.

But when he came north to Agdaness he heard
that Earl Hakon was in the firth, and withal
that he was at strife with the bonders. And when
Thorir heard tell of these things, then were matters
gone a far other way than he had been deeming ;
for after the battle with the Jomsburg vikings
were all men of Norway utterly friendly to Earl
Hakon for the victory he had gotten, and the
deliverance of all the land from war ; but now so ill
had things turned out that here was the earl at
strife with the bonders, and a great lord come into
the land.

CHAPTER LIII. THE FLIGHT OF EARL HAKON

NOW Earl Hakon was a-guesting at Middlehouse in Gauldale, but his ships lay out off Vig. There was a man named Worm Lyrgia, a wealthy bonder, who dwelt at Buness and had to wife one named Gudrun, daughter of Bergthor of Lund ; she was called the Sun of Lund, and was the fairest of women. Now the earl sent his thralls to Worm on this errand, to wit, to have away to him Gudrun Worm's wife. So the thralls showed him their errand, but Worm bade them first go to supper; and then or ever they had done their meat, came many men to Worm from the township, whom he had sent for, nor would Worm in any wise suffer Gudrun to go with the thralls. Gudrun moreover spake, and bade the thralls tell the earl that she would not come to him but if he sent Thora of Rimul after her ; a wealthy dame, and one of the earl's best-beloved.

So the thralls say that in such wise shall they come another time that both master and mistress shall repent them of their scurvy treatment, and therewithal gat them gone with many threats.

Then Worm let the war-arrow fare four ways through the country-side with this bidding withal, that all men should fall with weapons on Earl Hakon to slay him. He sent moreover to Haldor of Skerding-Stithy, and straightway Haldor let wend the war-arrow.

A little before the earl had taken the wife of a

man named Bryniolf, and had gotten great hatred
for the deed, and war had been at point to arise
thence.

So at this message of the war-arrow sprang up
much people, and made for Middlehouse; but the
earl had espial of them, and went his ways from
the stead with his folk into a deep dale which is
now called the Earl's-dale, and there they lay hid.

The next day the earl espied all the host of the
bonders. The bonders took all the ways, but
were most of mind that the earl would have
gotten to his ships, whereof was Erland his son
captain, the most hopeful of men.

But at nightfall the earl scattered his men,
bidding them fare by the woodland ways out to
Orkdale :

"No man will do you hurt, if I be nowhere anigh;
but send word to Erland to fare out down the
firth, and let us meet in Mere, and meanwhile
I will hide me well from the bonders."

Then departed the earl, and a thrall of his
named Kark was with him.

Now the water of Gaul was under ice, and the
earl thrust his horse into it, and let his cloak lie
behind there, and then went they into the cave
which has been called the Earl's-cave thereafter;
and there they fell asleep. But when Kark awoke
he told a dream of his : how a man, black and evil
to look on, passed by the cave's mouth so that he
was afeard of his coming in, and this man told him
that Ulli was dead. Then said the earl that it
was Erland would be slain.

Yet again slept Kark the thrall, and was

troubled in his sleep, and when he woke he told his dream : how he had seen that same man coming down back again, who bade him tell the earl that now were all the sounds locked. So told Kark his dream to the earl, who misdoubted now that this betokened him a short life.

Then he arose, and they went to the stead of Rimul, and the earl sent Kark to Thora, bidding her come privily to him. So did she, and welcomed the earl kindly, and he prayed her to hide him for certain nights till the gathering of the bonders went to pieces. Said she : "They will be seeking thee here about my stead both within and without ; for many wot that I would fain help thee all I may, but one place there is about my stead where I deem that I would not think of seeking for such a man as thou, a certain swine-sty to wit."

So they went thither ; and the earl said : "Make we ready here ; for we must take heed to our lives first of all." Then dug the thrall a deep hole therein, and bore away the mould, and then laid wood over it. Thora told the earl the tidings how Olaf Tryggvison was come into the mouth of the firth, and had slain Erland his son.

Then went the earl into the hole, and Kark with him, and Thora did it over with wood, and strawed over it mould and muck, and drave the swine thereover. And this swine-sty was under a certain big stone.

CHAPTER LIV. THE DEATH OF ER-LAND.

OLAF TRYGGVISON stood in up the mouth of the firth with five long-ships, and there rowed out to meet him Erland, the son of Earl Hakon, with three ships. But as the ships drew nigh one to the other, Erland misdoubted him that this would be war, and turned about toward the land. But when King Olaf saw the long-ships come rowing down the firth to meet him, he thought that Earl Hakon would be going there, and bade row after them in all haste. But when Erland and his folk were come to the land they ran the ships aground, and leapt overboard straightway and made for the shore. Then drave thither Olaf's ships ; and Olaf saw a man striking out for shore who was exceeding fair ; so he caught up the tiller and cast it at that man, and it smote the head of Erland the earl's son, and beat out his brains ; and there Erland lost his life.

Olaf and his folk slew many men ; some fled away, and some they laid hands on and took to peace, from whom they heard the tidings. So it was told to Olaf that the bonders had driven Earl Hakon away, and that he was fleeing before them, and that all his folk were scattered.

CHAPTER LV. THE DEATH OF EARL HAKON.

THEREWITHAL came the bonders to meet Olaf, and either side were fain of other, and they fall straightway into good friendship.

So the bonders take him to be king over them, and all with one accord go about to seek for Earl Hakon, and so fare up into Gauldale, deeming it most like that the earl will be at Rimul, if at any habited stead he be, because Thora was his dearest friend of all the dale folk. So thither fare they, and seek the earl within and without, and find him not. Then held Olaf a house-thing out in the garth, and himself stood up on that same big stone that was beside the swine-sty.

There spake Olaf to his men, and some deal of his speaking was that he would with wealth and worth further him who should bring Earl Hakon to harm.

Now this talk heard the earl and Kark, and they had a light there with them ; and the earl said : " Why art thou so pale, or whiles as black as earth ? is it not so that thou wilt bewray me ? "

" Nay," said Kark.

" We were born both on one and the same night," said the earl, " nor shall we be far apart in our deaths."

Then fared King Olaf away as the eve came on, but in the night the earl kept himself waking, but Kark slept and went on evilly in his sleep. Then the earl waked him and asked what he dreamed; and he said: " I was e'en now at

Ladir, and King Olaf laid a gold necklace on the neck of me."

The earl answered : " A blood-red necklace shall Olaf do about thy neck whenso ye meet. See thou to it ; but from me shalt thou have but good even as hath been aforetime ; so betray me not."

So thereafter they both waked, as men waking one over the other.

But against the daybreak the earl fell asleep, and speedily his sleep waxed troubled, till to such a pitch it came that he drew under him his heels and his head as if he would rise up, and cried out high and awfully. Then waxed Kark adrad and full of horror, and gripped a big knife from out his belt and thrust it through the earl's throat and sheared it right out. That was the bane of Earl Hakon.

Then Kark cut the head from the earl, and ran away thence with it; and he came the next day to Ladir, and brought the earl's head to King Olaf, and told him all these things that had befallen in the goings of him and Earl Hakon, even as is here written.

Then let King Olaf lead him away thence, and smite the head from him.

CHAPTER LVI. THE STONING OF EARL HAKON'S HEAD.

THEN fared King Olaf, and a many of the bonders with him, out to Nid-holm, and had with him the heads of Earl Hakon and Kark.

Now this holm was kept in those days for the

slaying of thieves and evil men, and a gallows stood there; and so thereto the king let be borne the head of Earl Hakon, and of Kark withal.

Then thereto went the whole host of them, and set up a whooping, and stoned the heads, crying out, that there they fared meetly together, rascal by rascal.

Then they let fare up into Gauldale and take the corpse of him and drag it away.

And now so great was the might of that enmity of the Thrandheimers against Earl Hakon, that no man durst name him otherwise than the Evil Earl; and for long after was this name laid on him. Yet sooth to say of Earl Hakon, for many things was he worthy to be lord; first, for the great stock he was come of, and then also for the wisdom and insight wherewith he dealt with his dominion; for his high heart in battle and his good hap withal, for the winning of victory and slaying of his foemen. And thus saith Thorleif Redfellson:

> Of no earl ever heard we
> Neath the moon's highway, Hakon,
> More famed than thou; Ran's fight-stem
> Gat fame from out the battle.
> Nine mighty chiefs to Odin
> Thou sentest; eats the raven
> The gotten corpses. Therefore
> Mightst thou be king wide-landed.

Most bountiful also was Earl Hakon. But most evil hap had such a lord in his death-day. And this brought it most about, that so it was that the day was come, when foredoomed was blood-offering and the men of blood-offerings, and the holy faith come in their stead, and the true worship.

CHAPTER LVII. OLAF TRYGGVISON TAKETH THE KINGDOM IN NORWAY.

NOW was Olaf Tryggvison taken for king at a Thing of all the people in Thrandheim over the land even as Harald Hairfair had held it. There rose up all the people thronging, and would hear nought else but that Olaf Tryggvison should be king.

Then King Olaf fared through all the land and laid it under him, and all men of Norway turned to his obedience ; yea, all the lords of the Uplands or the Wick, who had aforetime held their lands of the Dane-king, these became King Olaf's men and held their lands of him. In such wise he fared through the land the first winter and the summer after. Earl Eric Hakonson and Svein his brother, and others, friends and kin of theirs, fled the land, and went east to Sweden to King Olaf the Swede, and had good welcome of him, as sayeth Thord Kolbeinson :

> Short while, O scathe-wolves' scatterer,
> Wore ere the land-folk's treason
> Ended the life of Hakon —
> Weird wendeth things a-many !
> When the host fared from the Westland,
> Methinks the son of Tryggvi
> Came to the land that erewhile
> The staff of sword-fields conquered.

And again :

> More in his heart had Eric
> Against the great wealth-waster
> Than spoken word laid open,
> As from him might be looked for.

The wrathful Earl of Thrandheim
Sought rede of the King of Sweden;
Therefrom was no man running,
But stiff-necked grew the Thrandfolk.

CHAPTER LVIII. THE WEDDING OF LODIN.

THERE was one named Lodin, a wealthy man of the Wick and of good kin; he was oft on cheaping voyages, though whiles he went a-warring.

Now on a summer Lodin was on a cheaping voyage aboard a ship which he owned himself, and had plenteous merchandise therein. He made for Estland, and was busied with his chaffer through the summer. Now amidst the market there were brought thither many kind of wares, and many thralls were brought for sale. So there saw Lodin a certain woman who had been sold for a thrall, and as he beheld her he knew that she was Astrid, Eric's daughter, who had been wedded to King Tryggvi Olafson, howsoever she were unlike what he had seen her aforetime, being pale now, and lean, and ill-clad; so he went up to her, and asked her how it fared with her. She said: "It is a heavy tale to tell; I am sold at thrall-cheapings, and am brought hither to be sold." Then they gat known to each other, and Astrid knew Lodin and prayed him therewith to buy her and have her home with him to her kin.

"I will give thee a choice over that," said he; "I will bring thee back to Norway if thou wilt wed me."

Now whereas Astrid was hard bestead, and that she knew withal that Lodin was a doughty man and of good kin, she promised him so much for her freeing. So Lodin bought Astrid and brought her to Norway, and wedded her with her kindred's goodwill, and their children were Thorkel Nefia, Ingirid, and Ingigerd; but the daughters of Astrid by King Tryggvi were Ingibiorg and Astrid. The sons of Eric Biodaskalli were Sigurd Carlshead, Jostein, and Thorkel Dydrill; these were all noble men and wealthy, and had manors in the East-country. Two brethren who dwelt east in the Wick, one named Thorgeir and the other Hyrning, wealthy men and of good kin, wedded the daughters of Astrid and Lodin, Ingirid to wit, and Ingigerd.

CHAPTER LIX. KING OLAF CHRISTENETH THE WICK.

KING HARALD GORMSON the Daneking when he took christening sent bidding over all his realm that all men should let themselves be christened and turn to the right troth. He himself followed on the heels of that bidding, and used might and mishandling if otherwise men yielded not; he sent two earls into Norway with a great host, Urguthriot and Brimilskiar by name, in order to bid christening there, and folk yielded readily enough in the Wick, where had been Harald's rule, and there were christened many folk of the land. But after the death of Harald, Svein Twibeard his son gat speedily into wars in Saxland and Friesland, and at last in England. Then those men in Norway who had taken christening turned back again to blood-offering, as they had done afore, and after the fashion of them of the North-country.

But when Olaf Tryggvison was become king in Norway he abode a long while of summer in the Wick. Many of his kin came to him there, and some who were allied to him; and many there were who had been great friends of his father; and there was he welcomed with very great love.

So then Olaf called to speech with him his mother's brethren, Lodin his stepfather, and the sons-in-law of him, Thorgeir and Hyrning. Then he laid this matter most earnestly before them, craving that they should undertake it with him, and afterwards back it with all their might, to wit, that he will have the Christian faith set forth throughout all his realm. He saith that he will bring about the christening of all Norway, or die else: "But I will make you all great men and mighty, because I trust in you best of all, for kinship sake, and other ties."

So they all accorded to this, to do whatso he bade them, and to follow him herein whither he would, and all those men who would do after their rede.

So straightway King Olaf lay bare before all the people that he would bid all men throughout his realm be christened. They first assented to these commands who had afore pledged themselves, who were all the mightiest of those men who dwelt thereabout, and all others did according to

their example. So then east in the Wick were all
men christened.

Then fared the king into the north parts of the
Wick, and bade all men take christening; but
those who gainsaid him he mishandled sorely.
Some he slew, some he maimed, some he drave
away from the land.

So it came to pass that all through the realm of
Tryggvi his father, and the realm that Harald the
Grenlander, his kinsman, had held, folk gave themselves up to be christened according to the bidding
of King Olaf; and that summer and the winter
after was all the Wick christened.

CHAPTER LX.   OF THE HORD-LANDERS.

EARLY in spring-tide was Olaf stirring in
the Wick with a great host, and so fared
north into Agdir; and wheresoever he
came he called a Thing of the bonders and bade
all men be christened. So men come under the
faith of Christ, for there was none of the bonders
might rise up against the king, and the folk were
christened wheresoever he came.

Men there were in Hordland, many and noble,
come of the kin of Horda Kari. He had had
four sons: first, Thorleif the Sage; then Ogmund,
father of Thorolf Skialg, who was the father of
Erling of Soli; thirdly, Thord, the father of
Klypp the Hersir, who slew Sigurd Slaver, the
son of Gunnhild; fourthly, Olmod, the father of
Askel, the father of Aslak Pate a-Fitiar. And this

stock was the most and the noblest of Hordland.

Now when these kinsmen heard of these troublous
tidings, how the king was coming from the east
along the land with a great host, and was bringing
to nought the ancient laws of the people, and that
all who gainsaid him must abide penalties and
torments, then gathered these kinsmen together
among themselves, that they might look to it, for
they wotted well that the king would soon be upon
them. So it seemed good to them to meet all together well accompanied at the Gula-Thing, and have
there a summoning to meet King Olaf Tryggvison.

CHAPTER LXI.   ROGALAND CHRIS-
TENED.

KING OLAF summoned a Thing so soon
as he came into Rogaland ; and when the
bidding thereto came to the bonders they
gathered all together, a many people, and all armed.
And when they were met they fell to talking the
matter over, and appointed three men, the fairest
of speech in their company, to answer King Olaf
at the Thing, and speak against him, and say that
they would not submit themselves to any lawless
ways howsoever the king might bid them. But
when the bonders came to the Thing, and the
Thing was established, then stood up King Olaf
and spake to the bonders in kindly wise at the
first ; albeit it might be seen in his words that he
would have them take christening. This with fair
words he bade them ; but in the end was this

added against such as gainsaid him, and would not obey his bidding, that they shall abye his wrath, and punishment from him, and heavy ruin, wheresoever he might bring it about.

But when he had made an end of his speaking, then stood up he of the bonders who was the fairest spoken of them all, and at the outset had been chosen for that end that he might answer King Olaf; but lo, now when he would speak he fell a-coughing and choking so that no word would out of him, and down he sat again. Then arose the second bonder, and will nowise let his answer fall dead, howsoever ill the first hath sped; but when he began his talk such stammering fell on him that not a word would win out; and all fell a-laughing who heard, and down sat the bonder.

Yet arose the third and would say his say against King Olaf; but when he fell to speech he was so hoarse and husky that no man heard what he was a-saying, and down he sat again.

And so there was none left of the bonders to speak against the king; and whereas the bonders might get none to answer the king, none uprose to withstand him, and so it came about that they all accorded to the king's command, and the whole Thing-folk was christened or ever the king went his ways thence.

CHAPTER LXII. THE WOOING OF ERLING SKIALGSON.

NOW King Olaf made with his folk to the Gula-Thing, because the bonders had sent him word that they would give answer to his matter thereat. But when either side was come to the Thing, then would the king first of all have speech with the lords of the land. But when they were all come together, the king set forth his errand, bidding them take christening according to his command.

Then spake Olmod the Old: "We kinsmen have taken counsel together about this matter, and will be all of one consent herein. For if thou, king, art minded to drive us kinsfolk into such matters by torments, and wilt break down our laws, and wilt break down us beneath thee by mastery, then will we withstand thee to the uttermost of our might, and let him prevail who is fated thereto. But if, on the other hand, king, thou wilt speed us kinsfolk somewhat, then mayst thou bring it so well about, that we shall all turn to thee with hearty obedience."

The king saith: "What will ye ask of me to the end that the peace betwixt us be of the best?"

Answereth Olmod: "First of all, whether wilt thou wed Astrid thy sister to Erling Skialgson our kinsman, whom we now account the likeliest of all young men of Norway?"

King Olaf saith that himseemeth the wedding would be good, whereas Erling is of high kin, and the goodliest of men to look on; yet saith he that

Astrid must have a word in the matter. So the king laid the matter before his sister.

"Little avails it me," said she, "that I am a king's daughter and a king's sister, if I am to be given to a man without title of dignity. Liefer were I to abide a few winters for another wooing."

And therewith they left talking for that while.

CHAPTER LXIII. THE CHRISTENING OF HORDLAND.

BUT the king let take a hawk of Astrid's and pluck off all the feathers of it, and then sent it to her.

Said Astrid: "Wroth is my brother now."

And she arose and went to the king, and he gave her good welcome. Then spake Astrid and said that she would have the king deal with her matter according to his will.

"I was a-thinking," said the king, "that I had so much power in the land as to make what man I would a man of dignity."

Then let the king call Olmod and Erling and all the kin of them to talk with him; and the wooing was talked over, with such end that Astrid was betrothed to Erling.

Then let the king set a Thing on foot, and bade the bonders be christened; and now were Olmod and Erling leaders in pushing forward this matter for the king, and all their kindred to boot; nor had any boldness to gainsay it, and all that folk was christened.

CHAPTER LXIV. THE WEDDING OF ERLING SKIALGSON.

SO Erling Skialgson arrayed his wedding in the summer-tide, and thereat was a full many folk, and there was Olaf the King.

Then offered the king an earldom to Erling, but Erling spake thus : " Hersirs have all my kin been, nor will I have a higher name than they ; but this will I take of thee, king, that thou make me the highest of that name here in the land."

The king said yea thereto, and at their parting King Olaf gave Erling his brother-in-law dominion south-away from Sogn-sea and east to Lidandisness, in such wise as Harald Hairfair had given land to his sons, whereof is aforewrit.

CHAPTER LXV. THE FIRTHS AND RAUMSDALE CHRISTENED.

THAT same autumn King Olaf summoned a Thing of four counties north at Dragseid of Stad ; thither were to come the folk of Sogn and the Firths, of South-mere and Raumsdale. Thither fared King Olaf with a great host of men that he had from the East-country, and the folk withal that had come to him out of Hordland and Rogaland. But when King Olaf came to the Thing, there bade he christening as at other places; and whereas the king had with him a very great host, men were adrad of him ; and at the end of his speaking the king bade them have one of two choices, either take christening or make them ready for battle with him. But whereas the bonders saw that there was no might with them to fight with the king, they took such rede that all folk were christened.

Then King Olaf fared with his folk into North-mere, and christened that country. Thence he sailed in to Ladir, and let break down the God-house there, and take all the wealth and adorn-ment from the God-house, and from off the gods. A great gold ring also he took from the door thereof, which Earl Hakon had let make, and thereafter King Olaf let burn the House.

But when the bonders heard thereof, they sent forth the war-arrow over all the country-side, and called out an host and would go against King Olaf. Then King Olaf brought his folk down the firth, and stood north-away along the land, being minded for Halogaland to christen folk there. But when he came north to Bear-eres, then heard he of Halogaland that they had an host out there, and were minded to defend the land against the king. And these were the captains of that host : Harek of Thiotta, Thorir Hart of Vogar, and Eyvind Kent-cheek. So when King Olaf heard thereof, he turned about, and sailed south along the land.

But when he came south of the Stad, he went more at his leisure, but yet came in the beginning of winter right east-away into the Wick.

CHAPTER LXVI. KING OLAF WOOETH QUEEN SIGRID THE HAUGHTY.

NOW Queen Sigrid of Sweden, who was called the Haughty, sat there on her manors. And that winter fared men betwixt King Olaf and Queen Sigrid, whereby King Olaf set forth his wooing of her ; and she took it in hopeful wise, and the matter was bounden with troth-words. Then sent King Olaf unto Queen Sigrid that great gold ring which he had taken from the God-house door at Ladir, deeming that a most noble gift. But the appointed day for settling this matter was to be holden the next spring-tide at the marches of the lands amid the Elf.

Now while the ring which King Olaf had sent to Queen Sigrid was being praised exceedingly of all men, there were with the queen her two smiths, brethren. These handled the ring about, and weighed it in their hands, and then spake a privy word together. So the queen called them to her, and asked why they mocked at the ring ; but they naysay that. Then she said that they must needs in all despite tell her what they had found. And they said thereon that there was false metal in the ring. So she let break it asunder, and lo ! inwardly it was but brass. Thereat was the queen wroth, and said that Olaf would play her false in more matters than this one only.

That same winter fared King Olaf up into Ring-realm and christened there.

CHAPTER LXVII. THE CHRISTENING OF OLAF HARALDSON.

ASTA, Gudbrand's daughter, was speedily wedded after the death of Harald the Grenlander to a man named Sigurd Syr, who was king in Ring-realm. Sigurd was the son of Halfdan, who was the son of Sigurd a-Bush, son of Harald Hairfair.

Now Olaf, the son of Asta by Harald the Grenlander, abode with his mother, and waxed up in his childhood at the house of Sigurd Syr, his stepfather. But when King Olaf Tryggvison came into Ring-realm bidding to christening, then Sigurd Syr let himself be christened with Asta his wife and Olaf her son; and Olaf Tryggvison became gossip to Olaf Haraldson, who was then three winters old. Then yet again fared King Olaf south into the Wick, and abode there through the winter. And now had he been three winters king over Norway.

CHAPTER LXVIII. THE TALK OF KING OLAF AND SIGRID THE HAUGHTY.

EARLY in spring-tide went King Olaf east to the King's-rock to the appointed meeting with Queen Sigrid. And when they met they talked over that matter which had been set on foot in the winter-tide, to wit, how they would be wedded together, and things looked hopefully concerning it. Then spake King Olaf,

and bade Sigrid take christening, and the right-
wise troth.   But she spake thus: "I will not
depart from the troth that I have aforetime
holden, and all my kin before me; yet will I not
account it against thee, though thou trow in whatso God seemeth good to thee."   Then waxed
King Olaf very wroth, and spake in haste:
"What have I to do to wed with thee, a heathen
bitch?" and smote her in the face with the glove
he was a-holding.

Therewith he arose, and she too; and Sigrid
said, "This may well be the bane of thee!"

Then they departed, and the king went north
into the Wick, but the queen east into the Swede-
realm.

CHAPTER LXIX.   THE BURNING OF WIZARDS.

THEN fared King Olaf to Tunsberg, and
again held a Thing there, and gave out
thereat that all such as were known and
proven to deal with witchcraft and spellwork, and
all wizards, should get them gone from the land.
Then let the king ransack for those men about the
steads that were hard by, and bid them all to him.
And when they came there, among them was a
man named Eyvind Well-spring, who was the son's
son of Rognvald Straight-leg, the son of King
Harald Hairfair.   Now Eyvind was a spellworker,
and wise above all.   Now King Olaf let marshal
these men in a certain hall, and let array it well,
and made them a feast therein, and gave them

strong drink. But when they were drunken the king let lay fire in the hall, and the hall burned up with all them that were therein, save Eyvind Well-spring, who got out by the luffer, and so away thence.

And when he was gotten a long way off, he met men on his road, and bade them tell the king that Eyvind Well-spring was gotten away from the fire, and would never come again into the power of King Olaf, but would fare in the same wise as he had heretofore in all his cunning. So when these men met King Olaf, they told him even as Eyvind had bidden them. And the king was ill content that Eyvind was not dead.

CHAPTER LXX. THE SLAYING OF EYVIND WELL-SPRING.

WHEN spring-tide was come King Olaf fared out along the Wick, and guested at his great manors, and sent word throughout all the Wick that he would have an host out in the summer-tide to fare into the North-country. Then wended he north to Agdir; but when Lent was well worn, stood north again for Rogaland, and came at Easter-eve to Ogvalds-ness in Kormt-isle. And there was his Easter-feast arrayed for him, and he had hard on three hundred men.

That same night made land at the isle Eyvind Well-spring, with a long-ship all manned, and the crew were all spell-singers or other wizard-folk. So Eyvind went up aland with his company, and

they wrought hard at their wizardry, and made
wrapping of dimness, and thick darkness so great
that the king might not get to see them.   But
when they were come hard by the stead at
Ogvaldsness the day waxed bright there, and all
went clean contrary to Eyvind's mind, for the
mirk he had made by wizardry fell upon him
and his fellows, so that they might see no more
with their eyes than with their polls, and kept
going all round and round about.   But the king's
warders saw where they went, and wotted not
what folk they were.   So the king was told
thereof, and he arose and clad himself and all his
folk.   And when he saw where Eyvind and his
folk fared, he bade his men arm them, and go see
what manner of men these would be.   But when
the king's men knew Eyvind, they laid hands on
him and the whole company, and brought them to
the king.   And Eyvind told all that had befallen
in his journey.

Then the king let take them all and bring them
out into a tide-washed skerry, and bind them
there.   So there Eyvind and all of them lost their
lives ; and that skerry is thenceforward called
Scratch-skerry.

CHAPTER LXXI.   OF KING OLAF AND THE GUILES OF ODIN.

SO goeth the tale, that as King Olaf was feasting at Ogvaldsness, thither came on an eve
an old man very wise of speech, with a wide
slouched hat and one-eyed ; and that man had

knowledge to tell of all lands. Now he gat into talk
with the king, and the king deemed it good game
of his talk, and asked him of many matters; but
the guest answered clearly to all his questioning,
and the king sat long with him that evening. The
king asked if he wotted who Ogvald had been,
after whom that stead and ness were named. Said
the guest that Ogvald was a king and a mighty
warrior, who did very great sacrifices to a certain
cow, and had her with him wheresoever he went,
and deemed it availed him well for his health to
drink always of her milk. Now King Ogvald
fought with a king called Varin, and in that battle
fell King Ogvald, and was laid in howe hard by
the stead here, and standing-stones were set up in
remembrance of him, even those that yet stand
hereby; but in another place a little way hence
was the cow laid in howe.

Such things he told of, and many other matters
of kings and the tidings of old.

But when the night was far spent, the bishop
called to the king's mind that it was time to go to
sleep, and the king did after his words. But
when he was unclad and laid in his bed, then sat
the guest down on the foot-board of his bed and
talked yet a long while with the king; and ever
when one word was done deemed the king that he
lacked another. Then spake the bishop to the
king, saying that it was time to sleep; so the
king did according to his word, and the guest went
out. A little after the king awoke and asked after
the guest, and bade call him to him, but nowhere
might the guest be found. But the next morning

the king let call to him his cook, and him who
had the keeping of his drink, and asked if any
strange man had come to them. They said that
as they were getting ready the meat there came to
them a certain man, and said that wondrous ill
flesh-meat were they seething for the king's table,
and therewith he gave them two sides of neat
both thick and fat, and they seethed them with
the other flesh-meat.

Then sayeth the king that all that victual shall
be wasted, saying that this will have been no man,
but Odin rather, he whom heathen men have long
trowed in. "But," said he, "in no wise shall Odin
beguile us."

CHAPTER LXXII. A THING IN THRANDHEIM.

KING OLAF drew together much people
from the East-country that summer, and
brought his host north-away to Thrandheim, and stood up first to Nidaros.   Then he let
wend the Thing-bidding throughout all the firth,
and summoned a Thing of eight folks at Frosta ;
but the bonders turned this Thing-bidding into a
war-arrow, and drew together, both thane and
thrall, from out all Thrandheim.

So when the king came to the Thing, thither
also was come the bonder-host all armed.

Now when the Thing was established the king
spake before his lieges and bade them take
christening, but when he had spoken a little
while, the bonders cried out at him, bidding him

hold his peace, and saying that they will fall on him else and drive him away : "Thus did we," say they, "with Hakon Athelstane's Foster-son whenas he bade us such-like bidding, nor do we account thee of more worth than him."

So when King Olaf saw the fierce mind of the bonders, and withal how great an host they had, not to be withstood, then he turned his speech aside as being of one accord with the bonders, and said thus : "I will that we make peace and good fellowship together, even as we have done aforetime. I will fare thither whereas ye have your greatest blood-offering, and behold your worship there. And then let us take counsel together concerning the worship, which we shall have, and be all of one accord thereover." So whereas the king spake softly to the bonders, their fierce mind was appeased, and thereafter all the talk went hopefully and peacefully, and at the last it was determined that the midsummer feast of offering should be holden in at Mere, and thither should come all lords and mighty bonders, as the wont was; and King Olaf also should be there.

CHAPTER LXXIII.   OF IRON-SKEGGI.

THERE was one Skeggi, a rich bonder, who was called Iron-Skeggi, and dwelt at Uphowe in Yriar. Skeggi was the first to speak against King Olaf at the Thing, and above all the bonders did he speak against Christ's faith.

But on the terms aforesaid came the Thing to
an end, and the bonders fared home, but the king
to Ladir.

CHAPTER LXXIV. FEAST AT LADIR.

NOW King Olaf laid his ships in the Nid,
and thirty ships he had, and a goodly host
and great ; but the king himself was
oftest at Ladir with the company of his court.

But when it wore toward the time whenas the
blood-offering should be at Mere, King Olaf
made a great feast at Ladir, and sent bidding in to
Strind and up into Gauldale, and west into
Orkdale, and bade to him lords and other great
bonders. But when the feast was arrayed, and
the guests were come, the first eve was the feast
full fair and the cheer most glorious, and men
were very drunk ; and that night slept all men in
peace there.

But on the morrow morn when the king was
clad he let sing mass before him, and when the
mass was ended the king let blow up for a House-
Thing. And all his men went from the ships
therewith and came to the Thing. But when the
Thing was established the king stood up and
spake in these words : " A Thing we held up at
Frosta, and thereat I bade the bonders be christened ; and they bade me back again turn me to
offering with them, even as King Hakon Athelstane's Foster-son did. Wherefore we accorded
together to meet up at Mere, and there make a
great blood-offering. But look ye, if I turn me

to offering with you, then will I make the greatest blood-offering that is, and will offer up men ; yea, and neither will I choose hereto thralls and evildoers ; but rather will I choose gifts for the gods the noblest of men ; and hereto I name Worm Lygra of Middlehouse, Styrkar of Gimsar, Kar of Griting, Asbiorn Thorbergson of Varness, Worm of Lioxa, Haldor of Skerding-stithy."

Other five he named withal, the noblest that were, and saith that these will he offer up for peace and the plenty of the year, and biddeth fall on them forthwith.

But when the bonders saw that they lacked might to meet the king, they craved peace, and gave up the whole matter for the king's might to deal with. So it was agreed on betwixt them that all the bonders who were there come should let themselves be christened, and make oath to the king to hold the true faith, and lay aside all blood-offering. And all these men did the king keep for guests till they gave him hostage, son, or brother, or other near kinsman.

CHAPTER LXXV. OF A THING IN THRANDHEIM.

NOW King Olaf fared with all his host in to Thrandheim, but when he came up to Mere, thither were come all the lords of Thrandheim, such as most withstood christening, and these had with them all the mighty bonders who had aforetime upheld the sacrifices in that place. Great was the concourse of

men even as was wont to be, and after the manner
of what had been aforetime at the Frosta-Thing.

So let the king cry the Thing; and thither
went both sides all-armed. But when the Thing
was set up, then spake the king, and bade men
christening.

Then Iron-Skeggi answered the king on behoof
of the bonders, and said they would no whit more
than aforetime that the king should break down
their laws on them. "We will, king," quoth he,
"that thou make offering here as other kings have
done before thee."

At this his speaking made the bonders great
stir, and said that even as Skeggi spake would
they have it all. Then answered the king saying
that he would fare into the God-house with them,
and look at the worship whenas they made offering.
The bonders were well pleased thereat, and either
side fareth to the God-house.

CHAPTER LXXVI.   THRANDHEIM CHRISTENED.

SO now King Olaf went into the God-house,
and a certain few of his men with him, and a
certain few of the bonders. But when the
king came whereas the gods were, there sat Thor
the most honoured of all the gods, adorned with
gold and silver. Then King Olaf hove up the
gold-wrought rod that he had in his hand, and
smote Thor that he fell down from the stall; and
therewith ran forth all the king's men and tumbled
down all the gods from their stalls. But whiles

the king was in the God-house was Iron-Skeggi slain without, even at the very door, and that deed did the king's men.

So when the king was come back to his folk he bade the bonders take one of two things, either all be christened, or else abide the brunt of battle with him. But after the death of Skeggi there was no leader among the folk of the bonders to raise up the banner against King Olaf. So was the choice taken of them to go to the king and obey his bidding. Then let King Olaf christen all folk that were there, and took hostages of the bonders that they would hold to their christening.

Thereafter King Olaf caused men of his wend over all parts of Thrandheim; and now spake no man against the faith of Christ. And so were all folk christened in the country-side of Thrandheim.

CHAPTER LXXVII. THE BUILDING OF A TOWN.

KING OLAF brought his host out to Nidoyce, and there let he raise up a house on the Nid-bank, and so ordered it that there should be a cheaping-stead, and gave men tofts there whereon to build them houses; but he himself let build the king's house up above Ship-crook. Thither let he flit in the autumn-tide all goods that were needed for winter abode, and there had he a full many men.

CHAPTER LXXVIII.   THE WEDDING OF KING OLAF.

NOW King Olaf appointed a day of meeting with the kin of Iron-Skeggi, and offered them atonement thereat; and many noble men had the answering thereof. Iron-Skeggi had a daughter named Gudrun; and so it befell at last amid their peace-making that King Olaf should wed Gudrun.

But the very first night they lay together, so soon as the king was fallen asleep, she drew a knife and would thrust him through. But when the king was ware of it he took the knife from her, and leapt up from the bed, and went to his men and told them what had betid. Gudrun also took her raiment and all those men who had followed her thither, and they went on their way, and Gudrun never came again into the same bed with King Olaf.

CHAPTER LXXIX.   THE BUILDING OF THE CRANE.

THAT same autumn let King Olaf build a great long-ship on the beach of the Nid. A cutter was this, and many smiths he had at the building of it. But in the beginning of winter, when it was fully done, thirty benches of oars might be told in it; high in the stem it was, but nothing broad of beam. That ship the king called the Crane.

After the slaying of Iron-Skeggi his body was

brought out to Yriar, and he lieth in Skeggi's-howe by Eastairt.

CHAPTER LXXX. THANGBRAND FARETH TO ICELAND.

NOW whenas Olaf Tryggvison had been king over Norway two winters, there was with him a Saxon priest named Thang-brand; masterful was he and murderous, but a good clerk and a doughty man. Now whereas he was so headstrong a man, the king would not have him with him; but sent him on this message, to wit, to fare out to Iceland and christen the land there. So a merchant-ship was gotten for him, and the tale telleth about his journey that he made the East-firths of Iceland, Swanfirth the southmost to wit, and the winter after abode with Hall of the Side.

So Thangbrand preached christening in Iceland, and after his words Hall let himself be christened and all his household, and many other chieftains also; notwithstanding many more there were who gainsaid him.

Thorvald the Guileful and Winterlid the Skald made a scurvy rime about Thangbrand, but he slew them both. Thangbrand abode three winters in Iceland, and was the bane of three men or ever he departed thence.

CHAPTER LXXXI. OF HAWK AND SIGURD.

TWO men there were, one named Sigurd and the other Hawk; Halogalanders of kin were they, and had been much busied in chaffering voyages. On a summer they had fared west to England, and when they came back to Norway they sailed north along the land. But in North-mere they fell in with the fleet of King Olaf; and when the king was told that thither were come certain men, Halogalanders and heathen, he let call the skippers to him, and asked if they would let themselves be christened; but they gain-said it. Then the king would talk them over in many wise, and prevailed nought. So he threatened them with death or maiming; but nought for that would they shift about. So he let set them in irons, and they were with him a certain while holden in fetters; and the king often talked with them, but it was but labour lost. And on a certain night they vanished away so that none heard aught of them, or knew in what wise they had gotten away. But in the autumn-tide they turned up in the North-country with Harek of Thiotta, who gave them good welcome, and they abode the winter with him in good entertainment.

CHAPTER LXXXII. OF HAREK OF THIOTTA.

NOW on a fair day of spring-tide was Harek at home and few men with him at the stead, and the time hung heavy on his hands. So Sigurd spake to him, saying that if he will they will go a-rowing somewhither for their disport. That liked Harek well; so they go down to the strand, and launch a six-oarer, and Sigurd took from the boathouse sail and gear that went with the craft; for such-wise oft they fared to take the sail with them when they rowed for their disport. Then Harek went aboard the boat and shipped the rudder. The brethren Sigurd and Hawk went with all weapons, even as they were ever wont to go with the goodman at home; and they were both men of the strongest.

Now before they went aboard the craft they cast into her a butter-keg and a bread-basket, and bare between them a beer-cask down to the boat. Then they rowed away from land; but when they were come a little way from the isle, then the brethren hoisted sail and Harek steered, and they speedily made way from the isle. Then went the brethren aft to where Harek sat, and Sigurd spake: " Now shalt thou make thy choice of certain things: the first is that thou let us brethren be masters of our voyage, and the course of it; the second, that thou let us bind thee; and the third, forsooth, that we slay thee."

Now Harek saw in what a plight he was, being no more than a match for either of the brethren,

even were he arrayed as well as they ; so he made
that choice which seemed to him the best of a bad
business, to wit, to let them be masters of the
voyage. So he bound himself with oaths thereto,
and gave them his troth ; and Sigurd went to the
rudder, and they stood south along the land. The
brethren took heed that they should meet no man,
and the wind was of the fairest. So they made no
stay till they came south to Thrandheim, and into
Nidoyce, and there met they King Olaf. Then
let the king call Harek to talk with him, and bade
him be christened ; but Harek gainsaid him.

Hereof spake the king and Harek many days at
whiles before many men, at whiles privily, nor
might they be at one thereover. So in the end
spake King Olaf to Harek : " Now shalt thou go
thy ways home, nor will I be heavy on thee this
time, all the more as we are nigh akin, and withal
thou mayst say that I have gotten thee by guile.
But know of a sooth that my mind it is to come up
north there in the summer, and look on you Halogalanders, and then shall ye wot how hard I may be
on those that gainsay christening."

Harek seemed well content to get away at his
speediest this time. King Olaf gave him a good
cutter rowing ten or twelve oars a-side ; and let
array that ship as well as might be with all things
needful ; and he gave Harek thirty men, all doughty
fellows and well arrayed.

CHAPTER LXXXIII. THE DEATH OF EYVIND RENT-CHEEK.

SO Harek of Thiotta gat him gone from the town at his speediest, but Hawk and Sigurd abode with the king, and let themselves both be christened.

Harek went on his ways till he came home to Thiotta. Thence sent he word to his friend Eyvind Rent-cheek, bidding men tell him that Harek of Thiotta had come face to face with King Olaf, and had not let himself be cowed into christening; and again he bade tell him that King Olaf had it in his heart to come on them with an host next summer; and saith Harek that they must look to it to deal warily therewith, and biddeth Eyvind come to meet him as soon as may be.

But when this errand was set forth before Eyvind, he seeth that the need is instant to look to it that they be not tripped by the king. So Eyvind fared at his speediest in a light skiff, and but few men with him; but when they came to Thiotta, Harek greeted him well, and straightway gat they a-talking, Harek and Eyvind, on the other way out from the stead. Yet but a little while had they talked, ere King Olaf's men, who had followed Harek to the north, come upon them, and lay hands on Eyvind, and lead him down to the ship with them, and so sail away with Eyvind; nor stayed they their journey till they were come to Thrandheim and found King Olaf in Nidoyce. Then was Eyvind brought to speech with King Olaf, and the king bade him take christening like other men;

which thing Eyvind gainsaid. The king bade him
with kind words to take christening, showing him
many things clearly, he and the bishop also; but
none the more would Eyvind shift about. Then
the king offered him gifts and great bailiwicks; but
Eyvind would none of them. Then the king
threatened him with maiming or death; but it
availed nought to turn him.

Then let the king bear in a hand-basin full of
glowing coals and set it on Eyvind's belly, and
presently his belly burst asunder. Then spake
Eyvind: "Take away the basin, and I will speak
a word before I die." Said the king: "Wilt thou
now trow in Christ, Eyvind?" "Nay," said he,
"I may nowise take christening. I am a ghost
quickened in a man's body by cunning of the Finns;
and my father and mother might have no child
before that."

Then died Eyvind, who had been the cunningest
of wizards.

CHAPTER LXXXIV.   HALOGALAND CHRISTENED.

THE spring after these things, let King
Olaf array his ships and folk, and he himself sailed the Crane; a fair host and a
mighty had the king. So when he was ready he
brought his fleet out of the firth and then north of
Byrda, and so north-away to Halogaland. And
wheresoever he came aland, there held he a Thing
and bade all folk thereat to take christening and
the right troth.

No man durst gainsay him, and all the land was christened wheresoever he came.

King Olaf took guesting at Thiotta at Harek's, and there was Harek christened and all his folk. Harek gave the king good gifts at parting, and became his man, and took bailifries of the king and the dues and rights of a lord of the land.

CHAPTER LXXXV. THE FALL OF THORIR HART.

RAUD the Strong was the name of a man who dwelt in a firth called Salpt in God-isle. He was very wealthy, and had many house-carles; a mighty man, and there followed him great plenty of Finns whenso he had need thereof.

Raud was busy in blood-offerings, and full wise in wizardry; he was a great friend of a man named afore, Thorir Hart to wit; and they were both great chieftains.

Now when they heard that King Olaf was faring over Halogaland from the south with an host of men, they gathered men to them and called out ships, and gat a great company.

Raud had a mighty dragon with a head all done with gold, a ship of thirty benches by tale, and great of hull withal for her length. Thorir Hart also had a great ship.

So they stood south with their host to meet King Olaf; and when they met they joined battle with the king. Great was the battle, and men fell thick and fast: but the slaughter began to fall on

the Halogaland host, and their ships to be cleared ;
and then fell fear and terror on them.   Raud rowed
out to sea with his dragon, and so let hoist sail ;
for ever had he wind at will whithersoever he
would sail, which thing came from his wizardry.
But the shortest tale of Raud's journey is that he
sailed home to God-isle.

Thorir Hart and his folk fled in toward land,
and leapt ashore from his ship ; but King Olaf
followed them, he and his, and they also leapt
ashore, and chased them and slew them.   The
king was foremost, as ever when such play was
toward, and he saw where Thorir Hart ran, who
was the swiftest footed of men.   So the king ran
after him, and his hound Vigi followed him.   Then
cried the king, " Vigi, take the hart ! " So Vigi ran
forth after Thorir and was on him straightway.
Thereon Thorir made stay and the king shot a
spear at him.   Thorir thrust with his sword at the
hound, and gave him a great wound ; but even
therewith flew the king's spear under Thorir's
arm so that it stood out at the other side.   So there
Thorir ended his life, but Vigi was borne wounded
out to the ship.

But King Olaf gave peace to all who craved it,
and would take christening.

CHAPTER LXXXVI. THE JOURNEY OF KING OLAF TO GOD-ISLE.

NOW King Olaf stood north along the land, christening all folk whithersoever he came ; but when he came north to Salpt he was minded to sail in up the firth to find Raud, but foul weather and a squally storm raged down the firth. So there lay the king for a week, and ever the same foul weather endured down the firth, though without was the wind blowing fair for sailing north along the land. So the king sailed north-away to Omd, and there came all folk under christening. Then turned the king south again ; but when he came south off Salpt, again was there a driving storm with brine spray down the firth ; certain nights the king lay there, and still was the weather the same. Then spake the king to Bishop Sigurd, and asked him if he knew of any remedy hereto, and the bishop said he would try it, if God would strengthen his hands to overcome the might of these fiends.

CHAPTER LXXXVII. OF BISHOP SIGURD ; AND OF RAUD'S TORMENT-ING.

SO took Bishop Sigurd all his mass-array, and went forth on to the prow of the king's ship, and let kindle the candles, and bore incense. Then he set up the rood in the prow of the ship, and read out the gospel and many prayers, and sprinkled holy water over all the ship. Then he bade unship the tilt and row in up the firth.

Then called the king to the other ships, bidding them all row into the firth after him. But so soon as they fell a-rowing of the Crane, she made way up into the firth, and they who rowed that ship felt no wind on them, and quite calm stood there the walled-in track behind in the ship's wake, while on either side thereof whirled the driving spray so free, that because of it the fells might not be seen. But in that calm rowed one ship after other; and so fared they all day, and the night after, and came a little before daybreak to the God-isles. And when they came off Raud's stead, lo, there off the shore lay his great dragon. So King Olaf went straightway up to the house with his folk, and set on the loft wherein Raud slept, and brake open the door; then men ran in, and Raud was laid hand on and bound, but such men as were therein were slain or taken. Then went men to the hall wherein slept Raud's house-carles; and there some were slain, and some bound, and some beaten.

Then let the king bring Raud before him, and he bade him be christened. "Then," said the king, "will I not take thy possessions from thee, but rather be thy friend, if thou wilt be worthy thereof." But Raud cried out at him, saying that he would never trow in Christ, and blasphemed much; and the king waxed wroth, and said that Raud should have the worst of deaths. So he let take him and bind him face up to a beam, and let set a gag between his teeth to open the mouth of him; then let the king take a ling-worm and

set it to his mouth, but nowise would the worm
enter his mouth, but shrank away whenas Raud
blew upon him. Then let the king take a hollow
stalk of angelica, and set it in the mouth of Raud,
or, as some men say, it was his horn that he let set
in his mouth; but they laid therein the worm, and
laid a glowing iron to the outwards thereof, so that
the worm crawled into the mouth of Raud, and
then into his throat, and dug out a hole in the side
of him, and there came Raud to his ending.

But King Olaf took there very great wealth of
silver and gold and other chattels, weapons to wit,
and divers kinds of dear-bought things; and all
those men who had served Raud the king let
christen, or if they would not be christened he had
them slain or tormented. There took King Olaf
that dragon which Raud had had, and he himself
steered it, for it was a far greater and goodlier
ship than was the Crane. Forward on it was a
dragon's head, but afterward a crook fashioned in
the end as the tail of a dragon; but either side the
neck and all the stem were overlaid with gold.
That ship the king called the Worm, because when
the sail was aloft, then should that be as the wings
of the dragon. The fairest of all Norway was
that ship.

Now those isles wherein Raud had dwelt were
called Gilling and Hæring, but all the isles
together the God-isles, and the stream to the
north betwixt them and the mainland was called
the God-isles' stream. All that firth King Olaf
christened now, and then went his ways south
along the land, and in that his journey betid many

tidings told of in tale thereafter, how trolls and
evil creatures tempted his men; yea, whiles himself even. Yet will we rather write about the
tidings that befell when King Olaf christened
Norway, or those other lands he brought unto
christening.

So King Olaf brought his host that same autumn
to Thrandheim, and stood in for Nidoyce, and
there ordered his winter dwelling.

And now will I let write next what is to tell of
Iceland men.

CHAPTER LXXXVIII. OF THE ICE-LAND MEN.

FOR that same harvest came out to Nidaros
from Iceland Kiartan, the son of Olaf, the
the son of Hoskuld, and the son also of
the daughter of Egil Skallagrimson, which Kiartan
hath been called nighabout the likeliest and goodliest man ever begotten in Iceland. There was
then also Haldor, son of Gudmund of Madder-
mead, and Kolbein, son of Thord, Frey's priest,
the brother of Burning-Flosi; Sverting also, son
of Runolf the Priest; these and many others,
mighty and unmighty, were all heathen.

Therewith also were come from Iceland noble
men who had taken christening from Thangbrand,
to wit, Gizur the White, the son of Teit Ketil-
biorn's son, whose mother was Alof, daughter of
Bodvar the Hersir, son of Viking-Kari; but the
brother of Bodvar was Sigurd, father of Eric
Biodaskalli, the father of Astrid, mother of King

Olaf. Another Icelander hight Hialti, son of Skeggi; he had to wife Vilborg, daughter of Gizur the White. Hialti was a christened man, and King Olaf gave full kindly welcome to father and son-in-law, Gizur and Hialti, and they abode with him.

Now those Iceland men who were captains of the ships, such of them as were heathen, sought to sail away, when the king was come into the town, for it was told them that the king would christen all men perforce; but the wind was against them, and they were driven back under Nid-holm. These were the captains of ships there: Thorarin Nefiolfson, Hallfred the Skald, son of Ottar, Brand the Bountiful, and Thorleik Brandson. Now it was told King Olaf that there lay certain ships of Icelanders, who were all heathen and would flee away from meeting the king. So he sent men to them forbidding them to stand out to sea, bidding them go lie off the town, and so did they, but unladed not their ships [but they cried a market, and held chaffer by the king's bridges. Thrice in the spring-tide they sought to sail away, but the wind never served, and they lay yet by the bridges.

Now on a fair-weather day many men were a-swimming for their disport; and one man of them far outdid the others in all mastery. Then spake Kiartan with Hallfred the Troublous-skald bidding go try feats of swimming with this man, but he excused himself. Said Kiartan, "Then shall I try;" and cast his clothes from him therewith, and leapt into the water, and struck out for that man, and caught him by the foot and drew him

under. Up they come, and have no word together,
but down they go again, and are under water much
longer than the first time, and again come up, and
hold their peace, and go down again the third time;
till Kiartan thought the game all up, but might
nowise amend it, and now knew well the odds of
strength betwixt them. So they are under water
there till Kiartan is well-nigh spent ; then up they
come and swim to land. Then asked the Northman what might the Icelander's name be, and
Kiartan named himself. Said the other, " Thou
art deft at swimming ; hast thou any mastery in
other matters ?" Said Kiartan : "Little mastery
is this." The Northman said : "Why askest thou
me nought again ?" Kiartan answereth : "Meseemeth it is nought to me who thou art, or in
what wise thou art named." Answered the other :
" I will tell thee then : Here is Olaf Tryggvison."
And therewith he asked him many things of the
Iceland men, and lightly Kiartan told him all, and
therewith was minded to get him away hastily.
But the king said : " Here is a cloak which I will
give thee, Kiartan." So Kiartan took the cloak,
and thanked him wondrous well.]

CHAPTER LXXXIX.   THE ICELAND MEN CHRISTENED.

AND now was Michaelmas come, and the
king let hold hightide, and sing mass full
gloriously; and thither went the Icelanders,
and hearken the fair song, and the voice of the
bells. And when they came back to their ships,

each man said how the ways of the Christian men liked them, and Kiartan said he was well pleased, but most other mocked at them.   And so it went, as saith the saw, *Many are the king's ears*, and the king was told thereof.   So forthwith on that same day he sent a man after Kiartan bidding him come to him; and Kiartan went to the king with certain men, and the king greeted him well. Kiartan was the biggest and goodliest of men, and fair-spoken withal.   So now when the king and Kiartan had taken and given some few words together, the king bade Kiartan take christening. Kiartan saith that he will not gainsay it, if he shall have the king's friendship therefor; and the king promised him his hearty friendship; and so Kiartan and he strike this bargain between them. The next day was Kiartan christened, and Bolli Thorleikson his kinsman, and all their fellows; and Kiartan and Bolli were guests of the king whiles they wore their white weeds; and the king was full kind to them, and all men accounted them noble men wheresoever they came.

CHAPTER XC.   THE CHRISTENING OF HALLFRED THE TROUBLOUS-SKALD.

ON a day went the king a-walking in the street, and certain men met him, and he of them who went first greeted the king; and the king asked him of his name, and he named himself Hallfred.

"Art thou the skald?" said the king.

Said he: "I can make verses."

Then said the king : "Wilt thou take christening, and become my man thereafter ? "

Saith he : "This shall be our bargain : I will let myself be christened, if thou, king, be thyself my gossip, but from no other man will I take it."

The king answereth : "Well, I will do that."

So then was Hallfred christened, and the king himself held him at the font.

Then the king asked of Hallfred : "Wilt thou now become my man ? "

Hallfred said : "Erst was I of the body-guard of Earl Hakon ; nor will I now be the liege-man of thee nor of any other lord, but if thou give me thy word that for no deed I may happen to do thou wilt drive me away from thee."

"From all that is told me," said the king, "thou art neither so wise nor so meek but it seemeth like enough to me that thou mayest do some deed or other which I may in nowise put up with."

"Slay me then," said Hallfred.

The king said : "Thou art a Troublous-skald ; but my man shalt thou be now."

Answereth Hallfred : "What wilt thou give me, king, for a name-gift, if I am to be called Troublous-skald ? "

The king gave him a sword, but no scabbard therewith ; and said the king : "Make us now a stave about the sword, and let the sword come into every line."

Hallfred sang :

> One only sword of all swords
> Hath made me now sword-wealthy.
> Now then shall things be sword-some

For the Niords of the sweep of sword-edge.
Nought to the sword were lacking,
If to that sword were scabbard
All with the earth-bones coloured.
Of three swords am I worthy.

Then the king gave him the scabbard and
said : "But there is not a sword in every line."

"Yea," answers Hallfred, "but there are three
swords in one line."

"Yea, forsooth," saith the king.

Now from Hallfred's songs we take knowledge
and sooth witness from what is there told concerning
King Olaf.

CHAPTER XCI. THANGBRAND COMETH BACK TO KING OLAF FROM ICELAND.

THAT same harvest came back from Iceland to King Olaf Thangbrand the mass-
priest, and told how that his journey had
been none of the smoothest ; for that the Icelanders
had made scurvy rimes on him, yea, and some
would slay him. And he said there was no hope
that that land would ever be christened. Hereat
was King Olaf so wood wroth that he let blow
together all the Iceland men that were in the
town, saying withal that he would slay them every
one. But Kiartan and Gizur and Hialti, and
other such as had taken christening, went to him
and said : "Thou wilt not, king, draw back from
that word of thine, whereby thou saidst that no
man might do so much to anger thee, but that thou

wouldst forgive it him if he cast aside heathendom
and let himself be christened.   Now will all Iceland men that here are let themselves be christened ; and we will devise somewhat whereby the
Christian faith shall prevail in Iceland.   Here are
sons of many mighty men of Iceland, and their
fathers will help all they may in the matter.   But
in sooth Thangbrand fared there as here with thee,
dealing ever with masterful ways and manslaying ;
and such things men would not bear of him."

So the king got to hearken to these redes, and
all men of Iceland that there were, were christened.

CHAPTER XCII.   OF KING OLAF'S MASTERIES.

KING OLAF was of all men told of the
most of prowess in Norway in all matters; stronger was he and nimbler than
any, and many are the tales told hereof.   One, to
wit, how he went up the Smalshorn, and made fast
his shield to the topmost of the peak ; and withal
how he helped a courtman of his who had clomb
up before him on to a sheer rock in such wise that
he might neither get up nor down ; but the king
went to him and bore him under his arm down
unto a level place.

King Olaf also would walk out-board along the
oars of the Worm while his men were a-rowing ;
and with three hand-saxes would he play so that
one was ever aloft, and one hilt ever in his hand.
He smote well alike with either hand, and shot
with two spears at once.

King Olaf was the gladdest of all men and game-some. Kind he was and lowly-hearted; exceed-ing eager in all matters; bountiful of gifts; very glorious of attire; before all men for high heart in battle. The grimmest of all men was he in his wrath, and marvellous pains laid he upon his foes. Some he burnt in the fire; some he let wild hounds tear asunder; some he stoned, or cast down from high rocks. Now for all these things was he well-beloved of his friends and dreaded of his foes. Full great, therefore, was his furtherance, whereas some did his will for love and kindness sake, and othersome for fear.

CHAPTER XCIII. THE CHRISTENING OF LEIF ERICSON.

LEIF, the son of Eric the Red, who first settled Greenland, was come this summer from Greenland to Norway. He went to King Olaf, and took christening, and abode that winter with King Olaf.

CHAPTER XCIV. THE FALL OF KING GUDROD.

NOW Gudrod, son of Eric Blood-axe and Gunnhild, had been a-warring in the West-lands since he fled the land before Earl Hakon; but in this summer afore told of, whenas King Olaf Tryggvison had ruled over Norway four winters, then came Gudrod to Norway with many war-ships, and had newly sailed from England; but when he drew so nigh as to have inkling of Norway, he stood south along the land whereas King Olaf was least to be looked for, and sailed to the Wick. But so soon as he came aland, he fell a-harrying and beating down the people under him, bidding them take him for king. So when the folk of the land saw that a mighty host was come upon them, then sought men for truce and peace, and offered to the king to send the bidding to a Thing throughout the land, and would rather take him to guesting than have to bear the war of him; and therefore was there tarrying in the matter whiles the call to the Thing was abroad. Then craved the king money for his victual whiles he abode thus; but the bonders chose rather to give the king quarters for such time as he needed; which choice the king took and went guesting about the land with some of his folk, while some held ward over his ships.

But when the brethren Hyrning and Thorgeir, King Olaf's brothers-in-law, heard that, they gather folk and go a-shipboard, and so fare north unto the Wick, and come on a night with their company to where Gudrod was a-guesting; and there they fell on him with fire and the sword. There fell King Gudrod, and the more part of his folk; but they of them who had been at the ships were slain, some of them, and some escaped and fled away far and wide. And now are all the sons of Eric and Gunnhild dead.

CHAPTER XCV. THE BUILDING OF THE LONG WORM.

NOW the winter that King Olaf came from Halogaland he let build a great ship in under the Ladir-cliffs, and much greater it was than other ships that were then in the land; and yet are the slips whereon it was built left there for a token: seventy-and-four ells long of grass-lying keel was it. Thorberg Shave-hewer was the master-smith of that ship, but there were many others at the work; some to join, some to chip, some to smite rivets, some to flit timbers: there were all matters of the choicest. Long was that ship, and broad of beam, high of bulwark, and great in the scantling.

But now when they were gotten to the free-board Thorberg had some needful errand that took him home to his house, and he tarried there very long, and when he came back the bulwark was all done.

Now the king went in the eventide and Thorberg with him to look on the ship, and see how the ship showed, and every man said that never yet had they seen a long-ship so great or so goodly; and so the king went back to the town.

But early the next morning went the king and Thorberg again to the ship, and the smiths were already come thither, but there they stood doing nothing. The king asked them what they were about then; and they said that the ship was spoilt, for some man or other must have gone from stem

to stern cutting notches with an axe all along the
gunwale one by another. So the king went thereto,
and saw that sooth it was ; and he spake therewith,
and swore an oath that if he might find the man
who for envy's sake had spoilt the ship he should
surely die. " And he who will tell me thereof shall
have great good of me."

Then spake Thorberg : " I might tell thee, belike, king, who will have done this deed."

Saith the king : " I might look to thee as much
as to any man to have such good hap as to wot
hereof and tell me."

" Well, I will tell thee, king, who hath done it ;
I have done it."

Answereth the king : " Then shalt thou make
it good, so that all be as well as heretofore ; and
thy life shall lie on it."

So Thorberg went to the ship, and planed all
the notches out of the gunwale ; and thereon said
the king and all others that the ship was much
fairer on that board where Thorberg had cut it ;
and the king bade him fashion it so on either
board, and bade him have much thank for it all.

So thereafter was Thorberg master-smith of the
ship until it was done.

This ship was a dragon, and was wrought after
the fashion of the Worm, that ship which the king
had gotten in Halogaland, but bigger it was and
more excellent in all wise ; and he called it the
Long Worm, but the other the Short Worm.

On this Worm were there thirty-and-four
benches of oars. The head and the crooked tail of
it were all done over with gold, and the bulwarks

were as high as in a ship built for sailing the main
sea. The best wrought and the most costly
was that ship of any that have been in Norway.

CHAPTER XCVI. OF EARL ERIC HAKONSON.

NOW Earl Eric Hakonson and his
brethren, and many other noble kinsmen
of theirs, had fled away from the land
after the fall of Earl Hakon. Earl Eric fared east
into Sweden to Olaf the Swede-king, and had
good welcome of him, he and his; and King Olaf
gave the earl a land of peace there, and great grants
to sustain himself and his folk. Hereof telleth
Thord Kolbeinson:

> Short while, O scathe-wolves' scatterer,
> Wore ere the land-folk's treason
> Ended the life of Hakon—
> Weird wendeth things a-many!
> When the host fared from the Westland,
> Methinks the son of Tryggvi
> Came to the land that erewhile
> The staff of sword-fields conquered.
>
> More in his heart had Eric
> Against the great wealth-waster
> Than spoken word laid open,
> As from him might be looked for.
> The wrathful Earl of Thrandheim
> Sought rede of the King of Sweden;
> Therefore no man forsook him.
> Stiff-necked then grew the Thrandfolk.

Much folk resorted from Norway to Earl Eric,
who had fled away from the land before King
Olaf Tryggvison. So Earl Eric took such rede

that he gat him a-shipboard and went a-warring
to gather wealth for him and his men. First he
made for Gothland, and lay off there long in the
summer season, waylaying ships of chapmen who
sailed toward the land, or of the vikings else;
and whiles he went aland and harried there wide
about the borders of the sea. So it is said in
Banda-drapa :

> The Lord renowned thereafter
> Won mail-storms more a-many,
> That have we learned aforetime ;
> *The spear-storm bounteous Eric . . .*
> When wrought he Vali's storm-wreath
> Of the hawks of the strand of Virvil
> About wide-harried Gothland.
> *To him, and fight-gay wages . . .*

Then sailed Earl Eric south to Wendland, and
fell in there off Staur with certain viking-ships, and
joined battle with them. There won Earl Eric
the victory and slew the vikings ; as is said in
Banda-drapa :

> The steerer of the stem-steed
> At Staur let heads of men lie,
> The Lord such deed he fashioned.
> *The earl his wars and swayeth . . .*
> So then the scalp of vikings
> The wound-mew tore by sea-beach,
> There at the hard swords' meeting.
> *The land by gods safe-guarded.*

CHAPTER XCVII. OF ERIC'S WARRING IN THE EASTLANDS.

THEN sailed Earl Eric back to Sweden in harvest-tide and abode there another winter, but in spring-tide he arrayed his ships and sailed for the Eastlands. And when he came into the realm of King Valdimar he fell a-harrying, and slew menfolk, and burnt all before him, and laid waste the land; and he came to Aldeigia-burg, and beset it till he won the stead. There he slew many folk and brake down and burnt all the burg, and thereafter fared wide about Garth-realm doing all deeds of war; as is said in Banda-drapa:

> Fared thence the sea-flames' brightener
> King Valdimar's land to harry,
> All with the brand of point-storm,
> Thereat the fray grew greater.
> Men's awe, thou brok'st Aldeigia,
> And hard indeed the fight waxed,
> Betwixt the hosts thou camest
> East unto Garths: so knew we.

This warfare waged Earl Eric for five summers in all; but when he came from Garth-realm he went a-warring all about Adalsysla and the Isle-sysla, and there took he four viking-cutters of the Danes, and slew all the folk thereof. So saith it in Banda-drapa:

> Heard I where he the hardener
> Of the fire of the spear-sea
> In Isle-land sound the fray raised.
> *The spear-storm bounteous Eric . . .*
> The fight-tree, firth-flame's giver
> Cleared four ships of the Dane-folk.

So heard we the true story.
To him, and fight-gay wages . . .

O heedful Niord of the launch-steed,
With Gautland men ye battled
When ran the yeomen townward.
The earl his wars and swayeth . . .
The war's-god wended war-shield
Aloft all o'er the counties,
To men the peace he minished.
The land by gods safe-guarded.

Earl Eric went to Denmark whenas he had
been one winter in the Swede-realm; he met
Svein Twibeard the Dane-king there, and wooed
for himself Gyda his daughter; which wooing
came to wedding, and Earl Eric had Gyda to
wife, and the next winter they had a son hight
Hakon.

Earl Eric abode in Denmark in the winter, or
whiles in the Swede-realm; but in summer-tide he
went a-warring.

CHAPTER XCVIII. THE WEDDING OF KING SVEIN.

SVEIN TWIBEARD the Dane-king had
to wife Gunnhild, the daughter of Burislaf,
king of the Wends. But in these days even
now told of it befell that Queen Gunnhild fell sick
and died, and a little after King Svein wedded
Sigrid the Haughty, the daughter of Skogul Tosti,
who was the mother of Olaf the Swede, King of
Sweden; and with this alliance love also befell
between the kings, and well-beloved of them both,
and they of him, was Earl Eric Hakonson.

CHAPTER XCIX. THE WEDDING OF KING BURISLAF.

NOW Burislaf the Wend-king laid plaint before Earl Sigvaldi his son-in-law, that the treaty was broken which Earl Sigvaldi had made between King Svein and King Burislaf, to wit, that Burislaf should wed Thyri, Harald's daughter, the sister of King Svein, which wedding had never come to pass, because Thyri had said nay downright to the wedding with a heathen king and an old man. So sayeth Burislaf now that he will claim the treaty's fulfilment, and bade the earl fare to Denmark, and have away with him Queen Thyri for King Burislaf's behoof.

So Earl Sigvaldi slept not over that journey, but fared to meet the Dane-king, and laid the matter before him, and in such way the word of the earl prevailed that King Svein delivered Thyri his sister into his hands; and certain women went with her, and her foster-father, one Ozur Agison, a wealthy man, and certain other men withal. It was covenanted between the king and the earl that those domains in Wendland which Queen Gunnhild had had should be for a dowry to Thyri, and other great possessions should she have for jointure.

Sore greeted Thyri and went all against her will; but when the earl and she came to Wendland, then King Burislaf arrayed the wedding and took to wife Queen Thyri. But now that she was come among heathen men she would neither take meat nor drink of them, and such wise went matters for seven nights.

CHAPTER C. KING OLAF WEDDETH QUEEN THYRI.

NOW it came to pass on a certain night that Queen Thyri and Ozur fled away to the wood by night and cloud, and, shortly to tell of their journeying, they came to Denmark ; but there nowise durst Thyri abide, because she wotted well that if King Svein, her brother, heard of her being there, he would speedily send her back to Wendland. So they fared with heads all hidden until they came into Norway, and Thyri made no stay till she came before King Olaf Tryggvison. But he took them in kindly, and in good welcome they abode there. Thyri told the king all her trouble, and craved helpful counsel of him and a peaceful dwelling in his realm. A smooth-spoken woman was Thyri, and the king thought well of her ways, and beheld her that she was a fair woman ; and it came into his mind that this would be a good wedding for him. So thitherwise he turned the talk, and asketh her will she wed him. But whereas her fortune had fared in such wise, and she deemed herself right hard bestead, and saw on the other hand how happy a wedding this was, to be wedded to so noble a king, she bade him deal with her and her matter as he would. And so according to this talk King Olaf wedded Queen Thyri, and their wedding was held in harvest-tide, whenas he was come south from Halogaland. So King Olaf and Queen Thyri abode in Nidoyce that winter.

But the next spring would Queen Thyri be oft

bewailing to King Olaf, and weeping sorely therewith, how, for as great possessions as she had in
Wendland, here in the land had she no wealth such
as beseemed a queen : and whiles would she pray
the king with fair words to go get her her own,
saying that King Burislaf was so dear a friend of
King Olaf, that so soon as they met he would give
over to him all that he craved.   Nevertheless, all
the friends of the king, when they heard of this
talk, letted the king of that journey.

Now so tells the tale, that on a day early in
spring-tide the king was a-going down the street,
when by the market-place a man met him with
many angelica heads, wondrous big for that season
of spring ; so the king took a great stem of angelica in his hand, and went home therewith to the
lodging of Queen Thyri.

Now Thyri sat a-weeping in her hall when the
king came in ; but he spake : " See here the big
angelica I give thee."

But she thrust it aside with her hand, and spake :
" Harald Gormson was wont to give me greater
gifts ; and moreover he feared less than thou dost
now, to fare from the land and seek his own ; as was
well seen of him when he came hither into Norway
and laid waste the more part of this land, and won
to him all the scat and dues thereof ; whereas thou
durst not wend through the Dane-realm for fear of
King Svein my brother."   Then up sprang King
Olaf at that word of hers, and spake out on high,
and sware an oath, saying : " Never shall I fare in
fear for King Svein thy brother.   Nay, and if we
meet, he it is shall give aback ! "

CHAPTER CI.   THE MUSTER OF KING OLAF.

SO a little hereafter King Olaf summoned a Thing there in the town, whereat he set forth before all the people that he would have an host put off the land that summer, and would have a levy from every folk-land, both of men and ships ; and therewithal he sayeth how many ships he will have thence from out the firth. Then sendeth he messengers north and south along the land, by the outer and the inner ways, and let call out his folk.

Therewith let King Olaf thrust forth the Long Worm, and all his other ships both great and small ; and he himself steered the Long Worm.

But when men were dight to go aboard ship, so well arrayed and chosen was his company, that none should be aboard the Long Worm older than sixty or younger than twenty, and full closely were they chosen both for strength and stoutness of heart ; and the first set aside thereto were those of the body-guard of King Olaf, for these were chosen from all that was strongest and stoutest, both of folk of the land and of outlanders.

CHAPTER CII.   THE TELLING-UP OF THE WORM'S MANNING.

WOLF THE RED was the man hight who bore King Olaf's banner, and was in the prow of the Worm ; and next to him was Kolbiorn the Marshal, Thorstein Oxfoot also, and Vikar of Tenthland, the brother of Arnliot Gellin.

These were of the forecastle in the prow : Vakr of the Elf, son of Raumi ; Bersi the Strong ; An the Shooter of Iamtland ; Thrand the Stout of Thelmark, and Uthyrmir his brother ; these Halogalanders, to wit, Thrand Squint-eye, Ogmund Sandy, Lodvir the Long of Salt-wick, and Harek the Keen. These of Inner Thrandheim : Ketil the High, Thorfin Eisli, Howard, he and his brethren of Orkdale.

These manned the forehold : Biorn of Studla ; Bork of the Firths ; Thorgrim, son of Thiodolf of Hvin ; Asbiorn and Worm ; Thord of Niordlow ; Thorstein the White of Oprustead ; Arnor the Mere-man ; Hallstein and Hawk of the Firths ; Eyvind the Snake ; Bergthor Bestill ; Hallkel of Fialir ; Olaf the Lad ; Arnfinn of Sogn ; Sigurd Bill ; Einar of Hordland and Finn ; Ketil of Rogaland ; Griotgard the Brisk.

These were in the main-hold : Einar Thambarskelvir, deemed indeed by the others not ablebodied, whereas he was but eighteen winters old ; Thorstein Hlifarson ; Thorolf ; Ivar Smetta ; Worm Shaw-neb, and many other right noble men withal were on the Worm, though nought can we name them. Eight men there were to a half-berth in the Worm, all chosen man by man. Thirty there were in the fore-hold.

The talk of men it was that the crew of the Worm no less bore away the bell from other men for goodliness and might and stout heart, than did the Long Worm from other ships.

Thorkel Nosy, the king's brother, steered the Short Worm, and Thorkel Dydril and Jostein, the mother's brothers of the king, had the Crane; and either ship was full well manned. Eleven great ships had King Olaf from Thrandheim, and twenty-banked ships, moreover, and smaller ships, and victuallers.

CHAPTER CIII. ICELAND CHRISTENED.

NOW when King Olaf had wellnigh arrayed his host for sailing from Nidoyce, he appointed men throughout all Thrandheim to the stewardships and bailifries. Then sent he to Iceland Gizur the White and Hialti Skeggison to bid christening therein, and gave them a priest named Thormod, and other hallowed men; but he held as hostages four Iceland men such as he deemed the noblest, to wit, Kiartan Olafson, Haldor Gudmundson, Kolbein Thordson, and Swerting Runolfson. And now it is to be said of the journey of Gizur and Hialti, that they came to Iceland before the Althing and fared to the Thing, at which Thing was Christ's troth taken for law in Iceland; and that same summer was all manfolk christened there.

CHAPTER CIV. GREENLAND CHRISTENED.

THAT same spring also King Olaf sent Leif Ericson to Greenland to bid christening there; so that same summer he went thither. He took up a ship's crew on the sea who had come to nought, and were lying on the wreck of the ship; and in that journey found he Vineland the Good and came back in harvest-tide to Greenland, bearing with him thither a priest and teachers, and so went to guest with Eric his father at Brentlithe. Men called him thereafter Leif the Lucky; but Eric his father said that one thing might be set against another, whereas on the one hand Leif had holpen that wrecked crew, and on the other had brought that juggler to Greenland, to wit, the priest.

CHAPTER CV. EARL ROGNVALD SENDETH MEN TO KING OLAF.

NOW King Olaf and Queen Thyri abode in Nidoyce that winter wherein the king had christened Halogaland; and the summer before that Queen Thyri brought forth a man-child, begotten of King Olaf. Great was the lad, and of good hope, and was called Harald, after his mother's father. The king and the queen loved the lad much, and set their hearts on his growing up and taking the heritage of his father; but he lived not a full year from the time he was born, and a sore scathe they both deemed it.

That winter were there many Iceland men with
King Olaf, as is afore writ, and many other noble
men besides; and in the court also was Ingibiorg,
Tryggvi's daughter, the sister of King Olaf. Fair
she was to look on, lowly of mien, and kind to all
folk; faithful she was, great-hearted, and full
friendly. She loved well the Iceland men such as
were there, but Kiartan Olafson was the dearest
of them all to her; for the longest of them had he
abided with the king, and often talking to him she
deemed a delight, for wise he was and sweet of
speech.

King Olaf was ever glad and joyous with his
men, and oft he turned him to asking of the ways
and the glory of the mighty men of the realms
anigh, when men came to him from Sweden or
Denmark.

Now Hallfred the Troublous-skald was come
that summer from Gautland east-away there, and
had been with Earl Rognvald Wolfson, now come
to the dominion of West Gautland. Wolf the
father of Rognvald was brother of Sigrid the
Haughty, and King Olaf the Swede and Earl
Rognvald were cousins-germain. Now Hallfred
told King Olaf many things of Earl Rognvald,
saying how that he was a brave lord and a
masterful, bounteous of money, manly-minded,
and friendly. Hallfred said withal that the earl
would fain fall into friendship with King Olaf, and
had talked over how he would be a-wooing Ingibiorg, Tryggvi's daughter. And so that same
winter came west from Gautland messengers from
Earl Rognvald, who met King Olaf north-away in

Nidoyce. There they set forth the earl's errand before the king, according to the word that Hallfred had spoken, to wit, that the earl was fain to be very friend of King Olaf, and that he would speak of alliance with the king and would wed Ingibiorg his sister. Therewith the messengers brought to the king manifest tokens of the earl to make it plain that they did his errand faithfully. The king took their matter well, but said that Ingibiorg must herself be mistress of her wedding. Then talked the king this matter over with his sister, and asked her what her mind was herein ; and she answered thus : " I have abided with thee a while, and thou hast given me brotherly furtherance and loving honour in every place since thou camest into this land. Therefore will I say yea to whatso thou wilt have of me in my wedding ; yet indeed I look to it that thou wilt not give me to a heathen man."

The king saith that so indeed it shall be, and therewith he had speech of the messengers ; and this was determined before they went their ways, that Earl Rognvald should come to meet King Olaf in the East-country that summer, if he would become his very friend, and then should they themselves talk over the matter when they met.

So the messengers of the earl go back east on this errand ; but King Olaf abode that winter in Nidoyce with great glory and many men.

CHAPTER CVI. KING OLAF GOETH HIS WAYS TO WENDLAND.

THAT summer fared King Olaf with his host south along the land. Now there resorted to him many friends of his, and mighty men, such as were arrayed for faring with the king; and the first man of all was Erling Skialgson, his brother-in-law, who had a great cutter of thirty benches, and full well manned was that ship. There came to him also his brethren-in-law, Hyrning and Thorgeir, either of them steering a big ship; and many other mighty men followed him. Sixty long-ships had he as he fared from the land, and sailed south along Denmark through the Ere-sound, and so to Wendland. There he appointed a day of meeting with King Burislaf, and the kings met, and talked together over those possessions which King Olaf claimed; and all went in likely wise between the kings, and the claims that King Olaf deemed he had there were brought into a fair way to be paid. So King Olaf abode there long that summer, and found there a many of his friends

CHAPTER CVII. THE EGGING ON OF SIGRID THE HAUGHTY.

NOW King Svein Twibeard had then to wife Sigrid the Haughty, as is afore writ. Sigrid was the greatest foe of King Olaf Tryggvison, for this cause forsooth, that King Olaf had broken their plighted troth and smitten

her in the face even as is afore writ. Now she
stirred up King Svein busily to join battle with
King Olaf Tryggvison, and said that he had
enough against him, in that King Olaf had lain
by Thyri his sister without the leave of him :
" And never would thy forefathers have borne such
things."

Such like words had Queen Sigrid for ever in
her mouth, whereby at the last she brought it to
pass that King Svein was gotten ready to do by
her counsel.

So early in the spring King Svein sent men
east to Sweden to meet Olaf the Swede-king, his
son-in-law, and Earl Eric, and he bade tell them
that Olaf, King of Norway, had his fleet abroad,
and was minded to fare to Wendland that summer.
This word also went with the message of the Dane-
king, that the Swede-king and Earl Eric should
have out their host and go meet King Svein, and
that all they together should go join battle with
King Olaf Tryggvison.

Now Olaf the Swede-king and Earl Eric were
all ready for this journey; so they drew together a
great host of ships from the Swede-realm, and
brought that host south to Denmark, but came
thither when King Olaf Tryggvison had already
sailed east. Hereof telleth Haldor the Unchristened in the song that he made on Earl Eric :

> The kings' o'er-thrower dauntless
> In gale of flame of battle
> Called out much folk from Sweden.
> The king held south to battle.
> Fattener of carrion-hornets !

Then each and every yeoman
Was fain to follow Eric?
Drink gat the wound-mew seaward.

So the Swede-king and Earl Eric held on to
meet the Dane-king, and now joined all together
they had a marvellous great host.

CHAPTER CVIII. THE GUILES OF EARL SIGVALDI.

NOW King Svein, when he sent for that
host, had sent Earl Sigvaldi to Wendland
to spy on the host and the ways of King
Olaf Tryggvison, and to lay such a trap that King
Svein and his fellows might not fail to fall in with
him. So Earl Sigvaldi went his ways, and came
to Wendland and Iomsburg, and so went to meet
Olaf Tryggvison. So there was most friendly
converse betwixt them, and the earl grew into the
greatest good liking with King Olaf. Astrid, the
wife of the earl and daughter of King Burislaf,
was a great friend of King Olaf, which came about
much from their former ties, whereas King Olaf
had wedded Geira her sister.

Now Earl Sigvaldi was a wise man and a shifty,
and when he was gotten into the privity of King
Olaf's counsel, he ever held him back from sailing
from the east, and found hereunto, now one thing,
now another. But King Olaf's folk took it marvellous ill, being waxen very homesick as they lay
all dight for sailing and the weather boding fair
wind.

Meanwhile Earl Sigvaldi had privy tidings from

Denmark that the host of the Swede-king was now come from the east, and that Earl Eric also had arrayed his host, and that these lords would now be coming east under Wendland, and had appointed to waylay King Olaf by an isle called Svoldr; so that it behoved the earl to bring it so about that they might fall in with King Olaf there.

CHAPTER CIX. KING OLAF'S JOURNEY FROM WENDLAND.

AND now it got whispered about in Wendland that Svein the Dane-king had an host abroad, and speedily arose the rumour that King Svein would meet King Olaf; but Earl Sigvaldi saith to the king: "It will be no rede for King Svein to join battle with thee with the Dane-host only, so great an host as thou hast gotten; but if thou misdoubt at all that war besetteth thy way, then will I be of thy company with my folk, and time has been when the following of the Vikings of Iomsburg has been deemed of good avail for a lord: lo, I will get thee eleven ships well manned." The king said yea thereto; the wind blew light and handy for sailing: so the king let weigh anchor and blow for departing. Then men hoisted sail, and all the small ships made the more way, and sailed away right out to sea.

Now the earl sailed hard by the king's ship, and called out to them, bidding the king sail after him. "Full well I know," said he, "where are the deepest of the sounds betwixt the isles, and this will ye need for your big ships."

So the earl sailed on before with his ships; eleven ships he had; and the king sailed after him with his big ships, and he too had eleven there; but all the rest of the host sailed out to sea.

Now when Earl Sigvaldi was come sailing off Svoldr by the west, a skiff rowed off to meet him, and they told him that the host of the Dane-king lay awaiting them in the haven there. Then let the earl strike sail and row in under the isle. So sayeth Haldor the Unchristened:

> From the south came the king of the isle-folk
> With ships one more than seventy,
> The meet-stem of the wave-steed,
> He reddened sword in the murder.
> Whenas the earl had ordered
> The sea's knop-crownèd reindeer
> For a war-mote with the Scanings,
> Men's peace it flew asunder.

Herein is it said that King Olaf and Earl Sigvaldi had seventy ships and one whenas they sailed from the south.

CHAPTER CX. THE KINGS TALK TOGETHER AND TAKE COUNSEL.

NOW Svein the Dane-king and Olaf the Swede-king were there with all their host: fair weather it was, and bright shone the sun. So all the lords went up on to the holm with a great company of men, and they saw how a many ships together went sailing out to sea; and now see they where saileth a great ship and a brave. Then spake both the kings and said: "Yonder is a great ship and marvellous fair;

this will be the Long Worm." But Earl Eric answered and said : " Nay, this will not be the Long Worm."

And so it was as he said, for this ship was of Eindrid of Gimsar.

A little thereafter they saw where another ship came sailing much greater than the first. Then spake King Svein : " Now is Olaf Tryggvison afeard, and durst not sail with the head on his ship." Then saith Earl Eric : " This is not the king's ship, for I know it, ship and striped sail. Erling Skialgson owneth it. Let these sail on! for better for us shall be that rent and lacking in King Olaf's fleet than that yonder ship be there, so well arrayed as it is."

But a while after saw they, and knew Earl Sigvaldi's ships that turned them toward the holm.

Then saw they where three ships came sailing, and one was great. Then spake King Svein, and bade go a-shipboard, for that there came the Long Worm. Then said Earl Eric : " Many other great ships and glorious have they, beside the Long Worm ; bide we a while !"

Then gat many men a-talking, and said : " Earl Eric will not fight then, and avenge his father. Great shame is this, to be told of through all lands, if we lie here with this so great an host, and King Olaf saileth out to sea, out here past our very eyes."

But when they had talked this wise awhile, saw they where four ships came a-sailing, and one of them was a dragon full great all done about with gold. Then up stood King Svein and spake on

high : " This night shall the Worm bear me, and
I will steer her. And many men said withal that
the Worm was a wondrous great ship and goodly,
and great glory it was to let build such a ship.

But Earl Eric said so that certain men heard
him : " If King Olaf had no bigger ship than that
one alone, yet should King Svein never get it from
him with the Dane-host only."

Then drew the folk toward the ships, and struck
the tilts, and were minded to dight them speedily.

But while the lords were so speaking together,
they saw where came three full mighty ships
a-sailing, and a fourth last of all, and lo! it was
the Long Worm.

But those great ships which had sailed by afore,
and they deemed had been the Worm, were the
first the Crane, and the last the Short Worm.

But now when they saw the Long Worm all
knew her, and none had a word to say against it
that there was sailing Olaf Tryggvison, and they
went to their ships and arrayed them for onset.

This was the privy bargain struck between the
chieftains, King Svein, to wit, King Olaf, and
Earl Eric, that each should have his own third
share of Norway if they laid low Olaf Tryggvison ;
but whoso first went up on the Worm should have
all the prey to be gotten thereon, and each should
have such ships as himself cleared.

Earl Eric had a beaked ship wondrous great,
wherewith he was wont to sail a-warring ; and a
beard there was on either side the prow thereof, and
thick staves of iron down from thence all the breadth
of the beard, and going down to the water-line.

CHAPTER CXI. OF KING OLAF'S HOST.

NOW when Earl Sigvaldi and his folk rowed in under the holm, that saw Thorkel Dydril from the Crane and the other captains who went with him, how the earl turned his ships under the holm; so they struck sail and rowed after them, and hailing them, asked why they fared so. The earl said that he would lie-to for King Olaf: "For it looketh like that war awaiteth us."

So they let their ships drift till Thorkel Nosy came up in the Short Worm and the three ships that went with her. The same tale were they told; so they too struck sail and lay-to abiding King Olaf. But now when the king sailed in toward the holm, then rowed the whole host out into the sound to meet them. But when men saw that, they bade the king sail on his way, and not join battle with so great an host. Then the king answered with a high voice, as he stood up in the poop: "Strike sails! let no men of mine think of flight! never have I fled from battle. Let God look to my life! for never will I turn to flight."

And so was it done as the king bade; even as Hallfred sayeth :

> Still must the word be told of,
> Which, said the men foe-griping
> The king deed-mighty spake there
> To his lads at fray of weapons :
> The bower-down of Swede-ranks
> Forbade his trusty war-host
> To think of flight. The stout word
> Of the people's leader liveth.

CHAPTER CXII. KING OLAF ORDER-ETH HIS FOLK.

SO King Olaf let blow up for the gathering together of all his ships ; and the king's ship was in the midst of his battle, but on one board lay the Short Worm, and the Crane on the other. But when they set about lashing together the stems of the Long Worm and the Short, and the king saw them at it, he cried out on high, bidding them lay the big ship better forward, and not let it hang aback behind all ships in the host. Then answered Wolf the Red : " If the Worm shall lie as far forward as she is longer than other ships, then there will be windy weather to-day in the bows." Saith the king : " I wotted not that I had a forecastle-man both Red and adrad." Quoth Wolf : " Ward thou the poop with thy back no more than I the bows with mine."

Then the king caught hold of his bow, and laid an arrow on the string and turned it on Wolf.

Said Wolf : " Shoot another way, king, whereas it will avail thee more ; for thee work I that I work."

CHAPTER CXIII. OF KING OLAF.

KING OLAF stood on the poop of the Worm and showed high up aloft: a for-gilded shield he had and a gold-wrought helm, and was easy to know from other men : a short red kirtle had he over his byrny.

Now when King Olaf saw that the hosts were drifting about, and the banners set up before the captains, he asked : " Who is captain of the host over against us ? " So it was told him that there was King Svein Twibeard with the Dane-host.

Answered the king : " We fear not those blenchers ; in Danes there is no heart. But what captain is behind the banners out there on the right hand ? "

It was told him that there was King Olaf with the Swede-host. Saith King Olaf : " Better were the Swedes to sit at home licking their blood-bowls than setting on the Worm under your weapons. But who is lord of the big ships that lie out there on the larboard of the Danes ? "   " There is Earl Eric Hakonson," said they. Then answered King Olaf : " He will deem us well met to-day ; and we may look for full fierce fight from that folk, for they are Northmen as we be."

CHAPTER CXIV. THE BEGINNING OF THE BATTLE.

THEN fell the kings to the onset, and King Svein laid his ship against the Long Worm, and King Olaf the Swede lay outward from him, and grappled from the prow the outermost ship of King Olaf Tryggvison, but on the other side lay Earl Eric. And then befell a hard fight. Earl Sigvaldi let hang aback with his ships, nor thrust into the battle. So saith Skuli Thorsteinson, who was with Earl Eric that day :

> The Frisian's foe I followed,
> And Sigvaldi ; young gat I
> Life-gain, where spears were singing
> (Old now do people find me).

Where I bore reddened wound-leek
To the mote against the meeter
Of mail-Thing in the helm-din
Off Svold-mouth in the south-land.

And moreover of these tidings saith Hallfred :

Meseems the king, fight-framer.
That tide o'ermuch was missing.
The following of the Thrand-lads
Much folk to fleeing turned them.
The mighty folk-lord fought there
Sole gainst two kings full doughty,
And an earl for third foe had he.
Famed wont such things to tell of.

CHAPTER CXV. THE FLIGHT OF KING SVEIN AND OF OLAF THE SWEDE-KING.

THIS battle was of the sharpest, and great was the fall of men. The forecastle-men of the Long Worm and the Short Worm and the Crane cast anchors and grapplings on to the ships of King Svein, and had to bring their weapons to bear right down under their feet. So cleared they all those ships they grappled ; but King Svein and such of his folk as escaped fled into other ships, and therewith drew aback out of shot. So went it with this host as King Olaf Tryggvison had guessed.

Then in the place of them fell on Olaf the Swede-king ; but so soon as they came nigh to the big ships it fared with them as with the others, that they lost much folk and some of their ships, and in such plight drew aback.

But Earl Eric laid Iron-beak aboard the outer-

most ship of King Olaf, and cleared it, and cut
it adrift from its lashings, and then laid aboard
that one which was next, and fought till that too
was cleared. Then fell the folk a-fleeing from
the lesser ships up on to the bigger; but Earl
Eric cut each one adrift from her lashings as he
cleared it.

Then drew the Danes and Swedes into bowshot
again, and beset King Olaf's ships all round
about; but ever Earl Eric laid aboard the ships
and dealt in fight of handy-strokes; and ever as
men fell aboard his ships came other in the stead
of them, Swedes and Danes. So sayeth Haldor:

> Brunt of sharp swords betided
> All round about the Long Worm,
> Lads sheared peace long asunder
> Where golden spears were singing.
> 'Tis told that men of Sweden,
> And Dane-groves of bright leg-biters
> Him followed forth in the Southland
> At war-tide of his foemen.

Then waxed the battle of the sharpest, and
much folk fell; but in the end it came about that
all the ships of King Olaf Tryggvison were
cleared, saving the Long Worm, and all the folk
were come aboard it who were yet fit for fight of
his men. Then Earl Eric laid Iron-beak aboard
the Long Worm, and there befell fight of handy-
strokes. So sayeth Haldor:

> Midst a hard firth was gotten
> The Long Worm. There were cloven
> The moons of the galley's prow-fork
> Where blood-reeds clashed together.

Where the byrny-witchwife's Regin
Laid the board-mighty Beardling
Gainst Fafnir's side ; and the earl wrought
The helm-gale off the island.

CHAPTER CXVI.   OF EARL ERIC.

EARL ERIC was in the forehold of his ship, and a shield-burg was arrayed about him.

There was both handy-stroke and thrusting of spears, and all things cast that might make a weapon, while some shot with the bow or cast with the hand. But such brunt of weapons was borne against the Worm that scarce might any shield him, so thick flew spears and arrows ; for the warships lay on the Worm all round about.

But now were King Olaf's men waxen so wood, that they leapt up on the bulwark to the end that they might get stroke of sword to smite folk ; but many lay not the Worm so nigh aboard that they would come to handy-strokes ; and Olaf's men went most of them overboard, and took no more heed than if they fought on the plain mead, and so sunk they down with their weapons. So sayeth Hallfred :

Smiters of ring-wrought war-sark
Sank wounded down from the Adder
In the fray of arrows' peril ;
And nowise there they spared them.
The Worm shall long be lacking
Such lads as these, though glorious
The king may be who steers her
As 'neath war-host she glideth.

CHAPTER CXVII.   OF EINAR THAM-BARSKELVIR.

NOW Einar Thambarskelvir was aboard the Worm aft in the main-hold ; and he shot with the bow and was the hardest shooting of all men.   Einar shot at Earl Eric, and the arrow smote the tiller-head above the head of the earl, and went in up to the shaft binding.   The earl looked thereon and asked if they wist who shot ; and even therewith came another arrow so nigh that it flew betwixt the earl's side and his arm, and so on into the staying board of the steersman, and the point stood out far beyond.   Then spake the earl to a man whom some name Finn, but othersome say that he was of Finnish kin, and he was the greatest of bowmen ; and he said, "Shoot me yonder big man in the strait hold."

So Finn shot, and the arrow came on Einar's bow even as he drew the third time, and the bow burst asunder in the midst.   Then spake King Olaf : "What brake there so loud ?"

Answereth Einar : "Norway, king, from thine hands."

"No such crash as that," said the king ; "take my bow and shoot therewith."   And he cast the bow to him.   So Einar took the bow and drew it straightway right over the arrow-head, and said : "Too weak, too weak, All-wielder's bow !" and cast the bow back.   Then took he his shield and sword, and fought manfully.

CHAPTER CXVIII.   KING OLAF BRINGETH HIS MEN SHARP SWORDS.

KING OLAF TRYGGVISON stood on the poop of the Worm, and shot full oft that day, whiles with the bow and whiles with javelins, and ever twain at once. Now looked he forward on the ship, and saw his men heave up sword and smite full fast, but saw withal that they bit but ill; so he cried out aloud: "Is it because ye raise your swords so dully, that I see that none of ye bite?"

So a man answered: "Our swords are dull and all to-sharded."

Then went the king down into the forehold, and unlocked the chest of the high-seat; and took thence many sharp swords and gave them to his men.

But as he stretched down his right hand men saw that the blood ran down from under his byrny sleeve; but none wist where he was wounded.

CHAPTER CXIX. THEY GO UP ON TO THE LONG WORM.

NOW the most defence on the Worm and the most murderous to men was of those of the forehold and the forecastle, for in either place was the most chosen folk and the bulwark highest; but the folk began to fall first amidships. But now whenas but few men were on their feet about the mast, Earl Eric fell to boarding, and came up on to the Worm with fourteen men. Then came against him Hyrning,

brother-in-law of King Olaf, with a company of
men, and there befell the hardest battle ; but such
was the end of it that the earl drew aback on to
Iron-beak, and of those men who followed him,
some fell and some were wounded. Hereof telleth
Thord Kolbeinson :

> There was upraised the war-din
> Around the gory Hropt's walls
> Of the king's host : and there Hyrning
> Who turned the blue swords' edges,
> Gat good word. Ere it dieth
> Shall the high fells' hall be fallen.

And yet again was the battle of the sharpest, and
many men fell aboard the Worm. But when the
crew of the Worm waxed thin for the warding, then
Earl Eric fell on again to come up on to her ; and
yet again was his meeting hard. But when the
forecastle men of the Worm saw this, they went
aft and turned against the earl to defend them,
and dealt him a hard meeting. Nevertheless,
whereas there was so much folk fallen aboard the
Worm that the bulwarks were widely waste of
men, the earl's men came aboard on every side,
and all the folk that yet stood upon their feet for
the warding of the Worm fell aback aft whereas
the king was. So saith Haldor the Unchristened,
telling how Earl Eric cheered on his men :

> Back shrank the folk with Olaf
> Across the thwarts, when glad-heart
> The earl cheered on his war-lads,
> The doughty in the battle,
> When they had locked the ship-boards
> Around the King of Halland,
> Bounteous of sea-flame. Tided
> Sword-oath round that Wend-slayer.

CHAPTER CXX.　THE CLEARING OF THE LONG WORM.

NOW Kolbiorn the Marshal went up on to the poop to the king, and much alike were they in raiment and weapons, and Kolbiorn also was the fairest and biggest of men. And now once more in the forehold was the battle full fierce ; but, because so much folk of the earl was gotten aboard the Worm as the ship might well hold, and his ships also lay close all round about the Worm, and but a few folk were left for warding her against so great an host, now albeit those men were both strong and stout of heart, yet there in short space fell the more part of them. But King Olaf himself and Kolbiorn leapt overboard, either on his own board ; but the earl's men had put forth small boats and slew such as leapt into the deep. So when the king himself leapt into the sea they would have laid hands on him and brought him to Earl Eric ; but King Olaf threw up his shield over him, and sank down into the deep sea. But Kolbiorn the Marshal thrust his shield under him to guard him from the weapons thrust up at him from the boats that lay below, and in such wise he came into the sea that his shield was under him, so that he sank not so speedily, but that they laid hand on him and drew him up into a boat ; and they deemed of him that he was the king. So he was led before the earl ; and when the earl was ware that it was Kolbiorn and not King Olaf, then was peace given to Kolbiorn.

But even at this point of time leapt overboard

from the Worm all King Olaf's men that were yet alive; and Hallfred sayeth that Thorkel Nosy the king's brother leapt overboard the last of all :

> The waster of the arm-stone
> Saw the Crane floating empty,
> And either Adder : gladsome
> He reddened spear in the battle
> Ere the fight-daring, bold-heart
> Thorketil deft at swimming
> Fled from huge brunt of battle
> Offboard the wolf of tackle.

CHAPTER CXXI. OF THE WENDLAND CUTTER.

NOW as is aforewrit Earl Sigvaldi had fallen into fellowship with King Olaf in Wendland, and had ten ships with him ; but an eleventh there was whereon were the men of Astrid the king's daughter, wife of Earl Sigvaldi. But whenas King Olaf leaped overboard, then all the host cried the cry of victory, and therewith Earl Sigvaldi and his men dashed their oars into the water and rowed into the battle. Hereof telleth Haldor the Unchristened :

> From wide away the Wend-ships
> Drew o'er the sea together,
> And Thridi's land's lean monsters
> On the folk yawned iron-throated.
> Swords'-din at sea betided,
> Wolf's fare the erne was tearing,
> There fought the lads' dear leader,
> And fled full many a war-host.

But the Wendland cutter whereon were Astrid's men rowed away and back under Wendland ; and the talk of many it was then and there that King Olaf will have done off his byrny under water, and so dived out under the long-ships and swum for the Wendland cutter, and that Astrid's men brought him to land. And many are the tales told thereafter by some men about King Olaf's farings. Nevertheless in this wise sayeth Hallfred :

> I wot not one or the other,
> To call him dead or living,
> The soother of mews of clatter
> Of the sheen of Leyfi's sea-deer.
> Since either tale folk tell me
> For true, and this is certain
> That wounded must the king be,
> And tidings of him fail us.

And howsoever it may have been, nevermore thenceforward came Olaf Tryggvison back to his realm of Norway.

But thus sayeth Hallfred the Troublous-skald

> The man who said that living
> Was the folk's king, all his life long
> Was the point-shaking servant
> Of the guile-shy son of Tryggvi.
> And so folk say that Olaf
> Gat him from out the steel-storm—
> Ah, wide from truth their words are ;
> Woe worth that all is worser !

And again :

> When thanes fell on with folk-host,
> On the king the hardy-hearted,
> E'en as I learn, then would not
> Such luck befall his land's folk,
> As that the swayer of hand's ice,
> Of worth so manifolded,
> From such an host should get him,
> And yet folk deem it likely.

Still will some tell the wealth-wise
Of the king in battle wounded,
Or of his coming safely
Forth from the clash of metal.
But sooth from the Southland cometh
Of the Great Play and his slaying,
Nor many things now may I
With the wavering word of men-folk.

CHAPTER CXXII. OF EARL ERIC.

SO had Earl Eric gotten the Long Worm, and the victory, and a great prey; as sayeth Haldor:

Thither the Long Worm bore him,
The lord with helm becoifèd,
To the Thing of swords full mighty,
And the folk adorned their shipboard.
Right glad the earl took over
The Adder south in the war-din,
But Heming's high-born brother
Ere that must redden edges.

Now Svein, the son of Earl Hakon, had wedded Holmfrid, the daughter of Olaf the Swede-king. But when they shared the realm of Norway between them, the Dane-king, the Swede-king, and Earl Eric, then had Olaf the Swede-king four folklands in Thrandheim, both the Meres and Raumsdale, and Ran-realm from the Gaut-elf to Swine-sound. This dominion King Olaf delivered into the hands of Earl Svein on such covenant as the scat-paying kings or earls had held it aforetime of the over-kings.

But Earl Eric had four counties in Thrandheim, Halogaland and Naumdale, the Firths and Fialir,

Sogn and Hordland and Rogaland, and North Agdir out to Lidandisness. So sayeth Thord Kolbeinson :

> Wot I that, save for Erling,
> Most Hersirs erst were friendly
> Unto the Earls. Here sing I
> The Tyr of the flame of ship-land.
> Fight done, and all the land lay
> At peace north all from Veiga
> To Agdir south, or further
> Maybe. I chose words rightly.

> Now folk well-pleased of their ruler,
> To love their lot well liked them ;
> And he gave out he was bounden
> To hold hand over Norway.
> But Svein the king, the tale goes,
> Is dead now in the Southland,
> And his towns withal are wasted.
> But few of folk woe faileth.

Svein the Dane-king had still the Wick even as he had aforetime ; but he gave Earl Eric Raum-realm and Heathmark.

Svein Hakonson took earldom from Olaf the Swede. Earl Svein was the goodliest man ever seen. Earl Eric and Earl Svein both let themselves be christened and took the right troth ; but whiles they ruled over Norway they let every man do as he would about the holding of the faith ; but the ancient laws they held well and all customs of the land, and were men of upright rule and well beloved. Earl Eric was by far the foremost of the brethren in all authority.

EXPLANATIONS OF THE METAPHORS IN THE VERSES.

EXPLANATIONS

Of the less obvious "kenningar" (periphrases), preceded by a
list of abbreviated references.

B. Stud. — Sophus Bugge, Studier over de nordiske Gude og
 Heltesagns Oprindelse. Christiania, 1881-89.
FaS.—Fornaldarsögur Norðrlanda. 2nd ed., Reykjavík, 1886.
Fm.—Fafnismál, in N. F., pp. 219-226.
Fs.—Fornmanna-sögur. Kaupmannahöfn, 1825, etc.
Gh.—Guðrúnar-hvöt (Gudrun's Whetting), in N. F., pp. 311-315.
Grm.—Grímnis-mál (Grimnis[= Odin's]-lay), in N. F., pp. 75-89.
Hbl.—Hár-barðs ljóð (Hoary-beard's[= Odin's]-lay), in N. F., pp.
 97-104.
Hdm.—Hamðismál (Lay of Hamdir), in N. F., pp. 316-23.
H. H.—Helga kviða Hjörvarðssonar (Lay of Helgi Hiorvardson),
 in N. F., pp. 171-178.
Hm.—Hávamál (High-one's[= Odin's]-lay), in N. F., pp. 43-64.
Lex. poet.—Lexicon poeticum linguae septentrionalis, conscripsit
 Sveinbjörn Egilsson. Hafniae, 1860.
N. F.—Norræn Fornkvæði . . . almindelig kaldet Sæmundar Edda
 hins Fróða. Udgiven af Sophus Bugge. Christiania, 1867.
N. F. H.—A. P. Munch's Det norske Folks Historie. Christiania,
 1852, etc.
S. E.—(Snorra Edda) Edda Snorra Sturlusonar. Hafniae, 1848, etc.
Saxo.—Saxo Grammaticus. Ed. P. E. Müller. Hafniae, 1839-58.
Vk.—Völundar-kviða (Wealand's Lay), in N. F., pp. 163-170.
Vsp.—Völuspá (The Witches' Word), in N. F., pp. 1-11.
Vþm.—Vafþrúðnismál (Lay of the Riddle-Wise), in N. F., pp.
 65-74.
Y.—Ynglingasaga (Story of the Ynglings), in the present vol.

Page 16.

SEAS' sun: "djúp-röðull," Sun of the deep = gold.—
Forehead's moons: "enni-tungl" = eyes.

Page 21. Sire of As-folk: "ása niðr"= Odin, to
which the epithet reddener of shield: "skáldblætr,"=
"skjaldblætr," links itself appositively. Others take

"reddener of shield" as vocat., an apostrophe to a listener.—Scat-giver: "skattfœrir" = Sœming.—Giant-maiden: "járnviðja" = Skadi. Cf. S. E. i. 58: "Gýgr ein býr fyrir austan Miðgarð í þeim skógi er Járnviðr heitir; í þeim skógi byggja þær tröllkonur er Járnviðjur heita," *i.e.* a certain trollwoman dwells to the east of Midgarth in that wood which is called Iron-"with"; in that wood dwell the trollwomen who are called Iron-withies. For Skadi's kin, cf. S. E. i. 92: "Njörðr á þá konu er Skaði heitir, dóttir þjaza jötuns," *i.e.* Niord has her for wife who is hight Skadi, the daughter of the giant Thiazi, cf. Grm. 11 (N. F.).—Manhome: "Mann-heimar," according to Snorri another name for Sweden proper, to distinguish it from Godhome, or Sweden the Great = Scythia. Possibly, however, Snorri was mis-taken here. From the myth of Gefjon, Y. ch. v., it would seem that the parts of Sweden believed to be inhabited by giants were named Giant-home, Jötun-heimar; naturally, therefore, the remaining parts, in-habited by man, would be called Manhome.

For	Read
The warriors' friend	The sea-bone's folk's
And Skadi with him.	Friend and Skadi.
But she of the rock-lands'	But she, the goddess
Rushing snow-skids,	Of gliding snow-skids,

The sea-bone's folk's friend: "sævar beins skatna vinr" = Odin (in his character of Thiazi's son-in-law); sea-bone = stone, rock, hence rocky mountains, their folk = mountain giants. Goddess of snow-skids: "öndur-dís" = Skadi; cf. S. E. i. 94: "ferr hon (Skaði) mjök á skíðum ok með boga ok skýtr dýr; hon heitir öndurguð eðr öndurdís," *i.e.* fares she much on snow-shoes and with bow and shoots wild things; she is called snow-shoe goddess or snow-shoe maid.

Page 25. Windless wave of the wild bull's spears: "vindlauss vágr svigðis geira" = mead; thus: bull's spears = horns; their wave = the fluid, liquor, which is drunk out of them, here the mead of the vat, in the still deep of which Fjölnir was drowned.

Page 26. Durnir's offspring : " Durnis niðr " = a dwarf, Durnir being one of many Eddaic names of dwarfs, S. E. i. 470.—Sokmimir, a giant (S. E. i. 551, and n. 2). Sokmimir's hall = a hollow stone, cavernous rocks being regarded as the abode of mountain giants.

Page 27. Vili's (not Vilir's) brother : " Vilja bróðir " = Odin. Cf. S. E. i. 46 : " Börr fékk þeirrar konu, er Besla hét, dóttir Bölþorns jötuns, ok fengu þau III sonu : hét einn Oðinn, annar Vili, III Ve," *i.e.* Bör gat that woman who hight Besla, a daughter of the giant Bale-thorn, and they had three sons, one hight Odin, another Vili, a third Ve.—Men's over-thrower : " ljóna bági " = Vanland.—Jewel caster : " men-glötuðr " = Vanland.

Page 28. Will-burg : " vilja byrgi," prop. the chest, the breast = body.—The sea's brother : " sjávar niðr " = fire.—Baneful thief of the woodland : " mein-þjófr markar " = fire. Cf. S. E. i. 332 : " Hvernig skal kenna eld ? Svá, at kalla hann bróður vinds ok Ægis, bana ok grand viðar," &c., *i.e.* How shall fire be betokened ? Thus, to call it the brother of the wind and of Ægir, the bane and destruction of wood, &c.

Page 29. 1. Roaring wolf of gleed, or, better, roaring Garm of gleed : " glymjandi glóða Garmr " = fire. Garm, the name of the dog that watched the entrance to " Gnipa "-cave, Vsp. passim, Grm. 44.—Dog of the gleed = fiery devourer = flame.—Hearth-keel : " arin-kjóll," nave of the hearth = house, hall.

Page 30. 2. Roaring bane of Half : " dynjandi bani Hálfs " = fire, funeral burning. Half, a king of Hord-land, and famous sea-rover, about A.D. 700, N. F. H. i. 356, set upon with fire by his stepfather Asmund and, on escaping from the flames, slain by him together with his company, the famous Half's champions ("Hálfs-rekkar"), FaS. ii. 35-38. Half's bane = fire, S. E. i. 332. The earliest tradition was clearly that Half had been burnt to death.

Page 31. Glitnir's goddess: "Glitnis gná" = the Sun, a goddess among the Æsir, S. E. i. 118. Glitnir, the glittering region, the sky; also the heavenly palace of the god Forseti (President), S. E. i. 78, 102-104. Gná, a goddess in the service of Frigg, S. E. i. 116.—The sister of Wolf, the sister of Narfi: "jódís Ulfs ok Narfa" = "Loki's daughter," at the end of the strophe, *i.e.* Hel. Cf. S. E. i. 104: "Sá er enn taldr með Asum, er sumir kalla rógbera Asanna . . . . sá er nefndr Loki eða Loptr, son Farbauta jötuns . . . . kona hans heitir Sygin, sonr þeirra Nari eða Narvi. Enn átti Loki fleiri börn. Angrboða hét gýgr í Jötunheimum, við henni gat Loki III börn : eitt var Fenris-úlfr, annat Jörmungandr, þat er Miðgarðsormr, III er Hel," *i.e.* Further, among the Æsir is counted he, whom some folk call the slanderer of the Æsir . . . . he is named Loki or Lopt, son of the giant Farbauti . . . . his wife is hight Sygin, and their son, Nari or Narvi. Still more children had Loki. Angrboda hight a troll-wife in Giant-home on whom Loki gat three children : one of whom was Fenris-Wolf, another Jormungand, that is, Midgarth-worm, and the third Hel.

Page 32. Death-rod : "val-teinn" = sword ; he that tameth its hunger : "spak-frömuðr" = a warrior, here King Day.

Page 33. The fork that pitcheth the meat of Sleipnir : "slöngu-þref Sleipnis verðar" = hay-fork. Sleipnir, Odin's eight-footed horse, S. E. i. 70 : "Hestar Asanna heita svá: Sleipnir er baztr, hann á Odinn, hann hefir átta fætr," *i.e.* The horses of the Æsir are thus called : Sleipnir is the best, he is owned by Odin, he has eight feet. Cf. S. E. i. 132-4. Sleipnir's meat = horse fodder, hay.

Page 34. Loki's sister, read daughter : "Loga dís" = Hel. Cf. p. 31.—He who needs must tame the wind-cold steed of Signy's husband : "hinn er temja skyldi svalan hest Signýjar vers" = King Agni, hanged on gallows. Signy's husband, the famous sea-king Hagbard, whom

King Sigar had hanged on gallows (S. E. i. 522) for getting
disguised into bed with his daughter Signy, whose brothers,
Sigar's sons, Hagbard had lately felled in battle. His
death Signy so took to heart, that she burnt herself
and her handmaidens in her own bower. Cf. Saxo,
lib. vii. 341 foll.; S. E. i. 522; FaS, i. 180. Hence
Signy's husband's, *i.e.* Hagbard's, horse = the gallows
that bore the weight of his body. "Wind-cold," as an
epithet to a gallows, is derived from the name of the
tree on which Odin hung, "vingameiðr," "vindga meiði"
(dat.), the windy, to winds exposed tree, Hávamál, 138,
cf. Bugge, Stud., 1 Ser., p. 292 foll.

Page 39. The grim-heart horse of Sigar: "grimmr
Sigars jór" = gallows; corpse-ridden windy tree: "ná-
reiðr vinga meiðr," id.

Page 41. High-breasted hemp-rope Sleipnir: "há-
brjóstr hörva Sleipnir" = tall gallows.—The leavings of
Hagbard's goat: "Hagbarðs höðnu leif" = hang-rope,
halter. A doubtful "kenning." "The goat's leavings"
is supposed to mean the skin of a goat out of which
might have been made the halter with which Hagbard
was hanged.

Pages 43, 44. The little end of the sword that bull
beareth: "sveiðuðs mækis hlutr hinn mjóvari" = the
sword-point of the yoke reindeer; "ok-hreins lögðis oddr"
= the herd's head-weapon: "hjarðar mækir;" all mean-
ing a horn—the horn of oxen being the animal's weapon
(sword) of attack.

Page 46. Jotun's yoke-beast: "jötuns eykr" = wild
bull; its head sword: "flæmingr farra trjónu" = horn.—
Brows' temple: "brúna hörgr" = head.

Page 52. The mountain-tangle's biting sickness:
"hlíðar-þangs bit-sótt" = wood fire, fire.—Ship of the
hearth-fires: "brand-nór" = house; cf. hearth keel,
p. 29.

Page 53. Toft's-bark: "toptar nökkvi" = nave (navis),
hall.—Sea-heart: "lagar hjarta" = stone, hence = the
countryside or place called Stone in Esthonia.

III.   C C

Page 54. Gymir's song: "Gýmis ljóð" = the sea-god's lay, the murmur of the sea.

Page 56. The bane of Jonaker's sons : "harmr Jonakrs bura" = rock-slip, stones. Gudrun, daughter of Giuki, had with King Jonakr three sons, Sörli, Erp, and Hamdir. With her first husband, Sigurd Fafnir's-bane, she had a daughter, Swan-hild, afterwards married to King Jormunrek (Ermanaric), who had her trodden to death by horses. The sons of Jonakr undertook the revenge, and Sörli and Hamdir, having slain Erp on the way, made so good an account of themselves in the hall of Jormunrek, that they could not be overcome by weapons. Then Jormunrek cried out:

> Stone ye the men,
> Since spears won't bite,
> Nor edge nor iron,
> The sons of Jonaker.

And so they fell. Cf. Gh., N. F., 311, Hdm. v. 25, S. E. i. 366-70.

Page 57. Corpse destroyer, read copse destroyer: "heipt hrísungs" = the stone slip.—Hogni's bulrush: "Högna hrör" (*i.e.* "hreyr" = "reyr") = sword or spear. Hogni, a famous sea-king, cf. S. E. i. 432-34.

World's bones: "foldar bein"=stones, rocks. Cf. S. E. i. 48 : "þeir (Börs synir) tóku Ymi (—i. 46 : hinn gamli hrímþurs, hann köllum vær Ymi—) ok fluttu í mitt Ginnunga-gap, ok gerðu af honum jörðina; af blóði hans sæinn ok vötnin, jörðin var gör af holdinu, en björgin af beinunum, grjót ok urðir gerðu þeir af tönnum ok jöxlum, ok af þeim beinum er brotin voru," *i.e.* They (the sons of Bor) took Ymir (—the ancient rhyme-giant, him we call Ymir—), and brought him into the midst of Ginnung-gap, and made of him the earth ; out of his blood the sea and the waters, the earth (soil) being made of his flesh, but the rocks of his bones, grit and skries'-heaps they made of his front teeth and jaw-teeth, and of such of his bones as were broken.

Page 64. Reek-flinger: "reyks rösuðr" = fire.—House-

thief fiery-footed : "hús-þjófr hyrjar leistum . . . ."
= id.

Page 66. Temple-wolf: "hof-gyldir" = fire.—The
glede-, read : gleed-wrapt son of Forniot : "glóð-fjálgr
sonr Fornjóts" = fire. Cf. S. E. i. 330 : "Hvernig skal
kenna vind ? Svá, at kalla hann son Fornjóts, bróður
Ægis ok elds," *i.e.* How shall wind be betokened ? Thus,
to call it the son of Forniot, the brother to Ægir and fire.

Page 68. The hill-ward's helpsome daughter : "hallvarps hlífi-nauma," must mean Hel. We have followed
Egilsson's conjecture, who, instead of "hallvarps" reads
"hall-varþs," from "hall-varþr" ("hall-vörðr"), guardian of
rocks, rock-abider, a giant, Loki, whose "hlífi-nauma,"
helping or aiding daughter, Hel might well be named,
seeing that in the last fight of the gods all Hel's company
follows Loki—"en Loka fylgja allir Heljar sinnar" (S. E.
i. 190).—Elf of the byrny : "brynj-álfr"= man, here Halfdan Whiteleg.

Page 69. To the may (= daughter) of the brother of
Byleist : "til meyjar Byleists bróður" = to Hel. Cf.
S. E. i. 104 : "bræðr hans (*i.e.* Loka) eru þeir Byleistr ok
Helblindi," *i.e.* the brothers of him (Loki, the father of
Hel) are these, Byleist and Hell-blind.

Sea's bones : "lagar bein" = stones, cf. p. 57.

Page 70. The Thing of Odin : "þriðja þing," lit. the
Third-one's Thing or assembly = Val-Hall ; þriði, one
of Odin's names, S. E. i. 36.—Hvedrung's maiden :
"hveðrungs mær" = Hel. Hveðrungr, a giant (S. E.
i. 549), cf. "mögr Hveðrungs," the son of Hvedrung =
Fenris-wolf, the brother of Hel, Vsp. 55₅.

Page 73. Thror: "þrór" = Odin.

Page 99. 1. Fight-fish : "hjaldr-seið" = sword ; its
home-road : "vé-braut" = wonted path = shield ; the
sword's singing : "galdrar," thereon = weapon din, fight,
battle ; those who crave it (lit. its craving beams) : "æski-
meiðar" = rebels.—Heathland = "Updale Woods" of
the text.—War-din's raiser : "Grímnis gný-stærandi," lit.
increaser of Grímni's, *i.e.* Odin's, din = Harald Hairfair.

—Sea skates: " lagar skíði "=ships.—Horses that welter in wind-swept hall: "gnap-salar rið-vigg " = ships ; "gnap-salr " = exposed hall, windswept ocean, " rið-vigg " = rocking, rolling horse.

2. War-din's heeder: " þróttar hlym-rækr," lit. Thrott's, *i.e.* Odin's din's pursuer, strenuous fighter = Harald the king.—Wolf-pack's highway: "glamma ferðar tröð " = heath-land, the Updale Woods again.—Manscathe that meeteth the home-way unto the sea-log: " mann-skæðr mætir vé-brautar lagar tanna " = Harald, in his capacity of a victorious commander of the fleet; "tanni " = fir-tree ; " t. lagar," the fir-tree of the sea, ship; its " vé-braut," home-way, wonted path = ocean ; its "mætir," he who meets, *i.e.* braves it.

Page 100. Board-steed : " borð-hölkvir " = ship. "Hölkvir," the name of Hogni's horse, S. E. i. 484.— Wargear's wielder = Harald.—The red shields' voice : " rauðra randa rödd " = battle din, battle.

Page 102. Byrny's fowl : " bryn-gögl " =weapons for thrusting and cutting.—The din of Skogul : " Sköglar dynr " = battle. Skögul, one of the " Valkyrjur," S. E. i. 118-20.—Dyer of edges : " egg-lituðr " = King Harald.

Page 104. Stem of Hogni's daughter : " viðr Högna meyjar " = warrior, a warlike lord. Högni's daughter, Hildr, S. E. i. 432-36, here treated as the " Valkyrja " of the same name, S. E. i. 118.

Page 105. The friend of Lodur : " vinr Loðurs " = Odin ; his din = battle. — In Vsp. 18, Lodur plays with Odin the same part in the creation of Ask and Embla, that Odin's brother, Vili, plays in S. E. i. 52.

Page 109. 1. Frey's game : " Freys leikr " = warfare.

2. Feeder of the fight mew : " grennir gunn-más " = Harald Hairfair.—The linden's wild deer : " ölmr lindi-hjörtr " = ship, that " bounds over billow."

Page 110. Construe : Black gleaming swords of the followers of the mighty, *i.e.* of Harald, bit men.

Page 112. 2. Wolf-coats: " úlf-héðnar," the bareserks of King Harald, who defended the forecastle of his ship,

and wore wolf-coats for byrnies. Cf. Vatnsdæla saga,
ch. 9 (in Fornsögur, Leipzig, 1860).

3. Bold lord of the Eastmen = King of the Norwegians,
Harald Hairfair.—The brawny-necked king : Kiotvi the
Wealthy, King of Agdir.

Page 113. Odin's hall-tiles : "Svafnis salnæfrar " =
shields. "Svafnir," sopitor, one of the names of Odin
(Grm. 54); his "salr" = "Val"-hall ; its "næfrar" (from
"næfr," the rind of the birch bark) = shields. Cf. S. E.
i. 34 : "svá segir þjóðólfr hinn hvinverski, at Valhöll
var skjöldum þökt," so says Thiodolf of Hvin, that
Val-hall was roofed with shields. In proof of this the
present verse is quoted.—Gold staves : "auð-kylfur," lit.
wealth-clubs = men.

Page 114. Holmfolk: "Hólmrygir," the dwellers of
the islands belonging to Rogaland ; here, such of Harald's
wives as hailed from Rogaland.

Page 116. Gold-loader: "men-fergir," he who loads
his men with gold, a bounteous prince, King Harald.—
The grove of Nith-wolves' land-lace: "lundr Niðar-varga
land-mens" = King Harald. Nith, name of several rivers,
= river ; its wolf, the prowler thereof, a ship ; its (the
ship's) land = ocean ; the lace, ornament, jewel, therein
= gold ; the grove thereof = man, here King Harald.
Cf. K. Gíslason, Njála, ii. 380-388, and Finnur Jónsson, Kritiske Studier, 76-78. — Waster of the path of
the fish that playeth around the war-sword's isthmus :
"þverrir lögðis eiðs læ-brautar" = relentless warrior,
King Harald. The war-sword's isthmus = a shield
(which swords habitually cross) ; the shield's fish =
weapon(s) passing through and across it ; the shield-
fish's path = shield again ; its waster, a warrior, here
King Harald.

Page 118. Brave brother of the barons = Rolf Wend-
afoot.—Wolf of Odin's war-board : "úlfr Yggs val-bríkar"
= Rolf Wend-afoot. "Yggr," terrifier, one of Odin's
names, S. E. i. 86, Grm. 54 ; his war-board = shield ;
its wolf, destroyer = warrior, here Rolf.

Page 126. 3. Foot-thorn of the eagle: "il-þorn arnar" = claw.

Page 134. Ship's plain: "fleyja flatvöllr" = sea.—Geitir's way: "Geitis vegr" = sea. Geitir, a sea-king, S. E. i. 546.

Page 155. 1. Rider of the strand-steed: "blakk-riðandi bakka," *i.e.* riðandi bakka blakks = Harald Greycloak. Strand-steed = ship; its rider = captain, commander of a fleet.—Fight-fire's speeder: "róg-eisu ræsir" = Harald Greycloak. Fight-fire = gleaming weapon.

2. Folk's friend drave the fight-flames to gladden the choughs of the Valkyrs: "gumna vinr rak dólg-eisu at gamni gjóðum dísar" = Harald Greycloak pursued warfare with much manslaughter. Choughs of the Valkyrs = carrion birds, ravens.—The Frey of the land: "Foldar Freyr" = Harald Greycloak.

Page 156. Drift of battle's maiden: "drífa Mistar vífs" = weapon-fray, fight. This "kenning" is somewhat unsatisfactory, unless "Mist," a name of a Valkyrja, is taken as an appellative for battle. Another reading is: "drífa Mistar nífs" (= "hnífs" or "knífs"), the drift of Mist's knife, the shower of the battle-maiden's missiles, which is both full and correct. Mist, one of the cup-bearers in "Val"-hall, a Valkyrja, Grm. 36.—Swan of Odin: "svanr Jalfaðar" (one of Odin's many names) = raven, bird of prey.—Lurers to crows' wine (= blood), warriors; their covering = byrnies, coats of mail.—In his Kritiske Studier, pp. 81-84, Dr. Finnur Jónsson has made an ingenious attempt at restoring the second half of this strophe, in the translation of which we have followed Egilsson, Fs. xii. 26, Lex. Poet., convinced that it still awaits proper interpretation.

Page 157. 1. Speeder of gales of bow-drifts' fires; "él-runnr alm-drosar eisu," *i.e.* runnr eisu alm-drosar éls = King Hakon the Good. Bow-drift, flight of arrows; its gale, brunt of battle; the fire thereof, gleaming weapons; their speeder, warrior, commander in battles.

—Green ness (lit. snout) of the Seal-wound : "græn trjóna Sel-meina" = the green nesses of Sealand. Guthorm Cinder has known the name of Sealand only in the form of Selund, and takes it to be a compound of Sel = seal, and und = wound, hurt. Selund is the oldest name of the Danish island, which afterwards by mistaken folk-etymology went into Sealand, Siáland.— Plate-decked sea-steeds : "tingls marar" = ships.— Wand of slaughter : "vals vöndr" = sword ; its sender = man, here Hakon the Good.

2. Blackthorn of the onset : "sókn-heggr" = warrior, King Hakon.—The safe-guard of the Wend-host : "frelsi Vinda vals" = safe retreats, which the Wends might have had in Skaney. Cf. Gíslason, Udvalg af oldnord. skjaldekvad, p. 63.—Egilsson takes "safe-guard" to refer to the ships of the Wends.

Page 158. 1. Shielded by the skirt of Odin : "skyldir skaut-jalfaðar" = King Hakon. So Egilsson, who takes jalfaðar for gen. of Jalfaðr, one of the names of Odin ; his skirt = byrny. But the kenning may also be rendered : He who beshields the skirt-bear ; skirt ("skaut") = sail ; its bear = ship ; its skyldir, he who furnishes it with shields, goes a-warring on board her.—Gold-hewer : "gull-skyflir" = a bounteous man, King Hakon.

2. The helmet's (lit. onset-hat's) ice-rod's reddener : "sókn-hattar svell-rjóðr" = King Hakon. Helmet's ice-rod = sword.—Mind - gladdener : "geð-bætir" = King Tryggvi Olafson.—Oak-green maid of Onar : "eiki-grænt fljóð Onars" = land, territory. Cf. S. E. i. 320 : "Hvernig skal jörð kenna ? Kalla Ymis hold, ok móður þórs, dóttur Onars," *i.e.* How shall earth (land) be betokened ? Call her Ymir's flesh, and mother of Thor, daughter of Onar.

Page 159. Swegdir's hall : "S/segðis salr" = shieldburg, testudo clipeorum ; its breaker : "brigðandi" = ardent warrior, King Tryggvi. Svegdir, one of the princes of the Yngling race (Y., chap. xv.), or, it may be, some other hero of fame, renowned for an attack upon, or defence within a "skjald-borg," which, according to

S. E. i. 420, may be called "höll ok ræfr" = hall and roof.—Swan-mead's runners : "svan-vangs skíð" = ships. Swan-mead = sea ; the runner, skate, or skid of the sea = ship.

Page 160. War-shrine : "gunn-hörgr" = shield.— Sheath-tongues : "slíðr-tungur" = swords.

Page 166. Thiassi's offspring : "afspringr þjaza" = Earl Sigurd. It is stated (Y., chap. ix.) that Earl Hakon the Mighty, the father of Earl Sigurd, carried back the tale of his forefathers to Sœming, the son of Odin and Skadi, but Skadi was the daughter of the giant Thiazi, S. E. i. 92.—Gold-wounder : "fé-særandi" = one who shares gold, scatters wealth, a bounteous prince = Earl Sigurd.—Glaive god : "vægja vé" = Earl Sigurd.—Lord of fen-fire : "fens fúr-rögnir" = Earl Sigurd. Fen's fire = gold. Cf. S. E. i. 336 : "Hvernig skal kenna gull? Svá, at kalla þat . . . eld allra vatna," *i.e.* How shall gold be betokened? Thus, to call it the fire of all waters. The many kennings of this kind for gold must derive their origin from myths about the Rhine gold, the Nibelung's hoard (cf. Rínar bál, glóð, log, sól, tjör, &c.; see also S. E. i. 364).

Page 172. Eker of din of Valkyr : "gildir val-þagnar" = King Hakon.

Page 173. 1. Fight-moons : "víg-nestr" = shields.— Hand-warp, read hand-wrap : "handar-vaf" = that which covers the hand, a shield.—The Niord of the fire of wide lands of sound-steeds : "Njörðr brands víðra landa sunda-vals" [1] = King Hakon. Sound-steed = ship; its wide land = the sea; the fire of the sea = gold; its Niord (god) = man, here King Hakon.—Niord of the moon of roaring of the swords : "Njörðr nadds-há-raddar mána" = King Guthorm. Roaring of swords = battle; its moon = shield; the shield's Niord (god) = warrior, here King Guthorm.

2. Awer of bow-draught : "ægir alm-drauga" = King

[1] See Gíslason, Udvalg af oldnordiske skjaldekvad. Københ. 1892, p. 65.

Hakon; his brethren: "bræðr" = his brother's sons, the sons of King Eric. Bow-draught = bow-string.—Wound-fire's Balder = King Hakon. Wound-fire = sword; its Balder (god) = man, warrior.—Fight-seeker of the flood-craft = seeker of the flood-craft's fight: "böð-sækir flæða bríkar" = "sækir flæða bríkar böðvar" = King Hakon. Flood-craft's fight = naval battle.

Page 179. Gold waster: "málma þverrir" = King Hakon.—Host of sword song: "hjörva raddar herr" = war-host, army; sword song = battle.—War-flame: "róg-cisa" = sword; its speeder: "ræsir" = King Hakon. —The breeze of Mani's darling: "byrr Mána óskkvánar" = courage. Cf. S. E. i. 540: "huginn skal svá kenna, at kalla vind tröllkvenna, ok rétt at nefna til hverja er vill, ok svá at nefna jötnana ok kenna þá til konu eða móður eða dóttur þess," *i.e.* the mind shall thus be betokened, to call it the wind of troll-women (giantesses), and it is right to name thereto anyone (giantess) at will, and also to name the giants, and then to betoken the mind by (the wind of) a wife or a mother or a daughter of the giant named. Thus Máni was the son of the giant Mundilfœri, S. E. i. 56, Vfm. 23; his darling, therefore, a trollwoman, whose wind, breeze = "hugr," which means not only thought, mind, but also courage, valour. Finn Jónsson's interpretation, Kritiske Studier, 93.—Fray of spear-maids: "Snerra geir-vífa" = battle. Spear-maids = Valkyrjur.

Page 180. Fenrir's jaw-gag: "Fenris varra sparri" = sword, cf. S. E. i. 112: "Ulfrinn gapti ákaflega, ok fekkst um mjök ok vildi bíta þá. þeir skutu í munn honum sverði nokkvoru, nema hjöltin við neðra gómi, en efra gómi blóðrefillinn, þat er góm-sparri hans," *i.e.* The Wolf (Fenrir) gaped awfully and struggled about much and wanted to bite them. They slipped into his mouth a certain sword, the hilts of which stick against the lower jaw and the point against the upper; this is his jaw-gag.—Steel-storm: "málm-hríð" = battle; its trees, "meiðar" = men, warriors.

Page 181. Sheath-staff: "fetil-stingr" = sword.—
Byrny - meeting: "bryn-þing" = meeting of hosts in
armour, battle.

Page 182. Shaft - rain: "nadd - regn" = battle; its
Niord, god, war commander.—Rakni's roaring highway:
"Rakna rym-leið" = sea. Rakni, a sea-king of fame,
S. E. i. 548.—War-board: "gunn-borð" = shield.

Page 184. 2. War-weed: "her-váðir"= armour, byrny.
War-warders' leader: "vísi verðungar"=King Hakon.
"Verðung" = body-guard.

3. Flinger of the glitter in the she-giant's drift on Ice-
moon of sea-steed: "gim-slöngvir nausta-blakks hlé-mána-
gífrs drífu" = King Hakon. Sea-steed = ship; its Ice-
moon = shield; the shield's she-giant = axe; its drift on or
against the shield = battle; the glitter of battle = gleaming weapons; the flinger thereof = a warrior, here King
Hakon.

Page 185. 1. Vafad's weeds: "váðir Váfaðar" = byrny,
armour. "Váfaðr," one of the names of Odin = the
wavering one, the shifty wanderer, πολύτροπος.

2. Ring Tyr: "bauga Týr" = King Hakon. Tyr, one
of the "Æsir" or Gods; cf. S. E. i. 334: "Mann er ok
rétt at kenna til allra Asa heita," *i.e.* it is right to betoken a man by all the names of the "Æsir."—Shield-
bright burgs = bright shieldburgs: "skírar skjald-borgir"
= lines of warriors with bright shields aloft.

Page 186. 1. Tempest of slaughter-hurdles' Gefn:
"veðr val-grindar Gefnar" = battle. Slaughter-hurdle
= shield; its "Gefn" (one of the names of the goddess
Freyja, S. E. i. 114), a "Valkyrja"; her tempest = battle;
its speeder: "heyjandi" = man, warrior, King Hakon.—
Crafts-master of Odin's brunt: "kennir Njóts svips"=
King Hakon. Njótr, one of Odin's names, S. E. i. 86,
note 11, ii. 266, note 1 (cf. ib. 472, 556); his brunt (svipr)
= battle; its crafts-master (knower), a renowned warrior,
King Hakon.

2. Wound-wand: "ben-vöndr" = sword.—The squall
of the boar of Ali: "él galtar Ala" = sea-fight. Ali, a

sea-king of fame (S. E. i. 546); his boar = ship ; the squall
thereof = naval fight.—Hair mounds : " skarar haugar "
= heads, skulls.

Page 187. 1. Wolves' slayer : "varga myrðir " = King
Hakon. Wolves = misdoers.—Gold's well wonted scarer :
" vanr ótta gulls " = accustomed to scatter gold about, a
bounteous prince.

2. The Niord of Gondul who giveth drink to
Hugin : " Göndlar Njörðr, sá er gerði hugins drekku " =
Thoralf Skolmson (cf. p. 184). "Göndul," one of the
" Valkyrjur," hence, appellatively, fight ; the Niord (god)
thereof, a warrior ; " Huginn," one of Odin's two wise
ravens ("Thought," in fact) ; its drink, liquor = blood.

Page 190. 4. Wound-sea : " sár-gýmir " (cf. p. 54) =
oceans of blood.—Swords' nesses : " sverða nes " =
shields.—Flood of spears : " flóð fleina "=blood shed in
battle.

5. Red shield's [read : brim's] heaven : " roðnar (roðin-
nar) randar himinn " = shield.—Skogul's cloud storm :
" Sköglar skýs veðr " = brunts of fighting. Skogul's
cloud = shield ; the storm thereof = fight.

Page 191. 1. Spear-waves : " odd-lár " = blood flowing.
—Odin's weather : " Oðins veðr " = brunt of battle.

5. Geir-skogul, one of the " Valkyrjur," as is also
Skogul, p. 192, 1.

Page 193. 4. Fenriswolf ; see note to p. 31.

Page 198. 1. Battle-god's black falcons : "dólg-bands
dökk-valir "=ravens. Battle-god=Odin ; his black falcons = ravens.—Wound-reed : " benja reyr " = sword.

2. See note to p. 180.

Page 199. 1. Hords' land-ward : " Hörða land-vörðr "
= King Harald Greycloak.—Wounds' hail : " benja
hagl " = arrows.—Sheath-ice : " fetla svell," stiria baltei
= sword.

2. Uller of leek of battle : " Ullr ímun-lauks " = King
Harald Greycloak. Leek of battle = sword ; its Uller
(god) = man, warrior.—The seed of Fyris meadow :
" frae Fýris-valla " = gold. Cf. S. E. i. 396-98, where

the story is told, how Rolf Kraki was betrayed at Upsala by King Adils, his stepfather. "But Yrsa, the mother of Rolf, gave him an ox-horn full of gold, and therewithal the ring 'Svíagríss,' and bade him and his ride away to their host. They sprang to their horses, and rode down unto the Fyris-meads, and then saw how King Adils rode after them with all his host in full armour, intent on slaying them. Then took Rolf Kraki with his right hand the gold out of the horn and sowed it all about the road. And when the Swedes saw this, they sprang from their saddles and each one picked up what he caught hold of, but King Adils bade them ride on, himself riding as hard as he could, Slungnir, his steed, being the best of all horses. Now when Rolf Kraki saw King Adils riding close upon him, he took the ring 'Svíagríss' and flung it to him, and bade him take it for a gift. King Adils rode to the ring and lifted it with the point of his spear and slipped it up over the socket. But Rolf Kraki, turning back, saw how Adils bowed down (catching the ring) and said: 'Utterly humbled have I now him who is the mightiest among the Swedes;' and thereon they parted. By reason of this gold is called the seed of Kraki or of Fyris-mead."—The falcon's fell: "hauka fjöll" = hands, whereon the falcon sits.—The meal of the woeful maidens of Frodi: "meldr fá-glýjaðra þýja Fróða" = gold. Cf. S. E. i. 376: "King Frodi (Fridleifson of Denmark) went to a feast in Sweden to the king who was named Fjölnir. Then he bought two bondswomen who were called Fenja and Menja, being big women and strong. At this time were found in Denmark two quernstones so huge, that none might be found strong enough to turn them. Now such was the nature of the quern that it would grind whatever the grinder of it wished. That quern was called Grotti. Drop-chaps, 'Hengi-kjöptr,' is he called who gave the quern to King Frodi. King Frodi had the bondswomen brought to the quern and bade them grind gold and peace and bliss to Frodi. But no longer rest or sleep gave he to them than while the

cuckoo was silent or a song might be sung. And so it
is said they sang that lay which is called Grotti's-lay, and
ere the song came to an end they had ground an armed
host upon Frodi; and on that night there came the sea-
king called Mysing and slew Frodi, and took much
plunder; and then Frodi's peace came to naught. Now
Mysing took away with him both Grotti and Fenja and
Menja besides, and bade them grind salt; and at midnight they asked if Mysing was not growing weary of
salt; but he bade them grind on. But a little while had
they yet ground or ever the ships sank down, leaving a
whirlpool in the ocean where the sea falls through the
quern - hole."— Troll-wives' foeman: "mellu - dólgr" =
Thor; his mother = Earth; her flesh = mould, soil.

Page 200. 1. The coif-sun of the brow-fields of Fulla:
"fall-sól Fullar brá-vallar" = gold, the diadem of Fulla's
headdress. — Mountains of Uller's keel: "fjöll Ullar
kjóls" = hands. Uller's keel = shield (as, according to
the so-called Laufáss Edda, he owned a ship called
Skjöldr = shield; Lex. Poet., sub Ullr); its mountains =
hands, that lift the shield on high.—Sun of the river:
"álf-röðull elfar" = gold.—Corpse of the mother of the
giant's foe; cf. end of preceding note.

3. Speeder of skates of isle-mead: "skerja-foldar skíð-
rennandi" = seafarer, sea-king, here King Harald Greycloak.

Page 201. 1. Breeze of giant maidens: "byr þursa tœs"
= mind; cf. note to p. 179, breeze of Mani's darling.

Hawk-land's jewel: "val-jarðar men" = gold. Hawk-
land = hand.—Lair of the ling-worm: "lyngva látr" =
gold, here gold-ring. Ling-worm = serpent. The myth
of the serpent or dragon Fafnir underlies all "kennings"
of this kind.

2. Terror-staff of the jaw-teeth of Heimdall: "Ógnar-
stafr tanna Hallinskíða" = scatterer, destroyer of gold, a
bounteous lord, King Harald Greycloak. "Hallinskíði,"
one of the names of Heimdall. Cf. S. E. i. 100: "Heim-
dallr heitir einn . . . hann heitir ok Hallinskíði ok

Gullintanni ; tennr hans voru af gulli," *i.e.* Heimdall is the name of one (of the Æsir), he is also hight Hallinskidi and Goldentooth ; his teeth being of gold. Hence Heimdall's jaw-teeth = gold ; its terror-staff = destroyer, a man liberal of his wealth.

Page 206. 1. Swans of the Burden-Tyr : " svanir-farma-Týs " = ravens. Burden-Tyr = Odin (cf. S. E. i. 230) ; his swans = ravens.—Rooks' beer from Hadding's chosen : " Hróka-bjór Haddingja-vals " = blood. Hadding's chosen (ones) = war-host ; the rook thereof = bird of carnage, raven ; its beer = blood. The Hadding here mentioned is Hadding, son of Gram, legendary King of Denmark of mighty fame ; cf. Saxo, lib. i. 34-60.

2. The arm's (gold-) worm : "alnar ormr " = ring, bracelet.—Fish land : "ölun-jörð " = sea, ocean.

Page 207. 1. For "merry king " read merry lord, *i.e.* Earl Hakon.—Storms of Gondul : "Göndlar veðr " = fight, battle.—Red moon that is of Odin's (read : Hedin's) elbow : " rauðmáni Héðin's bóga " = war-shield.—Fight-sail : " róg-segl " = shield.

2. Swan(-fowl) of the heavy sword-stream : "svanr sverða sverri-fjarðar " = raven. Sverri-fjörð, lit. heavy sea ; heavy sword-sea = blood shed in torrents.—Shaft-storm of the spear-wife : " örva-drífa odda-vífs " = fight, battle ; spear-wife = "Valkyrja."—Hlokk's sail : "Hlakkar segl " = shield. Hlokk, a "Valkyrja." — Bow-hail : "bogna hagl " = showers of arrows.

3. Storm of Ali : "él Ala " = fight. Ali, a renowned sea-king.—Deft grove of the shield leek : " ræki-lundr randar-lauks " = warrior, Earl Hakon. Shield leek = sword.

4. Warder of waves' raven : " vörðr hranna hrafna " = commander of a fleet, Earl Hakon. Waves' raven = ship.

5. Mail-rain : "mél-regn" = shower of arrows.—Sword-storm's urger : "hjörs hríð-remmir = remmir hjörs hríðar " = commander in battle, Earl Hakon.—Vidur of gale of sea-steeds : " hald-Viðurr haf-faxa " = " Viðurr hjaldrs

haf-faxa" = commander in sea-fight, Earl Hakon. Sea-steed's gale = sea-fight; its Vidur (one of the names of Odin) the director, ruler thereof.—The High-one's tempest: "Hárs drífa" = battle. "Hár," one of Odin's many names.

Page 215. Spear-gale: "geir-drífa" = battle.

Pages 216-17. Helm-storm: "hjalm-gráp" = shower of arrows, brunt of battle.—Loft's friend's hall of friendship: "Lofts vinar vin-heimr" = "Val"-hall. Loft's friend = Loki's friend, Odin; his hall of friendship, friendly home = "Val"-hall.—Fiery rain of Odin: "skúr þróttar fúrs" = brunt of battle. "þróttr" = Odin; his fire = sword; the shower thereof = battle.

Page 218. Svolnir's dame: "Svölnis vara" = earth. Svolnir = Odin; his wife = earth.—Hind of birch-buds: "hind birki-brums" = goat.

Page 219. 1. Terns fin-tailed foreboders of long nets: "sporð-fjaðraðar spá-þernur langra nóta" = herring, the approach of whose shoals forebodes long nets being called into use.—Fire goddess = woman (apostrophe).—Silver-weeds of the ice-fields: "akr-murur jökla" = "murur jökla akrs" = herring. "Jökla akr" = sea, ocean surface; its silver-weed, the silver shining herring.—Wave-swine: "unn-svín" = ship, here fishing or herring boat.

2. Sea-heaven's folk: "ál-himins lendingar" = Icelanders. Sea-heaven = ice, covering the sea's surface.—Swimming firth-herd: "fjörð-hjörð" = fish, here herring.

Page 220. Herrings that leap from hands of Egil to Mar for sea-shafts sold I: "hlaup-síldr Egils gaupna selda ek Mæ við örum sævar" = my arrows I sold to Mar for herrings. Egil, the son of a king of the Fins and brother to Völund (Velent) (cf. Vk. introd., N.F. 163), was a most famous archer, and performed at the behest of King Niðuð (Nidung) the same feat of archery that Tell did at the bidding of Gessler (cf. Diðriks saga af Bern, ch. 75). Here real *arrows* are called the herrings that leap from archer Egil's hands, while real *herrings* are called the arrows of the sea.

Page 239. 1. God of hilts made meetly: "Mætra hjalta málm-Oðinn" = King Harald Greycloak. A more literal rendering would be God of the precious hilt-metal; hilt-metal = sword; its Odin, god, a warrior.

2. Glammi's steed: "Glamma sóti" = ship; its garth-wall: "garðr" = shield; its heeder = warrior, King Harald Greycloak. "Glammi," a sea-king of fame, S. E. i. 546.—The scatterer of the sea's flame: "sendir sjávar báls" = bounteous prince, King Harald.—The word-happy kings' friend: "orð-heppinn jöfra spjalli" = Earl Hakon Sigurdson the Mighty.

Page 241. Eyebrow's field: "brúna grund" = fore-head; the heeder of the silk-fillet thereof = one who wears such a band as a mark of social distinction, here Earl Hakon.

Page 242. 2. Thor's shrine-lands: "hofs lönd Ein-riða" = lands belonging to the temples of Thor. Ein-ridi, one of Thor's names, S. E. i. 553.—Hlorrid of the spear-garth: "geira garðs Hlórriði" = Earl Hakon. Spear-garth = shield; the Hlorrid = Thor (god) thereof, a warrior, here Earl Hakon.—Wolf of the death of the giants: "vitnir jötna val falls" = ship. The death of the giants = ocean, cf. S. E. i. 46-48: "Synir Börs drápu Ymi jötun; enn er hann féll, þá hljóp svá mikit blóð or sárum hans, at með því drekktu þeir allri ætt Hrímþursa," *i.e.* the sons of Bor slew the giant Ymir; but when he fell, then flowed so much blood from his wounds, that therewith they drowned all the kindred of the Rime-giants . . . . "þeir gerðu af blóði hans sæinn ok vötnin": they made of his blood the sea and the waters.

3. Fight-worthy folk of Hlökk's staff: "Her-þarfir Hlakkar ás-megir" (*i.e.* Hlakkar áss megir) = warriors, then men in general. "Hlökk," a "Valkyrja," here used appellatively for battle.—Mighty red-board's wielder: "ríkı rauð-bríkar rækir" = Earl Hakon. Red-board = shield.—Gold-waster: "auð-rýrir" = Earl Hakon.—Spear-bridge: "geir-brú" = shield.

4. Fight-board: "ímun-borð" = id.

Page 245. 1. Frey of Hedin's breezes: "Freyr Héð-ins byrjar" = Earl Hakon. Hedin, a sea-king; his breeze = fight.—War-brand's Uller (god): "branda Ullr" = Earl Hakon.

2. Hurdles smooth of Meiti: "Meita mjúk-hurðir" = ships. Meiti, a sea-king of fame, S. E. ii. 468.—Glad-denner of the sparrow of the shield-swarf: "svör-gœlir randa-sörva" = Earl Hakon. Shield-swarf = shield-filings, chipping-up of shields = battle; the sparrow thereof = raven, carrion bird. Gods (not god) of the wall of Hedin: "Ullar Hedins veggjar" = warriors. Wall of Hedin = shield.

Page 246. 1. The Narvi of the screaming of the shield-witch: "Hlym-Narfi hlífar flagðs" = "Narfi hlífar-flagðs hlyms" = Earl Hakon. Shield-witch = axe; its screaming = battle; the Narvi (a son of Loki, S. E. i. 104 = giant) thereof: war commander, Earl Hakon.—The need of the Ialk of snow-shoes: "þörf öndur-Jalks" = ship. Ialk, one of the names of Odin; the Ialk of snow-shoes = the god famed for snow-shoes, *i.c.* Uller. Cf. S. E. i. 102: "hann (Ullr) er bogmaðr svá góðr ok skíðfærr, svá at engi má við hann keppast," *i.c.* He is an archer so good and so skilled at snow-shoeing, that no one may contend against him. Uller's need = his ship, the name of which was Skjöldr = shield, which points to Uller's need being meant here to signify shield-hung ships, warships. The last two lines of the verse corre-spond to the prose-words, "The earl brought-to his ships by the land."

2. Fight-groves: "gunnar-lundar" = warriors, armed hosts.—The host of the ocean = King Ragnfrod's levies from Orkney.

Page 248. Meiti's sea-skate: "Meita skíð" = ship. "Meiti," cf. note to p. 245, 2.

Page 249. 1. The flickering flame of targe-field: "rið-logi rand-vallar" = vibrated, gleaming sword. Targe-field = shield.—Wolf-gladdener: "Ulf-teitir" = he who by carnage provides food for wolves; here

III.   D D

Earl Eric.—Blood-hawks: "blóð-valr " = raven, carrion bird.

2. Sand-Kiar: " Kjár sanda " = Skopti of the tidings. Kiar, a lord of Normandy (N. F. 163, cf. 283, 6), here used appellatively for lord. " Kiar sanda," lord of the sands, *i.e.* sea-side countries, therefore = hersir of the sea-marge in the preceding stanza.

The land's belt's fire's giver : " log-reifir land-mens "= " reifir land-mens logs " = Skopti of the tidings. Land's belt = sea ; its fire = gold ; its giver = bounteous man, liberal lord.—Steel-awer, perhaps better steel Ægir, god : " stál-ægir " = Earl Eric. Ægir, the god of the sea.— Din-bidder of the storm of stem-plain's raven : " stafns flet-bálkar hrafna dynbeiðir," *i.e.* " beiðir dyns bálkar stafns-flets hrafna " = Skopti of the tidings. Stem-plain, planities proræ = ocean; its raven = ship ; the storm (balkr) thereof = brunt of battle, naval fight ; the din thereof =clash of weapons.

The italicized line here, and those on pp. 346-48, form the so-called klofa-stef or cleft, split-up refrain of Eyjolf Dadaskald's poem, the Banda-drapa. Taken together, the five lines, of which the "stave" consists, form the following sentences in praise of Earl Eric :

> The land at gods' will draweth
> The spearstorm bounteous Eric
> To him, and fight-gay wages
> That earl his wars, and swayeth
> The land by gods safe-guarded.

3. The ale-skiff of the sea-worm : " öl-knarrar sjáfar-naðr " = hall, palace. Ale-skiff = beaker, bowl, in a collective, multiplicative sense ; its sea-worm = ship, *i.e.* nave, hall, palace.—Finn of the serpent's seat-berg : " linna set-bergs Finnr" = bounteous prince, King Harald Gorm-son. Serpent's seat-berg = gold ; its Finnr = Dwarf = a wealthy man, a bounteous lord.—The whetter of the Hild-storm : " Hildar él-hvetjandi" = " hvetjandi Hildar éls " = Earl Eric. Hild, a " Valkyrja " (S. E. i. 118) ; her storm = battle ; its "hvetjandi," a dauntless warrior, a war

duke.—The bride of Odin: "Yggjar brúðir" = earth, land, Norway, the preceding prose text stating that King Harald appointed Eric earl with dominion over Vingulmark and Raumrealm.

Page 250. The foe of the flame-flash of the yew-seat: "hati elds ý-setrs" = Olaf Tryggvison. Yew-seat = the seat of the yew-bow, the hand that holds and lifts it; the hand's flame-flash = gold; its foe = he who wastes, scatters it, a liberal, open-handed person.— Stout friend of Hord-folk = Olaf Tryggvison. Hord-folk stands here, pars pro toto, for the Norwegian nation; the poet must have chosen this folk-land in preference to any other because of the close alliance which afterwards took place between the great Hord-land chiefs, the kinsmen of Hörða-Kári and the family of Olaf Tryggvison, cf. ch. lxii.-iv.—Weed of Hamdir: "Hamdis klæði" = byrnies or coats of mail.—Clash of sword edge: "hjörva gnýr" = battle; its clouds: "ský" = shields.

Page 253. Corpse-banes: "hræ-skóð" (scathe) = swords.

Page 255. 1. Gold-shearer: "gull-skerðir" = bounteous man, Olaf Tryggvison.—Spear-gale: "geir-þeyr" (thaw) = battle.

2. Yoke-beasts of the ere-boards: "eykir aur-borðs" = ships. Aur-borð, which, for want of any technical term for it, we translate "ere-board," the board that drags through the ere = the sand or shingle, when a boat is hauled up on to the beach, is the second plank from the keel (bilge-plank?).—Grove of battle: "sig-runnr" = warrior, Earl Hakon. Helm of aweing: "hólm-fjöturs hjalmr" = "œgis-hjálmr," the terrifier's helmet. Cf. S. E. i. 356: "Fafnir hafði þá tekit hjálm, er Hreiðmar hafði átt, ok setti á höfut sér, er kallaðr var œgis-hjálmr, er öll kvikvendi hræðast er sjá," *i.e.* Fafnir had then taken the helm, which (his father) Hreidmar had owned, and all quick things dread who see it. "Hólm-fjöturr" = holm-fetter, island-belt = sea = "Ægir" = god of the sea, taken as an appellative =

sea. This verse, it would seem, was not made till the sound of œ in œgir = terrifier, and that of æ in Ægir had become identical in sound, but that was a long time after the death of Jingle-scale, which occurred shortly after A.D. 986.

3. Frost of murder: "morð-frost" = battle (where bodies of men are rendered stiff as if they were frozen).— Elf of the land of mirkwoods: "álfr myrk-markar fold-ynjar" = Norway, the land of dense, dim woods.

Page 256. 1. Heeder of storm of war-sark: "val-serkja veðr-hirðir" = "hirðir veðrs val-serkja" = Earl Hakon. War-sark = byrny, coat of mail; its storm = battle; its heeder = fighter, commander in war.—Fight-Niords of Hagbard's hurdles' rollers: "Hlunn-Nirðir Hagbarðsa-hurða" = fighters, armed host. Hagbard, a sea-king (cf. note to page 34); his hurdle = shield; the roller thereof = sword; the Niords (gods) whereof = armed men.

2. Ragnir of garth of spear-flight: "garð-Rögnir geir-rásar" = "Rögnir geir-rásar garðs" = the Emperor Otto. Garth of spear-flight = shield; its Ragnir = Odin (S. E. ii. 472), ruler, wielder, a warrior.—Fight Vidur: "gunn-Viðurr" = the Emperor Otto. Viðurr = Odin (Grm. 49). —Sea-horse rider: "vágs blakk-riði" = "riði vágs blakks" = sailor, shipmate, man, here the Emperor Otto.

3. Flame of Thridi: "log þriðja" = gleaming sword; its din: "þrymr" = battle.—Stirrer of ernes' craving: "arn-greddir" = "greddir arna" = he who rouses the eagle's greed with corpses of the slain, here Earl Hakon.

Page 257. The fray-Thrott of the sound steed: "sæki-þróttr sund-faxa" = Earl Hakon. þróttr (pith), one of Odin's names. Fray-Thrott = fight god, a warring lord. Sound-steed = ship.

Page 259. 1. Bole of the gear of Hedin: "draugr Heðins vaða" = Earl Hakon. Hedin's gear = byrny, coat of mail; its bole = warrior, man.—Corpse-fowls: "hræ-gammar" (vultures) = ravens.—Tyr of pine-rod's hollow, or rather: Tyr of pine-hollow's rod: "Týr tyrva teinlautar" = "Týr tyrva-lautar teins" = Earl Hakon. Pine (like "askr," "lind") = sword; its hollow ("laut") = shield; the shield's rod ("teinn") = sword; its Tyr (god), a man, warrior.

2. Wild-fire of the sword-vale: "hyrr hjör-lautar" = sword. Sword-vale ("hjör-laut") = shield; its wild-fire ("hyrr"), the flashing sword.—Sörli's roof: "Sörla rann" = shield. Sorli, son of King Jonaker, slain in the hall of Ermanaric, Hdm. 31.—Sleeping-loft of ling-fish: "lopt lyngs barða" = gold. Ling-fish = serpent; its sleeping loft = gold. Cf. the myth of Fafnir, Fm., Story of the Volsungs, S. E. i. 356-60.

3. God of the gale of Frodi: "Ass Fróða hríðar" = Earl Hakon. Frodi, a sea-king of fame, S. E. i. 546; his gale = battle; the god thereof = commander, war duke.

Page 260. Speeding-stem of the (sea-)steed of rollers: "hleypi-meiðr hlunn-viggja" = King Olaf Tryggvison. Steeds of rollers ("hlunn-vigg") = ship; its speeding-stem = sailor, skipper, sea-king, commander.—Birch of fight-sark: "birki böð-serkjar" = host in armour, an army. Fight-sark = byrny; its birch (collectively, birch-wood) = an host in arms.

Page 261. 1. Troll-wife's steed ill-waxen: "Ljót-vaxinn Leiknar hestr" = wolf. Leikn = a troll-wife; her steed, riding-horse = wolf. Cf. N. F. (H. H.), 176: "Heþinn fór einn saman heim or scógi iólaaptan oc fann trollkono; sv reið vargi oc hafði orma at taumum," *i.e.* Hedinn went alone together home from the wood Yule-eve and found (met) a troll-wife; she rode on a wolf and had snakes for reins.—The dusky stallion whereon Night-rider fareth: "blakkt kveld-riðu stóð" = wolf.

2. Corpse awl (probe): "val-keri" = sword; its skin ("líki") = sheath.

3. Nourisher of spear-shower: "nærir nadd-skúrar" = a war-leader, warrior, Olaf Tryggvison.

Page 262. Bow-trees' dread: "ý-drauga ægir" = Olaf Tryggvison. Bow-tree, the tree that upbears the bow =

archer, warrior, man.—Choughs of the storm of spear-cast : "gjóðar geira hríðar" = carrion birds, ravens. Storm of spear-cast = battle ; the chough thereof, carrion fowl.

Page 268. Mew of Mornir: "már (mór) Mörnis" = ship. Mornir, a sea-king ; his mew = ship.—Powers of the hall of mountains: "bönd berg-salar" = guardian spirits. Hall of mountains = cave.

Page 273. Steel stems: "stála meiðar" = an host under arms.—The stem of the steed of the meadow of Sveidi: "Sveiða vangs vigg-meiðr" = "meiðr viggs Sveiða-vangs" = Earl Hakon. Sveidi, a sea-king of fame (S. E. i. 546) ; his meadow = the sea ; the steed thereof = ship ; the stem thereof = sailor, master, commander at sea.

Page 274. Shield-maple: " skjald-hlynr" = Earl Hakon.

Page 275. Fifth-board steeds: "hrefnis stóð" = ships, fleet. "Hrefni" = the fifth plank from the keel.

Page 277. (Sea-)mews of the glow-home: "mævar glæ-heims" = ships. Glow-home, the glittering region = sea ; the mews of it as such = ships.—The steed of the sea-brim, or rather, gunwale : "barms vigg" = ship.

Page 278. 1. Land-rulers: "jarð-ráðendr " = the Earls Hakon and Eric.—Wasters: "eyðendr" = the vikings of Jom.—Sword-elf : " sverð-álfr " = Earl Sigvaldi.

2. Sewing: "sœing" = thing sown, byrny.—Flame-Gerd : "gims Gerðr" = woman.—Bent boughs of the shoulder : "bjúg-limir herða" = arms, hands.—Din of Fiolnir's fires: "gnýr Fjölnis fúra" = battle. Fjölnir = Odin, S. E. i. 38, Grm. 47 ; his fire = gleaming sword.—Byrny's Vidur : "brynju Viðurr" = Earl Hakon. Vidur = Odin, cf. p. 256, 2. Clattering war-sark of Hangi : "hryn-serkr Hanga" = byrny, coat of mail. Hangi = he who hangs, a hanged person, here = Odin. Cf. Hm. 138 :

Veit ec at ec hecc	I wot, that I hung
Vindga meiði a	On the windy tree
netr allar nio,	Nights all nine together,
geiri vndaþr	Wounded with spear
oc gefin Odni,	To Wodan given,
sialfr sialfom mer.	Self unto myself.

Odin's clattering war-sark = byrny.—Weltering steeds of the sea-stream, better: of Rodi's stream or roost: "rið-marar Róða rastar" = ships. Róði, a sea-king of fame, S. E. i. 548; his stream, roost = sea.

3. The ring-weaved shirt of Sorli: "hring-ofinn serkr Sörla" = byrny; for Sörli, cf. p. 259, 2.

Page 283. Hugin's fellows' feeder: "verð-bjóðr Hugins ferðar" = warrior, fighter, here Earl Hakon. Hugin, one of Odin's wise ravens; its "ferð" = company, fellowship = ravens.—Dog of thong sun: "sól-gagarr seilar" = "gagarr seilar-sólar" = sword. Seil, thong, strap to which the shield was attached (τελαμών); its sun = shield; shield's dog = sword.—Wight spear-stems = able-bodied fighters, the Norwegian army.

Page 288. The sea-lime's urger's folk-play of the fire of head of Hedin: "lög-skundaðar lindar = lagar-lindar skundaðar fólk-leikr Hedins reikar fúrs" = great battle. The fire of Hedin's head = gleaming helmet; its folk-play = general agitation, battle, national fight. Sea-lime = ship, whose urger = Earl Hakon, whose great, national fight = the battle of Hiorung-wick.

Page 298. Ran's fight-stem: "folk-runnr Ránar" = "Ranar-fólks runnr" = sea-rover, fighter at sea, here Earl Hakon. Ran = goddess of the sea, S. E. i. 338; Ran's fight = sea fight. The stem of fight = warrior, man.

Page 299. 1. Scathe-wolves' scatterer: "mein-rennir varga" = "rennir mein-varga" = Earl Eric. "Mein-vargar" = robbers and evil-doers, the Joms-vikings.—Staff of sword-fields: "lindar láð-stafr = "stafr lindar láðs" = Earl Hakon. Sword-field = shield; its staff or stem = a man.

Page 339. Niords of the sweep of sword-edge : "svip-Nirðir sverða " = warriors.—Scabbard all with the earth-bones coloured (lit. scabbard of earth's leg): " umgerð jarðar leggs" = stained, painted scabbard. Earth's leg = earth's bone = stone (cf. sea-bone, p. 21, and world's bones, p. 54), here in the derived sense : stone-colour, stain.

Page 345. See notes to pp. 299-300.

Page 346. 1. Mail-storm: "málm-hríð " = battle, cf. p. 180.—Spear-storm bounteous: "geira veðr-mildr," *i.e.* "mildr geira veðrs" = fight eager.—Vali's storm-wreath of the hawks of the strand of Virvil : "Vala garðr vala Virfils strandar " = sea-fight. "Virvill" (= Huyruillus, Holandiae princeps, Saxo, lib. iv., 178-79), a sea-king (S. E. ii. 469); his strand, *i.e.* haunts = sea ; the hawks thereof = ships ; Vali, a sea-rover, his storm-wreath = battle ; his storm-wreath of the hawks of Virvil's strand = sea-fight.

2. Steerer of the stem-steed : "stýrir stafn-viggs" = Earl Eric. Stem-steed = ship.—Wound-mew : " unda már " = raven.

Page 347. 1. Sea-flame's brightener : "lægis log-fágandi," *i.e.* "fágandi lægis logs " = one liberal of his wealth, Earl Eric.—Brand of point-storm : "brandr odd-hríðar " = sword. Point-storm = battle ; its brand, *i.e.* flame = gleaming sword.

2. Hardener of the fire of the spear-sea : "fúr-herðir fleina-sjávar," *i.e.* "herðir fúrs fleina-sjávar " = doughty fighter, Earl Eric. Spear-sea = blood ; its fire = gleaming weapon ; the hardener thereof = he who tempers his steel in blood.—The fight-tree, firth-flame's giver : "fólk-meiðr vága fúr-gjafall," *i.e.* "gjafall vága-fúrs " = boun-teous Earl Eric. "Vágr" = bay, firth ; its "fúrr," fire = gold.

Page 348. O heedful Niord of the launch-steed : "hlunn-viggs gæti-Njörðr " = sea captain, Earl Eric. Launch steed = ship ; its heedful Niord (god) = com-mander.—War's god : " Hildar áss " = Earl Eric. Hildr, used with appellative force, = battle.

Page 359. Dauntless in gale of flame of battle: "él-móðr gunn-bliks," *i.e.* "móðr [= móðugr] gunn-bliks éls" = Earl Eric. Flame of battle = flashing weapon; its gale = fight, battle.—Fattener of carrion hornets: "feitir hræ-geitunga" = fighter, warrior. "Geitungr," Dan. geding, Swed. geting = hornet; but S. E. ii. 488 gives it as the name of a bird. Hence carrion hornet = raven.

Page 360. Wound-mew: "sára már" = raven.

Page 362. Meet stem of the wave-steed: "mætr meiðr unn-viggs" = King Olaf Tryggvison.—Sea's knop-crowned reindeer: "lagar hún-hreinar" = ships with knopped mast-heads.

Page 368. 1. Wound-leek: "sár-laukr" = sword.—Mail-Thing: "málm-þing" = weapon mote, battle.—Helm-din: "dynr hjálma" = fray of battle, fight.

Page 369. 1. Dane groves of bright leg-biter: "danskir runnar fráns legg-bita" = Danish warriors. Leg-biter = sword.—Him, *i.e.* Earl Eric, followed, etc.

2. Hard firth: "harðr fjörðr" = heavy sea, *i.e.* severe brunt of fight.—Moons of the galley's prow-fork: "tungl tingla tangar" = shields. Tingl = figure-head; the prow-fork (lit. pair of tongues) thereof, the converging beams of the prow upholding it.—Blood-reeds: "dreyra reyr" = swords.

Page 370. 1. The byrny witchwife's Regin: "bryn-flagðs Reginn" = Earl Eric. Byrny witchwife = axe; its Reginn, dwarf, S. E. ii. 470, Vsp. 12, = warrior.—Fafnir = the Long Worm.

2. Ring-wrought war-sark: "baugs megin-serkr" = ring-wrought coat of mail.—Adder: "naðr" = the Long Worm, cf. p. 377.

Page 373. 1. Hropt's walls: "Hropts toptir" = shields; "Hroptr" = Odin.—High fells' hall: "hárra fjalla höll" = heaven.

2. Halland for Haðland = Haðaland, *i.e.* Hathaland; the king thereof, Olaf Tryggvison.—Sea-flame: "haf-viti" = gold.—Sword-oath: "Vápn-eiðr" = battle-fray.

Page 375. 1. Waster of the arm-stone: "úgræðir arm-grjóts" = Thorkel Nosy.—Either Adder = both the Long and the Short Worm.—Wolf of Tackle: "snæris vitnir" = ship, here the Long Worm.

2. Thridi's land's lean monsters: "þriðja hauðrs þunn galkn" = swords. Thridi, Third-one = Odin (S. E. i. 36); his land = shield; its thin monsters, devouring beasts = swords.—Wolf's fare (lit. bait): "gera beita" = dead corpses.

Page 376. 1. The soother of mews of clatter Of the sheen of Leyfi's (sea-)deer: "hungr-deyfir dyn-sæðinga Leyfa dýr-bliks," *i.e.* "deyfir hungrs sæðinga dyns Leyfa dýrs bliks" = feeder of ravens. Leyfi, a sea-king of fame (= Leifi, S. E. 548); his deer = ship (bounding over wavy sea); the ship's sheen = shield; the shields' clatter = battle; its (the battle's) mew = carrion bird, raven; the soother thereof, a man, here Olaf Tryggvison.

2. Point-shaking servant of, etc.: "odd-bragðs árr" = captain, commander in battle.

3. Swayer of hand's ice: "stýrir mund-jökuls" = Olaf Tryggvison. Hand's ice, prop. silver, silvern ornaments, here jewels in general.

Page 377. 1. Some tell the wealth-wise: "sumr seggr segir auðar-kenni," *i.e.* tell me, the poet, Hallfred Troublous-skald.

2. Thing (= encounter) of swords: "hrings þing" = battle. Hringr = sword, S. E. i. 566.—Heming's high-born brother, Earl Eric, cf. Story of Ol. Tryggvison, ch. xix.

Page 378. 1. Tyr of the flame of ship-land: "fasta-Týr far-lands," *i.e.* "Týr far-lands fasta" = Erling Skialgson. Ship-land = sea; its fire (fasti) = gold; the Tyr (god) thereof, a bounteous lord.

THE END.

CHISWICK PRESS:—C. WHITTINGHAM AND CO., TOOKS COURT, CHANCERY LANE.